THE RIVER UNDERGROUND

Western Literature Series

THE RIVER UNDERGROUND

An Anthology of Nevada Fiction

EDITED BY

Shaun T. Griffin

UNIVERSITY OF NEVADA PRESS

Reno & Las Vegas

Western Literature Series

University of Nevada Press, Reno, Nevada 89557 USA

Manufactured in the United States of America
Text design by Kaelin Chappell
Cover art by Karen Kreyeski, "Lenticular Clouds Over Nevada,"
pastel painting, 2000

Library of Congress Cataloging-in-Publication Data
The river underground : an anthology of Nevada fiction /
edited by Shaun T. Griffin.
p. cm. — (Western literature series)
ISBN 0-87417-364-7 (pbk. : alk. paper)
1. American fiction—Nevada.
2. Short stories, American—Nevada.
3. Nevada—Social life and customs—Fiction.
I. Griffin, Shaun T. (Shaun Timothy), 1953– II. Series.
PS571.N3 R58 2001
813.008'09793—dc21 00-011395

The paper used in this book meets the requirements of
American National Standard for Information Sciences—
Permanence of Paper for Printed Library Materials, ANSI Z39.48-1984.
Binding materials were selected for strength and durability.

First Printing
10 09 08 07 06 05 04 03 02 01 5 4 3 2 1

FOR

Thomas Flagg

WHOSE GROUNDBREAKING WORK

ON THIS ANTHOLOGY

WAS NOT IN VAIN

AND

Robert Laxalt

FROM ALL OF US

The editorial mind is nothing if not flexible.
The good editorial mind, that is.

—HAYDEN CARRUTH

The Best of Possible Worlds

Nevada is my adopted state and I will defend it to the death. Nowhere in the Union is so low and comfortable a way of life available as in the One Sound State, the Hard Money State, the Sagebrush State. It is, among other things, the only state in the Union with no public debt, no income, inheritance, sales, or other nuisance or confiscatory state imposts. It is the only state where gambling, high, wide, and handsome, flourishes around the clock, and one of two—Louisiana, I think, is the other—where the saloons never close. Storey County, where I reside in the seedy grandeur of a Victorian mansion, is so poor that no offense requiring a jury trial ever reaches the bar of justice. Malefactors, including a recent murderer, are booted across the county line and told not to return.

Best of all, there are hardly any people in Nevada, only about one inhabitant for every square mile, which is as dense a population as I, after twenty-odd years on Madison Avenue, care to put up with. When, from my dressing room in the morning, I look across the 175 miles separating Virginia City from the Reese River Mountains, I can comfortably reflect that there are hardly twenty-odd people in the intervening countryside.

As I say, Nevada is the best of possible worlds.

—LUCIUS BEEBE, 1953

Contents

Acknowledgments xvii

Preface xix

ROBERT LAXALT

From a Balcony in Paris 1

STEPHEN SHU-NING LIU

The Yellow Crane 17

RANDALL C. REID

Little Strokes 25

HART WEGNER

Cockshut Light 35

JOHN H. IRSFELD

excerpt from *Little Kingdoms* 57

JOANNE MESCHERY

Why Do Things Die in the Country 75

BILL MOODY

Rehearsal 93

PHYLLIS BARBER
Mormon Levi's 101

FRANK BERGON
excerpt from *Shoshone Mike* 117

H. LEE BARNES
Stonehands and the Tigress 129

RICHARD WILEY
excerpt from *Soldiers in Hiding* 147

DONALD BERINATI
The Excellent House 161

MIKE HENDERSON
Harmonica Man 175

ADRIAN C. LOUIS
Abducted by Aliens Inside Her Brain 187

MARILEE SWIRCZEK
A Time to Gather Stones 197

EILEEN CLEARY
excerpt from *Ringgold's Run* 203

STEVEN NIGHTINGALE
excerpt from *The Lost Coast* 219

THOMAS R. TURMAN
A Sunset 227

DOUGLAS UNGER
excerpt from *Leaving the Land* 235

MONIQUE LAXALT
excerpt from *The Deep Blue Memory* 253

TERESA JORDAN
St. Francis of Tobacco 277

JOHN ZIEBELL
Yellowjackets 293

SAM MICHEL
Willows 309

VERITA BLACK PROTHRO
Porched Suitcases 323

ERICA HECTOR VITAL
excerpt from *Natural Causes* 339

Acknowledgments

The editor would like to thank the following publications for granting permission to reprint the stories or novel excerpts in this collection:

STORIES

"Cockshut Light," by Hart Wegner, from *Weber Studies,* Fall 1996; "Stonehands and the Tigress," by H. Lee Barnes, from *Clackamas Literary Review,* Spring 1998; "From a Balcony in Paris," by Robert Laxalt, from *Cosmopolitan,* August 1964; "Rehearsal," by Bill Moody, from *Las Vegas Review-Journal,* 1990; "Little Strokes," by Randall C. Reid, from *Seattle Review,* 1989; "Why Do Things Die in the Country," by Joanne Meschery, from *The Best of Intro,* 1985; "Willows," by Sam Michel, from *Under the Light: Stories,* by permission of Alfred A. Knopf. © 1996 by Sam Michel.

NOVEL EXCERPTS

Reprinted from *Leaving the Land,* by Douglas Unger, by permission of the University of Nebraska Press. © 1984 by Douglas Unger; *Little Kingdoms,* by John H. Irsfeld, by permission of Southern Methodist University Press. © 1989 by John H. Irsfeld; *The Lost*

Coast, by Steven Nightingale, by permission of St. Martin's Press, LLC. © 1996 by Steven Nightingale.

EPIGRAPH

The Lucius Beebe Reader, edited by Charles Clegg and Duncan Emrich, by permission of Ann Clegg Holloway, literary executor. © 1963 Lucius Beebe.

Preface

CHRISTMAS DAY 1995

I carried the manuscripts that would be a book of fiction to my house—maybe a half mile from the office. The sun was shining bright, it was forty degrees, no wind, an altogether glorious day. The satchel weighed fifteen pounds. I was struck by the alchemy about to take place: from the bulk of a large cloth handbag would come a small book.

DECEMBER 1996

One year ago, when I wrote the preceding journal entry, there were many titles before me. I came to them out of a sort of reverence. How could I not? These books and stories were the backbone of my interest in this project.

Shortly after completing *Desert Wood* in 1991, I wanted to begin editing this book, but other writing commitments would not permit me. So I began reading the many authors that laid the foundation for this anthology—Walter Van Tilburg Clark, Lucius Beebe, Sarah Winnemucca, Dan DeQuille, Mary Austin, Mark Twain, and others. I quickly realized my labor would never be finished and reconciled myself to working slowly at first. As I moved closer to the actual editing, I was counseled by several writers "not to go digging over old bones." After much thought, I finally agreed, and hence this volume spans the period from the 1930s to the present (most of the writers were born in the forties and fifties).

To gather the short stories and novel excerpts, I sent notices to all of the state's libraries, colleges, and newspapers. Many people helped me track down writers throughout Nevada and beyond. And some, despite all manner of requests, declined to submit. To give focus to the anthology, I asked that only mainstream literary fiction be submitted (e.g., all other fiction—detective, mystery, romance, science fiction, and juvenile—was not considered). Hence the absence of Bernard Schopen, David Eddings, and writers from other genres.

This anthology represents the best fiction I could find by *Nevada* writers. All of the authors represented here are either current or former residents of the state. In a word, they are wedded to this place by birth, livelihood, or affliction—meaning a place not chosen but endured. Although the fiction is not necessarily based in Nevada, all of the writers have at one time or another called this state home.

Thematically, the book is organized around one central criterion—truly inspired writing. Thus the selection process for it paralleled that for *Desert Wood*: the writers have (or have had) a solid connection to Nevada, and their writing is of the highest quality.

The stories also appealed to some sense of humanity—whether the lost dignity of the Western Shoshone in *Shoshone Mike,* or the fragile cultural allegiance of a first-generation Japanese American during World War II (*Soldiers in Hiding*), or the loss of innocence—ultimately, the characters demonstrate self-respect in the face of unrelenting erosion of their basic humanity. Just as many of the stories chronicle our cantankerous and wrongheaded lives, they are grounded first in the everyday, in the mulch and make-do of the bulldog world. They mean something to the reader because, in my opinion, they resist artifice and move to the human plane of a vulnerable, fallible central character. This is their redemption: they succeed on human terms.

A further point of clarification: while this book is intended to be a collection of short fiction, several novel excerpts are included as well, since they closely fit the scope and purpose of this anthology: the best writing by authors from Nevada.

To the last page, I was not prepared for the joy and sorrow that would come. Nearly every story and novel excerpt is different from the others, and each commands attention. An unintended mixture of voices, they're established and young, his and hers, equally strong strands of family from the four compass points. This anthology is more than the sum of its geographical and cultural origins—from Ely to Lovelock, Basque to Paiute, Irish to Italian, Texan to Illinoisan. The roots of the fiction in this book lie in our ancestral labors—roaming, farming, hunting, and yes, warring. Each writer has gathered the mystery of his or her tabernacle, his or her precise economy of words, and put the "bear in the kitchen," to spend that great line from Faulkner.

I am indebted to all. They taught me to read again, at first for pleasure, and then for the subtle reverberation of recognition that comes when we reach below our knees and braille the tracks of those before us. The question I repeatedly hear these writers ask, it seems to me, is can fiction do any real good in our lives? My answer is yes, if we listen and read with open eyes. If we read as if the words are more than entertainment, more than markers of the busy mind, perhaps the sense of these stories will sink in and guide a footstep to the next warm hand. If not, this book is still worth the journey. Sentient beings cannot unfold their time without the comfort of reading.

My first thanks go to the writers—they have left a legacy of fine storytelling—and it has once again made me a believer in the veracity of Nevada letters. Before *Desert Wood* was published, few people suspected there was a substantial body of Nevada literature worth reading. This volume offers further illustration of the depth of the work being done. I hope others who open this book come to enjoy the wonder of such prose as this.

There is little doubt that these authors will make their mark; some already have—Laxalt, Irsfeld, Meschery, Bergon, Louis, Unger, Wiley, and others. But each brings a new fascination to language and literary life in this state. I urge all who read this sampling to journey on to other works by these writers. There are more than veins to be mined here; there is hard rock from which these words emerge. As editor, as reader, as caretaker of all things storming to the center of this small book, I offer it now as one might offer bread to a friend.

Few books come into the world without a great many hands holding them up along the way. This one is no exception. From the beginning I had the encouragement of many people, and without them, this project would not have come to fruition. I thank each of them: Tom Radko, and later, Margaret Dalrymple, for their unfailing curiosity, abiding friendship, and support; Robert Laxalt, who agonized long hours with me over the scope and breadth of this book and who finally graciously agreed to submit a short story himself, thereby generously passing the baton to the next generation of Nevada fiction writers; the many writers in the volume and so many more, who, if it were a perfect world, would be here too, especially John Irsfeld, Douglas Unger, Randall Reid (who nearly twenty years ago knocked me out with a story he read at the Blue Mailbox cafe in Reno), Adrian Louis, Monique Laxalt, my dear friends and fellow writers Don Bush and Gary Short; and special collections librarians Robert Blesse (UNR) and Peter Michel (UNLV). More than a small portion of the credit goes to my family—they endured the absence of a husband and father much longer than anyone should have to.

Careful readers will recognize the anthology's title comes from Walter Van Tilburg Clark's song lyrics in "The Sweet Promised Land of Nevada." I thank him and Hayden Carruth for suggesting that I turn to the Nevada poets of Carruth's generation to find a title.

It was only after nearly finishing the volume that I learned of its predecessor from Bill Moody, the former Las Vegas writer and jazz musician. In 1988, after two years' work, Thomas Flagg, together with John Irsfeld and Hart Wegner, edited the manuscript *El Dorado: Fiction from Nevada.* Though it never saw print, I am indebted to them for their early editorial work, which in turn made this volume possible. In a word, one of the many hands holding this book up is grace—as with so many books, it took the labors of three men and thirteen years for it to gestate and finally be born.

No doubt I missed some deserving authors and certainly will find my fingerprints on the delicate matter of choice. Like so many anthologies, it will ultimately be completed in the reader's imagination, and clearly I struggled over the inclusion of several strong fiction writers from this state—writers who have been recognized for their talent in a number of venues. Other limitations prohibited a bigger book, but in truth I chose the best writing I could find *for this particular collection.* All of the selections contribute in some fundamental way to the book as a whole. There is no solace in making these editorial decisions, save the hope that, in time, all good writing finds its way to print. Perhaps in a future volume of Nevada fiction. Nevertheless, this effort remains true to its origins—the best book I could make.

POSTSCRIPT:
23 DECEMBER 1998

I have closed the book
have named the terrible
admonition of its searching:
the river underground.

Shaun T. Griffin
December 1995–December 1998
Virginia City, Nevada

THE RIVER UNDERGROUND

ROBERT LAXALT
(1923–   )

There are writers for whom the bloodline speaks loudest: "My father was a sheepherder and his home was the hills"—thus the opening echo from *Sweet Promised Land.* Born the second of six children to Basque immigrants, Robert Laxalt began life at the base of the eastern Sierra Nevada, and that landscape has been the compass point for his long life in letters. Considered by many to be Nevada's finest living writer, Laxalt has carved a reputation for the clean, spare prose of a master. Indeed, when *A Man in the Wheatfield* was published, the *New York Times* compared him to both Hemingway and Steinbeck. His shadow looms large in Nevada: the founding director of the University of Nevada Press, brother to the statesman Paul Laxalt, and distinguished teacher to all those who came looking for inspiration. A former boxer, UPI correspondent, horseman, and dear friend of Walter Clark, he ferments a room with memory yet defers when asked what makes his many novels succeed. As a writer, he never confuses the two poles of self and other. Instead he keeps looking for a way to get that magnanimous humanity on the page, the rugged self-assurance of a father in the hills and a mother as resolute as the Pyrenees from which she came. Quiet, direct, and honest. In many ways his fiction belies the ardor of a man who woke early to write for nearly fifty years—

from freelance journalism to the finest nonfiction and short-story markets. Throughout it all, he has remained a conscientious presence in the artistic and cultural life of this state. If ever there were a novelist whose words were crushed hard against the stone of experience, it is Robert Laxalt.

Time of the Rabies. Reno: University of Nevada Press, 2000.

A Private War: An American Code Officer in the Belgian Congo. Reno: University of Nevada Press, 1998.

The Basque Family Trilogy (slipcase). Reno: University of Nevada Press, 1997.

Dust Devils. Reno: University of Nevada Press, 1997.

A Lean Year and Other Stories. Reno: University of Nevada Press, 1996.

A Time We Knew: Images of Yesterday in the Basque Homeland. Reno: University of Nevada Press, 1995.

A Cup of Tea in Pamplona. Reno: University of Nevada Press, 1985.

Nevada: A Bicentennial History. New York: Norton, 1977; reprint, Reno: University of Nevada Press, 1991.

In a Hundred Graves: A Basque Portrait. Reno: University of Nevada Press, 1972.

Nevada. Reno: Coward/McCann, 1970.

A Man in the Wheatfield. New York: Harper and Row, 1964; reprint, Reno: University of Nevada Press, 1987.

Sweet Promised Land. New York: Harper and Row, 1957; reprint, Reno: University of Nevada Press, 2000.

The Violent Land: Tales the Old Timers Tell. Reno: University of Nevada Press, 1952.

From a Balcony in Paris

THE ROOM WAS ON THE FOURTH FLOOR, or *troisieme étage* in the French way of doing things, and it looked down on a narrow street that ran along the side of the hotel. The street was crowded with afternoon activity, but he had not come out to watch that.

The room had suddenly become monstrous to him, and Clete had escaped by the simple device of stepping out on the balcony. Through the high, open doors behind him, he could hear his wife crying. He gripped the iron railing with both hands. "If there's one lesson I will one day get through my thick head," he said to the street, "it is that nobody has ever listened to anybody in the world, not even Christ."

He had not traveled much, but enough to have learned that places never turned out the way you thought they were going to. The travel folders and the postcards were all selective lies. They showed none of the poverty, and they didn't smell, like the Congo marketplace that had looked so colorful from a distance but was something else when he got inside. He had talked his head off trying to convince her of this. But how does one describe poverty in a foreign land without ending up making it attractive?

Though they had been separated on the boat train from Le Havre, and sat across the aisle from each other, he had seen the beginning cracks in the castle walls she had set for herself. Those walls had been twenty years in the building, and he could have talked another twenty years instead of the six months he had, and still not torn them down.

He had been forced to talk to an effeminate law clerk in a checked outfit, with a woman's eye and ear for gossip, who was telling him what *really* happened behind the scenes on the liner, and his wife had sat facing a professor who was showing off his textbook French and, whenever she turned her head to stare out the window, who looked hungrily at her tapered legs.

They had passed an unending succession of squalid stone hovels and fields where bent old women in long black worked side by side in the dirt with their husbands. In one way, if the sky had been gray outside, it would have been more like mood paintings, and so better. But the sun was bright and the fields were green, and against this, the poverty was jarring in its reality.

She was a grown woman with her fair quota of shattered illusions. But not this one yet. In this one, she was a woman with a child's illusion carefully shaped from the time she had picked up her first Daphne du Maurier primer. As she kept up a pretense of conversation, he had watched the frantic lines that only he could recognize make their tiny appearance in her planed face. *Good,* he had thought in an instant's vindictiveness. Then, in remorse as quick, *Why does it always have to hurt you so much, and finally me?*

Somewhere in the rude and angry confusion of the French depot, when he had gone a little insane himself trying to locate thirteen pieces of baggage filled mostly with the party dresses he had told her she would never wear, she turned completely off. In the taxicab ride through the Paris streets to the hotel, she had stared frozenly ahead, seeing nothing.

The hotel was a typical tourist trap with a nice front graced by potted trees. She had almost brightened at that, but finally it did her more harm than good. Because then they had passed beyond the front into the dim and musty dungeons of corridors that led to their room.

She was calling him. "Clete, please come back." He held out, as he knew he would, until she cried the words, "Don't leave me alone." Then he gave up the balcony and went inside.

Unlike most women, she never looked the worse for crying. Tears seemed to wash her face clean as sleep and leave her at least outwardly serene. She was sitting on the edge of the bed. It was so high off the floor that her feet did not touch. "Feeling better?" he said.

For a moment, he thought she was going to start crying again. "Of course I'm not feeling better," she said. "How can you even think that?"

"I didn't come back in here to get blamed again."

"I'm not blaming you," she said. "I only wish you could have warned me it was going to be like this."

"I tried to tell you."

"Not really," she said. "I wasn't ready for this . . . this filth." Now that she had found the word, he knew that everything she saw would be painted by it. The expectation made him a little sick.

"Have you looked at this room?" she said.

"I know what it's like."

"You *don't* know what it's like," she cried. "You never look at anything you don't want to see. You just pretend it isn't there, and it goes away. How very convenient. Like having a magic wand."

Knowing what was going to happen if he did, but doing it anyway because there was no other choice but to go on making the same mistakes, he regarded her from a great height. Her anger turned on like a dark flare in her eyes. Leaping off the bed, she clutched at his sleeve. "For once in your blinkered existence, I'm going to make you look. I'm going to make you see unpleasantness."

When she was angry, she made gestures like a very bad actress. "Do you see that ugly thing we're supposed to keep our clothes in?" She swept her arm at the huge armoire that stood like a brown giant against the wall. "The shelves are lined with newspapers," she said angrily, "and there have been *things* in there."

He tried to shut off his mind as she went through the stained rug they were standing on, the drapes that had once been blue velvet but were now black with dirt, the coverlet on their bed, and what was worse, the bathroom. He was not very successful. "What the hell did you expect?" he said to her. "After all, it's Paris."

"After all, it's Paris!" she screamed. "Are you blind to me, too? That's exactly what I mean. It *is* Paris."

Leaving her hysterical on the bed, Clete escaped to the balcony again. The helplessness that he feared most in life was beginning to gnaw at his legs. She was getting to his vision. The street below, already caught in shadow, was not the street he had been looking at a few minutes ago. It was just a street of dirty shop windows and dreary people. He watched it sullenly, and then a movement in red and gold caught his eye.

A girl was leaning against the wall on the other side. She had her hands on her hips, and her blond hair was tousled on her head in calculated disorder. In the late afternoon press of shoppers and people going home from work, a man who looked like a government clerk was forced to pass close by her. She spoke to him, and he said something over his shoulder. She tossed her chin after him like a pouting child.

In spite of himself, Clete's interest quickened. He scanned

the sidewalk carefully to see if his guess would prove out. He seized at it like salvation. By some incredible stroke, the balcony overlooked a prostitutes' street. Up the block from the coquettish blonde was a heavy-breasted mulatto who leaned against the wall and looked out at the passing men with contemptuous lips. And on the corner down the street, there was another whom he did not recognize as one at first, because she was older and wore a proper print dress and made no advances, but simply walked back and forth on her beat.

Oh, God, this is better than a floor show, thought Clete. He went inside to get a chair so that he could settle down to watch it. She was sitting on the bed with her chin cupped in her hands.

"I want a drink," she said.

Clete paused with the chair in his hands. "It's a little early."

"I don't give a damn what time it is. I want a drink."

Clete looked at the balcony, and then at her. He compromised by ordering the drinks first and then taking the chair out on the balcony. She acted as if she didn't know he had gone.

The room was high enough that voices from the street did not carry up. He could see the actions of the prostitutes, but he could not hear their words, so it was like a play in pantomime. None of them seemed to be having much luck. Not even the blonde, who was getting more brazen as the afternoon shadows deepened.

She was venturing out from her wall to walk a few steps with the men. They either shook their heads or ignored her altogether. Then, unexpectedly, one of them stopped to talk. They stood in serious negotiation for a while. Nobody else passing by seemed to notice or even to care.

Clete held his breath. Then the man turned away abruptly and went on down the street. The blonde shrugged and returned to her wall. Her skirt was stretched tight as a sail across her rounded little bottom.

"Clete, the boy is here," his wife called.

"Well, pay him, then."

"But what if he doesn't speak English?"

"Talk to him in French."

She sounded panicky. "But I'm afraid to."

Swearing under his breath, Clete relinquished his chair and went inside. She was straightening her dress. "Are you proper now?" She looked at him evenly, and he went to the door. The boy, who was an old man, brought the drinks in and set them down on a straight-backed chair.

"Combien?" said Clete. He paid the old man, hesitated, and then tipped him despite the service charge.

"That was easy," she said.

"Well, of course it's easy."

"But you've had the practice, and I haven't." She surveyed the room. "You're going to have to bring your chair inside. There's no place to sit."

Clete felt a sense of loss, and then an idea occurred to him. "Let's have our drinks on the balcony. It's nice out there."

"Oh, I couldn't do that," she said. "Not out in public."

"Who the hell cares?" he said. "This is France."

She thought about it a moment and brightened. "All right," she said. "Let's do it, then. Anything to get out of this awful room."

When they were settled on the balcony, Clete looked casually for the blonde. She was nowhere to be seen. Forgetting himself, he stood up and searched the street corners. The mulatto was still leaning against her wall, and the proper prostitute in the print dress was strolling back and forth on her corner. *Dammit all. She scored and I missed it!*

"What are you mumbling about?"

He sat down a little sheepishly. "Nothing."

"It would have to be something to make you angry." Because

she was watching the people on the street, she did not press it. "Have you ever seen so much littleness?" she said. "Little people and little bikes and little cars."

"I had a Frenchman tell me once it's because our diet is enriched, and theirs isn't," said Clete. "He said it's like a horse. The more grain you give him the bigger he grows."

She wrinkled her nose. "I don't like being compared to a horse."

"You don't ever have to worry about that. Not with your body."

"That's nice, even if you don't mean it."

He looked at her. "But I do mean it."

"Shut up and pay attention to the street," she said, laughing for the first time. "On second thought, don't. There are too many attractions down there."

He glanced at her sharply to see if she suspected. If she did, her face did not reveal it.

"You know," she said, "at first I thought I'd never seen so many pretty women in all my life. But they're not really so pretty. It's the way they dress and do their hair. It's . . ." She searched for the fixing word. "It's dramatic."

He made a sound of assent. There was a little hotel near the street corner, and the blonde was coming down the stairs. There was a man with her. They parted without a word, and the blonde came back up the street to her post. When she passed the mulatto, she said something to her, and they both laughed. Clete grinned to himself, too. He stood up. "Let's have another drink."

"All right," she said detachedly, as if she were thinking about something. He went inside and ordered another drink.

"Clete," she said when he came back. Her voice was strange. "Those are prostitutes down there."

He was defensive. "Well, of course they're prostitutes."

"And you've been watching them all this time."

"What's wrong with that? It's the French scene."

"How could you?"

"Because it's like life," he said. "You tell me I never look at reality. Well, that's as real as it's going to get down there. Now you look at it for a while."

She was still too stunned to be angry. "I can't," she said.

"Why not?"

"I don't know," she said. "I'm a woman. It's different for a woman."

It occurred to Clete that the unspoken understanding that lay between women, far deeper than between men, had never been made so clear to him before, as at this moment when one woman was watching other women sell themselves.

Down the street, it looked as though the mulatto was in business. A muscled young man, with his sleeves rolled up to his elbows, was leaning over her. One arm was propped intimately against the wall. She was not dismayed by the flaunting of his strength. If anything, the dark tilt of her head was more contemptuous than before. They talked for a moment, and then the young man suddenly laughed and moved away down the street. The mulatto had only been showing off, after all.

"I'm going inside for a while," she said.

"You don't want to watch, then?"

"If I do," she said, "it's going to bother me for a long time. I'd better go inside and think about it."

Clete pulled back his outstretched legs as she passed. He was not angry, but ashamed somehow, as though he had been caught doing something he shouldn't. He looked morosely through the bars of the balcony. Traffic was beginning to thin out with the dinner hour. The blonde was getting more bold, and the playful switching of her hips was something to see. Clete found that he was not very interested in her anymore. She had scored, and that was that. But the others had not, and he felt a sense of lacking for them. That was how everything went. The more flamboyant, the quicker the success.

There was a knocking on the door. It was the boy with the drinks. There was a pause, and then he heard her footsteps crossing the floor. Clete stayed where he was, really pleased, listening to the murmur of French and the tinkling of glasses.

"Clete! How much do I tip?" Her voice was only a little unnatural.

"If it's new francs . . ." he began, and then decided to go inside. It was just too complicated to explain. He took a coin out of her hand. The boy, who could probably speak English, was tactful enough to thank her instead.

"I almost did it," she said. Her cheeks were flushed.

"You did do it," said Clete. "All I did was hand him the tip." He mixed the drinks elaborately. "Shall we have them outside?"

"Well, I certainly don't want to drink alone in here."

It was subterfuge, and he went along with it. "You're sure you don't mind?"

"It wouldn't make much difference if I did."

When they were settled, he searched out the mulatto. She had not moved, but was leaning against her wall in the same pose she had struck from the beginning. Clete made a sound of sympathy.

"It's not dark enough yet," she said.

Startled, he looked at her. "What're you talking about?"

"Well, she's the dangerous type, or at least she likes to think so. That's her forte. It has to be nighttime for that to take. Men don't like danger in the daytime."

Clete laughed in amazement. "You're right, you know."

"Of course I'm right," she said. "I'm a woman."

"What about the other one?" asked Clete. "What's the psychology of a prostitute in a proper print dress?"

"Why, I haven't seen her yet," she said, leaning forward to follow the direction of his gaze.

The prostitute on the street corner was still strolling back and forth on her beat. She walked almost sedately, with her head held erect and looking forward, so that at times she seemed to melt invisibly into the passing people.

"Oh, no," she said, turning away quickly in pain. "I didn't want to see her."

"I'm sorry," said Clete. "I shouldn't have pointed her out to you." After a while, he said, "She bothers me too."

"Why does she bother you? I'm really interested."

"I'm not sure," said Clete. "Except that she makes me mad. What in the hell is she doing out there if she's not going to hustle?"

"It wouldn't work anyway. She hasn't got a prostitute's heart."

"Then what the hell is she doing out there?"

"God, what a question to ask!"

"All right," said Clete. "Then you tell me."

"If you can't see it," she said, "it won't do any good for me to tell you."

Clete accepted the rebuke in silence. "We'd better eat dinner," he said sulkily. "It's getting late."

"Wait a minute," she said. "I want to see this."

An American had appeared at the end of the street. He was wearing a raincoat with the collar pulled up, and his hands were plunged deep in his pockets. His purpose in coming to this street was so apparent in his every movement that he might as well have been wearing a sign. In spite of it, he walked ashamedly, weighed down with the heavy load of inhibitions of his American circumstance.

"I'll bet you a drink," she said to him. "Which one do you think will get him?"

"This time I don't want to look," said Clete. "He's so indecent he makes me disgusted."

"Now you know how I felt a while ago," she said. "Come on, which one do you choose?"

"I'll take the blond sex kitten."

"You're wrong. She's much too obvious for him. I'll choose the dangerous one instead."

The American passed the prostitute in the proper print dress without even noticing her. The blonde saw him coming the instant he rounded the corner. She stepped out into the middle of the sidewalk to block his progress. But she overplayed her game when she began tugging him by the arm. He disentangled himself from her grasp and fled down the street.

By the time he reached the next corner, his pace was slowed. The mulatto was waiting for him. As he approached, she said something to make him pause uncertainly. He fumbled in his pockets, and there was the flare of a match. Then he took a cigarette, too, and was lost. The mulatto enveloped him like a spider. After a moment, they went up the stairs together into the little hotel.

Clete took her to dinner at a sidewalk restaurant on the Champs Elysees. They had entrecôte and red wine, and after the wine, she spoke in animated French with the waiter.

When they walked home through the dim streets, she said, "The City of Light."

Clete felt the gray weight of the old, uncared-for buildings and the darkness. "Don't," he said. "They didn't mean it that way."

"But you do think of them together," she said.

When they were near the hotel, she had an inspiration. "Let's walk down the prostitutes' street."

"No," said Clete. "I'd rather see them from up there."

"There you are, escaping reality again."

"Maybe I am," said Clete. "But if I see them up close, I may not like them, and I like them now."

They mounted to the fourth floor on the rickety *ascenseur* and were plunged again into the maze of dark, oppressive hallways that led to their room. "The French stink," she said. "They really do."

Clete did not argue with her. The wine had worn off, and the helplessness was gnawing at him again. But this time he could not be sure whether it was because of her or if it had been his fault from the beginning. As soon as they got to the room, he ordered double brandies and went out to the balcony. She handled paying for the drinks with ease.

Clete sipped his brandy and allowed himself to become absorbed with the street. Business was picking up. The evening strollers had emerged like ants from somewhere, and the blonde and the mulatto were scoring regularly. There was a curious detachment in the attitudes of the men about it all. They seemed to approach the transactions as dispassionately as though they were deciding on what movie to go to.

From time to time, Clete sought out the prostitute in the print dress, and as promptly turned away. She was having no luck at all.

"I wonder what they say to men, exactly how they proposition," she said. "It's not like a private seduction, where everything is understood. It has to be in words. I've tried to imagine, but it all sounds so crude. And it can't be that, either."

Before she could pose the question, Clete said, "Don't ask me."

"Oh, but you know," she said. "All men know." She went on musingly. "There are so many things I don't know. I wonder what kind of lives they have at home. I wonder if they take Sundays off and go to church, if they have children at home, if they tuck them in and say, 'Bye, bye now. Mommy has to go to work.'"

Clete laughed. Now, curiously, it was she who was helping him. "You're getting whimsical," he said.

"Well, maybe I am," she giggled. "But I really do wonder."

They both fell silent as the same scene unfolded. A man and his wife and a child had rounded the corner. They had obviously been window-shopping. The woman and the child paused at a fashion store, and the man strolled on ahead. The blond prostitute, seeing a man unattached, stopped him on the sidewalk. She had no sooner begun talking to him when his wife and child joined him.

The blonde stared perplexedly at the family group, and then they all burst into laughter. The blonde went back to her wall, still almost doubled over, and the family continued on its way, the man and his wife leaning against each other in their hilarity.

"What a terrible city," she said, but not condemningly at all. She stood up. "It's time to go to bed."

Clete lay staring into the darkness as the sounds of the street diminished, until finally, the only sound was the hollow clicking of heels on the sidewalk, like a lonely drumbeat in the night.

He turned in bed and, quite by accident, touched her. It was like an electric shock between them. They made love then as they had not known it for many years.

Long afterward, the clicking of the heels wakened him, and he began to get out of bed. She stirred drowsily. "Are you going out on the balcony?"

"Yes, just for a minute."

"Clete," she mumbled. "Everything is going to be all right with me now. Will you thank them for me?"

Clete went out on the balcony. "Now, how do you figure that?" he said to himself.

The street was deserted, except for them. The night mist had come in, and the sidewalks and the buildings glistened with the wetness. They were all alone, walking with measured pace as on appointed rounds. Now they had on raincoats, and even the blonde was subdued. Over on the corner, the prostitute in the print dress paused for a moment before a shop window. In the window's reflections, she touched at her hair, and moved on very quickly.

And Clete remembered Africa in the war, and the first night he had seen the old crones of prostitutes sitting like gray death on the curbstones. They had called out in cracked voices that terrified him. Then he remembered what loneliness was.

STEPHEN SHU-NING LIU (1930–)

The son of a hermitic painter of water lilies, Stephen Shu-Ning Liu was born in Fuling, China, near the Yangtze River. His grandfather, a poet and Mandarin scholar, taught him the Chinese classics. In 1952, shortly before the Cultural Revolution, Liu left for San Francisco. In nearly five decades of hard work since that time, he has received numerous literary awards, published widely, and earned his Ph.D. in English from the University of North Dakota. He is widely regarded as Nevada's finest living poet, and he was the first Nevada writer to receive a fellowship in creative writing from the National Endowment for the Arts (1981–82). He was the first poet to appear on the cover of *American Poetry Review*, and his poetry was featured in *Seneca Review*. An avid bird photographer, he has returned to China four times, most recently to the island of Hainan, where the poet Su Tung-p'o was exiled in the eleventh century A.D. The following story received the NEA/PEN Syndicated Fiction Project Short Story Award. In 1993 Liu was inducted into the Nevada Writers Hall of Fame. Since 1973 he has taught English at the Community College of Southern Nevada, and for the past five years, he has been writing his autobiography. He lives with his wife, Shirley, in Las Vegas.

My Father's Martial Art and Other Poems. Reno: University of Nevada Press, 1999.
Dream Journeys to China. Beijing, China: New World Press, 1982.

The Yellow Crane

He calls himself a bird, a chickadee perhaps, that flies home across the Pacific. It has been forty summers since he last walked these cornfields. Landscapes appear different after the Revolution that ravished and ransacked the countryside like a Siberian hurricane. Through his made-in-USA sunglasses, he searches in vain for the banyan grove his ancestors had planted, the underbrushes where he used to pick strawberries, and the stone lions by the main gate. To his chagrin, he sees only arteries of the earth after months of drought. Skeletal conifers and bamboo twigs lie everywhere. Tall foxtails have blindfolded the lotus pond that once mirrored his face; cracked crannies on the wall gape at him like dusty eye sockets of the elders.

The timid steps of the visitor wake up the brick house from its decades of sleep. The front porch is half hidden in disheveled sugarcane stalks, and the grape awning has collapsed. The greenhouse has been reduced to a pile of debris. His homestead reminds him of a wrecked ship where waves have washed away almost everything. A rotten smell lingers in the hall. The rooms are dark and empty; most windows are sealed in nails, dust falling from the shattered ceilings. There had been times of looting and plunderage.

The house falls back into blunt silence when the traveler steps out into the afternoon sun and into the field. A curious crowd has been waiting for him. The sudden return of the native has alarmed people in the village. Some hundred indurate eyes shoot straight at him as though he were a rare animal from a foreign land.

"Can anyone tell me where my father is?" the gray-haired stranger hears his own voice. His question bounces back to him from a rampart of hard faces. The farmers remain calm, with their mouths closed like clamshells. The late Cultural Revolution has taught them one last lesson: mind your own business.

"Is he dead or alive?" the intruder insists his inquiry. "My father was your landlord. You called him 'the generous Earth Fairy.' Do you remember? He had never offended anybody. Some of you had never paid your rent for ages. Where is he? Tell me, please."

Again, silence. What can those onlookers say about his father? During the years of Land Reform, most of the landlords were publicly beaten up and abused—some hanged in trees, some starved to death, some sent away to hard labor camps. No one knows the whereabouts of his father. The old gentleman simply disappeared.

The traveler reaches for a tiny piece of painting in his pocket. He bought it at the hotel because the image of a yellow-eyed crane is in it. The bird rests on one leg among the lotus flowers, its long beak pointing out toward the sky, its wings spreading and shimmering in the last sun. The painter seems to say, "Look, my bird is going to fly!" Incidentally, the traveler's father was a painter of birds, especially the crane with yellow orbs, at the hillside that remained inactively dreaming in the lurid sun of the South.

Now he waves his silk artwork at the crowd. "My father was not a slave driver," he says, "nor was he a land shark. He was an artist, too busy painting his birds. Some of you received this kind of painting as a gift from him. How could you forget his greetings on New Year's festivals? He always laughed aloud, almost like a honking crane. There were good times. But what has happened to him? Is he dead or alive?"

Not a soul in the crowd dares to break the silence with a word or gesture. Their eyes appear uneasy in the sweltering summer afternoon. The traveler feels the heat that sweeps against him and brings forth odors of festered clovers and crops. He turns, and, like a somnambulist, he is on his way to Lion Head Mountain, north of the village.

Country roads grow narrow behind him. From the slopes he looks back: the small village sits there in the haze like an invalid. His father had often mentioned the mountain. He told his son that someday he would give up his land and would join the Chief Monk at the monastery on the mountain's peak, and that he would live in the world of Zen, a world without memories of pain or sadness. And each day he saw his father sitting on a cushion of reeds, cross-legged. The middle-aged man sat there like an Indian Buddha, breathing in the candlelight. He said that he had seen, many times, the splendors of his Western Paradise. Once he sat on the cushion, day or night, he would not budge a whit even if the house caught on fire. Yet in his hours of meditation, he would stretch out his arms like a cat, or pull his limbs together like a spider, or lift up his head like a crane with its beak above the water. The boy watched his father doing all these on the cushion. His dead-water-calm spirit, he said, would occasionally escape from his body, light as willow catkin, floating away far beyond the house, toward Lion Head Mountain. At times he said his flesh and bones would evaporate in the summer's heat; at times he said he would shrink into a grain, into the mouth of a lotus flower. And one night the boy heard his father say that he would go away from home, riding a yellow crane.

As if in an intimate dream, the traveler ascends the trails, where the limpish fungus and cow parsnips forever cover the earth from summer's heat. Myriads of wild daisies spread before him like a welcome carpet. With their trembling fingers, more aspen leaves usher him farther into the forest, into the fragrance of pine trees. To his left, about a mile from the trails, he discovers a hamlet with red barns against bamboo groves. A temple's steeple gleams by the waterfalls. Somewhere near the wooden bridge, the snow-white petals of a fruit tree are falling; on the lake there is a fishing boat with its dark nets flowing quietly over the sunlit waves. The landscape soothes and exhilarates him. He halts his steps, his eyes feeding on the scene once alive in his father's watercolor paintings. Now the monastery looms above the distant cliffs, no bigger than a bird nest. The sky tilts toward him. He feels a little dizzy. He has not had any food since morning. Quite fatigued after hours of climbing, he pillows his head against a mossy rock. A few minutes later, he is attacked by a mass of cold air. But he does not know it. His entire body becomes warm in the sun, a kind of familiar sunlight at the hillside, where he stands four feet tall, with his hair cut short across his forehead. In his morning robe, his father, as usual, talks to him as though he is old enough to understand the philosophy of a hermit.

"How do you like the crane in my painting? I painted the bird because I love the poem. Let's hear it, son."

The boy's eyes flash in comprehension. As he had done it before, he chants the verse mechanically:

> Riding his yellow crane,
> The ancient Bard had gone!
> Forever gone, with his crane,
> The tower stands here alone,
> And the white clouds float on
> For a thousand years, in vain . . .

"Very good! Not a word missed," his father says. "It's a wonderful poem. The Chief Monk said the Yellow Crane is the soul of man. The day will come, and we will be gone with the bird, far away from this world of vanity."

The painter has barely spoken his words when the spring sun, without any warning, flinches and oozes into a bank of clouds. Shadows rise, advancing toward the hillside like angry armies. His father turns away to grasp his paintings in the wind. The boy leaps into the air to rescue his father's works, but he falls on his back and feels the cold moss where he has been dozing off for a few minutes.

Jumping to his feet, he cries aloud, "Ah, Father, I know you're here. Don't hide from me. I know you're here." No answer: only the wind that roars through the pine trees. The wind had roared long before his father's time, long before this mountain was formed. It is late. The sun sinks fast behind the ridges. The slant trail leads him to a cluster of humble houses, all made of brown bricks and timbers. It could be an abandoned mining site or a place of hermits. No one sees him approaching. No dog barks. "I must go to someone and ask for a drink of water," the traveler says to himself. And for some time he has been sauntering among old graves, where tombstones had crumbled in last winter's storms. Just a few yards ahead of him something stirs in the bushes, something that lifts up heavily into the sky with a prolonged shrill. He draws back, holds his breath and watches the movement of that enormous flier with its legs dangling like pendulums, its eyes glowing copper-yellow in the last ray of the sun. It soon disappears over the woods. The wayfarer stands there at a loss. The evening deepens. And the graves, the hamlet, the monastery over the cliffs, the traveler himself, all melt away into a darksome mystery.

RANDALL C. REID
(1931–1992)

For nearly twenty years, Randy Reid taught English and creative writing at the University of Nevada, Reno. When he wasn't teaching or working with students, he turned to his own fiction. His stories were published in books and literary journals throughout the country (from *Prize Stories 1973: The O'Henry Awards* to *Antioch Review*), yet, to his credit, he remained an unassuming writer. One particular December evening in 1978 has stayed with me to this day. Though it was snowing outside, the Blue Mailbox cafe in Reno was filled, and the story he read was so vivid it bordered on poetry. Reid was a literary writer whose work and life ended all too soon after a long struggle with cancer, but he nearly always had a kind word for other writers, and he helped scores of them along the way—Judy Kohler, Greg Jones, and Valerie Varble among them. In his fiction, he was concerned with the "endless, nocturnal conversation of marriage," to quote Cyril Connolly. When he succeeded, the dialogue—frequently tinged with desperation—was unwavering in its portrayal of our delicate struggle to find love in a less-than-loving world.

Lost and Found. New York: Simon and Schuster, 1975.

Little Strokes

RUTH KEPT HER HANDS TIGHT ON THE WHEEL, trying to watch both the rain-blurred highway and the silent man who sat crouched against the door. The sealed letter from the clinic lay on the seat between them.

"You're not being committed," said Ruth. "Remember that. You are voluntarily undergoing treatment for an illness."

"You sound like the doctor," he said.

"All right," she said. "What's wrong with that?"

"You're my daughter, not my doctor."

"Of course," she said. She stretched her neck, peering through the streaked windshield. Her smock was too tight under the arms, and she felt swollen and clumsy, as though her limbs had grown short while her body thickened with the child.

"I'm scared," he said.

"It's not Bedlam," she said. "It's a hospital where they cure people."

"It's the looney bin," he said. He sat up, fumbling in his pockets until he found a cigarette. The trembling fingers bent again and struggled with a match. The match broke. He tore another match from the book, but now his hands shook so badly that he could not bring them together. She watched him stab and stab, his whole body beginning to tremble. He turned to her. "Please . . . ," he said. But as he spoke the cigarette dropped from his lips to the floor. He bent over, groping for it.

"Let it go," she said. Carefully, she lighted another cigarette and passed it to him.

"They'll give me shock," he said.

"I don't think so."

"They've got to promise," he said. "I won't go unless they promise."

"Dad," she said, "they won't give you anything you don't need."

Then, abruptly, he was silent. She could see him vanish, his eyes turning blind and his face crumpling as though all life had been pumped out from within. She knew that if she spoke now he would not hear or answer, but she knew that this too would not last. Whatever region he had fled to was no happier than any other, and soon he would be driven back, back into speech, panting as if he were being pursued.

She reached over, removing the dead cigarette from his lips. She knew, but she did not understand. Three months before, without any warning, he had appeared unshaven at the door. "I've been sick," he said, and that was all. He did not explain how he had come two hundred miles, nor what had happened. They led him in and put him to bed on the couch. "What is it?" Ed had asked. "I've never seen him like this." "I don't know," she said. Nor, it seemed, did he. "It's my heart," he said, "it's too much liquor, it's my nerves." But she had doctors come, and they found nothing wrong with his heart. She kept liquor from him, but he did not improve. Then the question, the question she asked so often: "Dad, it's not liquor and it's not your heart. What is it? What's wrong?" Always the same response—the look of terror, the sudden tremor of the hands, the small voice saying, "I don't know, I don't know." So there were other doctors; weekly, she took him to the psychiatric section of a public clinic. But he did not improve. Cigarette burns appeared like stigmata on his fingers, and his shins were scarred and blackened from bruises he had not even felt. Some days he would not leave the house. "It's their eyes," he said. "I'm afraid of people's eyes." There were days when he sat almost without moving, days when he drank pots of coffee, pitchers of iced tea, a half gallon of wine, as though nothing could fill the void within him. "You've got to love me," he said. "You've got to love me." "I do," she said, but this was not enough. He would cry out for her at night, and she would get up, knowing that Ed was awake beside her and that his patience would suffer this too without protest.

She slowed for a red light. He sat up, blinking at the other cars. "Are we there?"

"No," she said. "It's fifteen miles yet." She glanced at her watch, for to her, too, it seemed they had been driving for hours.

"You know," he said, "I think I can make it."

"Good."

"I mean without the hospital. I think with a little more time to get on my feet . . ." His voice trailed off, and he sat looking at her, his face like that of a child who expects to be refused.

"We don't have any more time," she said. "The baby's almost due."

"I could help," he said. "I could help with the housework."

She did not answer. That morning, he had not been able to put on his socks or tie his shoes.

"Does . . . does. . . ." He frowned, closing his eyes. "Does . . . does he—*God damn it.*"

"What's wrong?"

"His name, I can't think of his name."

"You mean Ed?"

"Does Ed like me?"

"He's always liked you. He's always spoken well of you."

He paused, his hands playing with the letter from the clinic. "How about you?"

"Dad," she said, "you know I love you." The words no longer meant anything to her. They were a sound he required, a sound that soothed him, and by now they were a habit, perhaps even a lie.

But the words seemed to have worked. She saw his face relax, almost smiling. He had moments of sudden health, moments when it seemed that a haircut and a change of clothes were all he needed to be cured.

"Are you happy about the baby?" he said.

"Yes," she said. "Of course."

"It's a funny thing, having a child." He paused, his mouth slightly open, as if to test the shape of other words. "Do you remember when you were little? When you used to get in bed with us because you had nightmares? Your mother got tired of it. I remember when she made you stay in your own bed and you got so scared you screamed. I heard it. My God, the neighbors could hear it. Your mother said, 'Frank, she's eight years old. She's got to learn to sleep by herself. She's got to learn not to be afraid of the dark.' And I said, 'She won't ever learn it being shut up in there alone.' I said that. And I went in there and sat by your bed all night long. Your mother said, 'You'll spoil her, Frank. I hope you enjoy sitting up with her every night.' And I said, 'My God, Alice, don't you know what it's like to be afraid of the dark?'"

She drove on in silence, watching the billboards loom and vanish.

"Do you remember that?" he said. "Yes," she said. "I remember." She had always thought some violence would claim him, something careless and bloody like that fall from the roof that had split and scarred his brow so long ago. Or like the finger he had sliced off in the band saw, making a toy chest for her room. But instead a subtle change now seemed to possess his features, a change more terrifying because so slight, because it was still the same face and she had to recognize it.

"It's Ed, isn't it?" he said. "He made you do this."

"No." After a moment, she said, "And I'm not doing it. You are."

"What if I don't get well?"

"You will."

"But what if I don't?"

"Dad," she said, "you will be under the care of doctors. They'll find what's wrong and they'll know what to do about it."

"How do you know?"

"I know."

She glanced again at her watch and then stared mindlessly at the road.

"Do you suppose—" he said. "Do you suppose we could have a little drink?"

"No."

"I've got to."

He stared at the windshield as though the arcing path of the wipers entranced his eyes. "Your mother," he said. "She always thought a little drink was damnation."

"You're not a drinker, Dad. Not really."

"Maybe not," he said. "Maybe not, but I want one now."

He grabbed the door handle. As she stabbed at the brake, she felt the car swerve on the wet pavement, and she heard the squeal of other tires behind her. She wrenched the car around and sent it skidding onto the shoulder of the road. It rocked, tipped, and settled back. The traffic whipped past them, but she did not turn to see.

"You almost killed us," she said.

He crouched against the door, his frightened eyes staring at her. Her hands were shaking, and she felt the shock of fear pass into nausea. For a moment, she was afraid she would have to get out and be sick by the edge of the road.

"God damn you," she said. "Ed didn't want me to drive because of the baby, but I said yes, he'll feel better if I take him. And you try to kill us."

He did not answer. She waited until her hands stopped shaking, and then she stooped heavily and picked up the letter from the clinic, replacing it on the seat.

He cleared his throat. "I want out," he said.

"Just put me out," he said. "Right there by the side of the road. Just put me out and forget me."

"Ruth," he said, "I'm not going to get well."

"Yes, you are."

"No. Something happened. I don't know what, but something happened. I've been in a mess before, but not like this. Before, it was my fault . . ." His words died, and when they began again she winced at the terror in his voice. "I just can't do anything. Do you know what that means? *I just can't do anything.*"

She was silent, remembering the clinic doctor's question: "Has your father had any strokes?" She had said no, not that she knew of. "His tests indicate possible organic damage to the brain," said the doctor. "Or perhaps not. We don't know. But at his age, it is always a possibility."

"Dad," she said. For an instant she wavered, but then she closed her mind as decisively as she could close her eyes, and when she spoke, her voice was firm. "You're just fifty-nine years old. You've got a lot of life ahead of you. That's why I'm taking you to the hospital, and that's why you're going to submit yourself voluntarily to treatment."

She switched on the ignition and turned the car onto the highway, its wheels slipping in the mud.

"Do you love me?" he said.

"Yes," she said.

The rain had stopped, and she reached up to turn off the windshield wipers. Ahead, she saw the blinking yellow light of an intersection. "We're almost there," she said.

She turned off the highway, following a narrow road through orchards and fields. The bare limbs of winter trees stood up against the sky, gaunt and rain-blackened, dark as the wet earth about their roots. Yet here and there the ground was hidden by yellow mustard blossoms and the new green of grass. It will be spring soon, she thought.

Another turn, and the hospital appeared before them—a sprawl of old brick buildings rising above the orchard trees. She swung the car into the gravel parking area.

"See," she said. "It's a nice place. Trees and lawns."

But as they climbed the steps to the administration building she was not so sure. The dark lobby seemed to funnel like a cave before them, and behind her she had seen patients in faded khakis trudging along like the remnants of a defeated army.

She paused at the lobby desk to ask directions, then turned down a dim corridor to her right. He followed her, stumbling, letting her pull him by the arm.

"Walk," she said. "Stand up and try to walk."

But he would not. He did not resist her, but he was like a horse being led, contributing no volition of his own.

The office was empty. "Sit down," she said, pointing to the single chair. He sat. Aside from the chair, the tiny room contained only a desk and a green filing cabinet. It could have been a closet, a cell, a public toilet.

"Ruth?"

"Yes."

"You wouldn't have me do this if you didn't know it was right, would you?"

"No," she said. "No, I wouldn't."

He subsided then, but as they waited, she saw him begin to shift and twitch in the chair. *Please,* she thought, *please hurry.*

At last the doctor came—a shabby, fat man who seemed to carry fraud or failure like a scent about his person. She gave him the letter. He opened it and let his face assume the practiced, depthless gravity of a mortician.

The doctor folded the letter. "You are Frank Talbot?"

A quick nod, like a small convulsion.

"And it is your wish to be admitted here?"

Another nod.

"Very well. Would you please read this application and then sign at the bottom?"

Her father held the paper, its edge rattling against the wire basket on the desk.

"Is something wrong?" said the doctor.

"I can't read it."

The doctor nodded. "Your signature will be sufficient."

Ruth watched her father's fingers bend and grapple with the pen. The pen scratched and caught. The doctor glanced at him, noting, without comment, the violent tremor of the hands. Then the pen moved, and the long, wretched scrawl continued, ending with a wavering flourish as he crossed the final *t.* He handed the pen to the doctor and slumped exhausted in his chair.

"Thank you, Frank," said the doctor. He picked up the paper, examining the signature. "Thank you," he said again.

There were other questions then—date and place of birth, marital status, occupation, record of military service. Her father's voice broke and faltered, until at last she took over for him and supplied the final answers herself.

The doctor paused, checking over the forms he had completed. He nodded and shifted his gaze from the papers to the people. His eyes were veiled, discreet, but she felt the sudden need to answer them.

"He wasn't always like this," she said.

"Of course," said the doctor. He stood up. "I will send an orderly to take your father to the ward." He left the office.

"Do you think he liked me?" said her father.

"Yes," she said. She put a hand on his shoulder.

"I wouldn't do this for anyone else," he said. "Not anyone else on earth. Do you know that?"

Ruth dropped her hand. She stood looking at the floor, her fingers rubbing idly at a cigarette burn on the edge of the desk.

"Yes," she said at last. "I know that."

When the orderly appeared, she gave her father's shoulder a final squeeze. "I've got to go now, Dad," she said.

"Wait," he said. "What are they going to do?"

"Just take you to the ward."

"Do you love me?"

"Yes, Dad."

The orderly took her father's arm, and she began to back out of the room.

"Wait, do you love me?"

"Yes," she said. She turned and walked quickly down the hall, but his voice pursued her, an idiot sound. "Do you love me? Do you love me?" She turned the corner. The voice rose and broke, demanding of doctors, nurses, patients, and the echoing halls themselves, "Do you love me? Do you love me?"

She hurried through the lobby and down the steps. "No," she said. "No, I don't." But she knew that even this lie would not help.

HART WEGNER
(1931–   )

As a boy in Silesia, in an eastern region of Germany (which later became a part of Poland), Hart Wegner lived in a prewar Europe that would inform his fiction for a lifetime. As do so many immigrant writers, he has had to choose between the unsettling distance of two homes—one past and one present but neither truly home. Out of this long journey have come words that are sparse, meditative, and, at their best, evocative of a time most would not remember, save those like Hart who cannot forget their country's sorrow. For more than thirty years, he has taught German, comparative literature, and film studies at the University of Nevada, Las Vegas. His fiction has frequently been published in *MSS* (the journal edited by the late John Gardner) and in other American and—in translation—European journals. He was twice cited on the honor roll of some of our finest foreign-born authors (from the Pushcart Prize and the *Best American Short Stories*), and he was the first Southern Nevadan to be inducted into the Nevada Writers Hall of Fame. Currently, he is finishing a novel, *The Dragon*, and starting on a novel set against the background of present-day Vienna. The following story is taken from *Off Paradise*, a collection of interwoven stories about an immigrant family living in Las Vegas.

Off Paradise. Reno: University of Nevada Press, 2001.
Houses of Ivory. New York: Soho Press, 1988 (distributed by Farrar, Straus, and Giroux).

Cockshut Light

"YOU WERE ELEGANT," Mother was talking to Father while she dragged a wicker chair to the foot of his bed. Martin wanted to help, but by the time he had lifted the sleeping dog from his lap, Mother was already cranking down the hospital bed. After the amputation of Father's left leg, Mother had ordered an electric bed for the living room rather than leaving him a day longer in the hospital.

"Before you get comfortable, help me slide him up. But don't hurt yourself. He looks thin, but he has a heavy skeleton."

Martin winced. He didn't like it when she talked about Father's heavy skeleton, although she'd done it as long as he could remember, usually in men's clothing stores when they had gone shopping with Father. When Martin slipped his arm under his father's back, it felt moist and warm where it had lain on the egg-crate pad. Like lifting up a hen, he thought and remembered how as a child, he had carried chickens around their yard by putting his hands in their wing pits. With his left arm Martin clasped Father to his own chest, while supporting himself with his right hand in the warm hollow his father's head had made in the golden-yellow pillow. Mother liked bold colors, and when she saw something dull or gray, she would ask, "How can I bring some life into it?"

She unbuttoned Father's pajama top. "Can you hold him for another moment?" Together they pulled his jacket off. The flesh of his arms had shrunk so much that his elbows were large knobs. She toweled him and shook baby powder over his bent back and held on to him with one hand while with the other she plucked a freshly laundered jacket off the sofa. When they lowered him onto the yellow pillow, Father smiled at Mother and Martin.

"That's done," she said and smiled at her son. Every morning when he came by on his way to work she proudly presented Father to Martin, alive, well cared for, and doing as well as one could expect from a man who had celebrated his ninetieth birthday and had been disabled since the first of the big wars. Martin knew that in spite of all she was doing for Father, the coldness from his swollen foot was rising. Not only was it chilling his one remaining leg, but it was moving upward until his whole body lay cold.

Martin kissed his father and turned away while his father patted Nini, who stood upright resting her forepaws on the rail of his bed.

"Ah, that's done," Mother sighed while she propped a pillow for her back into the wicker chair. It wasn't comfortable for her, but she wouldn't give it up, because it had been Father's favorite chair before his illness. When he still drove, she had picked out carpet squares in colors she liked from sample bins and had sewn two flat pillows for him. Then he had to give up driving. Now the sun was fading the golden metallic paint on Father's Toronado that had been parked too long in the same spot. While Father lay sick she refused to accept rides to go shopping, just as she hadn't left Father's room during his six weeks in the hospital. When the surgeon—who was to take Father's leg—had asked Martin why his mother stayed day and night in the hospital room, Martin had apologized that his parents were

"Old Country people." *And so am I,* he had wanted to add, but he had just stood there in his fine American suit and had said nothing. When he later thought that he should have done it, he wasn't even sure that it would have been the truth. Was he an Old Country *mensch,* a man of the New World, or something entirely different?

"Yes, you *were* elegant." Mother talked toward the bed. Pushing her shoulders back against the hard pillow, she turned to Martin. "It keeps going through my mind. When we first met . . . on the stairs, he wore a tailored suit. Very fashionable. Midnight-blue with a handkerchief in his pocket that was blossom-white. It was during a weekend conference at the Elisabet Gymnasium. The next day he wore a different suit."

"What color was the other suit?" Martin always liked to hear about the church conference where his parents met.

"Dove-blue."

"I remember he had three suits made all at once," Martin said.

"How would you know that?" Mother asked. "You were just a child."

"*I* was the one he took to his fittings. You two are not the only ones who remember. The tailor shop was on the second floor. I can still see us walking up the steep, narrow steps."

"Maybe they just seemed steep because you were a child. How old could you have been?"

"On the big day when the suits were ready, *I* was with him, but I can't remember if we were still living in the apartment on Pulststrasse or had we already bought the house?"

"Don't strain yourself, it doesn't matter," Mother consoled him. She often told him, "Remembering is hard work, so don't try so hard to remember."

"I *was* with him that day, but how could he have carried three suits? We didn't have a car, not until America when you bought the dark-blue Plymouth. Maybe the tailor delivered them. What was his name?"

"Janek!" Father called out before Martin could remember. Since Father didn't speak much anymore, Martin was startled to hear his voice, dulled by the pillows enclosing his face.

"The druggist on the corner . . ."

"Duvineau," Mother answered triumphantly.

Duvineau, the cluttered drugstore, where Martin got the bird pictures he collected and glued in an album with cream-colored pages. Mother kept buying Chlorodont and with each tube he got a new picture. Every day he looked at the birds in his album, and when he had enough empty toothpaste tubes he melted them down to cast lead soldiers.

"Next to Duvineau was the Engel butcher . . ."

"And across the street was the bridge to Tschansch." Martin spoke quickly so he could better the others at remembering.

"We took the bridge when he had to go to the . . ." Mother stopped in the middle of the sentence.

When we had to go to the cemetery, that's what she was going to say, Martin thought. "On the footpath curving from the top of the bridge we rode a sled. Not often . . ." It was the same sled they had packed with everything they could carry when they were preparing to flee. Mother, Grandmother, and Martin had waited by the sled for Father while they listened to the rumbling of the artillery fire. They were going to pull the sled and go west. When Father came home he argued angrily that they would freeze to death or die from exhaustion in some snowdrift by the side of the road. He made them unpack the sled and carry what they could to the railroad station.

"And the Dietrich baker . . . Now, these are all the houses between Duvineau's and the railroad station. We remembered them all." She sighed as she settled back in her chair.

With eyes closed he listened to his mother as she shifted in her uncomfortable chair while she tried to keep the wicker from creaking.

"What are you thinking?" Martin asked without opening his eyes.

"An die Heimat."

He knew that she meant Silesia and not Germany, although one had been part of the other. Years ago, when he was learning English, he had made a file of definitions. *"Heimat"* he had to file in German, because he couldn't find a fitting translation. "Home" meant something else, "back home" reminded him of a Frank Capra film and seemed fitting only for America, while "homeland" was a word for immigration and census forms. After a few years he had given up trying to explain the meaning of *"Heimat"* to his American friends. How much sense could such a word make to people who moved every few years after having a garage sale of what they didn't want to take along? He was shocked when he noticed the coincidence that in his file index the *"Heimat"* card came directly between "heaven" and "hell."

"What was I wearing when I met Father? It doesn't come to me right now." She bowed her head as she concentrated on a night almost sixty years ago. "It used to be that I could ask Aunt Bertel and she would know, because in those years she tailored everything that I wore. After she was gone, I could still ask Aunt Lydia, because we were always together, even on the night when I met Papa. Now I'm the only one left of those who know.

"When Aunt Bertel saw Father, she said to me, 'This man is of nobility.' Just like that. Not, this man *looks* like a nobleman or *acts* like one, no, he is. That humpbacked little woman knew, the way she knew many other things." With her head lowered, she drifted again into the past.

"He asked me to dance." Laughing softly, she reached under the blanket to pat Father's foot. "And then he came back and asked me for a second dance."

Through the years he had heard about the meeting on the stairs, when Mother saw Father for the first time. After reading the story of the Nibelungen, he had imagined the meeting on the stairs as having been of the same importance as that of Kriemhild and Brunhild on the steps of the cathedral in Worms. Even as a child he had understood it to mean that great things would happen, but he had hoped that for his family's sake they wouldn't be all blood and fire as they had been for the Nibelungen.

"Ah, the stairs," Mother said as if she had read his mind as she so often did. "It was a church conference with a Saturday night dance. Hat in hand, Father was walking upstairs, while my mother and Lydia and I were going down. Midnight-blue. Now I remember." She laughed with satisfaction. "My dress was of midnight-blue velvet, and the stairs were as wide as those leading to the ballroom of a palace."

Martin remembered the stairs well. When he was nine his father had enrolled him in that same school—Elisabet—and he had told his son that the school had been founded in 1292. Martin knew that Father, a practical man, didn't enroll his son at Elisabet because he once had danced there with Mother. He had selected this preparatory school over others in Breslau because its location made it easier for Martin to commute. But Father had planned in vain. Soon after, the school was turned into a military hospital because it was so close to the railroad station where the casualties arrived from the Russian front.

"He had such masterful green eyes."

"Ah, yes . . ." Father sighed.

"Don't you make fun of me." She patted his foot under the blanket. "Next day in church he wore his dove-blue suit." She lowered her head. "I have never forgotten." The dog, shivering in her dream, whimpered on Martin's knees. He gently shook her awake.

"Poor Nini." Mother patted the blanket of the sickbed.

"Ah, yes, after that Sunday service he waited two weeks before he came running." She gave Father's leg a squeeze. He laughed among his pillows. "Listen to him," she said proudly. "Laugh! It's good for you. Yes, he came running all the way to Waldenburg where I was living with my parents. Two hours by train . . ."

"What did you do?"

"We walked together."

Father *did* like to walk, Martin thought, in spite of his leg wound that he had brought home along with other wounds from the First World War. The few photos they had left from home were mostly walking shots. On an outing Father would screw his Agfa camera onto the tripod, set the timer, and then—at his cue—the three of them smiled as they strode in measured steps toward the ticking camera.

When Martin was old enough Father took him on walks in the evening. They walked along the fence of the wooded Walter estate. Between a hedge and the rail line to Breslau, the path led to a pond where they often turned around to go home.

One evening they heard shots.

"They are hunting birds," Father said.

"So late?" Martin asked fearfully. "It's almost dark."

"The birds fly at dusk." Father took him by the hand and they walked on. After a few steps they heard rustling in the dry leaves. Crouching down, Martin saw a big bird huddled under the hedge. From a toothpaste picture he could tell that it was a pheasant: the feathers of its back were iridescent and the reddish wings flecked with gold. What hadn't been on the picture was the crimson stain on one of the wings. Martin was kneeling by the hedge—his face close to the wounded bird—when a boot came down and pressed the pheasant against the wire fence. Forced into the mesh, the bird's shiny feathers had turned into square golden pillows. The bird was stretching its neck toward Martin and opened its beak to crow. Its eyes were glowing yellow in the fading light, when, without warning, the hand of the beater reached down and twisted the pheasant's neck. Once more its wings tried to fly, but only a few feathers twitched among the golden pillows shiny with blood. Martin couldn't get up. He told himself later that he must have heard the fragile, white-banded neck snap, but what he remembered most sharply was the whir of wings above his head. He kept kneeling while he listened to the sound of the wings growing faint and then to the silence afterward, until his father pulled him up and drew him toward the railroad crossing and the pond. The hedge along the path bore snowberries, glowing white in the failing light like lanterns during the Night of the Dead. Martin stripped off a handful of white berries and dropped them on the hard-packed earth. Then he stomped on each berry and made it explode with a crack.

"They aren't going to shoot anymore. It's too dark." Father pulled him along. When Martin didn't stop crying, his father walked up the railroad embankment and picked a sorrel leaf. From his breast pocket he pulled a handkerchief, blindingly white in the near darkness, and rubbed the leaf on both sides. Then he held it out for the boy.

Their house was dark because Mother had already pulled down the light-tight black shades so enemy planes couldn't spot them. The blackout badge in the shape of a magpie spread a greenish glow on Martin's lapel. At their front door Martin spat out the sorrel juice that had gathered in a sour pool under his tongue. When they sat at the dinner table he couldn't get himself to swallow any food. Before he went to his cold bedroom he unpinned from his jacket the magpie badge that Father had brought back from Bad Elster, a spa where he had been for a cure. Martin thought it strange that a spa where his father bathed in health-restoring waters along with other invalids should be named after a carrion-eating bird. Shivering in his bed, he pressed the pin with a cupped hand against the bulb of the lamp on the nightstand. With wings spread, the bird glowed brightly like an angel, but when Martin sniffed it, the magpie smelled like sulphur on the head of a match.

He leaned back in his chair, his mouth puckered as if he were still chewing the sorrel of long ago. Mother looked up when he cleared his throat.

"My mind drifted. On one of our walks Papa and I went to look at the new palace. My grandfather had worked there as secretary to the prince. In the new palace they had built a hall of mirrors especially for the emperor, but it didn't get finished in time for his visit. The Silesian prince had married Daisy, a girl from England with long golden hair, blue eyes and beautiful skin. She was a real princess, although her father had been no more than an officer. Daisy always wanted to go back to England. She understood what it meant to be homesick.

"Long before I met Papa, Grandfather had been invited to the birthday party celebration of the princess. Daisy, the greatest beauty of them all, drew the winning numbers of the raffle, and Grandfather won a painting of Eve under the apple tree framed in *Ebenholz*."

Martin hadn't heard "ebony wood" since Grandmother had told him fairy tales of princesses whose long hair glistened like ebony wood in the moonlight.

"When the prince proposed to her at a ball in London, she told him that she didn't love him. Her family needed money, and there was talk that Hans the Magnificent, as they called the Fürst von Pless behind his back, bought Daisy for a string of pearls six yards long."

Folding a pillowcase, she kept smoothing the yellow linen in her lap over and over.

"I had pearls of my own." She took off her glasses and rubbed her eyes. "They were almost real, but I never cared about jewelry. When we had to flee, I didn't even take my amethyst pendant because we barely got away before Breslau was declared a fortress. When our refugee train finally arrived in Waldenburg, Aunt Lydia immediately asked me: 'Did you bring your amethyst?'" Mother shook her head. "We were still sitting on our suitcases, and Lydia asked about the amethyst, while I was sick with worry about what might be happening to Papa, who had stayed behind in the fortress."

A mighty fortress is our God, Martin thought, *a good armor and weapon.* And they were still fighting in the ruins of the fortress Breslau on the sixth of May 1945, after everybody else in Europe had given up on the war.

Behind the pillows Father breathed faintly. Was he asleep or was he listening to the stories from the past?

"It *was* a beautiful violet stone. So clear."

"I remember your amethyst." Sneaking into his parents' bedroom—he wasn't supposed to be there at all—Martin had pulled out the drawer of Mother's dressing table, but only far enough so that he could peer into it. With a pounding heart he watched the amethyst shoot purple rays from its dark cave in the drawer of the table.

He shook his head like Nini when she came out of the water. Most of the time he tried not to think of Silesia and their losses. "And Daisy?"

"For the sake of the pearls she moved as a very young woman into a strange country. When she married Hans Heinrich the Magnificent she was just a little younger than I was when I married Papa. She was eighteen and I . . ."

"You were twenty."

"Moving to Brockau was for me like going to a strange country. Waldenburg, where I grew up, was surrounded by hills, mountains, and forests, while Brockau sat in potato and sugar beet fields, flat and gray as a slate board. We still wrote on slate in the first grade."

"I did too."

"Before your papa took me to Brockau he gave me a colored brochure like a travel agent might. It described Brockau as 'the Garden City,' while it was in reality a town of railroaders, built around the shunting yard." She laughed. "Not an ordinary railroad station, but the biggest freight yard east of Berlin. But you know all of that anyway."

"I was so young when we had to leave . . . and that was a lifetime ago."

"The Brockauers were proud of their freight yard, except during the war, then they worried that it might attract the bombers. Most of them rented apartments from Papa's company. I still remember the day when I went for the first time to your father's office. Every man behind the counter and those behind their desks looked at me. They stared because I was new in town, the one their boss had married. Father was the comptroller and sat on the board of directors. I was proud to be married to Papa. Men pulled their hats when they saw him walk by, even if he was walking on the other side of the street. But I did feel alone in the new town. Daisy von Pless must have felt like that too. But one day the empress befriended her when she heard Daisy play the piano in a remote room of the palace. . . . We too had a piano. Too bad you didn't learn how to play. Do you know that the empress I am talking about was the mother of Kaiser Wilhelm II?"

Martin shook his head.

"Although no empress befriended me, I had Papa and later moved my mother down from Waldenburg and she brought her father with her, but we soon had to bury him in our cemetery."

"I went with you to the graveyard. When you weeded his grave and watered the flowers I played near the back wall, by the heap where they threw the old decorations."

It had grown dark in the room.

As a child he had hated nightfall. At dusk, he was called in from the garden where he liked to play all day. Often his parents made him sit with them in the living room without turning on the lights. When Martin asked why he had to sit in the dark, Mother answered by calling it "our twilight hour." His parents wanted him by their side and to be as quiet as they were while night was falling. He looked longingly across their big garden toward the highway and the rail line into Breslau. In better light he would at least have been able to watch the big storage tanks of the municipal gas company and been able to tell which one was rising and which one was sinking into the ground. Father and Mother put up their legs while they were listening to the radio that played softly in the twilight. Caught on the glass doors of the bookcase was the last gleam of reddish light, like the fire in the kitchen stove when it was about to die.

For Martin darkness came too slowly. If his parents would just let him twist the light switch so that he could read. While he had to sit with his parents in the deepening dark he welcomed even the yellowish glow of the radio dial as if it were a porthole in the brick walls. If he could just see if anything was happening in their garden, but Father's large mahogany desk wouldn't let him stand close to the window. He knew that by now all of the chickens had gone into the henhouse, although he wondered how they knew when it was about to get dark, because they certainly weren't very smart in other ways. Before the light had faded most of them filed quietly through the door while some dodged through the open hatch and flew up to their perches. They all knew, the old ones who couldn't fly anymore and had to wobble up the slanting board with the cleats nailed to it, as well as the young ones, they all knew when it was time.

One night he asked if he could leave the room.

"Why can't you sit quietly with us?" his father had asked.

As if he had always known the answer to this question Martin answered immediately, "Because my heart beats too fast."

On another night he finally couldn't wait any longer, and he turned on the light. In the soft glow of the lamp over the dining table he saw his father and mother holding hands.

"Too early," was all Father said. Guiltily, Martin switched off the light, as if he knew that he had broken a spell.

Sometime after the killing of the pheasant he became ill. As an unusual favor, granted only because of his sickness, he was allowed to sleep in the living room. It had the best stove in the house. As an even greater favor he was given permission to keep a light on during the night by his makeshift bed on the sofa. He had asked that Father's brass desk lamp with its shade of green silk be put on a chair next to the sofa. "You are pampering the boy," Father had grumbled, but Mother had prevailed.

Because his throat was so sore that he couldn't eat, Mother put a jar with strawberries from their own garden under the lamp with the green shade. From time to time during the night he would spoon some strawberries. Even now he could feel the strawberries in their cold, sweet juice sliding down his aching throat.

In the middle of the night, when he was sure that no one would come into the living room to check on the patient, Martin opened his book on wild birds. He didn't turn anymore to the picture of the red-and-golden pheasant but went instead to the page with the black-and-white magpie. When his lips were forming the Latin words *pica pica,* he had to laugh because it sounded like a chicken pecking. Although the laughter hurt his throat, he hoarsely muttered "pica pica" again and again. Because of the shortages of food, part of their garden had been fenced as a chicken run. Among the brown Rhode Island laying hens, he imagined the black-and-white magpie, its head tilted as if it were eyeing a kernel. After Martin's family had fled from Brockau—women and children first—Father had slaughtered the chickens and had taken them to his aunt in Breslau, who stayed in the city after it had been declared a fortress. Friends had last seen her walk out of her burning house, and then she was lost forever. The magpie was pecking away at them all.

Nini moaned, her belly resting on Martin's thighs.

"How can a dog sleep so much?" Mother asked.

"Maybe with her it's the way it is with Father."

"I guess she is getting to be an old dog."

He didn't want to think of Nini as being old. True, a grayish cast was dulling her big black eyes, but he told himself that it was only visible in a certain light. At home they had a saying for taking care of a task that had been put off for a long time: *alte Hunde totschlagen,* to slay old dogs. He never liked Mother to say that, just as he didn't like her to talk about Father's heavy skeleton. Stroking Nini, he entwined his fingers in her pale curls as if that way he could hold and keep her forever.

He was back in the glow of the green light, lying on the sofa with his bird book that told him magpies mate for life. He liked that, because it sounded like Father and Mother, who had never been separated, but another part of the description puzzled him. Within a day after one bird of a magpie couple has been killed, all the other magpies flock together and the survivor selects a mate from that group. How do they tell each other that someone has died? How do they know? Propped up by extra pillows so that he could breathe easier, he imagined the silent council of birds. At the center of the circle stood the magpie with its head tilted, looking at each of the birds and choosing solemnly, as if it were a meeting on the stairs.

When he was too tired to keep the large book from closing, he would hold the magpie pin to the bulb and watch the bird glow brightly. He wondered why he liked its phosphorescence, because everybody knew that these birds were thieves, but its glow made up for the many silent dusks in the living room.

"Do you want me to turn the lights on for you?" Martin asked, softly, so that if his Mother should be asleep, he wouldn't wake her.

"No."

"Whatever happened to Daisy?"

"She became paralyzed and the prince divorced her. At the palace they never finished the hall of mirrors, not even by 1914, and what wasn't finished by then . . . And by 1918, after the war had been lost, all the horses were gone. The prince had been proud of his stud farm, but now the stables stood empty. And all of that devastation was just after the first war. . . ."

In his family too many stories were told that ended with "and after 1918"—then came a deep sigh—or "after 1945," followed by a sigh or more often by silence.

"You know, much has happened to us, but we were always happy as long as we were together. Even then."

Martin knew what she meant by "then": the time at the end of the war and the time right after when they had been together every hour of their days, walking across Germany, every step toward Silesia. During the day they pulled a handcart, and at night they slept wherever they could. He had liked barns best, but it wasn't often that a farmer would let them in.

"Until one day they told us that we weren't allowed to go back to Silesia." Maybe Mother knew what had gone through his mind.

He heard a sigh from Father's bed. Was he listening or had he sighed in his sleep?

"*Never.* That we would *never* be allowed to go back to Silesia," Martin added.

A helicopter clattered over their house, and he followed the fading sound as though it mattered, as once the whirring of pheasant wings had.

"When we heard that our house had been burned to the ground, there was nothing left to hold us in Germany because in West Germany we were strangers anyway and the time was right to go to America. They had taken our home from us and everything in it. What we had left was our lives."

The slamming of a car door made Nini growl. She was becoming heavy, and Martin twisted around in his chair. Now that he faced the sofa, he was looking at the golden cardboard wreath with a "50" in its center. Martin had put it on the wall for his parents on their anniversary celebration, and his mother had never taken it down. The year after their golden wedding he had bought a single "1" at a florist shop and stuck it into the wreath in front of the much larger "0." Every year he changed the numbers. Now a cardboard "4" leaned from the wreath, as if it were ready to fall.

"But hasn't everything turned out to have been a blessing?"

The headlights of a passing car swept over the wreath and made the leaves shine golden above his mother's head. In the flash of the sudden glare he had seen how her hand had settled like a shadowy bird on his father's foot.

He listened to the rhythm of her breathing and hoped that she had fallen asleep. What a blessing? A friend who had visited Polish Silesia had taken pictures of the garden that once had surrounded their home. The house was gone, and all that was left of it was a grassy mound. A rusting pump, from which they had carried water for the garden, and the brick henhouse were the only things that had survived. The fruit trees had been cut down in the garden, which was now overgrown with weeds. Travelers coming back had reported that the bricks from the burned-out ruin of their house had been taken to the east, maybe even as far as Russia. That the stones had been used to build other houses had consoled him for a while, but not tonight. He wanted to be back in the railroad town that once had dreamed of being a garden city. Tonight he wanted to walk into the sunset across land flat as a slate toward the violet cone of the Zobten mountain. He wanted to have his home back, the house of his childhood, the garden where he had run on paths bordered by wild strawberries, white and red.

He thought that he had accepted the losses and had made peace, but tonight the past stared at him, its bright yellow eyes undimmed by darkness and unclouded by time.

He saw himself standing in the snow, his head turned eastward toward the grumbling of the artillery that had grown louder with every day. He stomped his feet, but the cold crept up his legs. His mother lingered with the house key in her hand. It was January, and so it was getting dark early. She couldn't bring herself to lock the front door of their house. Impatiently Martin flicked the cord of the sled as if it were a jump rope. He couldn't wait for the adventure to begin.

Now he understood how it had been. On the afternoon of her thirty-fifth birthday his mother had gone into exile, once again, as she had done when she left her home in the mountains for their house in the plains.

Martin was sitting with his back to the night that was flooding through the window. Among the shadows of the living room he saw their home being eaten by fire. The flames were licking into the secret places until they reached deep into Mother's dresser that hid her amethyst and burned the violet gem to a yellow stone.

On the way to the railroad station they had passed the gray houses of the tailor, the druggist, and the butcher for the last time. They carried all they could, and then they waited on the same platform where Martin used to wait for the train that would take him to school. Now their bundles were lying in the snow while they waited for the train that would take them from home forever.

Why bother to remember? Often Martin had asked himself that question, but tonight he thought that he had found the answer. As long as they could remember, the row of houses between the drugstore and the railroad station would stand. His mother would buy toothpaste and soap, his father would stand tall as he was fitted for suits, and Martin could be poised with his sled at the top of the embankment of the road leading across the bridge. And only when the last one of them forgot or when death took their last body to be buried somewhere in the sunshine in America, only then would the gray houses crumble and, as if in a dream, fall silently and be dust.

"But we always sang." She began to hum a melody he knew from long ago. They had sung "Come to the Vineyard" in the evenings, when the night had stood across the road like a black wall and it was time to look for shelter.

"Come to the vineyard." She sang in a low voice as if she were murmuring an incantation. "Come all you harvesters, arise. Can't you hear the trumpet's blare? Soon it will be midnight."

She had stopped, but her voice kept hanging in the dark and again he saw the summer roads as they were traveling east, clustered around the cart as if they needed to protect their last possessions with their bodies. Martin pulled on the crossbar of the shaft, Mother walked on one side of the cart, Father on the other, and both of them leaned their shoulders into the load. Grandmother walked behind, holding on to the tailgate. And they sang.

What will I do without them?

Martin couldn't bear it any longer, and he switched on the lamp by his chair, but only to its first stage.

In the pale light he saw his mother bent forward. With her eyes closed, she was humming while she stroked Father's foot. She had to keep his blood flowing through yet another night, so that in the morning she could present him once more to his son.

"Too early," Martin murmured.

"No, leave it on. I have to get up."

"I should go."

"Yes, get some rest. You have to take good care of yourself. You are all that we have left."

Bending over the chrome rail, he kissed his father's dry, feverish mouth. A puff of his father's breath felt as if a small feather was brushing against Martin's lips.

"Until morning," Martin said. As if it were an answer, he heard a sigh rise from the yellow pillows.

Martin was standing in the open door with the dog at his heels, when he heard his mother half whispering and half chanting, "Soon it'll be midnight." But he did not turn back for a last look, because he knew that the song was not meant for him and that, once again, he was being shielded from what was about to happen.

JOHN H. IRSFELD
(*1937–*)

Although John Irsfeld was raised in Texas, he has lived in the Silver State since 1969, when he joined the English department at the University of Nevada, Las Vegas. Like so many before him, Irsfeld had to write many novels to find the one that emerged as his story; his first published novel, *Coming Through,* was his fifth. In 1981, when Larry McMurtry published an otherwise scathing essay on Texas writers, he hailed Irsfeld as one of only three writers from the Lone Star State to watch. He called the three "smart, tough, skilled, and educated" (the other two were Max Crawford and James Crumley). Their books, he said, "are our Outlaw books, critical, hard-bitten, disrespectful to the point of contempt." For a man who was by then in the administration at UNLV, this must have come as sweet nectar. Although anchored in the bloody lore of a West Texas crime spree, *Little Kingdoms* is a novel about passion. Vanzandt, the smart one, Pembarton, the looney con, and Chooey, the small bird of a man beating his life out in their hands, break out of prison to carry out a final revenge. Told from the three characters' points of view, this early section lays the groundwork for the coming terror and their eventual unraveling. Lately, Irsfeld told me he is a "recovering writer." I hope that means he is writing again, now that he is chair of the English department after a long time away.

Rats Alley. Reno: University of Nevada Press, 1987.
Little Kingdoms. New York: Putnam, 1976; reprint, Dallas: Southern Methodist University Press, 1989.
Coming Through. New York: Putnam, 1975.

Little Kingdoms

(EXCERPT)

Vanzandt

WE'VE COVERED A LOT OF MILES on the ground but according to the map we've put only about three hundred, a little less I figure between us and the slam.

It may be foolish to be taking these back ways; I don't know if it's best or not. Less traffic but still we're probably far enough away by now, almost across the state.

I finish my coffee and wait at the door while Pem pays the bill and gets candy bars for Chooey and cigarettes for himself. I have the map folded in my pocket underneath the coat I stole this morning from that man's apartment. A bachelor. His car still there, but his place empty. On a vacation, it looked like. All the signs.

The clothes were good. Not the best, but good. The coat pulls across my back at the shoulders. Reminding me it's not my own. Chooey looks like a kid at Halloween with the coat he got. Same man, but a funnier coat. And Chooey's small. Pem is just about the same size, if you measure them carefully with your eye you can see, but he seems bigger. Chooey's not about to explode like Pem seems always on the edge of doing. I'll keep the map.

Out in the car, I can see coming down the long hill the fall of the lights on the cars. I see some extra ones here and there, but mostly they are truck lights outlining the edges of the cabs and trailers. I keep waiting for that flashing, in the dark like now.

"Well, what do you think?" Pem asks me as we climb in and buckle up just in case it gets rough later.

"Well, what do you think?" I say. I know Pem wants to hear me tell him what we'll do. What I think we'll do. But if I try to force it it won't go. Pem won't buy it.

"Come on, Vanzandt!" he says. He's already getting touchy and it's only been twelve hours. It's going to get close before it's over, I guess, tight between us, him and me.

Before it's over, too. I wonder just how we'll work this all out before it's over. I want to make my stop. I've got to make my stop. I will. And then I'll go with Pem. It's just . . . it's just that I don't care anymore. After that. I don't want to go back to jail. Another month of that, another six months, another year . . . soon . . . it would kill me. Just the going around again of the going around. Jail's just like being out in all that's bad of being out except the choices.

"I think we ought to cross to Clovis, then head into somebody's wheat field or a dry irrigation canal and try to get some sleep for a while. Then later on, toward first light, I think we ought to try to slip on by what we know'll be waiting for us there."

"The Highways?"

"Don't you figure?"

"Yeah. I . . . Yeah."

He does now.

He doesn't speak for a while, nor do I, as we drive in the full dark night on the falling highways of eastern New Mexico, down out of the hills that rise behind us here. The traffic is light now, out here away from everyone and everything. There is no moon yet, yet there will be soon. We could have picked—Pem could have picked—a darker time for our escape. I can see when I glance aside forms of rocks and goats beyond the fences in the fields made up of scrawny trees, bushes, and hard grass.

In the back Chooey has finished his candy bars now and has stretched out across the seat to sleep. It's probably more of a shame about Chooey than it is about me or Pem. Surely Pem. Surely me. More of a shame. Chooey liked it there. He could have found someone else, someone after Pem had gone. I still don't see why Pem brought him along. Unless to underline or dignify the certainty of his going, of his passing, of his death. Not tonight, perhaps, and not tomorrow night. But before too long Pem knows and I know, even if Chooey doesn't know, that what we've embarked upon is the last try for some meaningful act in our otherwise foolish, wasted lives. If I can explain and if Pem can . . . if Pem can point out to old man Tucker where he erred, then Pem and I will be happy, I think. It doesn't matter what's going to happen. Only if it happens when it should. Not tonight, not tomorrow night, but . . . sometime soon after.

"You think they'll sure enough be out there on the highway, stopping cars?"

"Wouldn't you be if you had Homer's old job, knowing all the things you said after your trial and while you was in?"

"But goddamn, Vanzandt! That's been four, coming on five years ago!"

"I haven't forgot. You haven't forgot."

"That's right too. But then we never had nothing else much on our minds in there."

I suppose old Pem wants even this for nothing, like everything else. Here he is, on his way to his last statement, his final signature, the capstone to his life, and he wants it free for nothing.

"They might be out for wetbacks, too," Pem says.

I do not answer him. They might be. But if they are, we'll be the wetbacks.

The moon is rising now ahead of us in the dark. It creeps above the line of darkness beyond and below which it was hidden like a great blood-yellow yolk, as big as the earth itself as it crosses the horizon, growing smaller and whiter as it rises in the night sky.

We drive on in silence. Chooey begins to snore from the safety and calm of his sleep and ignorance in the seat in back. Pem nods from time to time, I see, on the seat beside me. He will not, of course, lean against the door and go to sleep outright, as if it made some sort of difference to the world.

We are like a little family driving home after a late outing, an outing that adds up to a lot of years inside, counted all together there.

Even though inside is not that bad.

It's not outside, and there are limits to your roaming.

We pass through a sleeping Clovis and suddenly, beyond it in the dark, we are there. We are home, we three. We are back in Texas.

Pembarton

DARK NOW . . . BEST AT DARK . . . CANNOT SEE TO SEE. . . .

Hidden here inside this white car with Chooey and Vanzandt . . . they'll never find us. Though I wish we had the guns . . . he wouldn't let me get them after the clothes this morning and some cans of soup in the punk pad where we got the car. No, he said, there's no need now for guns or either after till we've gone there where I've got to go. I told you, he said, I would come with you only on that condition, first we had to go where I have to go and see the one I have to see there. Yes, I said,

I know but we're out now don't you see and they've guns. If we don't have them they won't. I know that they won't, he said. Kill us, that's what they won't. I don't care, I say. Guns, we've got to have guns and we're going to get some. Chooey in the apartment with us there looking at himself in the punk's mirror wearing the punk's clothes. Van's already fixed the car so it will go and he's come in after us and found some clothes that he can wear. No, he says again, no. I think for a moment I will just take him; I could. I could count on Chooey too I suppose for help but then I look up carefully at him. He is dressing now, putting on the funny coat that is too tight for him across the shoulders and I can see his eyes, distant, strange; that, and fuck I think what the fuck. Should I ruin my hands and maybe get my ass wasted over this now when we're out and all but home free? And . . . no I figure no let's just let it be. I'll have all the time later if I want to or need to; I can do it then after he's made this crazy visit to that little place and seen whoever it is there. I asked him once inside before we ever left, maybe three four months now, who it was. I didn't really care, partly just showing my interest to make some fucking conversation to him, trying to find out something about what made him decide to take the chance. I'd tried to get him to go with me before and he never would. He always said there were things he would have to have agreed to that he knew I couldn't buy and I never asked. I always figured sooner or later the son of a bitch would come around . . . but the weeks passed and the months, day after dead-ass day the same thing, the same thing, and so I went back again to see him. He was in the library then. He'd been transferred from the shop too sometime after they took me out for fighting with that fucking nigger . . . they'd of left me alone a little longer I would of made two niggers out of that one, split down the middle with a metal lath like a chicken, a nigger chicken; he wasn't that, though, he liked that action, I'll give his ass that. He was just as ripe to waste my ass as I was to waste his and then them fuckers stopped it, goddamn, only because the hacks was coming. They spread the word as fast as we do who's doing what to who and when and sometimes even why. They'd of let us kill each other and swore to hold each other's lies up but the hacks come and so they broke us up. I'm just as glad. I guess it wasn't really killing that I wanted to do, not that it makes a shit to me about that anymore; it was just to be doing something real and not just lying there inside that son of a bitch. Those laths was somebody's mistake; how they had us even moving them that day I'll never understand. So then they transferred me and him too, the nigger, and I never seen Vanzandt for a long time, I don't remember now, and finally I remembered about him saying he couldn't come with me if I went because there was things he'd have to say we'd have to do that he didn't figure I would go for. Then I finally got to go to the library when he was there. The first two times I missed him: once he was off assigned to some shit detail somewhere else; the other, where was he, sick call or some fucked-up place. I don't remember; finally, the third time is charm, I found him there behind the desk pasting checkout slips in books given to the library by some school someplace. They were all fucked up, the books, but good enough for us I guess they figured. They were working on them, trying to fix the backs and shit, and Van was pasting in those fucking labels one after the other just as calm and regular, you'd of thought he was outside someplace and liked doing it. Finally I got a chance to talk with him, and said you know that thing we talked about before. What? he says, like he didn't remember none of it. That outing, I says, that you couldn't go on with me because you'd have to have it certain ways you knew I wouldn't go for. Yes, he says, I do, I remember that. Nothing has changed, he says, it would still have to be like I said before. What would it have to be, I said? No guns, he said, and we go do my bidness before we go do yours, then anything you want to do is fine. I'm ready. I'll help or hold or drive or whatever, he says. You must be out of your fucking head, I say, no guns. No guns? How long do you think we'd last out there without no guns? I don't know, he says, but if we ain't got no guns they probably won't kill us and I can't get killed until I've done this thing that is the only thing I'd leave here for, surely not to help you kill old man Tucker just because he told the truth that got you throwed in jail forever. No guns, I say again, I can't believe it. You are crazy as a fucking shoat. Maybe, he says, but I know what I've got to do and I can't do it if I'm dead and so if I'm going with you then it's got to be like I say until I've done my chore and errand and then like I say I'm with you, anything goes, I don't give that much of a shit anymore anyway... but first he said, he turned to me looking somewhere off just past my face at something behind me or in his head one, but first I've got to have my way. I said, Jesus, you are flat crazy in this fucking library. And him back all the time now, back pasting them checkout labels one after the other, one after the other in that fucking stack of books. He takes one off a stack, pastes a fucking label in the son of a bitch, puts it in another stack, then takes another one and another one and so on, you'd think he'd want to go just to get away from those fucking books. I start to leave. I don't know if I want air crazy fucker with me out there anyway, I say. He smiles then for the first time. Don't worry, he says, if you do have me with you I won't be the only crazy one out there. I know what he means; they're all over the place. Is why you've got to do it to them before they do it to you. I'll think about it. I'll let you know, I say. Fine, he says, pasting those labels, stacking those books, looking back again at his work, ignoring me now like I wasn't even there. I mosey around a little in there, fucking around so I don't have to go back to the fucking laundry where they've got my ass now washing come off sheets. He never does look up again and directly I get tired of the fucking library and go back to work, finally. I seen what I knowed all along. I wanted him with me because he knows shit. He knows what's going to happen before it happens sometimes. He claims he just thinks like the other feller and I see that satisfies him but can't nobody think that good that often about how the other feller's going to do or where he's going to go or what he's going to say. No, there's more to it than that, I'm convinced. Was then for sure what changed my mind. OK, I told him one day back in the library, it's your way. No guns. Just a car and some clothes; that's all until you've made your little trip to see whoever it is, do whatever it is. Fine, he says, not excited or nothing and never asks me no questions or nothing about my plans. Don't you want to know what we're going to do when? No, he says, just let me know. I've got no preparations to make, no good-bye letters to write. Even who's going with us, I say? No, he says, whatever you say. Only just enough to make it in one car that I can drive. I can't drive two of them. I laugh and tell him Chooey is all. He doesn't say nothing. I don't know what I expected him to, what I thought he'd say; if he gave a shit one way or the other about Chooey he didn't show it, didn't say nothing. Finally I said, I'll let you know. OK, he said, and that was it. I didn't fuck around there anymore that time. That goddamn library gives me the creeps, if anything does. He does, sometimes, he does. Then the time came. Out we went. Everything just like it was supposed to be, during that little lull I call the shit lull of a morning after chow and before work starts. Everybody's smoking them up and taking a shit, guards, everybody; and we made it just like we knew we could make it. Chooey was the key man and Van didn't know. If he'd of known that, if he'd of asked, he might of said No, I don't know, but it was Chooey I got to work for the padre and Chooey was the one who got the keys that we got the copies for that let us into the chapel that gave us the way outside. It was just too loose that morning, that's all, just too loose. They didn't have their chains as tight as usual and off we went; even the drivers were gone from the truck, we didn't have to stiff them. It was beautiful, really beautiful. That fucking garbage truck went *wham*! backwards through the gate. Then this morning that fucking Van still said no guns. I thought as soon as he got outside there wouldn't be no problem, but the son of a bitch is crazy, he stuck to it. No, he said, and I figure, what the fuck, he's stuck on this crazy shit just like I'm stuck on old man Tucker's ass and I figure OK, what the fuck, he's probably right. Maybe I ought to care more about getting old man Tucker than some dumb highway patrolman out in the middle of the fucking desert someplace and so I back away. OK, I say, OK. You're probably right, that was the deal, that was the deal. Only he don't say I know I'm right or you fucking A that was the deal, he don't say shit, but just buttons up that jacket too tight for him across the shoulders there still looking like a con even in the punk's clothes. There. Well, are we ready then, I say? Sure says Chooey, sure says Van, heading toward the door. And out we go to the liquor store for money... at least he let me get that. I'm surprised the fucker didn't make me go on an air diet like he's on. But he's right, just like I knew he was about the other things, he's right. Here we are coming into Texas now, our third state, our second line, and we're still at it, still going where we're going into the dark. Somewhere up here we'll ditch the car and sleep the night and then skirt the Highways that'll be out there... we know they will. I don't know how we missed them in New Mexico. Those fuckers are usually all over the place out there, eight feet tall with their goddamn big hats on, checking everything that moves, even the fucking rabbits. But Van never said nothing about them so I didn't either and sure enough they weren't there. After this is over, after Tucker's dead in hell, I'll go to Mexico I think just hit one whorehouse after another until I die of whiskey and beer or bad pussy one. Old Chooey. I think I'll show old Chooey what a woman's hole is like . . . Chooey may change his mind about love and life inside. . . .

Later

VANZANDT SLOWED THE CAR and then pulled over onto the wide gravel margin of the highway. Pembarton woke up suddenly, his head jerking upright followed immediately by the trunk of his body.

"Yeah," Pembarton said as if in answer to some question.

"Sleep good?" asked Vanzandt.

"No," Pembarton said shortly, "I wasn't asleep. Just resting my eyes."

He paused and looked around almost wildly, his eyes shining in the darkness from the lights of the dashboard until Vanzandt shut them off when he shut down the engine.

'Where are we?" Pembarton said, trying to control his voice.

"We're home," Vanzandt said, opening his door and getting out of the car. It was not very cool outside, but it was cooler than it had been during the day. The heat from the highway contrasted noticeably with the cooler temperature of the air up at the level of Vanzandt's face. He walked to the front of the car, paused a moment, and then came around to Pembarton's side.

Chooey remained asleep in the backseat, oblivious to all that was going on, whatever it was.

Pembarton opened his door and got out.

"What is it, goddamn it?" he asked. "Why'd you stop?"

Vanzandt turned away from Pembarton while the latter

spoke. He unzipped his pants and began to pee into the grass growing along the edge of the gravel shoulder.

"I don't know," Vanzandt said, a strange tone to his voice, a strange feeling inside him. He couldn't tell how he felt or describe to himself, much less to anyone else, what it was he did feel, what the feeling felt like. But something... was up ahead, he knew that. He could not tell how he knew. He could backtrack and figure out some reasons that agreed with what he knew, but they weren't what caused him to know. They were simply consistent after the fact.

They had been driving inside the Texas line for some time now, he had no watch, he wasn't sure how long, and they had not passed any highway patrol roadblock or checking station. He knew they should have. But he knew they should have in New Mexico too and they had not. Yet in New Mexico he had known they wouldn't and here he had not known until now, suddenly, that they were going to. Now he knew that up the long rise ahead of them, down in the pit of the valley on the other side, sat three or four or maybe even half a dozen highway patrol cars, waiting for him and Pem and Chooey to come bouncing over the crest of the hill in their white Chevrolet.

He zipped his pants up. Pembarton was beside him now, peeing also into the grass in the dark.

"The Highways," Vanzandt said as he turned back toward the car.

"Yeah?" said Pembarton, suddenly with a different tone in his voice. This was why he'd wanted Van to come along in the first place. He knew he could do it. He'd seen Van do it a dozen times when they worked in the shop together inside. Once they'd been gambling, six or seven of them shooting craps on the table they were making to hold a topographical map of the state for the warden's office. The map itself was being made in hobby crafts, but they were making the table for it in the shop.

The project had already called for much travel back and forth between the shop and hobby crafts and had opened up many interesting liaisons, personal as well as commercial.

Vanzandt wasn't gambling. He was standing near a wall about three or four feet away from Pembarton, who was the closest person to him. Vanzandt simply stood and watched and said nothing.

Then he looked up and appeared to sniff the air, almost like an animal.

"What?" Pem had asked over his shoulder.

"Here they come," Van said. He was already drifting away.

"Who?" said Pembarton.

Some of the other gamblers had gotten in on the last of the conversation now. Apparently more than one of them knew that if Van said they were coming, they were sure enough coming. The game dissolved in the bright morning light of the prison shop.

The hacks who had been paid to let the men gamble realized only after everyone else what was going on and so they themselves were the last to scurry to their proper stations.

Forty-five seconds after Vanzandt's last words the floor hack entered with two visiting dignitaries and several extra guards mounted for the occasion.

Later, when everyone was gone and the shop had returned to normal, Pembarton had asked, "How'd you do that?" Vanzandt simply shrugged. He did not answer.

Now Pembarton finished peeing into the grass and zipped up and turned back to the car. He could just barely see through the side window of the right-hand back door of the Chevrolet the outline of part of Chooey's body. Chooey continued to make crooked Z's in the moonlight, still unaware of anything.

Pem joined Vanzandt, who was leaning against the side of

the car, looking up the long rise from time to time and then back down again into the moonlit darkness at his feet.

"You know how many there are?" Pem asked, a solemn tentative tone to his voice.

"No," said Vanzandt. "Not for certain. Maybe half a dozen cars, though. Maybe that many."

"Well," said Pembarton. "What do you think?"

Vanzandt looked back up the hill again. A pair of double headlights crested the hill and bore down toward them, illuminating even more brightly than the moon the darkness of the night. The car sped by without slowing down or dimming its lights, its blue-and-yellow license plates crowded with numbers and the tiny funny letters that spelled out "California."

"Going home," said Vanzandt.

"Fucking queers," said Pembarton.

Vanzandt leaned forward and started back around the front of the car. "Let's go find a place to sleep," he said over his shoulder.

"Awright with me," said Pembarton, opening his door and getting in.

Vanzandt turned the car around in the highway and then switched on the lights once they were heading out in the direction from which they had come.

Chooey turned over and groaned in the backseat when the car started moving again. Pembarton turned to look at him.

Chooey had his hands together as if in prayer, stuffed down in between his thighs. His knees were brought up in a fetal crouch. He worked his mouth as if he were nursing on a bottle.

"Old Chooey," said Pembarton just out loud. "Even in his sleep."

Within a quarter of an hour Vanzandt found a graveled road to cut off on. A sign said Fluvanna.

They drove until they found a quiet, likely-looking spot and then Vanzandt pulled the car off the road.

"No need to hide in the fields, I don't think," he said.

"Don't you worry that the local boys will be out looking for some action?"

"Not tonight," said Vanzandt, getting out of the car. "You take the front seat," he said to Pembarton before he shut the door. "I'll sleep out here."

Pembarton started to speak. He didn't want the front seat. He didn't want to sleep outside on the ground either, but because Vanzandt had offered him the car seat he suspected there was good reason for a smart person to decline it. Vanzandt didn't allow him the option, though. He shut the door quietly but quickly behind him, cutting off any chance for answer. Pembarton was too tired to think it out clearly so he didn't lower his window to say anything. He watched as Vanzandt disappeared into the moonlit dark over on his side of the car, into the direction of the field.

Then, lulled by the childlike sounds of sleep coming from the backseat, Pembarton lay over on the seat himself, his head under the steering wheel, his short length pulled up the little it was necessary, and there he went to sleep, quickly, smoothly, as if he were an innocent and had thus no reason for sleep to be denied him, even temporarily, like most of us, while conscience and memory strive to rectify a view of life and of the past.

Vanzandt went straight from the car perhaps fifty feet into the field and there he lay down, on his back, crushing over stalks of the growth there to cushion him. He did not go right to sleep, but it did not take him long. Before he turned out the light, he tried to see where they should go in the morning and how they should get there. He had to make his visit, and he wanted to do that first. They could make it there tomorrow.

They were almost on a line with it now. All they had to do was travel due east and they would hit it.

He could see in his mind the old-fashioned white frame house sitting beside the country road. It was a standard shotgun construction made of white shiplap and screen wire and corrugated iron. It sat up on piles of stacked bricks. Inside lived his wife, Opal. Tomorrow he had to see her and try to explain to her why he had done what he had done to her daddy. He hoped she would give him more of a chance to explain than her silence to his letters during the past four years indicated she would. He could not see that she would. But then, he had not been able to tell either that all of this was going to happen before it had, before he had done what he had done. Any more than he could tell before he had done it that he was going to do that, either, to her daddy.

He would just have to try.

He closed his eyes, but the stars and the moon were still up there, shining whitely down on him and Pem and Chooey and the top of the white Chevrolet that glowed in the dark like foxfire not far from where he lay.

JOANNE MESCHERY
(1941–)

The daughter of a Methodist minister and a Texan by birth, Joanne Meschery grew up traveling the West, finally putting down roots in the small community of Fallon. After studying at the University of Nevada, Reno, and the Iowa Writers' Workshop, she returned to Truckee to write and raise a family. An avid cross-country skier and hiker, she writes in a small cabin in the Sierra Nevada, where silence is its own reward. A former Stegner fellow, she has written three novels that have won widespread critical acclaim (*A Gentleman's Guide to the Frontier* was a finalist for the PEN/Faulkner Award), and she is the recipient of two National Endowment for the Arts Literature Fellowships. In 1999, she was inducted into the Nevada Writers Hall of Fame. Since 1991, she has been the fiction writer in residence at the University of Arkansas (during the fall semesters). Her fiction comes quietly to haunt like the breath of darkness before dreams.

Home and Away. New York: Simon and Schuster, 1994; reprint, Berkeley: University of California Press, 1998.

A Gentleman's Guide to the Frontier. New York: Simon and Schuster, 1990.

In a High Place. New York: Simon and Schuster, 1982.

Why Do Things Die in the Country

ELIZABETH WAKES IN THE NIGHT, startled, not knowing where she is. She has done this before, struggling from sleep in unfamiliar rooms where beds seem to face the wrong way and her eyes cannot find the door. She sits up and pushes the sheets back. The dog stirs beside the bed. "Rufus," she whispers, and the Labrador's tail beats on the rug.

She remembers. She is at the ranch, her sister's house, and the baby is sleeping in the room with her. Gen and Steven had told her to sleep in their bed. "The best bed in the house," Gen said. Elizabeth had changed the sheets, her fingers tracing the pale yellow stains on the mattress pad.

Elizabeth opens the window and smells alfalfa and sage. Occasionally she hears a car on the country road, someone going home. The road ends out there, just before the mountains. "We never see a face we don't know," Steven had told her. "Except in the fall. Then they come all the way from Southern California to hunt on the marsh."

In the summer there are egrets on the marsh. Tomorrow I'll drive out in Gen's car and see them, she thinks. Then she stretches and smiles, knowing she won't go anywhere. For two days she has not left the ranch.

She stands at the window waiting for a breeze. Beyond the road she sees headlights in a field, and she listens for the low drone of the harrowbed and bailer. Steven's second crop will be ready soon, she thinks. And the barley. Steven and Gen had taken Elizabeth to see the barley field before they left. "Everybody out here is watching this field," Steven told her, snapping off a spike of the pale golden barley. He rolled the dark kernels into her palm. "Barley. It's never been raised here before." She had crushed the kernels in her fingers. "All I can smell is alfalfa," she said. "A nurse crop," Steven said, pointing to the patches of alfalfa in the field. "Barley has a better chance with alfalfa in there." When they went back to the car, Gen stroked Elizabeth's hair. "You know," Gen had said, "your hair is almost the color of that field."

Toward morning the baby wakes and Elizabeth takes him into bed with her. It was the same yesterday. The birds noisy in the trees and the sun bright as though it were noon. Elizabeth puts the baby to her breast and watches his face grow red from sucking. She runs her fingers along his head, feeling the soft dark hair, more like cotton than silk. She had nursed her two girls until they were twelve months. "In my day it was the bottle," her mother said. "I put you and your sister on the bottle the day you were born and you grew up well adjusted, didn't you? The next thing I know, you'll be joining the La Leche League. A radical group, the La Leche League." "You're a cow," her husband, Carl, teased. "You always have too much milk." When they made love, blue-white drops ran from her breasts.

Elizabeth leaves the baby sleeping between the pillows and goes to the kitchen. Gen and Steven's little dog stretches in front of the door. "How does it feel to sleep in the house?" she asks, bending to scratch the dog behind his ears. Steven doesn't allow dogs in the house. "Animals belong outdoors," he says.

She sings softly as she makes coffee.

> The wife takes the child,
> heigh-ho the dairy-o
> The wife takes the child.

Elizabeth is relieved to be here alone with the baby. Gen and Steven had come in from camping at the lake to meet her plane. "Are you sure you don't want to come with us?" Gen had asked as they drove to the ranch. "We'd call everything off if it weren't that the second crop will be ready in a few days. It'll be a while before we can get away again." Elizabeth had told them to leave her; she had wanted them to leave her. "Rufus and I will watch the ranch for you," she had said. She was tired. Very tired, she said, and there would be time for visiting when Carl and the girls arrived.

She sits at the kitchen table, and the dogs push their noses beneath her nightgown, along her thighs. These days are like secrets to her. Like the stains on the mattress pad or the soiled places where her nightgown wound tight and crumpled between her legs in the night.

Elizabeth's mother had made her a nightgown when the baby was born. She brought the gown to Elizabeth in the hospital. It was wrapped in lavender tissue with a note that said, "Dear Girl, Three babies are enough." Her mother had sewn the hem of the nightgown shut. Carl brought yellow rosebuds and a pamphlet for her to read. "Many couples find sexual intercourse more pleasurable following vasectomy," she read. Sometimes at night, Elizabeth wakes up, her legs pushing, flailing, under the blankets and she thinks the hem of her nightgown is sewed shut.

Elizabeth gives the dogs water from the sink and unlocks the door. The gray kitten hangs on the screen, its yellow eyes startled. "So you want to come in after all," she says. There are three kittens. Barn cats. "They're wild," Gen had told her. "The kids spend hours hunting those kittens." The kitten spits and drops from the screen, its tail stiff as it skitters across the yard. Behind Elizabeth, the dogs slip on the waxed kitchen floor and jump at the screen. "Be still," she scolds, following the dogs outside. "If you don't behave, I'll lock you out of the house tonight."

She looks down the dirt lane to the country road. It is a two-lane road with abrupt shoulders and greasewood growing on each side. Beyond the irrigation ditches and the alfalfa fields is the desert and the houses the government built for the Indians. They built six houses, wood frame and painted in pastel colors. Yellow, pink, and blue houses with concrete steps leading out to dust, to the Nevada desert. Nothing has changed since she was here last. The government has built no more houses.

She walks across the yard to the sheds and dust puffs between her toes. Another hour and she will have to put on her sandals. Yesterday she danced across the yard to the strip of lawn in front of the house, her feet burning. "No, today I'll stay in my gown," she says, pouring pellets of grain for Gen's rabbit. The big doe bangs up against the back of its hutch. "You won't care, will you? I won't even wash my face. I'll be dirty all day. Here," she says and lifts the cotton gown around her waist. She runs her finger beneath the crescents of her hips. It is wet there. She is already beginning to sweat. "I'll be sour here. Do you smell it?" She laughs. "And tonight I'll bring all of you into the house. Everyone will sleep in the house tonight." She thinks of all of them together in the house. The dogs. The wild kittens. Even the chickens. The rabbit will stretch its long legs out behind it and lay under the covers in her bed. In the morning there will be mounds of dry, rattling droppings on the sheets and the room will smell of sour milk.

She feeds the chickens and surprises the gray kitten as she

passes the sheds. The cat sits on the hood of Gen's car. It must be cooler there, she thinks. She walks beyond the shed and climbs up into Steven's tractor.

Heigh-ho, the dairy-o
The wife takes the cat.

It is a new tractor, huge and green with a closed-in cab, all windshield. She turns the key and pushes a cartridge into the tape deck. Steven is proud of this tractor. It has air conditioning and bucket seats. There is no music in the house except for the radio. Still, she is tired of these songs. She played them all yesterday, sitting there drinking iced coffee and tapping out time on the steering wheel.

Maybe today she will catch the horse. Walter, they call him, an old horse Gen brought home from the auction. "For the kids," Gen said. But the children don't ride him. "He's mean," Steven said, "spooky." She pulls alfalfa from the field and waves it over the fence. "Come here, boy." But the horse jerks his head, walleyed, and gallops toward the canal. She throws the alfalfa after him. "Have it your way, Walter," she yells. "You think I'm chasing you today, you're crazy."

Then she hears the pickup. It turns off the county road and flashes bright orange between the trees along the lane. She starts back for the house. The dogs run ahead of her, barking, as the pickup stops in the yard. She begins to run. Each time her feet come down in the dust, she feels the ache in her breasts.

"Sorry to bother you," the man says, looking at her closely, leaning over the open door of the pickup. "I thought Steve was out of town. He asked me to check his barley while he was gone. Didn't Steve and Gen go out to the lake?"

She wonders why he doesn't wear a hat like Steven. Like the other ranchers, their faces brown with bright white lines across their foreheads from hats pulled down against the sun. She brushes her nightgown away from her legs and crosses to the lawn, smoothing her hair. Behind her, she hears the baby crying in the house. "Excuse me," she says. "I'll just get the baby."

The baby blinks, working his head from side to side as though blinded by the bright sun. "Looking for something to eat, are you?" Elizabeth whispers to the baby as she walks to the truck.

"You've got a pretty baby there," the man says, whipping his car keys softly against his Levi's. But he is looking at Elizabeth.

She wipes the sweat from her forehead with the back of her hand and smiles. Carl had told her once, "The prettiest women in the world are the ones who don't know they're pretty." He had said it more than once, teasing her; bunching her long yellow hair up in his hands as if he would splash it over his face like water.

"Yes," she says, "he's a very pretty baby."

"I wanted to bring this package down." He reaches into the pickup. "It's been sitting out beside the mailbox for almost two days now. Not a good idea to leave things out there on the road."

"I should have picked up the mail," she says. She notices how his full lower lip is sunburned, skin flaking at the edge. "I haven't been up to the road. I guess I forgot about the mail." Then she laughs as she sees the package. "It's from me. I mailed that to Gen last week. Isn't that funny?"

The man's hair gleams reddish-black in the sun and his skin is white where the collar of his shirt stands away from his neck. Freckles grow into one another on the back of his hands like rust. The western shirt is tight across his ribs so that he looks narrow and thin.

"Oh, that's me," she says quickly. "Elizabeth Brender. We're moving, you see, and these are just some things, some things I wanted to give Gen." She laughs again. "You know how it is when you move. You get rid of everything."

He looks from the package to her, and she sees that he is younger than she thought. Maybe younger than she is. "You here by yourself?" he says.

"Gen and Steven will be back soon," she says. "And I have the baby. David," she says, propping the baby up in her arms.

"Well, I'm just down the road. That trailer behind the old schoolhouse is mine. We like to keep an eye on things for each other out here. You need anything, call me. I'm in the book. J. R. Worthen." He opens the screen door and sets the package just inside. His face reddens as he turns back to her.

"About the only thing you could do for me now is catch that horse. He could use a good ride," she says and smiles.

"Walter," he says, eyes fixed on her breasts. "You'd better forget about riding old Walter. That horse has been proud cut. Indians used to do it a lot. Makes a horse ornery."

"Proud cut?" she says and thinks she should offer him a cup of coffee, something to drink. He looks to her like a man who is always thirsty. She makes these distinctions—a silly habit. Carl makes a joke of it. "Your crazy nature," he says. "You want to nurture everybody." It is her way. The baby is hungry, thirsty, and she makes him full. She has done this for all of them. For the girls, for Carl. Most of all for Carl.

"Yeah," J. R. Worthen says, and looks off toward the yard. "When they cut old Walter they didn't take it all. He still has feelings. Makes a horse nervous."

She watches him walk around to the pickup.

"I'll be going into town this afternoon. Anything you want, give me a call."

She goes through the house to the bedroom and lays the baby on the bed. She hears him pull out of the yard and then stop. Maybe he's coming back, she thinks. I'll give him a cup of coffee. Then the truck moves on. She stares at the large wet stain on her nightgown, the fabric clinging to the hard nipple.

"Did you like our company?" she says, unpinning the baby's diaper. "Mr. Worthen. J.R. Maybe a real cowboy." She holds the naked baby. "We're in the Wild West, my man."

She runs lukewarm water into the bathtub and sits on the toilet seat listening to the splash. The room smells like sulphur. "How can they drink this water?" she says to the baby. "It smells worse than we do."

She leans back in the tub and holds the baby's hands, letting him drift over her, his head between her breasts.

> Sail baby dear far over the sea,
> but don't forget to sail home again to me.

Her feet push against the tub, sending slow waves onto the baby's chest. She drizzles water from the washcloth over his hair as he finds her nipple. His hands slip on her breasts. His feet curl along her thighs. She opens her legs and her hair flutters beneath the water like feather grass.

She towels and powders the baby carefully and puts him in his infant seat on the bathroom floor. "Now," she teases, "what shall I wear for you today? But, of course, my darling, I will be natural." She puckers her lips, lifting her hair before the mirror. "A prairie woman? Yes, yes." She pulls on fresh blue jeans and a pale print blouse. "And cantaloupe from the garden for lunch."

She holds a piece of cantaloupe to the baby's mouth and he begins to suck, his tongue pushing the cantaloupe into Elizabeth's fingers. "This young man needs solids," the doctor told Elizabeth when she took the baby for his checkup. But she hasn't taken the unopened cereal box from her shoulder bag. "Never mind," she says as the cantaloupe falls onto the kitchen table. "I'm all you need."

She snaps the elastic band of the sun hat under the baby's chin and carries him outside. He sits in the infant seat in the middle of the dusty yard. She wheels Gen's bicycle from the shed. "Are you ready?" she calls. "Ready," she answers.

She comes full speed across the yard, yip-yipping to the dogs at her heels. She spins circles around the baby and brakes abruptly. Dust settles over the baby's toes. "You want more? I'll give you more." She disappears behind the shed and then pedals out, her hair flying. "My grand finale," she yells, passing the baby. Her arms shoot out. She jams her feet to the handlebars. The front tire bounces against the fence and she laughs, dropping one leg. Everything is quiet. It is too hot for noise. She wipes the sweat from her face and listens to her breathing. The baby is asleep.

She looks back to the house, straining as she hears the faint ring of the telephone. The bicycle folds under her as she kicks away from the fence. She thinks of the cowboy; of the bright orange pickup. Maybe it is J. R. Worthen calling to ask if she needs anything from town. She will ask him to get her Canadian bacon and a carton of soft drinks. "People in the country give you your privacy, but they don't forget you," Steven had said.

"Where were you, honey? The phone must have rung ten times."

"Carl, where are you?"

"The girls and I are in Reno. We'll be there in an hour."

"You couldn't . . ." She wonders why she is startled, alarmed. She looks toward the screen door, seeing; knowing how it will be. The room a rush of noise. Touching, all of them touching her, and Carl kissing her until she feels the soft inside of his lips. She presses her mouth hard against the receiver.

"Just teasing, sweetheart. I wish we were. You O.K.? You sound a little funny. Everything O.K.?"

She thinks she should tell him that Gen and Steven are gone;

that she is alone. "Everything's fine. I was outside, that's all. I didn't hear the phone. Where are you?"

"Rock Island, Illinois. I figure three more days' driving. I've been stopping early so the girls can swim, but I'm going to drive late tonight and make some time. Be glad you flew with the baby and Rufus. It's so damned hot. How's David, anyway?"

"He's fine. I left him outside; he's asleep. I should bring him in."

"Wait a minute. The girls want to say hi."

Their voices are high and sweet. Small, uncertain voices. "Is that you, Mama?" they say. "We got new bathing suits. Daddy forgot the old ones in the motel." "Tell Mama you love her," Carl says to them. "Why are you there, Mama?" the little one says.

The baby wakes as she carries him into the house. "Go back to sleep," she says, patting him under the sheet. "Everything's all right. Maybe we'll have company. Would you like to see the cowboy?"

She makes the iced tea very strong. It should be strong with sugar. Or maybe he would rather have beer. She crouches in front of the refrigerator but sees nothing except a can of orange drink. The closet pantry is well stocked, but there is no beer. She takes out potato chips and a small package of beef jerky. "Cowboys live on jerky," she says. She believes he will come.

She arranges the damp bath towels in the bathroom and rinses out the tub. The cloth shade at the window sucks against the screen, full of sun. It is the only noise she hears. She would hear his pickup on the road, hear him turn down the dirt lane, shifting into low gear. "No one cares if the house is clean," Carl says. But she hates to be caught with things out of place. She cleans the toilet bowl carefully.

Then she takes off her blouse and washes her face, her neck, under her arms. She takes off her bra and lays the cold washcloth over her chest. She will be sorry when her milk is gone. Her breasts will be small puckered things then. "It doesn't matter what they say. Your breasts are never the same after you nurse," her mother says. Her mother gives her creams in tiny blue jars. "You're almost thirty, Elizabeth. You must start taking care of yourself. A woman has to do these things. Thirty is a lovely time for a woman. For your birthday I'll give you a day in a beauty shop. You'll feel like a million dollars. A woman your age shouldn't wear her hair like a teenager."

In the spring she had taken her mother for a drive. They drove to Chatham for lunch and later they walked along the beach. "The clouds are beautiful," she said. "Thank you," her mother said.

When she married, she bought identical toothbrushes, not caring if they got mixed up. She had let her hair grow down her back. She makes herself a glass of iced tea and goes to the bedroom. Gen keeps her scissors in the narrow drawer of the sewing cabinet. Elizabeth listens for the sound of the pickup and watches out the window, sipping her tea. The baby has turned over on his back, eyes open, staring at the yellowed ceiling. "Too hot to sleep," she says as she changes him. She presses her finger on an ice cube and then runs the finger along his mouth; his gums. "Well, come on, my man. You can watch me cut my hair."

The baby is in his seat on the bathroom floor. "You're not watching," she says, letting her hair fall into his lap. Hair the color of barley. She cuts it chin length. Strand by strand, a towel draped over her shoulders. Then she moves the scissors up, closer to her face. "Shall we go shorter?" she asks as more hair falls onto the towel. "A shorter look for the mature woman?" She takes the scissors higher, feeling the cold steel against her temples; her forehead. Too much time left, she thinks. I could live for fifty more years. Her reflection blurs in the mirror.

"Dear Mother, Cancel the day in the beauty shop. I feel like a million dollars."

She puts the baby on the kitchen table and pulls the strap of the infant seat tighter across his stomach. The she sits at the table, her head on her arm, her arm wet from crying. "Don't worry," she says after a while, and looks up at the baby. "Mama loves you." She thinks of Carl; of the girls. "I love all of you." The room is quiet; the baby's eyes are fixed on a bright calendar hanging on the pantry door. She follows his gaze to the calendar. "Have a happy day," she reads and laughs.

The baby startles, jerking his hands and feet as she makes a bolting movement from the table. Still laughing, she ruffles the hair around her face. "Do you like it?" she says. She takes a package of chicken from the refrigerator. It is still half frozen, and she sets it in the sunlight. "I think he'll notice that my hair is different. You can't put much past a cowboy." She winks at the baby.

> Whoopie ty yi oh, whoopie ty yi ay.
> One man's work is another man's play.

"I think we'll make a cake," she says to the baby. "A chocolate cake; it's almost my birthday. What do you say? Maybe he'll come for supper. People in the country eat supper early."

There is no vanilla for the cake. She licks batter from her fingers and looks through the cupboards again. "We'll just have to borrow some. Down the road," she says. "We'll find a place to borrow some. What are neighbors for?"

The yard is dark with shadows. "It might rain," she says, looking up at the clouds. "Wouldn't that be something." It is almost cool in the shed. Gen's car is covered with fine dust. The keys are in the ignition. "We never lock anything," Steven had said. "No need." She lays the baby on the seat beside her and turns the key. The engine grinds. A slow sound, deep, as though the car had not been driven in weeks. She tries the key again and hears a slapping noise. "Damn," she says, turning off the ignition. "What if there was an emergency, something happened to the baby, and I couldn't get out of here?"

She fumbles angrily with the hood latch. "Stuck here in the middle of nowhere." The dogs push around her legs, their tails thumping against the wheels. The heavy hood goes up easily. She sees gray fur. Pieces of red, of orange, of slippery white. It is all over the fan, the hood, like vomit. "They're wild," Gen had said. "The kids spend hours hunting those kittens."

She pushes the hood down slowly and leans her weight over it, making sure it is closed. "Rufus, come." She takes the baby in her arms. "We don't have to have vanilla." She brings the dogs inside and greases the cake pans. He had said his name was in the book. The oven is on, the kitchen hot. "You need anything, call me," he had said.

"This is Elizabeth Brender," she says when he answers. "Gen's sister. I killed one of the cats; the gray one. It was in the car. In the engine. I didn't know."

"Not your fault," he says. "Crazy barn cats." His voice is clear, soft. "Things like that happen out here. I can't keep a dog. They get hit or wander off. Don't worry about it. You want me to come over and clean it up?"

"I think it's all right," she says after a moment. She smells the cake in the oven. Chocolate. Maybe they will eat it warm without icing.

The baby cries, arching his back, his face red and moist. She takes him out of the infant seat and lays him on a blanket in the living room. "Don't cry, baby." She turns him onto his stomach. "I'll be right back."

The dogs follow her. She feeds the rabbit first. Then the chickens. Pellets of grain flow onto the ground. I'm feeding them too much, she thinks. They'll get sick. But she keeps feeding them. "Eat," she says to the dogs, but they don't touch their food. She brings them back into the house.

She takes the cake pans from the oven and puts them on racks to cool. Soon he will come to see if everything is all right. She sits cross-legged on the floor and puts the baby to her breast. His hair is wet from crying. "It's going to rain," she says. "You'll feel better then."

Her legs grow numb under her. When the baby dozes, she pinches his feet softly and he begins to suck again. She doesn't let him stop, even when her breasts are empty. The dogs settle down. They lie on the rug breathing, sighing, their eyes half open. She keeps the baby on her breast long after he has fallen asleep.

She puts the baby in his crib and closes the bedroom curtains. The light is dusky in the room; her bed unmade. She runs her fingers across Gen's bureau. Dust as fine as the powder she uses for the baby. She pulls the sheets from the bed and lies back, feeling the quilted diamonds on the mattress pad. She turns over, her face in the pale yellow stains. Then she changes the sheets.

Maybe he is waiting for the dark to come, she thinks, as she snaps on the kitchen light. Tonight there will be no sunset, but it will be cool. She begins to fix the chicken. He will like this chicken, chicken baked slow in the oven with herbs. She will fix corn and mashed potatoes. And tomatoes from the garden.

She has only to wait for the chicken to bake. It is good that he hasn't come too early. They might find it hard to talk if he came too early. She could tell him about moving, about how they are all coming across the country to California. She could tell him how, every night, her little girls jump on motel beds. Jump from bed to bed in their underwear until they are sleepy. She will ask him why he does not wear a hat and why he cannot keep a dog.

She studies the handwriting on the package and then carries

it into the living room. She unwraps the package on the floor and pulls the tape from the cardboard flaps. "Get rid of this stuff," Carl had said. "Send it to Gen. She wants another baby." The clothes still smell of baby powder and mild soap. They are little things with ribbons. Sometimes when the girls play loud running games in the house, Elizabeth goes to her bedroom and shuts the door. When they come looking for her, she asks, "Where are my babies?"

It begins to rain. She walks to the screen door. The smell of the desert is strong, the dust pungent. Then the hail comes; it rattles off the roof, bounces on the cement steps. The dogs move behind her, nosing at the screen. She holds her hand out the door and icy beads sting her fingers, her palm.

When she comes back from checking the baby, it has stopped. "A dirty trick," she says to the dogs. "Maybe it will still rain."

She lays the little clothes out carefully around her on the rug. "When I was small my mother gave me baby clothes, old baby clothes." She pets the dogs. "I put the clothes on the cats. I dressed them up and rode my bicycle down the street with the cats in the basket. My mother took a picture."

She doesn't let the phone ring long, but closes the door to the baby's room before she answers it.

"Steve's lost his barley," J. R. Worthen says. "I just drove out there. Figured it couldn't stand the hail. It's all down."

"What?" She looks out the window as if she could see the barley field.

"Damned freak storm. Two more days and Steve could have harvested that barley."

He is saying something about insurance. "Act of God Insurance," he says, but she barely hears him.

She doesn't bother to put on her sandals. The dust is cool as she runs to the shed. The baby will be all right, she thinks, as she lifts the hood of the car. She looks around the shed for a shovel, a rake. Then she runs back to the house. The baby is still asleep. She takes the broom from the closet and calls the dogs back inside.

There is not much light in the shed. She uses the broom carefully at first, brushing at the fan. Then she uses the stick end, working the broom faster and faster.

The car starts on the second try and she backs out of the shed. Steven will be angry, she thinks. But it's not my fault. None of this is my fault.

She leaves the car and moves through the long stalks. She feels the barley under her feet. It is almost too dark to see and she squats down between the stalks, feeling with her hands. The kernels are tiny in her palm, the size of hailstones. She rakes them up in her fingers and rubs them between her hands. Everything around her smells of barley.

She wonders, as she gets into the car, if anyone will plant barley again. She rolls the window down and feels the rain on her arm as she drives. The house is not far away; she could have walked to the field. The baby will be sleeping when she gets home. She slows the car, her foot barely touching the accelerator. The road ends out there; it ends before the mountains. In a few days she will tell Carl all of this. She turns down the lane. She will tell Carl nothing.

The yard lights are on, blazing from the sheds and the front of the house. She sees the pickup parked near the fence. She will ask J. R. Worthen why there is nothing left; why do things die in the country? The dogs run alongside the car as she pulls into the yard. They jump at the open window.

She walks past the sheds. The chickens make low, alarmed noises as she opens the gate to their pen, sweeping an arc in the dust. The rabbit trembles as she slides back the roof of the hutch. She raises the crossbars on the fence and the horse stamps in the dust. They are all safe. She calls to them as she moves back across the yard. "Go to sleep," she says. The dogs run ahead of her to the house.

It is as though the lights in the yard are trained on her or as though, suddenly, she has stepped into the path of a car's headlights. She thinks of them on the highway. He is driving late tonight, hurrying to get there. Once, walking home in the dark, walking fast because her mother was waiting up, a car stayed behind her, its engine so quiet that she heard only the gravelly sound of the tires, the sound of sprinklers running on someone's lawn. She did not dare to move out of the headlights or to turn around.

BILL MOODY
(1941–   )

After growing up in Southern California, Bill Moody moved to Las Vegas in 1974 and lived there for more than twenty years. He has worked as an editor, a teacher, a disc jockey, and for three decades, he has been a jazz drummer. Like the poet Hayden Carruth, Moody's love of jazz led him to work on a book on the subject. In the late 1980s he worked as the managing editor of *LV: The Magazine of Las Vegas*. Later, he began writing detective fiction and against nearly insurmountable odds sold his first novel based upon three chapters and an outline (*Sound of the Trumpet, Death of a Tenor Man,* and *Bird Lives* were reviewed in the *New York Times Book Review*). For many years, the venerable voice of Southern Nevada's university radio station, he hosted the *Jazz Traditions* program. Today, he teaches English at Sonoma State University, writes, and plays jazz long into the night.

Bird Lives. New York: Walker, 1999.
Sound of the Trumpet. New York: Walker, 1997.
Death of a Tenor Man. New York: Walker, 1995.
Solo Hand. New York: Walker, 1994.
Jazz Exiles. Reno: University of Nevada Press, 1993.

Rehearsal

"I HATE THESE THINGS," Old Folks says as he unpacks the electric bass guitar. I watch him perform the electronic ritual, admiring his unhurried movements done with surprising grace for a man his size. His arms stretch the thin fabric of his T-shirt as he snaps the cord into the amplifier and adjusts the volume.

Old Folks would be more at home stroking two hundred years of German wood, walking in rich, dark tones, but Ozzie's jazz, if it can still be called that, lends itself to the Fender.

In the harsh glare of the stage light, Old Folks's shaven head is dark and smooth, like polished mahogany. His eyes reflect the fatigue that comes with surviving thousands of one-nighters with Basie, Duke, and even a stint with Miles. Old Folks was there once, like a footnote in a chapter of jazz history. But he's tired now and must be, according to Ozzie, disposed of.

His real name is David Lee Burroughs, but no one remembers that now. He was dubbed Old Folks—by me, I suddenly recall—after the song, and because he's twice the age of any of us. Ozzie included. He takes the kidding about his name good-naturedly, but I wonder how he will react to Ozzie's plan.

There are disturbing rumors about Old Folks that he once served a year for assault, but no one has asked about them or wants them confirmed. His gentle manner seems to belie such a reality. But Emerson Barnes, Ozzie's manager, claims they are true. Nearly killed a man, he says, but Emerson is prone to exaggeration. I think to tell us was for effect, to keep Brian and me on edge, but the possibility looms heavily on my mind as I wonder if Old Folks suspects he will not play a single note on this opening night.

The Scenario is complex and, sadly, I'm to play a small part in its denouement. Despite his credits, Old Folks has not worked out. Not since a San Francisco concert, when Ozzie nearly destroyed the dressing room over Old Folks's failure to measure up to his expectations.

Two weeks' notice is the way it usually goes, but despite his being a major star, Ozzie is too insecure to confront Old Folks directly, honestly. Bowing to his wife's demands—a friend of a friend just happens to need work—Ozzie has instead chosen to humiliate Old Folks and cover up his own mistake.

I light a cigarette and watch the bartender stack glasses in a metal rack. The empty seats and booths seem to mock us. I'm anxious for this farce to be over, but even for this Ozzie is late. My impatience is transmitted to the drumsticks as I tap out idle rhythms on the cymbal. We all know our lines, the stage directions have been decided on, but everyone seems reluctant for the play to begin.

Someone has left the door open to the showroom lounge. Heavy black drapes, pulled nearly across the entrance, muffle the sounds of bells, groans, delighted cries, and the drone of a hundred conversations that filter in from the casino. Tonight a maitre d' will guard the entrance like a sentinel and admit the chosen few who have reservations. But now, except for the stage lights, the lounge is dark and deserted.

Old Folks and I sit alone on the stage waiting for Ozzie and

Brian to arrive and put truth to the sign at the entrance that reads: REHEARSAL IN PROCESS. So far there is none.

From behind the drums, I can see a pit boss roaming restlessly among the craps tables. A woman with flowing blond hair and a paper cup full of coins pauses at the entrance, glances in, then walks on impatiently.

It's cold outside and more snow threatens. This I know from an early-morning tramp through the woods. But here, inside the casino, without windows or clocks, I feel trapped, like a time traveler caught in a void. I wonder now why I have agreed to be a part of this. There is still time to back out, I tell myself.

"So where's the man?" Old Folks asks. He's settled on a bar stool and runs mammoth hands over the strings of the bass guitar that's cradled across his lap like a shotgun. His eyes flick from the entrance to me.

"You know Ozzie," I say, carefully avoiding his eyes, sure that my own will betray the knowledge of the scene about to unfold. Somehow I know he senses what is coming. He grunts in response and scans the music on the stand before him.

It's a difficult arrangement, Ozzie's new opener, and finished by Brian only two days ago. It too will play a part in the farce, designed as it is to unmask and degrade Old Folks. No one disputes his musical ability, but sight-reading is a long-forgotten skill, and his failing is the wedge Ozzie will use to drive Old Folks away.

And what of my own complicity in this plot? Old Folks deserves more than this sham Ozzie has planned. But I have agreed. Why? Is this what I wanted from music? Suddenly I want to be out in the snow again, feel the crisp, clean air on my face, gaze across the expanse of Lake Tahoe, but I'm too late. We both look up as the drapes are thrust aside.

Emerson Barnes strides in, trailed by Brian and, finally, Ozzie himself, wearing a ski jacket and dark glasses, as if his escape will be made through the snow.

"All right, fellas, let's do it." Emerson smiles with the confidence of a prosecuting attorney whose case is in the bag.

Brian takes his place at the piano, but for a moment he doesn't seem to know what to do. He is paler than usual, and I can see beads of sweat on his forehead. He thumbs through the music and strikes the keys, then finally pulls out the new arrangement, as if he has just discovered it.

I don't envy Brian his role, but he has made his choice. He likes being a conductor. Bending to Emerson's insistence and Ozzie's promises, it is Brian who will actually break the news to Old Folks. That's how we agreed it would go.

"Let's try the new opener," Brian says casually. He tries to catch my eye, but I look away. I won't help him. He's made his choice and I've made mine. Suddenly I want Old Folks to succeed, but as Brian counts us in, Old Folks is already in trouble, scuffling with the fast tempo, the notes that can be only a blur before his eyes.

Ozzie sneers in my direction, as if I'm responsible. Maybe I too will be gone before the night is over.

Brian stops us. "Can we try that again? Watch the key change at letter A," he says, never looking at Old Folks. Brian is an excellent musician, but he lacks moral strength. I wonder why I haven't noticed before. It is fear, I realize, that drives him.

Old Folks stumbles again. Impulsively, I make a deliberate error and regret it at once. I'm only prolonging the agony, but Old Folks glances at me with what I take to be a look of surprised gratitude. Ozzie glares; Emerson turns away for a moment. This is not in the script; I'm holding up the proceedings. "Sorry," I say, raising my hand.

We start again. Ozzie joins us after the first eight bars and miraculously, Old Folks is right on the money. Shaken, it is now Ozzie who stumbles over a phrase. He tries to press on but drops out and lets the microphone dangle at his side.

"C'mon, man, that's not it," Ozzie says. Old Folks seems to know what I want to tell him: if he could see behind Ozzie's dark glasses, he would find fear.

"What's the problem?" he asks. The hint of a smile crosses his face.

"The problem is you played a wrong note." He stares at Old Folks defiantly.

Old Folks grins openly. He knows Ozzie is bluffing. "Which one?" Ozzie is a gifted singer, blessed with a booming voice, but he knows little about music. He looks to Emerson for help.

"Maybe the tempo is wrong," Emerson suggests. He nods to Brian, who sits rock-still at the piano, staring at the keyboard as if the answer lies somewhere there.

We try again, and this time Ozzie is taking no chances. He doesn't even bother with his entrance. "No, no, no," he says. He drops the microphone on a chair, jumps off the stage, and starts for the exit. On cue, Emerson rises and follows. At the door Ozzie and Emerson confer briefly in a halfhearted manner that fools no one, certainly not Old Folks, who stares into the darkness.

Ozzie then disappears through the drapes. Shrugging and shaking his head, Emerson returns. "Man's under a lot of pressure," he mumbles just loud enough for us to hear. He calls Brian aside, who seems terrified now that the moment is at hand.

Old Folks looks at me. "What is this all about?"

I can do no more than shrug and feign a sudden interest in the height of one of my cymbals.

After an appropriate amount of time, Emerson pushes Brian forward. He looks to me for support, but I only stare back impassively, fearing for Brian but resolved to go no further. I know I will pay for it later.

"Ah, look," Brian begins, "Ozzie is a little upset. He says he can't . . ." His voice trails off under Old Folks's baleful glare. Rising from the stool, Old Folks towers over Brian.

"Yeah?"

My eyes dart to the open case on the floor near Old Folks. I realize I'm looking to see if there's a weapon inside.

"I'm sorry," Brian stammers. "Ozzie says he can't open with you." Mission accomplished; Brian retreats behind the piano.

Old Folks sits down and bows his head. His shoulders slump. He nods silently, and for the moment there are only the filtered sounds of the casino and glasses clinking as the bartender, oblivious to the little drama being played out, continues to work. Finally Old Folks turns towards me. "Well, I guess we knew this was coming, didn't we?"

I have no answer, but his smile makes me uneasy. The stories about Old Folks flood through my mind but I only sit dumbly and wonder how I allowed myself to be a part of this, sick inside with the knowledge that the new bassist, flown up from Los Angeles this morning, is now standing by in his room, awaiting word from Emerson to join the rehearsal.

Emerson stands rigid, steeling himself for Old Folks's reaction, but it is nothing more than to pack his bass guitar, quietly shut the case, and slowly step down from the stage. Emerson moves aside for him to pass but not before he slips an envelope into Old Folks's hand.

Old Folks never breaks stride until he reaches the heavy black drapes at the entrance. He stops then, and looks back. I'm sure it is me he gazes at, then he is gone, lost in the casino crowds. The rest of us know Ozzie is by now securely locked in his room and won't appear again until the first show.

Brian's sigh of relief is audible. He starts to speak, but Emerson cuts him off. "I'll call John," he says, breaking the silence. "You can run down the show with him, Brian."

I get up and walk off the stage. "Where are you going?" Emerson demands.

"Out, upstairs. I've had enough rehearsals for one day."

"Man, you still don't know what's happening, do you?" Emerson's voice is full of contempt, but I don't care now. I'm already out the door, pushing through the throng of gamblers toward the elevators.

On my floor there's a cart in front of Old Folks's door. Inside, a maid is pulling sheets and blankets off the bed. She barely glances at me. "You lookin' for that big fella, he's already gone," she says.

I nod and race back to the elevators. I stab at the Down button, but when the doors open, Old Folks is waiting. The bass and a battered suitcase look like toys in his massive hands. My first impulse is to back out, but the doors have already closed behind me.

"I saw you goin' up," Old Folks says. He presses the Down button and stares at me impassively. "They got somebody else lined up, right?"

I nod, admitting my own guilt, hoping it will absolve me of my sins for knowing about the plan, not telling.

Old Folks grins suddenly. "One thing, man," he says, " I won't forget this."

I stand silently, taking in his words, feeling reprieved but not understanding. Does he plan revenge on Ozzie or has he simply sensed my discomfort, understood my motives?

When we reach the lobby, he steps around two couples talking loudly about dinner plans. Old Folks turns and smiles at me, then disappears into the crowd. The couples look at me questioningly.

"It's all right," I say. "I'm going up."

PHYLLIS BARBER
(1943–)

Born in the Rose de Lima Hospital in Basic Townsite (what is now Henderson), Phyllis Barber is among a handful of native Nevadans whose names are synonymous with Western letters. Through her fictional accounts of Southern Nevada, she has brought renewed attention to the literary landscape of the region. Just as she has done in "Mormon Levi's," it is the halting breath of anticipation that remains long after the reading is over. She has published her fiction widely (*Kenyon Review, North American Review*) and received many honors in the past decade (Associated Writing Program Award Series Prize, first prize in the Utah Fine Arts Literary Competition). In 1996 she rode her bicycle from Colorado to Illinois before her knee gave out. From 1990 until 1999, she taught in the Vermont College Master of Fine Arts Program and recently was a guest on the *Today Show* as a writer who was affected by the draw of the Las Vegas culture—a sharp contrast to the Mormon culture in which she was raised and steeped. She now makes her home in Park City, Utah.

Parting the Veil: Stories Based on Mormon Lore. Salt Lake City: Signature Press, 1999.

How I Got Cultured: A Nevada Memoir. Athens: University of Georgia Press, 1992; reprint, Reno: University of Nevada Press, 1994.

And the Desert Shall Blossom. Salt Lake City: University of Utah Press, 1991; reprint, Salt Lake City: Signature Press, 1993.

The School of Love. Salt Lake City: University of Utah Press, 1990.

Mormon Levi's

TIGHT, LIKE TWO LONG CIGARETTES rolled in denim. We call them white Levi's, Mormon Levi's, but they're actually albino beige. I suck in my stomach, zip up my pants on the way to the window in my bedroom, split the venetian blinds to check the night and see if Shelley's pulling into my driveway. Not yet. I walk down the stairs and see my long legs reflected in the mirror at the bottom. Daddy Long Legs. Leggy legs. Legs made for walking and dancing the whole night through.

Where did you say you were going, Mattie? my mother asks as she pretends to dust the piano with the dishtowel in her hands.

To the movie.

What's playing?

A western.

I hear Shelley's horn. Thank heavens. I'm out of here. Out the door. Bye, Mom.

Remember your curfew, Mattie. And don't be chasing after those boys you think are so neat. You know better.

My eyes brush past my mother's eyes and the picture of Jesus on the wall behind her. Sun rays coming out of his head. Light like the sun on his forehead. Jesus is always looking over someone's shoulder it seems. Sure, Mom. Bye.

The door sounds final as I slam it, sealing me off from my house. I'm released into Friday night.

Hey, Wondah Woman, Shelley says after I slam the door of her brown Plymouth that looks like a tank. She backs into the street that separates me from the desert: the rim of Las Vegas, the edge of the plate. My house is in the last subdivision in town. The desert is my front yard.

Hey, Wondah Woman yourself, I say. Tonight's the night.

Shelley turns the radio up until the sound is bigger than the car and the street. "Stairway to Heaven." I settle back against the seat and drape my arm over the open window. We're off to hunt for Rod and the King, our non-Mormon, forbidden boyfriends. Forget the movie. Find somebody who knows the plot. We're off to the Bright Spot to wait for the boys.

They're at the Tracks right now, the place where the manly men of Las Vegas High drink on Friday nights, throwing Teddy Beer cans off the trestle while the Ch-Ch-Chiquitas of LVHS cruise the Spot, in and out of the driveway, circling, trolling.

As me and Shelley turn in at the magic driveway under the blinking, rotating sign where the BRIGHT shines brighter than the SPOT, we're looking for the heart of something that probably won't be here until the boys are. We check out who's with who, who's not with who, who's in their own car, who borrowed from M and D. We cruise some more, floating on shock absorbers, big tires, the night pouring into the windows, waiting.

It's 8:45. They're usually back from the Tracks about 9:30. So after we bump over the drive-in's speed traps for the sixth time, we dip into the gutter and out onto Charleston. We head for Fremont Street, past Anderson's Dairy, past the Little Chapel of the West, then turn left onto Fremont, toward the big vortex of light near the Union Pacific depot, the razzle-dazzle that never fails to take the words out of my mouth. The Golden Nugget. The Horseshoe. Those zillion bulbs of light.

Shelley switches the station to an oldies show. Chances are . . . , some sixties guy croons as we stop for a red light at Third and Fremont. My composure sort of . . .

How does somebody's composure sort of slip? I ask Shelley before the singer can finish the sentence. It either does or it doesn't.

True, Shelley says. But Johnny Mathis says so. It must be believed.

Funny, Shelley . . .

Hey, don't look now, Mattie, but some slime just pulled up next to us on your side of the car.

Some wanna-be Elvis with a souped-up Ford idles at the stoplight. Come along and be my party doll, he sings like we're his audience. I look at Shelley and roll my eyes. Then I stare straight ahead. He doesn't exist.

Shelley turns up the volume to drown out his, and Johnny's velvet amps my blood and the yearning for the One and Only. I've been waiting for a long time. My hand outside the window can feel the velvet. It tickles the tips of my fingers, the nerve endings. All I can think of is The Man Who Just Might Be Mine, the King.

We cruise past the marquee at the El Portal. *Way Out West,* Shelley says. That's the name of the movie, Mattie. Don't forget it when your mother asks you in the morning. Say it after me. *Way Out West.* She exaggerates her lips.

Way Out West, I mimic her, laughing. Shelley's the best, even if my mother thinks she's a bad influence on her rare gem of a daughter. It's good Shelley isn't afraid of my mother—the Lioness of Righteousness, the Defender of Virtuous Reality. God bless Shelley. The Primo Chiquita.

A car full of shaveheads from Nellis pulls up next to us and pins us with their air force eyes, like we're ground targets in the desert. One whistles a two-finger whistle. Another sticks out his tongue and wiggles it. Yuk, Shelley says. She tries to speed up when the light changes, but the traffic is packed like sardines. She's bumper to bumper with a Dodge wearing Iowa plates.

I've seen enough rubberneckers from Iowa, she says as she tap-dances her foot on the brake.

We're stuck in the intersection, and I feel squirmy like an amoeba under a microscope. Horns honking. Everyone stalled. The Nellis boys next to us, a bunch of prying eyes. I keep my head forward, but notice with my side eyes that one of them is opening the back door of their dull black car and is lunging toward our Plymouth, making like a primate for the entertainment of his friends. I roll up my window and lock my door just before the primate lands on the side of the car and plants a blowfish kiss on the glass. I can hear the rest of the guys in the car laughing like crazy.

Hey girls, he's yelling in between planting slobbery circles across the window. Pussy for me, girls? He puts his hand over his crotch, jiggles his family jewels, sucks in his breath with his teeth tight together.

Don't pay him any attention, I whisper as I turn away from the window, maintaining my cool, hardly breathing.

The blowfish moves over to the windshield and mashes one side of his face against the glass. I act as if I'm talking to Shelley with a permanent left-hand angle to my head. He mounts the hood of the car. He's crawling on his hands and knees, panting like a dog in 120-degree heat.

Go find another fireplug, I shout as loud as I can, which isn't too loud, then cover my face with the side of my hand. I'm laughing. I shouldn't be.

This isn't all that funny, Shelley says to me. Get off the car, she yells to him. You stupid jerk.

I'm trying to fold up in my elbows and arms, trying to be serious and angry like Shelley, but the flyboy's eyes. They're hollow. There's a famine there.

Luckily, the traffic starts to move, and, as Shelley creeps forward, she hits the brake, hard. He slides back, almost loses his balance, then leaps into the street. He gives us the finger before he becomes a reflection of the flashing lights.

My heart is beating in my throat. There's not enough air in Shelley's car. Shelley, let's get out of here.

Mattie, I'm doing the best I can. One more block.

In one block, we'll hit Main Street, the end of Fremont Street, the place where we can turn left and get back to the Bright Spot, where we can hold our breath for something important, like Rod and the King, even though they'll be drunk. Drunk enough to give the finger to all worldly inhabitants plus the moon and the stars as they speed down the highway. Drunk enough to call us Bitch One and Bitch Two.

I love it when they talk like that, words from the Forbidden City. Their words are like bold fingers on my neck, brushing over my breasts, down to my belly button. I can taste their words, and it doesn't matter what they call us, because they need us—our arms, our lips, our necks, our breasts, though we don't plan to give them anything past the neck. We are, after all, Mormon girls in Mormon Levi's, saving our sacred bodies for The Big Event called temple marriage.

But just when we turn left onto Main, I notice a patch of blood on my Levi's. Oh no, I say to Shelley. My period, right now, right this minute. White Cross Drug, Shelley. Can you believe this happened on Friday night?

Shelley steers the big boaty Plymouth into the parking lot of

White Cross Drug. She pulls up next to a long, long, stretched-out Cadillac sparkling in the streetlights. I crane my head and peer into the car. Some Big Sugar Daddy, maybe. I see something sparkling in the backseat, and when the door opens, a showgirl steps out with a cardigan draped over her shoulders. The little sweater doesn't really cover her costume. White satin. A vee down to her navel, big breasts like cantaloupes pushed together. Rhinestones glued over the tops of her eyebrows, eyes smothered with aqua shadow and pencil and mascara, more rhinestones glued to her neck, making two arrows that point to her breasts. Her headdress looks like an albino macaw sprinkled with diamonds.

Wow, I say to Shelley. I'm speechless. I wish I could trade places right this minute, have breasts as big as hers, wrap my head in silken turbans, tie gauzy scarves around my torso every which way.

Stop gawking and go get what you need, Shelley says. We don't have all night, remember. Your mother said twelve sharp, sharp, sharp. She asked me last week to start bringing you home on time. She blames me, your best friend and protector and buddy.

Yes, sir, I salute her. I feel the crossroads of the seams against my crotch as I push open the door with my shoulder, unfold into the darkening night, step on the asphalt that still holds the heat of the day.

Mother, I think as I look for the right aisle. Ever vigilant Mama mia. Mama owl. I start humming "Stouthearted Men," her favorite song about men who fight for the right they adore.

The showgirl is standing under the feminine hygiene sign. She has rhinestones down the seams of her white net hose. She must be in between shows. She's picking up a box of Tampax. Wow. Both of us on the same day. The same time. This must be portentous. The Ides of Something. I try not to look at her as she turns back toward the front of the store, but I can't help myself. There's too much to look at.

Up close I can see the lines of things. The outliner on her lips, the eyeliner, the penciled mole on her cheek. And I'm not sure why, but when she looks at me, I wish she wouldn't have. When she does, I can see two human eyes behind the blinking aqua eyelids. I can see two-in-one people walking down Aisle 5 of the White Cross Drugstore: one underneath a graceful feathered headdress and pushed into surprising places by the limits of the white satin costume, the other looking out at me and wow, do her eyes remind me of my dad talking about the windows of the soul. She's real. Wow. Her eyes briefly graze my face as she passes, leaving me with feelings I don't understand.

After I pay for the Always pads and push through the glass door, I can't stop thinking about those eyes. Standing alone on the sidewalk, I watch the back end of the long Cadillac flashing its right blinker, halos around the taillights, the body of the Caddy wrapping around the corner and turning right toward the Strip. I think her eyes remind me of the picture of the sad Jesus nailed to the wall of my Sunday school class. Maybe that's blasphemy, Jesus in drag, but he seems to be everywhere, staring out of the strangest places.

Suddenly I feel laced and larded with thoughts of redemption, salvation, and eternal life. Maybe Shelley and I should try to get Rod and the King to change their ways: go easy on the beer, be more responsible. She and I are, after all, instruments of God.

We don't drink. We don't smoke. We go to church twice on Sunday and once during the week.

But, Shelley is honking her horn. Hurry up, she yells out the open window. Let's move. And my ears tune back into Friday night and the strains of "Yellow Submarine" on Shelley's radio. There might be true love waiting for me at the Bright Spot. Remember?

What took you so long? Shelley asks as she turns left onto Las Vegas Boulevard and back toward the Bright Spot.

Slow checkout line, I say. I don't want to talk about the showgirl's eyes. Pull around to the back, someplace where it's dark, I say to Shelley. After she does, I unzip my Levi's, pull down my pants, pull the strip of paper from the back of an Always Super, and stick it to my panties. There's that spot of blood on my Levi's, but it's in a place that shouldn't be noticeable.

What is this yucky stuff anyway that shows up every month? I say to Shelley. And then, without wanting to, even while Shelley's answering me, I'm thinking of Jesus again. Him on the cross. The crown of thorns and pearls of blood on his forehead. And I think of the soldiers staring up at him. And other soldiers carrying shields that aren't big enough to cover their bodies. Arrows. Cannons. War and blood and innocents being massacred. But it's time to hurry up and get back to Friday night. My pants are even tighter when I zip them up again.

I'm ready. Let's hit the Bright Spot, I say, beamingly beamish girl that I am.

You going to buy me some gas for a change? she says, smiling her cheesy smile, her teeth lighting up the car like a neon Cheshire cat.

Sure, I say, money being a sore spot between us, me never having anything extra. There's six of us kids, and my mother cans every living thing except lizards so we can eat right. How about $2?

Wow, you're loaded, Mattie. Shelley rolls her eyes back and sucks in her cheeks. Her famous fish face.

Don't knock it. It's something.

The jumping neon on the Bright Spot's sign is still going

round and round the circular sign. The lights keep traveling the same old same old, and I wonder if there will ever be a moment when something will interfere with this geometrical pattern—six bulbs to a row, each row marching one by one into the light? Could these bulbs ever try another route? Is this world made of uninterruptible patterns? Unleavable sockets? Can anything or anybody dare to be different?

Shelley parks in Stall Number 16. The carhop slides a cardboard ticket under the windshield wiper. Cherry lime rickey, we both say in unison. We'd both like to add french-fried onion rings, but we don't have enough money. We don't care about food, anyway, though. We're still waiting, listening to all the radios as cars cruise the Bright Spot. "You Are So Beautiful." "Lady of the Blue Rose." "Imagine."

When do you think they'll get here? Shelley asks as she guzzles the last of her cherry lime rickey through her straw. Her red hair reflects the lights on the Bright Spot sign, and speckles of light dance across her bangs.

I tap the bottom of my glass to coax the last of the shaved ice to fall into my mouth. They better hurry, I say, getting tough, like I'll leave if they don't show. Fat chance.

And suddenly they're back, leaning into the windows of Shelley's Plymouth. Rod and the King. Their faces are red. They look like they're feelin' good. Park your car, they say. Come with us, you women, you broads.

I gotta take a whiz first, the King says. Too many Teddy Beers. He laughs. He makes a move with his hand like he's gonna whip his jewels out from behind his zipper right then and there and do it in the bright lights. But he winks at me and walks off for the bathroom. He's so lanky and tall and knows how to move those thin little hips of his. I'm holding my breath again. Hurry back, I whisper, then think about the science of pelvises.

Too much hard work at the Tracks, Rod says as we walk toward the King's car. Lifting those cans takes a lot of muscle. Like Olympic weight lifters, you better believe.

As soon as the King returns, we all slip into the magic car, the silver streak, Shelley and me in the backseat, Rod at shotgun, the King driving. I wish I was up there with him. I'd slide so close to him, I'd barely leave him room. I want body contact. But instead I watch the back of his head as he drives, the steady rhythm of the streetlights illuminating his olive neck, his dark hair like a Bedouin's, the perfect desert boyfriend, someone who might ride a camel and wrap scarves around his head if he had some. Why don't you get your ten-pound-weakling body to the gym? the King is shouting to Rod as we pass Health World, the new gym in town. He punches Rod in the shoulder.

Muscles, Rod says as he puts a beer can next to his biceps. The only kind of muscle I need, he says.

The King is slapping the seat with his hand. He's laughing as if Rod just told the last joke on earth. He's punching his buddy in the arm and the car is running on autopilot.

Watch where you're going, I want to say, but don't. I bite my tongue. I want to fit this time and this moment. Usually, Mormon girls are out of place. Our Mutual Improvement Association teachers gave us cards that said "Dare to Be Different." They thought this would encourage us to be daring enough not to fall into the morass of the world and the pit of the hell-bound, daring enough to live by the Truth. But I took the cards to mean I should be different from the way anybody told me I had to live life. Dare to be different from everything.

So I don't care if our car is weaving slightly as the King drives from streetlight to streetlight. Life is to be lived now, so why spend it preparing for the next one, hoping I'll be God's Little Darlin'? He holds the steering wheel with two thumbs, and I wish again I could be by his shoulder and see into the night better than I can from the backseat. The stars are shining more brightly the farther we pull away from the center of Las Vegas.

Where are we going? I ask as I lean on my elbows against the front seat.

The lake, the King says. Something new.

What would really be new, I say, is to drive to the stars.

Well, aren't you something? the King says to me.

Did my voice sound sexy when I said "stars"? I wonder. Is that what he means? Or does he think it's a cool idea to drive to the stars? When we get to the lake, maybe he'll want to change places with Shelley. Sit in the backseat with me.

Today's the day, Rod sings, the Teddy Beers have their picnic.

Tonight's the night, I say.

The radio blasts as we whip down Boulder Highway toward the man-made lake called Mead, which buries skeletons of Moapa Indians and Mormon pioneers and the bones of their houses. I've heard about this in Sunday school. The King accelerates. I close my eyes and imagine we could leave the ground any minute and take an aerial highway and blast through the stringy night clouds highlighted by the moon. I feel the power of speed, the moan of the tires spinning faster than light traveling.

I look over at my best friend, Shelley, whose jaw is tight. We both laugh, yet, steel-nerve Shelley's gripping the seat with clawlike hands. Her face looks white in this light. The desert hills whip by like ghosts, the marker posts by the sides of the road, white dominoes falling behind the path of the car. Chances are, I hum.

I like the idea of leaving the ground, leaving my father's Dale Carnegie and Norman Vincent Peale speeches. He won't allow me to say anything unkind about someone unless I say three nice things. We live the Golden Rule at home. We believe in all good things, we seek after these things. Life is one big bud of goodness, I've been told, yet, sometimes it's a maximum-security prison to have to smile and be loving all the time. To be inside those invisible bars of goodness that catch sunlight and keep me true to my word, true to the covenants with God. A cage of golden sunlight, golden plates, and golden birds who can't sing because their feathers are solid. Golden angels who can't fly because they're made of gold.

I think of myself giving my testimony in Sacrament meeting. "I know this Church is the only true Church on the face of the earth and that Joseph Smith is the Only True Prophet." Believing, believing, yet here I am, the velour air rubbing across my face and arms and making me want to unbutton my shirt. Open up to the night air. Save me, somebody.

Maybe tonight we'll bust free to the new religion of time and space. We're going fast enough. Fly, King, I whisper so he can't hear me. Step on the accelerator. My veins are drunk with you.

Have a swig, Rod says, reaching across the seat and handing his Teddy Beer to the King. He takes a long swig and heads into the night.

Shelley and I are leaning against the backseat, our legs spread wide. I'm looking at two large white Vs. Our legs in the shadow of the car. Our legs that look like bones in this moonlight. I love the wind that's whipping my hair and tangling it and blinding me with its thickness. Hair in my mouth, whipping around my ears. Hair is the only thing I can feel right now. Sometimes it slaps my cheek and stings, but I like the almost feel of cutting into my skin, my skin that's so innocent, my face that tells lies to my mother and says righteous prayers in church on Sunday. I'm a Pharisee. A whited sepulchre in white Levi's. Me. I touch my mouth. It can't wait until we stop somewhere so it can kiss the King. French-kiss him. Feel his tongue in my mouth. It can't wait to be bruised from kissing too hard, and I feel throbbing against the tight seam between my legs. Our bodies will wrangle with each other, roll on some sand at the lake, though I know it's only a rocky beach. I can't wait for him to get hard and push against me and my pelvis bone and the cloth of the Mormon Levi's.

But I know I'm still a good girl. I want to live with Jesus someday. Shelley, too. We're saving ourselves like stamps or coins or something valuable, even though we're crashing through the night, headlights cutting the dark into ribbons. I have a hunch we're both thinking that someday soon we'll be more careful. Do what our parents ask us. But this Nevada night. It sucks us in like a vacuum cleaner, and we're on the edge of something big.

The King takes another sip of the beer, tossing his head back for one second too long. The car swerves onto the gravelly shoulder of the road and fishtails from side to side. Careening, lurching, jerking, tipping, swaying, righting itself. The King finally gets control and pulls the silver Pontiac back into the southbound lane of the two-lane highway. We're still headed south. Both Shelley and I have one hand flat against our chests. With the other hand, we're holding each other's arms tighter than a fistful of cash.

Damn, that was beautiful, Rod says. Damn, damn. He's slapping his knees and pulling the ring top of another beer. Sweet little Teddy Beer, he says. Good little Teddy. Take care of me. Make me happy. He's stroking the side of the can as if it were a stuffed animal he had when he was a kid.

Give me another sip, the King says. Rod reaches across the front seat, his arm silhouetted against the windshield and the rocks and hills that look like grotesque shapes of elephants and desert camels we're passing on the lake road. Beer, beer, wonderful beer, he chants while the King takes more time with this swig. The King accelerates even more. We're heading for a rise in the road, the mound of the railroad track looming large ahead of us, and suddenly the sharp definition of double yellow stripes seem to be rising straight up to the sky.

Jesus and Mary, Rod says. Holy shit! Will you look at that Monster Rise in the Road? Holy holy shit. Rod's eyes are big as he holds his beer can in midair and looks at the King with a mouth caught by the hook of surprise.

Hey, you women back there, the King is yelling. You want love, do you? You want excitement? Well, hold on to your seats. We're gonna take air. A little foreplay, girls and boys.

Floor it, Rod says, leaning into the windshield to watch the ground rise. Go for it.

Maybe we'll sail when we hit the top of the mound because our car isn't a car anymore. I look at Shelley, who looks back at me. Our faces are blanks. We're here. On the ride. We accept our fate as the King steps on the pedal, pushes it to the floor, and we head for the high point in the road, the place with a railroad cross shining back at us. The radio is blasting.

I grab Shelley's hand and hold it tight, and together we lay our heads back and surrender, just like we used to do on the Roll-O-Plane at the carnival. Maybe we'll land like a jet on the other side. Maybe we'll keep flying. If that's the case, maybe Jesus will be waiting for us with open arms.

I squeeze my eyes shut. I squeeze Shelley's hand and brace my feet against the floor. I love you, Shelley, I whisper. You're my best friend ever. If I don't have anything else that matters, I have you.

You're the best, Shelley says, wrinkling her nose as she squeezes her eyes tightly. I peek at the black mountain of road soaring in front of the headlights, then slam my eyes shut again.

Jesus, we just might be coming to you. Hold those arms wide open. We're leaving the desert and maybe we'll get to look into your eyes and see if they really are sad, and if they are, we can ask you why.

FRANK BERGON
(1943–   )

Ely native Frank Bergon has worked hard to capture the West of the American imagination. His books chronicle our fascination with wide-open spaces and terrifying circumstances—whether frontier justice or nuclear storage, they remain a plea for our very survival. Although he was trained as a Stephen Crane scholar, his first passion is the vast Great Basin, a passion that he undoubtedly acquired from Wallace Stegner when he was a fellow at Stanford. *Western American Literature* called *Shoshone Mike* the best Western since Walter Van Tilburg Clark's *The Ox-Bow Incident,* but for me, it is really a book about the end of an era—the Shoshone who lived in the Humboldt Range. The book's namesake and central character, Shoshone Mike, must keep his family on the move to stay alive, but just as he realizes in this excerpt, there is no home left, no land on which to live. Bergon's recent novels continue to call into question the ethics of survival in a "barren land." When he is not writing at his mountain cabin in Colorado, he teaches English at Vassar College. He was inducted into the Nevada Writers Hall of Fame in 1998.

Wild Game. Reno: University of Nevada Press, 1995.
The Temptations of St. Ed and Brother S. Reno: University of Nevada Press, 1993.

The Journals of Lewis and Clark (editor). New York: Viking, 1989; reprint, New York: Penguin Nature Classics, 1995; reprint, London: Folio Society, 2000.

Shoshone Mike. New York: Viking Press, 1987; reprint, New York: Penguin, 1989; reprint, Reno: University of Nevada Press, 1994.

A Sharp Lookout: Selected Nature Essays of John Burroughs (editor). Washington, D.C.: Smithsonian Institution Press, 1987.

The Wilderness Reader (editor). New York: New American Library, 1980; reprint, Reno: University of Nevada Press, 1994.

The Western Writings of Stephen Crane (editor). New York: New American Library, 1979.

Looking Far West: The Search for the American West in History, Myth, and Literature (coedited with Zeese Papanikolas). New York: New American Library, 1978.

Stephen Crane's Artistry. New York: Columbia University Press, 1975.

Shoshone Mike

(EXCERPT)

EVERY DECEMBER MIKE RETURNED to the same bend in the creek at the mouth of Rock Creek Canyon. Hides went back on the domed willow frame. Shredded bark and grass lined the floor. Smoke twisted from the small campfire and spread out above the river willows. The year completed, the circle of travel closed, Mike and his family were ready for the winter.

In the wickiup when the snow was falling, Mike told stories to his family in various voices, as he once did during the winters at Fort Hall. To his children Mike was anything but silent. He laughed and talked into the night.

Mike's children lay on the warm, spongy floor of the wickiup and sometimes drifted to the edge of sleep. The wickiup smelled of smoke mixed with a stronger smell from the dried fish and venison stacked on the floor along the inside walls of the hut. Whether they slipped into sleep or out of sleep, they could hear the voices of Coyote and Wolf and their father, still talking.

In the beginning Wolf wanted to make everything easy and pleasant for the people, but his younger brother, Coyote, tried to make them work hard as they must do today. Wolf had all the animals shut up so the people could easily take what they wanted, but Coyote released the animals so the people had to go hunting. The people ranged through the country in individual families. There were no tribes, there were no bands. There were no chiefs. Families occasionally came together for a seasonal hunt, and an old and experienced man might emerge as a temporary leader. In the winter, groups of families camped together but went their separate ways in the spring. They all spoke the same language. To themselves and each other, they were simply the people, the Newe.

Wolf said, "The Newe shall not die."

"Why shouldn't they die?" Coyote asked. "Surely they must die."

Wolf said, "There will be two deaths then. After a man dies, he'll die again."

"No," Coyote said. "There ought to be only one death so that when a man dies, he shall stay that way."

They argued for a long time. Finally Wolf said, "Coyote, I agree with you about having only one death. It will be that way."

Shortly after, Coyote's son became sick and was near death. Coyote went to his brother and said, "Wolf, when you were giving orders, didn't you say we should have two deaths? Well, Wolf, I agree with you on that one. I like that idea."

Wolf said, "Don't be foolish."

Coyote began to cry and begged his brother to change the rule. He said, "I didn't think my son was going to die right away. Please change the rule."

Wolf said, "No, don't be foolish. When we make a rule we must keep it."

Afterward, Coyote felt sorry for the people and taught them how to cry and cut their hair when anyone died. Coyote told them that the dead go to another place. It's pleasant there, where the dead go, but they would still rather be with the living.

When Wolf and Coyote were talking, Wolf said, "Let there be no menstruation," but Coyote thought it proper that women should menstruate. So Coyote took some blood and threw it at his daughter. She began to menstruate and went to the menstrual hut, where Coyote taught her what she must do.

Wolf thought people ought to be born without copulation, but Coyote disagreed. "Fucking is better," Coyote said. "People should be born from the womb." So the world became as it was, a satisfactory place to live in.

ON ROCK CREEK, nights were icy, the moon cold white, but the morning winds began to come through the canyon without bite. Each day the places on the horizon where the sun rose and set grew farther and farther apart. The dried food they had eaten all winter was almost gone. The boys caught a winter-starved rabbit in the snow and roasted it whole. The winds grew warmer. The ice broke up in the creek. Trout swam in the creek and squirrels pushed themselves out of the ground. Their noses quivered as they looked at the world with quick dark eyes. Green clover appeared along the stream. Shoots of wild onions and the light green leaves of young lettuce thickened on the canyon floor. After the winter, they tasted like sunlight and spring water. Birds were flying around everywhere.

Mike's boys waded into the cold water and trapped trout with their hands. In earlier years they stayed until the first salmon ran up Rock Creek. They sliced the pink flesh from the bones and hung it along the creek on drying racks made of willows. But the salmon quit coming up Rock Creek when Milner Dam was built in the Snake River.

Then Mike and his family moved southward. Timing was everything. They could not harvest biscuit root before its seeds ripened, otherwise the root would spoil. Sego bulbs could be dug up while their yellow-core lilies still blossomed, but bitterroot only after its ghostly rose flowers dried and fell. Everywhere the ground offered something to eat. Mike and his family climbed to higher country, near Gollaher Mountain. They replenished their strings of horses with mustangs captured from the wild herds. The boys went to work running horses for ranchers. The women and children dug camas bulbs with crooked-nosed sticks hardened in the fire. The stick went into the ground a few inches from the plant. The stick jerked and the white bulb popped out of the ground. The women lightly steamed some bulbs for meals and cooked and pounded others for the coming winter. As the days grew hotter, the course of the sun shifted northward each day, pointing toward the coming cold. The women dug pit ovens in the ground. On the oven floor of stones a hardwood fire burned down to hot coals. The women raked the coals and covered them with grass, then added a layer of sego bulbs. They filled the pit with alternate layers of bulbs and coals and grass, covered with dirt. After the bulbs were baked, the women pounded them into flour or flattened them into cakes to be later recooked in boiling baskets. They roasted camas bulbs, removed the black outer layers, and squeezed the bulbs into warm, sugary macaroons hung away from the children to dry.

Fruits ripened. The air hummed with mosquitoes. Mashed serviceberries dried in the sun. Golden currants and red currants and black currants ripened in the lower valley. They were cooked into puddings. As the fall advanced, chokecherries hung in heavy dark clusters on bushes in the mountains. The seed harvest arrived and the women moved from crop to crop to gather the seeds of the quick-blooming plants before they scattered in the wind. Sometimes a day or two made all the difference. They worked deliberately but without hurry. The women hit the withered plant heads. Seeds showered into gathering baskets. Sunflower seeds, and grains from wild wheat and rye, the round black seeds of rice grass, and the tiny seeds of pickleweed—all were parched, hulled, and ground into rich flour.

Nive told her daughters that the flour of the white people tasted like alkali dust because they did not feed air to the flour. Seeds came from the ground. Fire heated them, stones cracked them. Flat winnowing baskets tossed them into the air so that wind blew away light chaff and flowed around the seeds before they were ground into flour. The same was done to crickets. In the cool mornings before they could jump, crickets lay in bunches in the grass, and children gathered them in handfuls. Roasted on hot coals, tossed in the air, they were ground like seeds into flour. Even chokecherries lay spread out on willow racks so the air could flow over and under and all around them.

In the fall, processions of clouds moved across the dark blue sky. The places on the horizon where the sun rose and set moved closer together. The women watched the sky day and night for signs. All across the land bright yellow flowers of rabbitbrush looked like lights. The men brought back fat rabbits and deer. They took sinews from the backstraps and legs of the deer; they cut the meat into strips and hung it on willows to dry. They cooked the tasty neck of the deer for the children. The women scraped hair from the hide and washed the skin. Tied to a tree, the wet skin was twisted with a stick until it was wrung dry. The women rubbed and smeared the deer's own oily brains into the hide to soften it.

Mornings grew colder. It was time for the last harvest. Mike and his family moved to the mountains for pine nuts. They stopped in Tecoma, the small railhead near the Utah border where Nive's sister lived. Other families from Tecoma and Fort Hall joined them for the harvest. They struck the nuts from their hard cones and roasted them. Even as the women prepared the nuts for storage, they cracked open roasted shells with their teeth and tasted the rich nut that would be mashed into gravy during the winter. Nive and her daughter Henie also gathered yarrow and other medicines that ripened at the same time as the pine nuts. Henie was the daughter who paid closest attention to how her mother did things. She was always watching. In the evening her father played the hand game with the other men and sang as he gambled. Nive gambled too. The people faced each other in rows, and their wavering voices rose and fell in pulsing rhythms. Henie felt the songs move into her body as the gamblers swayed back and forth.

Later she sat with her family where willows enclosed their camp the way a willow basket enclosed water. Smoke rose from the fire and spread over the darkening camp. The voices of the people sitting on the earth were low. Other people in the distance could be heard laughing and joking, telling stories. Mike smoked his short willowstem pipe in the dark. As he smoked, the green soapstone bowl glowed red. He'd picked wild tobacco from the earth in late fall and mixed it with tobacco from the store. Fire made the tobacco burn. Henie watched her father. Covering his head with a blanket and sitting outside facing east, he made himself into a mountain. The tobacco and fire and air around him became part of his head and rose into the cold air. Mike began to sing:

> Old mountain, old mountain,
> So strong, ay, ay,
> Moving through fog,
> Ay, ay, moving through fog.

Overhead, the white stars had gathered in thousands and covered the sky like snow.

HARD, DARK DAYS FOLLOWED. Winter was long and cold. Ten of Mike's horses died. In the early spring, when Mike and his family again camped in a canyon at Gollaher Mountain, their remaining horses were weak and without feed. In late April, Dell Hardy saw five of Mike's family about two miles east of

San Jacinto. They were all afoot. Old Mike was slightly stooped. He wore tattered overalls and his face was wrinkled with age. One of his sons walked beside him, a short, bowlegged, heavy-set man in his late thirties. His black hair, cut square across his forehead, was braided in the back and worn looped around his neck. Shuffling behind the men were two dark-headed women, wrapped in blankets, one carrying a small baby on her back, the other carrying a bundle. They walked toward the cattle company store, where they could buy on credit. At the store, Allie Patterson said that Old Mike and his family came on foot to the store several times that spring because their horses were too poor to ride.

In May, Mike's horses grew stronger, and his boys were getting ready to run mustangs to replace the horses that had died over the winter. During the day they let the horses graze for feed but drove them into brush corrals at night. One day his son Jack was driving the horses to camp when someone shot him from his horse. Mike saw two of his sons carrying Jack into the camp. They put him on the ground and cut away the overalls below his knee. Blood ran into the dust, turning it black. Jack's leg bent at the knee and it bent again below the knee where the bone was broken. The bone was sticking out of the blood and skin. Nive pressed poultices of mashed yarrow against the wound but the blood kept coming, and Mike heard the blood in his son's throat as he breathed. Nive worked hard with new poultices. She and her daughters were crying, their voices rising and falling in wails. Mike looked at his son's eyes and saw that they were dead.

Mike's other sons rode out and paid death with death. When they returned they said they had found five men and a woman camped in a draw. Corralled in the draw were stolen horses, and the men and woman must have thought Jack had discovered them. They had a fight with the men and they shot one in his brains and his heart. They knew they killed him and they knew who he was, Frankie Dopp, one of the white boys they'd played with as kids. Everything was crazy now. The other men they fought were men they had worked with when they were running horses for ranchers. Frank Tranmer was someone Mike had known for the past twenty years, ever since he'd left the reservation. The other man was named Nimrod Urie. Those men shot his son. His son's blood lay on the ground. Everything was out of order.

Everyone was crying as Mike washed his son, painted his face, and dressed him. He wrapped him in a blanket and tied it. On horses they dragged the wrapped body above the canyon and buried it in the rocks. With knives and sheepshears Nive and her daughters hacked their hair short. Jim cut off his braid and threw it away. Mike cut his hair and smeared ashes on his face. He lifted his face and wailed in a high-pitched cry until his voice broke and he sobbed with his face in his hands. He burned Jack's clothing and bedding. Nive burned rabbitbrush to keep all the ghosts away. They were all crying now—my brother, my son—but no one said his name for fear he would think they were calling him back. "Go away," his mother said. "We loved you when you were here. Your place is somewhere else now."

"Don't bother our dreams," Mike said. "Just be happy where you are."

That night Mike's sons—Nogoviz, Wonig, and Hogozap—returned to the white man's camp and drove horses from their brush corrals. Riding some of the horses and driving the rest, Mike and his family rode from Gollaher Mountain toward the west under a dim moon. Mike knew what would happen to him if he stayed in that country. It would be his word against a white man's. He made his family hurry, and they left behind their wagon, some pots, the wagon jack, and everything that was too heavy or clumsy to carry on horseback. They turned loose

Jack's favorite bay mare as well as some of their own weak horses. They left Jack's riding saddle and the saddle tree for his packhorse. Mike hung them in an aspen tree not far from where his son was shot.

Mike made his way westward, dropping south of the Owyhee Mountains and staying north of the Humboldt River. They stayed away from the few far-flung settlements and ranches in that open country. They had left before the spring and fall harvests and were without supplies. They moved across north-central Nevada and took what they needed from isolated sheep and cattle camps left empty during the day. They moved into the more populated country north of Golconda. They passed Paradise Valley, crossed a desert valley, and stopped at the Lay brothers' ranch to trade for some old harness. They made camp in a canyon and spent several days running horses. They now had a string of about twenty horses, including the ones taken from the stolen bunches at Gollaher Mountain. One day an Indian hunter approached the canyon, but Wonig and Hogozap rode out to keep him away from the horses. In the afternoon they saw clouds of dust raised by buckaroos running horses to the south. They moved out of their camp and headed toward less populated country. They crossed the Jackson Mountains through Rattlesnake Canyon, the massive purple head of King Lear Peak hidden from view to the north. They passed pale sand dunes shaped by the wind into delicate tufts and fluted ridges. They moved into country of lava rock flows, disintegrated volcanic fissures, and steaming hot springs. They rode out onto the flat, white, shimmering floor of the desert. Layers of dried mud peeled up from the desert floor like paper. Crusted with salt, the ground cracked, and beneath the hooves of horses brittle salt grass near hot springs snapped like hundreds of tiny twigs. The burnt and torn hills of the Black Rock Range came closer, and the volcanic rock yielded to the Harlequin Hills and the Calico Mountains. They were now more than two hundred miles from home. To the south the flat desert mirrored the sky like a distant sheen of blue water. Even the hills were reflected in that waterless lake. At the ends of the vast horizon the edges of the earth fell away into a curve. The country was full of ghosts, spinning in the distance in the form of dust devils. Mike did not know where in this country he would ever find a place to live.

H. LEE BARNES
(1944–)

For three decades Lee Barnes has lived in Las Vegas, where he teaches English at the Community College of Southern Nevada. A Westerner by birth and choice, he received his M.F.A. at Arizona State University. His fiction largely focuses on Vietnam, that strange and sometimes dis-tasteful parable now part of our collective history. The characters for whom he has the most affection are the ragged ones, scudding their way through the jungle. Always, there is a bit of surreal to the stories—whether baseball with the enemy or the mythic cat that fills this story. His fiction has been widely published in such journals as *Writers' Forum, Clackamus Literary Review* (where he won the 1997 fiction award, judged by Ron Carlson), and *Orange Coast Review.* He was the former fiction editor at *Red Rock Review* in Las Vegas and now concentrates on writing and teaching.

Gunning for Ho. Reno: University of Nevada Press, 2000.

Stonehands and the Tigress

THE ELONGATED COMBE was an obstacle course of tangles and elephant grass riddled with booby traps and tunnels and punji stakes; a free-fire range open to mortar attacks and ambushes; a habitat for spiders and mosquitoes and leeches, and for snakes—cobras and little green vipers called two-step death. Second Squad, Third Platoon marched uphill in single file, like worker ants lugging great burdens up an endless climb. They attacked the bitter ascent with machinelike apathy.

The climb had been most difficult during the last minutes through a monotonous curtain of vegetation, palm leaves the width of a man's chest and tree trunks the girth of mine shafts. The grunts, as they were called, had humped three hours now, puffing out air like draft animals. Sweat blackened their fatigues and burned into the fine cuts left by razorlike edges of the dense grass. Young and sinuous, they were capable of enduring great hardship, which they often did.

Halverson halted them in a rocky clearing atop a ridge. He told them to take a break. They tossed off their helmets and eased out of their web gear, dropping backpacks, the shoulder straps gravid with smoke and concussion grenades, and cartridge cases. They wiped away sweat with green bandannas and drank from canteens. Some sprawled out straddle-legged on the spot and lit cigarettes while others found shade and a tree trunk to lean against.

Stonehands removed his helmet. His forehead glistened with sweat as he gazed out at the depression below, where the valley opened and the verdant treetops ran to a horizon that blurred into a blue sky. He kept his M-60 ready, two belts of ammo wrapped in bandoliers across his shoulders, one feeding the chamber of the machine gun. A tall man with long, powerful thighs, he was solid and flat in the chest, and wide and stooped at the shoulders. His name was Walter Harvey, but he'd not been called that since jump school, where he'd dropped two opponents in the first rounds of his only fights—two pickup matches.

Stonehands watched Donatello suck on a cigarette and sprinkle his trouser cuffs with repellent. The size of an average Vietnamese, he was a wiry little man who would husband insect spray and batteries and recycle cigarette butts like a miser, then turn around and blow his pay on beer and boom-boom girls in Quang Ngai. Donatello hailed from New York, a place, so far as Stonehands could tell, where the populace distrusted everyone but politicians.

"Shoulda stayed at Benning and boxed," he said and pointed at Stonehands's M-60. "Instead you're humpin' that pig."

Stonehands listened absentmindedly. He thought about a particular boy, one he'd thought of a lot lately. He was stumped as to why after months of humping hills and sweeping villages, of seeing bodies burned or riddled with holes, the boy in Hai Drong came to mind so often. Why not Howkert, who'd been found in a gutter in Quang Ngai City with strips of skin sliced from his chest?

Hai Drong had been unremarkable as operations go—two sniper rounds, a captured VC turned over to the ARVN. Only the boy made it different. He'd come straight up the middle of the road on a rough-hewn crutch, smiling a gap-toothed smile like he was the local Welcome Wagon, his left arm gone, his left leg off at the knee. As he moved, his body listed to the right and he swung his good leg forward violently like a cricket hopping on one leg.

They'd fed him candy and canned peaches, given him cigarettes and watched him smoke. He'd called each of them Joe. They'd named him Sammy, a name he seemed to like. Someone crowned his head with a fatigue cap, and when it was time to go, he followed along as if one of them. *Di di mau,* he was told —no go with Joe. He'd struggled to keep up, hopping fiercely down the same road, following with the smile glued to his face as if that could change their minds. Then he fell and sat in the middle of the road and watched them leave.

"Be in fat city in Benning, Stoners. That colonel liked you," Donatello said so loud Stonehands had to look.

He licked his lips. "Sure could use some grape soda. Sure could."

Stonehands grunted. He'd never boxed again after his mother insisted he see a preacher and get a job "helping out"—her exact words. He'd explained there were no such jobs, that the army expected men to be tough. She stated that she hadn't raised her boy to hurt men with his fists.

A few yards away Drammel stood, field-stripped his cigarette, and unbuttoned his fly as he eased into the bush.

"Watch out a snake don't bite you," Donatello said.

Drammel shook off Donatello's comment and entered the vine tangle to urinate. An instant later he hurried out, buttoning up as he charged through the bush. He looked at Stonehands, then Halverson, and stuttered as he did when excited. "A mockin' funky hole while pliffin' by the ease."

Drammel was shy and twisted words—speaking in tongues, Donatello called it. His phobias included snakes and spiders and needles. Halverson sat him down to take a few deep breaths. Once he understood that Drammel had found a monkey hole, Halverson ordered the squad to set up a fire perimeter.

"Stonehands, bring that pig over here."

Stonehands stood by the mouth of the hole and kept his M-60 at the ready as Donatello removed his necklace, a silver chain from which dangled a lucky tiger's claw. It had been given to him by a prostitute in Quang Ngai. He handed it to Halverson along with a pack of cigarettes and took the flashlight Halverson offered but not the .45. He said using it would just blow the wax out of his ears. He crawled to the hole and peered in. He said it didn't seem to be a tunnel, didn't drop straight down like most and was shallow—six to seven feet deep.

Halverson said, "Check it out anyhow."

Donatello squirmed in and vanished. An instant later, he shouted, "Well, damn." At once, a tiger cub with rosettes on its back shot out, clawing at the ground. Donatello held a rear leg firmly in his grasp. He quickly stuffed the flashlight in his trousers and lifted the cub into the air by the nape of the neck, where it hung limply.

Stonehands, who'd grown up around bears and deer and owls, understood, as Donatello never could, the gravity of removing the cub. "Tell him to put it back, Hal."

"Cute, ain't it? No harm," Halverson said, tickling the pink of its ear. The cub seemed to like the attention. Halverson grinned as Donatello handed it over. Halverson scratched the tuft on its chin. Donatello hung the tiger's claw around his neck and reached for the animal.

Stonehands shook his head. "Put it back 'fore its mama come," he said.

"Well, you just shoot her, Bro." Examining his prize, Donatello licked his wrist where the cub had clawed him.

"How you gonna feed it?" Stonehands asked.

"What's with you?" Donatello asked. "I'll hook onto some cat chow." He tussled with the cub as he wrapped it in his bandanna. "That'll keep him from scratchin'." He stuffed it inside his shirt so that only its head stuck out.

AT THE FORWARD FIRE BASE Donatello scavenged three bags of powdered milk and a jar of honey and drained the syrup out of a can of fruit to feed the cub. Men came to the tent to see. It was a welcome break from the monotonous low drama of war and the petty annoyance of fear. It was a piece of home, a pet, something not yet ruined by the war. The captain stuck his head inside for a peep and reminded the men that a regiment of North Vietnamese was operating in the A Shau. He didn't mention the cub, which meant he wasn't going to cause a stir.

One man donated a poncho liner, another had two cans of evaporated milk sent by an aunt from Milwaukee. Still another said the cub was a sign, good luck, and should be made the company mascot. Donatello said Drammel was the company mascot and dangled his claw necklace in front of the cub, which lay on its back swatting at it. When the visitors left, the squad lit a joint. As the weed passed from hand to hand, Donatello romped with the cub. He asked what to name it, and the squad began compiling a list, the favorite name being Butter.

McPherson, a sad-faced kid from the First Squad, said the Montagnards believe a tiger has supernatural powers, that it is, in part, animal, human, and spirit.

"Whata you know?" Donatello asked.

It sounded like a challenge, and McPherson, being timid, seemed apologetic when he explained he'd read it somewhere.

"Where?" Donatello demanded.

Jurgens, a spec four from another platoon, said, "I know somethin' about tigers."

Donatello said, "Let McPherson finish."

"I read about animal myths," McPherson said. He seemed to wait for Donatello to take issue, but Donatello was distracted by the cub, which had found its footing and was trying to run away.

McPherson swallowed and explained that according to the story the tiger had descended from kings and queens who ruled the forest before the coming of the Annamese and is driven to mate because its spirit can pass into the heaven of kings only if it leaves behind posterity.

"That's it?" Donatello said.

McPherson gave a nod.

Donatello said, "That's dumb."

Jurgens nodded knowingly. "Ain't either. Tigers," he said, "ain't other animals. Not here. Had me a shack-up in Quang Ngai who told about a princess."

Fists stuffed in his pockets, Stonehands stood to the side and listened as Jurgens told the legend of a princess who ran away with a lover, a Radai, a great hunter-warrior, rather than marry the Annamese king she was promised to. The couple was tracked down by the king's soldiers and the Radai dismembered, his remains strewn over the highlands. Thereafter, Jurgens explained, the princess refused to eat, died, and was sent to the spirit world on a pyre, though he called it a "pier." According to his boom-boom girl, the tigress leaped out of the flames and killed the Annamese king. Always hungry, she had, he claimed, "roamed the jungle ever since in search of her lover's spirit."

Donatello gathered the cub in his arms. "Fairy tales are for kids. Besides, what does a pier have to do with tigers?"

"Uh, uh, he means a pu-pu-pyre," Drammel said.

"It's cute," Jurgens said, "but I wouldn't want to meets its mama, even if she is a goddamn princess."

The others were skeptical and joked about it, but Stonehands felt something resonant in these stories. Ain't right to mess with the natural, he thought, but a lot of things weren't right. Howkert, the boy, the vc. The image of the boy on the crutch came like a curtain closing his mind to anything else.

Donatello stood up from playing with the cub. "Thinks I'm his mommy. Whachu think of the name?" he asked.

Stonehands blinked but didn't answer.

"Well, man, what about Butter?"

He said. "It's bad. You hear what those boys said."

"You superstitious, Stonehands? Is 'at what's buggin' you? You scared of a little cub?"

Stonehands saw nothing wrong with superstition. Luck, it seemed to him, had everything to do with everything.

"S-s-s-Stonehands a-ain't a-afraid of nuh-nuh-nothing," Drammel said.

"Didn't you hear, Bro?" Donatello said to Stonehands. "It's unlucky to be superstitious." He laughed and looked at the others. "Get it?" He clutched the cub to his chest.

Stonehands was tired. He shook his head and left to be by himself. As he reached his tent, he was met by Halverson, who told him he had last watch.

"Been humpin' all day," Stonehands said.

Halverson shrugged. "Sorry. The listening post. You got four hours of shut-eye."

Now with more important matters facing him than thinking about a tiger cub—three hours of blackness at a listening post—Stonehands lifted the tent flap and crawled in. He lay on his left side but couldn't get comfortable, then flipped to his right, which was no better. He tried to think of something pleasant to whisk him into sleep, but he saw the boy again, hand outstretched for candy, and the cub swatting at the claw. These two fused into a picture of Howkert sitting next to him saying he was through. Through?

Stonehands hadn't understood at the time what Howkert

had meant. His had been crazy talk, rambling words about the only thing to live for and finding love and never seeing things the same. Stonehands closed his eyes and saw the narrow trail to his home in the Smokies, a turn in the path, and his house on the right, its windows open, a bluebottle fly buzzing by his head, and smells.... In the dream the boy came hopping down the road, but the road led to Stonehands's home. Then the boy was engulfed in a ball of darkness that swirled violently like a cyclone.

STONEHANDS AWOKE AND SAT UPRIGHT IN THE DARK. Grofield shook his shoulder. "You awake, Harvey?"

"Yeah, Sarge."

"You sure? You were talking in your sleep."

"I'm sure."

"Come on, then," the platoon sergeant said.

Stonehands pulled his boots on, tied them, and crawled out. Grofield took Stonehands's M-60, handed over an M-16, and told him to follow.

A fog had crept over the valley and sealed it in. At the perimeter, a guard spread the concertina and handed over a commo wire. Running the wire through his palm, Stonehands walked in silence, with Grofield a step behind. Two hundred meters later they reached the listening post, a foxhole large enough to accommodate one man and equipped with a field telephone.

Smith challenged them. Grofield said, "Slick silver." Smitty told them to advance and said he was glad to leave—the fog and all. "Times I felt I wasn't alone," he said.

Stonehands sank down into the damp hole and called in a brief commo check. By the time he finished, the fog had swallowed Grofield and Smitty. Left alone, he touched the commo wire, then laid the barrel of the M-16 on the sandbag.

The first hour seemed to go quickly. He thought about anything he could but the boy. He recalled the soldier he'd boxed at Benning, a white youngster with a boy's face and a man's body, the one he was afraid to hit because where he came from blacks didn't hit whites. He'd knocked him to his knees, then held him from going down until the referee urged him to a neutral corner so the count could begin. Later the soldier had congratulated him, had shaken his hand and smiled affably as if they were now friends.

Stonehands thought he heard footsteps nearby somewhere in the damp night. He concentrated, trying to locate the sound, but heard nothing. The fog-heavy air quelled sound. In this soup Charley could walk up on him before he'd hear anything. He'd heard of soldiers going crazy at a listening post but figured they just didn't have strong minds or had just had enough of combat. Maybe, like his buddy Howkert, they were merely looking to escape.

He missed Howkert, Howkert the reader who would quote Camus and Sartre, the hippie who'd been drafted, who'd come to 'Nam with a what-the-hell shrug and a medic's bag and more guts than sense. "Why not?" he'd said. "I hear the dope's good." He had a way of seeing things that made the lunacy of war seem absurdly logical—like the old wood carrier they'd stumbled upon on the way to Dak Chat, an old man who stepped on a toe-popper, a mine meant to shatter the foot and ankle. Howkert had treated the wound and called for a dust off. As they waited, he'd asked the interpreter to ask if the old man was authorized to sweep minefields, if he held a union card. The interpreter said he didn't understand. "That's the trouble with this country—no unions," Howkert had said.

Howkert hadn't deserted because he was a coward. One thing Stonehands and the others were certain of was that Howkert was brave. But he'd deserted. What would he have thought of the boy who'd lost both limbs on the left side—

both, so that no matter what aid he used to walk, he would always list to the right. How would Howkert see it?

A noise distracted Stonehands, indistinct, but sound nonetheless. He was sure, so certain he pressed the rifle butt into his shoulder and looked out over the barrel. Something was out there, an animal, a deer or wild pig. But the sound was gone, and eventually he lowered the M-16. This hadn't stopped being a forest just because of the war.

The fog was hypnotic. His eyelids drooped from staring into the dark. To keep alert, he tried to recall every movie he'd ever seen. That proved tiring. In the distance five-hundred-pounders fell to the west somewhere over Laos, Operation Arc Light. He counted explosions, seven in all, dropped from B-52s so high up their engines were silent.

"Think strong," Stonehands muttered as he cranked the field phone to make a commo check. The voice on the other end seemed uninterested. Anything out there? No, nothing, except fog and . . . noise. "Nothin'," Stonehands reported. That was the last human sound for another hour.

He remembered on the march to Hai Drong—the ARVN soldiers taking over the prisoner, slapping him and shouting. The VC, helpless to protect himself, had balled up on the road. His enemies had merely seen that as an excuse to use their feet. They kicked the side of his head as if practicing soccer, straight on or sideways with an instep or backward with a heel. His squad mates, ashamed that they'd handed over the prisoner, talked about shooting the ARVN soldiers and turning the prisoner loose, but that was crazy talk. Still, they were ashamed and angry. You could see it in their eyes. Perhaps that's why they'd taken to the boy so quickly—to make up for their shame.

But the boy had brought them only more shame.

Stonehands turned his attention to what he thought was movement in the fog, a swirling current. A wind. A sound. No, just imagination. Think strong. Stay awake. As a boy he'd memorized facts about presidents. His mother had bragged on him to her friends, called him into the kitchen to show the skeptics, especially Naomi Slaughter, the county Mrs. Know-Everybody's-Business. Learning facts was a trick, but they'd stayed with him. Now he drew them up—Andrew Jackson, birth date March 15, wife's name, wife's name?—Martha, no, Mary. Rachel—yes. He wasn't sure. Jackson followed by Van Buren. No one knows about him. Next was Polk. No, Tyler.

Again he heard something moving out there and had a passing desire to call out. He choked the rifle stock and listened but heard only his breathing and an annoying sound in his ears. At first he couldn't figure out where the sound came from, then realized it was in his head. It was an alarm.

As the animal circled, Stonehands, keeping his M-16 ready, wheeled in time with it. They moved cautiously, like strangers testing a dance step. It coughed—not a cough exactly but something low and guttural that seemed to vibrate out of its belly. Each of its circles became more attenuated. Though it was mostly shadow, Stonehands could identify its shoulders and its head with small half-moon ears.

He checked the safety, squeezed the rifle, thinking to use it—just shoot—but that presented a different set of problems. The enemy was somewhere, a regiment perhaps, hiding in shadows, or maybe they were ghosts. Maybe all of this is shadows or, as Howkert had said, shadows without essence. If so, what is the tiger? Doesn't matter. He'd see if a ghost bleeds.

Stonehands listened to its breathing, fast and heavy, double his, perhaps. He appealed to God that it didn't make sense, his dying this way, that he'd come to fight Charley, and if he was to die, Charley should do it. Strong mind, he thought, and over and over repeated in his mind the names—Tyler, Polk, Taylor; Tyler, Polk, Taylor—like a novena.

On tottering knees, he stood up to look around. He considered calling the command bunker. And say what? There's a tiger here. What could anyone do? They'd just think he was scared. Hell, he was.

IT SEEMED GONE—A HALLUCINATION, perhaps, as the boy might have been, and the prisoner and Howkert. What did Smitty say? Felt he wasn't alone. Alone gets to you. Causes delusions. A man could imagine anything, seeing what he'd seen in 'Nam. That boy might show up in the Smokies looking for a home, another shadow looking for its essence.

The animal materialized again, a vague shadow. Some initial fear gone, Stonehands waited, rifle at the ready. Twice it stepped out of and retreated back into the fog. The third time it appeared, Stonehands felt an odd sensation, a knowing of sorts. He knew for certain it was a she as she circled.

He recalled an encounter on a trail near his home when a similar sensation had guided him to a deer trapped between a tree and a boulder. He'd talked to the deer gently to slow its struggle until he could free it. It had stood, dazed, its bulblike eyes staring at Stonehands until he flapped his arms and sent it scurrying into the brush. But this was no whitetail deer, or even an ordinary tiger.

The beast stopped. Stonehands tried to swallow, but his mouth and throat had gone dry on him. She inched so close that the feel of her was on his flesh. His skin prickled as if she'd brushed him. Be quick, be strong. Taylor, Fillmore . . . Pierce. Her flicking tail grazed his cheek. It was like the touch of an icicle. In the next instant, before he could recover, she retreated into the fog.

He took a deep breath and blinked. He recalled the tale of the princess, the restless spirit of the tiger that must leave one behind to ensure a way into heaven. No legend. Just an animal, a big one. He wondered why he hadn't shot her and if she would return. He didn't have to speculate on that question long. All he had to do was look over his shoulder.

She faced him, opened her broad mouth and bared her teeth without uttering a sound. How she'd gotten behind him he had no idea, but she was there, and he could taste the animal smell, see the vapor of her breath swirl in the fog. He pointed the M-16 at the triangle-shaped nose, which was so close now he could see it move as she breathed. What amazed him most was her enormous head, like a moon with tufted ears. Time orbited around such a creature.

Neither he nor the animal moved. A thought occurred to him, something said about Armstrong and the moon, how a man could effortlessly break any earthly jumping record, but the results of a leap were unpredictable because he couldn't control his own body away from Earth's gravity. That was how Stonehands felt. He couldn't miss, but he couldn't pull the trigger either.

Then, as if unburdening herself of a great heaviness, she dropped to the ground no more than a foot from the foxhole, yawned once and stared away from him into the fog. Her breathing was slower now, and from inside her rose a deep rumbling purr that prickled the hair on his arms.

He forgot everything but her. There was no sense of the world, no sense of the past or the future. Just his breathing and her deep rumbling. Occasionally she'd flick her tail. She was so near he could reach out and stroke her. How would she react?

She lay calmly beside him. Relaxed now, he recited presidents' names all the way up to Grant, and explained how Mark Twain had found Grant living in poverty. He described the boy with no left arm and half a leg, the VC they'd captured, and told her how Howkert had gone over the wall to be with a boom-

boom girl in Quang Ngai, a girl he'd planned on running away with—though there was no place to run when you were a six-foot-two-inch American, a deserter.

Sometime later she rose into a crouch, her powerful legs locked, ready. He held the rifle but had no intention of shooting. Her body twitched. She flicked her tail once again and an instant later bolted into the fog.

What would he tell his squad? Who would believe it?

A roar broke the stillness. Then a man dashed by, chattering like a lunatic in Vietnamese, followed quickly by another. A third North Vietnamese tripped on the parapet and toppled into the foxhole, his AK-47 striking the side of Stonehands's helmet. Stonehands gripped the soldier by his neck, said he was sorry, then with a powerful twist of the hands, snapped the cervical cord. He heard more soldiers emerge from the fog and laid the dead soldier aside to ring up base camp.

He whispered into the mouthpiece, "Jus' put ever'thing right on top'a me."

He cloaked his shoulders with the dead man and sank down into the pit. He heard the distinct pop, a mortar round leaving the tube. A moment later the ground became a flash pot; the sound traveled through his bones; he felt a stabbing pain in his right eardrum. He clasped the dead man, closed his eyes, and prayed.

IT WAS STILL DARK, but not pitch-black as before. The air smelled of nitrate. The ground remained immersed in fog, and smoke hung just above the fog, trapped by the dense net of limbs and leaves. He'd lost sense of time and fact. The barrage could have been ten minutes or two hours. He couldn't say. He listened for evidence that the enemy was gone or still there—something, a sound, but there was nothing.

He slowly rose up. The dead man on his shoulders was a painful weight, but one he was grateful for. As he readied to toss the body off his back, he felt it lift away. He hoped for a bullet to the head, a quick death, but when he opened his eyes and peered out, he caught a fleeting glimpse of the tigress dragging the dead man into the fogbank.

The phone line was severed, so he waited until dawn to crawl out of the foxhole. When at last sunlight infiltrated the forest, he saw through the fog men lying in grotesque poses. Thin vapors of smoke curled out of the ground like spun silk. Flies appeared to do their mischief. At the edge of the trees the tigress sat staring at him, her expression bland. She lay down, rolled to her side and began licking her paws. He thought of the legends mentioned in the tent and grasped at last what Howkert knew the night he'd gone over the wire, what it was like to be summoned.

Stonehands walked, paying no mind to the bodies he sidestepped or the ground rent by craters or the blood that trickled from his ear. These obstacles, inconsequential parts of an aberrant world, matters of limited possibility, were measurements of a past he saw evaporating with the fog. At the perimeter, he shouted the password several times, gave his name, said he was coming in and told them not to shoot. The platoon swarmed about him, patted his back and asked what had happened. Drammel told him his ear was bleeding, said it without stammering.

The lieutenant pushed his way to the front. "How many?" he asked.

"Sir?" Stonehands looked uncomprehendingly at him, shook his head and grabbed Donatello by the arm.

"Easy, pal," Donatello said. "We thought you'd bought it—*chet roi.*"

"Where's the cub?" Stonehands asked.

"Hey, Bro . . ."

He lifted Donatello off his feet and stared into his eyes. Donatello pointed to a nearby bunker.

Stonehands swooped the cub up and walked toward the woods, his long strides devouring earth. The lieutenant ordered him to stop, but Stonehands paid no attention, and when Halverson caught up and told him to go back, Stonehands merely shook his head. Donatello hurried behind, telling him to put the cat down, that it wasn't his. Stonehands fired a single glance that sent Donatello reeling backward. No one made any further attempt to stop him. At the wire he threw his rifle aside and a few steps farther disappeared into a fogbank at the edge of the forest.

AT THE INQUIRY DONATELLO CLAIMED Stonehands had returned a week later and caught him by surprise in the latrine, just appeared out of nowhere with the cub in his arms.

"What did he want?"

"To have me tell his mother he wouldn't be coming home."

"That's all?"

"That's all, sir."

"Anything else you'd like to add, soldier?"

"No, sir." Donatello looked at his squad mates. He swallowed. "Yes, sir. His eye was on the woods. He kept watching like someone who might miss a bus, worried like. Something kept moving back and forth in the shadows. I can't be sure, but I think it was a tiger."

"But you aren't sure?"

"No, sir."

The board—a colonel, a major and two captains—looked at one another. Saying soldiers love to make up stories, the colonel dismissed the inquiry. Officially Stonehands went mad in the A Shau Valley, was missing in action and likely dead. That's what Donatello later told Stonehands's mother.

BRIEF FACTS: *In the thick forests of Southeast Asia, the black and gold striping of the Bengal tiger serves to make the great cat virtually invisible to the human eye. Occasionally a hunter stalking one ends up being the prey. Several official reports from Vietnam spoke of encounters with tigers, especially among grunts who humped the mountainous rain forests. A marine was once dragged from his foxhole near the* DMZ *in 1966 but fought the animal off with a K-bar knife. In 1969 army* PFC *Michael Mize was dragged away by a Bengal while standing watch at a listening post west of Pleiku. His remains—a skeleton, some shredded flesh, and his dog tags, upon which dangled a tiger's claw—were found the next day. Walter "Stonehands" Harvey is one of 1,568 missing in action still unaccounted for. A neutral investigator sent to account for* MIAs *heard rumors of a giant running in the forests with a tigress. Laotians had seen them playing in the streams, splashing one another like children at play. They couldn't say if the man was black or not. He was a giant. Wasn't that enough?*

RICHARD WILEY
(1944–)

Washington State native Richard Wiley has spent a good deal of his adult life living abroad—in Korea, Japan, Nigeria, Kenya, and other countries. Not surprisingly, his fiction is anchored in the larger world. His first novel, *Soldiers in Hiding,* was such a refreshing departure from the prevailing tastes in contemporary fiction that the PEN/Faulkner committee said, "Easily the most original piece of American fiction to appear in years," when *Soldiers in Hiding* received the award in 1987. The sadly misguided allegiance of the two central characters, Jimmy Yamamoto and Teddy Maki, both U.S.-born Japanese Americans who were playing music in Japan when World War II broke out, left me feeling stripped and alone—a reader without a country. In some elemental way, the novel harks back to remind us that we are flesh first, and must abide by the choices we make. His later novels continue to explore the themes of Americans abroad, and the long novel he recently completed, *Commodore Perry's Minstrel Show,* gathers these threads together to reflect an even greater cultural imagination. After working in Nairobi, Wiley moved to Las Vegas in 1989, where he now teaches at the University of Nevada.

Ahmed's Revenge. New York: Random House, 1998.
Indigo. New York: Dutton, 1992; reprint, New York: Plume Contemporary Fiction, 1993.
Festival for Three Thousand Maidens. New York: Dutton, 1991; reprint, New York: Plume Contemporary Fiction, 1993.
Fools' Gold. New York: Alfred A. Knopf, 1988.
Soldiers in Hiding. Boston: Atlantic Monthly Press, 1986.

Soldiers in Hiding

(EXCERPT)

MAJOR NAKAMURA MADE ME HIS AIDE. News of our encounter with the guerrillas reached the Manila headquarters, and soon we received instructions to desist, to worry about the open areas of the cities and towns where we were stationed, to let the guerrillas stay in the woods, to give them that terrain as their own. We waited a week for Ike or any of the others to return and then we were ordered to move, transferred southwest to the province of Bataan. There were prisoners there and we were being called to guard them. The guards they had, it seemed, were in need of some time to themselves, a bit of open warfare for their psychological well-being.

Jimmy grew more silent in the days after Ike's death. Now that I was aide to Nakamura we rarely saw each other, and by the time we got to Bataan I was too busy to worry about what he thought of my miraculous return. If he knew I'd run, I wasn't ashamed. If he was beginning to feel we should shoot like all the other Japanese, that was his problem. While working for the major I was ensured of staying away from the front, and because I had survived such a brutal battle, I had all his confidence. I carried my clipboard, the same one Ike had used, and I walked about the camp doing my duties. Jimmy spent his free time with his face pressed against the wire, staring in at the poor prisoners of war.

Most of the prisoners at Bataan were American, and because of my duties as aide I often came in contact with them. The conditions under which the prisoners lived were bad. Many people in America are still convinced of the brutality of the Japanese, but part of it was that we simply didn't know how many prisoners there would be, we didn't have the tools to handle them, not enough food, not enough housing. And running a camp was hard work. It was easy to get angry.

When I came into contact with the prisoners, I kept my knowledge of English to myself. I was responsible for supplies and security. When I walked among them my heart went out, but what was I to do? If I told them I was one of them they would despise me, and there was no way they could help me get back home. If I told them merely that I spoke English they would want to talk to me and the quaver in my voice might give me away, letting them know the feelings of sympathy I had for them and weakening my position with the major.

One day when I got to Major Nakamura's office there was a man from Los Angeles standing at tired attention in front of him. The man was the commander of a new group of prisoners, and had presented the major with a list of demands for better treatment, with requests for a change of diet, for better toilet facilities, for a place that the men could use for physical exercise. The American did not know it, but Major Nakamura was embarrassed. He'd been an elementary school principal before the war and had recently wondered aloud whether he'd ever be back in the school again. The man spoke to the major through an interpreter, a Filipino whose face did not change no matter what was said.

"He's a prisoner. Tell him not to forget his position," Nakamura told the man to tell the American. "These Americans . . . If we Japanese were being held captive we'd know how to act."

"War has rules," the man told the American. "Obey them."

Major Nakamura had gained a wide and unreasonable reputation as a disciplinarian, but in truth he was a meek man whose mind was set on surviving the war as much as mine was. He wanted to get home to his wife and family once again, to busy himself with the dainty discipline of the elementary school. Still, he knew belligerence when he heard it, even if the language used was English, and as the man from Los Angeles talked on, the major got madder.

"Watch out," he said. "I have my orders. I will not have rowdiness." But when the man heard the translation all he did was laugh. He had not been a prisoner long. He still had a modicum of meat on his bones.

"What?" said Major Nakamura.

The interpreter looked from one man to the other, but neither spoke. "He didn't say anything," the interpreter told the major.

"He laughed. Doesn't he know that his life is in my hands? Tell him not to laugh. Tell him if he laughs again I'll kill him. See how he likes that."

When the interpreter repeated what the major had told him, the man from Los Angeles kept quiet, but in a moment he said, "Obey the international rules for keeping prisoners," and he turned to try to leave before the major had said he could go.

"No!" shouted Nakamura. "You can't go until I give the order! Have you no sense of the way things are, of the relationship between conqueror and defeated during war? Don't you know how you are supposed to act?"

The major shouted and the guards at the door pushed the man back into the room. He sighed and said nothing after that, but he stood with his hands on his hips.

"Arms akimbo!" the major shouted, suddenly looking at me. "Japanese people hate arms akimbo! He knows that too, doesn't he?"

The Filipino interpreter had lost the line that the major was taking, and when the major ordered the man to put down his arms the interpreter told him to surrender his weapons.

"We don't have any weapons," the man said. "We just want fair treatment. Tell him we just want fair treatment."

The interpreter told the major what the man had said, but by this time things were completely confused. Only I knew what was really going on, but I didn't want to talk, didn't want to tell this man that not only was I a fellow citizen of his, but I was from the same town, perhaps the same stretch of city.

"I will not tolerate arms akimbo," Major Nakamura told the man very slowly. "It is something I will not have." He was leaning over his desk and speaking directly to the man now, the interpreter pushed aside. Out in front of the room where we were talking, the American soldiers of the man's company were waiting in the dust. The sun beat down on them, but the guards would not let them come into the shade. Everyone could hear the major yelling. When I looked through the window I could see Jimmy standing near the tired, defeated Americans. He had a rifle slung over his shoulder and was staring at the group and at the window where I watched him.

"Maki," the major shouted. "Come here. Maybe you can make this man understand."

"I'd prefer not to speak to him in English," I said. "It will undermine my effectiveness later."

"He's standing arms akimbo, look at him. Tell him to stop. That is what I can't stand about Americans. They are defeated, but they act as if somehow they are better than we are. It's too much."

"The major wants you to put your arms at your sides," I said quietly, looking at the American directly for the first time. "He feels that your posture is defiant and would prefer that you act the part of the conquered soldier rather than that of his equal."

The man from Los Angeles was startled at what I'd said, but without comment he dropped his hands to his sides and then looked back at Nakamura.

"That's good," Nakamura said, talking to me. "Now I want you to put this man and his men in separate housing. We might make an example of this man. It seems every time I look through the fence I see someone standing arms akimbo. I want this guy in the center of the yard for a while. The heat will make him lower his gaze when he speaks to a Japanese officer."

Without looking at the man from Los Angeles again I went outside and told the guards what they should do. The American soldiers were all about my age. They'd been prisoners for a long time, but had been transferred in from somewhere else. When Jimmy heard that the group's leader would be kept in the center of the yard he looked at me, but when the time came he lowered his rifle and marched them away. The whole thing was disgusting. Major Nakamura had been milder in the jungle region than he was here, and I had some trouble now, picturing him as an elementary school principal. Jimmy and I had been with him for the entire time we'd been in the Philippines, and until this day he had not raised his voice, either at a prisoner or at a soldier of his own.

A day passed and the major still made the man from Los Angeles stand in the center of the courtyard. At times it seemed that he wasted more energy than the man did, constantly getting up and walking to the window to see if his prisoner had moved. Jimmy and five others were made to guard the man in rotation, night and day, and though the man was sometimes allowed to sit down, the major had gone out and drawn a circle around him saying that he'd be killed if he stepped or fell across the line.

A few days passed and the man from Los Angeles seemed to grow more defiant. His men could see him when they walked about their barracks, and he seemed to take strength from the shouts that they gave him, from the sentimental, football-field mentality that they had. The major had cut the man's rations to a minimum, so it was surprising how long he lasted. After the first few days I could tell that the major wanted the affair ended, for he had seen in the American a willingness to see it through. He sat at his desk, sitting tall so that he could see the thin shape of the man's head, the way it waggled occasionally all loose on his still shoulders. Unable to sleep, Nakamura would rise from his mattress and stand at his window in the humid darkness just to see the slumped shoulders of the man in the moonlight. I knew, on about the fifth day, that if the man did step across Nakamura's line, the major was ready to kill him. The body of the sari-sari store woman had made the major retch, yet now he was willing to murder this man over a test of his will.

Late one night when the major was at his customary position, a worried look upon his face, nose pressed against the dirty glass of his office window, he saw something that broke the stalemate of the situation. Jimmy was on duty, standing facing the tall American, his rifle loosely held in his hands. Nakamura's eyes were rimmed red, I am sure, yet they were keen, and what they saw was Jimmy's hand coming up and something passing between it and the American officer's mouth. The major got out his field glasses and watched for the movement again and saw the brown band of a Japanese candy bar folded and tucked back into Jimmy's pocket. He was beside himself. He paced his room furiously for a few moments, then sneaked out his side window and came around to the general barracks where I and the others were sleeping.

"Psst," he said. "Everybody up. Keep quiet, don't turn on the lights." He sneaked around from mat to mat shaking our shoulders and whispering in our ears. "What we have here is mutiny," he told me after I was finally on my feet and awake. "Your friend has been feeding the prisoner. He has been supplementing his strength with Japanese candy!"

When we heard what the major was saying we looked at one another. "Get your guns and let's go," the major whispered, so we stepped behind him, silent as snakes, and wound around the side of the barracks until we were gathered in the gray courtyard a few meters away from them. I could hear English spoken softly, just a word or two, before the major stepped forward and shouted, before a switch was thrown that flooded the entire area with light.

The major marched forward and slapped Jimmy as hard as he could across the face. "Scoundrel!" he shouted. "Traitor!"

Jimmy fell down, but got up immediately, blood coming a little from his lower lip. Everyone's eyes were still trying to adjust to the light.

"Empty your pockets!" the major ordered, but Jimmy stood swaying a moment, so the major hit him again. The American officer looked on. His face had changed in the five days since I'd seen him closely.

"You," shouted the major, "will be shot! And you," he said, turning to Jimmy, "will do the shooting!"

The major pushed his own hand into Jimmy's pocket and then carefully smoothed out the creases in the crumpled candy wrapper.

"Where were you born?" the major screamed, looking straight at Jimmy.

Jimmy paused, then said, "Los Angeles." He spoke in English and silenced the already dead-quiet crowd.

The major looked from one to the other of them. The American inside the circle was skinnier than he had been in the office the week before. If Jimmy'd given him candy he couldn't have given him much.

The major turned to all of us, the candy wrapper held up

above his head. "We have a traitor in our midst," he said. "Yamamoto even speaks English when he is asked a question in Japanese." He stood a moment until his hands began to shake. His fury had forced his thoughts from him, but finally he shook his head and said, "In all my years as a school principal I never ran up against anything as awful as this."

The major was in charge but was out of control. The American officer had been crouching when we'd approached him but was able to stand, his long legs bringing him high above the rest of us. Jimmy still held his rifle on the man, trying to act the part of the proper guard. When the major regained himself he looked a long moment at Jimmy. He raised a short finger and pointed at the prisoner.

"Shoot this man, Yamamoto," he said. "Shoot him now."

The American seemed to know what was happening for all of a sudden he backed out of the major's circle and took a step or two to his right.

"Wait," he said.

The major's finger followed the man a moment, then he lowered it and called my name. I had been standing in the very back of the group of newly awakened soldiers. When he called me I felt a chill, though I was sweating and though the night was hot.

"Yes, sir," I said, softly beside him.

"Go to the barracks and bring a blindfold. Bring something with which to pin it behind this man's head."

"Wouldn't it be better to wait, Major?" I asked. "In the morning perhaps all this will seem less serious."

"We will resolve it now," the major said. "You Americans really stick together, don't you?"

"Yamamoto merely felt sorry for the man, I'm sure. Really, he's as Japanese as . . ."

"Go!" the major said, swinging around, red-eyed again. "Or maybe, Maki, I'll find myself another aide as well."

I jumped a little when he shouted at me, but stepped away quickly while he turned his attention back to the two Americans. In his office it was easy to find the blindfolds, but I held back a little, hoping that time would cool the major off and maybe save the life of the man from Los Angeles. I could see them standing, waiting for me, through the window. Jimmy had been so stupid. In another day the major might have let the man slink back with the others, and that would have been the end of it. Now he was decisive, had locked us all on his course. As the men were waking up, they began to chatter and he didn't stop them. The American in the center of the circle was gauging his chances as slim, I was sure. Even from the window I could see him bobbing about, his feet nervously scraping back and forth across Nakamura's old line.

"Maki!" the major shouted, so I went back fast, the whole box of blindfolds in my hands.

"Surely, sir . . ."

"Tie the blindfold quickly."

I walked up to the shaking soldier and held a blindfold up to his eyes.

"Wait," he said. "I'll be good."

He tried to turn his head away from me, so the major had a couple of the others hold him until I could secure the thing tightly behind his neck. "Try not to worry," I whispered.

Before the major turned to poor Jimmy again, he had another idea. He called to the guards who walked the ground around the American barracks and told them to bring all the prisoners out.

"We'll let them watch," he said. "One lesson and we won't have a bit of trouble for weeks."

The guards were afraid to go inside the building where all the Americans were sleeping, so they shouted first, ordering those on the inside to turn on the lights. It took nearly ten minutes for the prisoners to be brought, single file, out into the courtyard, but when they were lined across from us the major seemed satisfied and drew another circle around the poor man, using the tip of his boot. All the Americans watched in sullen silence.

"Yamamoto," said the major.

Poor Jimmy had been standing there all this time, weakly holding his rifle. He was such a silent man, such a private one, that even during this moment, even when the essence of confrontation was upon him, he remained within himself. He had his rifle and it struck me that he might murder the major instead. He might turn the thing on us all.

"Yamamoto," the major said once more.

Jimmy walked a ways toward the major, then back near where I was standing with the wilting prisoner.

"It was only a candy bar," he said. "An extra one. Nobody wanted it."

The major walked to the prisoner and turned him around so that he was facing the others of his kind, all of them standing there in their drab Japanese issue, their poor pants all high water, the sleeves of their shirts too short.

When the major touched him the American said, "Ahh." Then with all the timbre gone out of his voice, all of its character missing, he said, "Please . . ."

There was no noise now, no talking. All eyes, those of the Japanese soldiers and of the American prisoners, were on Jimmy. The major made all of us stand at attention, then he backed away from the prisoner and waited.

Jimmy walked up to the man and said, "I'm going to have to shoot you now." He held his rifle to the man's head, its barrel just touching his clumsily cropped hair. Time passed. The American shook. I, in my position at the edge of the platoon, was holding my breath. The major did not move. Only Jimmy, absurdly, seemed calm. When he put the rifle down he turned back toward us and unbuttoned the top button of his shirt at the same instant.

"No," he said, very calmly and in English.

When the prisoner heard him he jumped a little and all of the other Americans began to talk. I remember Jimmy had a slight smile on his face. When he spoke he broke the tension so completely for the Americans that their words came out harshly at us, like taunts. Major Nakamura stood still as the noise slapped against his ears. His face was red again, but this time he was not locked in indecision. He pulled his side arm from its holster and, walking over to where Jimmy was, put the barrel of it to Jimmy's temple and fired. Jimmy's smile did not leave his face as the small-caliber bullet passed through his brain. He seemed to stand an instant longer than he should have, then he fell at the feet of the blindfolded soldier, who, when he'd heard the shot, had nearly fallen himself. No one moved. I remember thinking at the precise moment of Jimmy's death how hot it was and how odd the events had been that led him to the end of his life, here in the Philippines, far from the streets of Los Angeles, far from increasingly evil Japan. We were all frozen into the postures that the sound of the shot had put us in. The major held his handgun in the air where Jimmy's head had been. The voices of the Americans sank into the walls of the jungle and the prisoner stood, knees locked, in the center of that awful circle. Perhaps Nakamura was mad then, for he moved before any of the others did. He picked up the rifle that Jimmy had let tumble when he died and held it up to the stone-still troops. His handgun still hung from his limp other wrist and he waited, looking right at me.

"Maki," he said, finally. The awful rifle blurred to my vision but nevertheless danced before me, like a cobra. I didn't move, so he walked over to where I stood and placed the rifle gently in my hands. "Your turn," he said. "Save yourself. Shoot him."

He was coaxing in the way he spoke to me and I could detect no anger in his voice. Jimmy's body lay before the American he was to have shot. His mouth was pursed as it was when he played his trumpet. I was walking, before I realized it, up to where the soldier stood, his back to me. The rifle's chamber was full, but there had not been time for the tension of an execution to build once more. I raised the gun when the major took a step backward, away from me. It had a hair trigger, not connected to the weight of the moment. The man seemed relaxed before me, and the Americans on the far side did not seem hostile to my action. There was a languid sense of levitation in me and I closed my eyes. I seemed to float. And I did not come back down to earth immediately. Not even with the sound of the report.

DONALD BERINATI
(1946–)

Eastern Sierra carpenter and outdoor enthusiast Donald Berinati has been writing short fiction for many years. His stories have the rugged themes of man-in-the-world, but with a core of tenderness. At his best they ring true to a greater theme of man-in-the-West as caretaker, not the empty colonial exploration of so many before him. Living as he does in the rough-and-tumble world of construction, he is fully aware of the irony of being a writer: there are so many calloused hands from which to choose. When he's not building a house, he spends his evenings in Reno, at a poetry reading or in a bookstore, hoping to find one more taste of good writing before he returns to his mountain home.

FOR BOB STEPHAN

The Excellent House

BOB WORKS IN MUD. He covers cracks and joints in drywall. He's done mud for more than fifteen years and doesn't like to think about it. Bob has just buried his dog down by the shallow alkaline lake that, like his youth, is disappearing.

He pulls up to a large house in his small truck. The house is new, an old friend's, and Bob has not done any of the work here. All the interior walls are stucco, and Bob Sculley is a man who knows his limits, has stayed away, until now, when there are problems and he has been called.

It is an October day in the eastern Sierra, and he is happy to make the drive south from the small town where he lives to the larger one where he works. The mountains sit in a bright rest period, a notch of quiet like the one they get in the spring. Skiing has not yet arrived and the summer people are gone, back to school and to jobs in places Bob has been to, even lived.

BOB OPENS THE SWING DOORS on the back of the camper shell, the glass lights in them smeared with noseprints, leans with one hand on each door, and takes a breath. He was about to help Franklin out, as he had to for the last years of his beagle's life.

Big Ed comes up behind him, in a hurry as he's always been, as most contractors are, now to have Bob fix the curved wall that isn't curved quite right. Bob steps back and latches the doors.

"Sorry about Franklin, Bob. Just heard yesterday."

Bob nods and walks with Ed, looks at his watch as he crosses the threshold and says he would have been eighteen next month. The entry to Big Ed's house gives him instant pause—inside the front door, he faces a wall. Bob realizes it is a hallway that goes left and right, and frowns.

"Over here," Ed says. He leads Bob down the short hall to the left and points toward the outside corner of the wall. The radius of the corner looks fine to Bob, good enough for Ed's house, he thinks. He steals looks. It is a tall, wood-ceilinged place, twelve feet or so where he stands, and he knows it would be hard to hold a good line for that length.

Big Ed has just married an interior designer, and she, fifteen years his junior, is different. The first and last time Bob met her was skiing, before she and Ed had met, and she was electrifying—that is, her colors were. Lime, orange, yellow—even the black seemed to jump. The rest of her was unremarkable but for her eyes, a champagne color, just like his own daughter's. But she is not Maggie; she is pretty, correct, as many are these days, and rich, and dumb as a rock. She is also alive.

"What time was that?" Bob asks.

"Three thirty-seven yesterday. It moves a minute or so a day."

Ed nods and they both watch the sunlight on the walls. Bob washes them with a quick eye that spots depressions and bumps, disturbances of line. He nods and speaks quietly, feels the hush that large spaces, like churches and libraries, bring. "Looks like they did a nice job." The two-story room beyond, which he guesses is the living room, is big, thirty by forty or so, and is dressed in electric colors, vertical and horizontal stripes that are the rage. He is afraid to go into the bathroom.

This is what has happened to this town, exactly what has happened. The people are now from the south and do not see mountains the way he has. To Bob, they appear to see only themselves in their houses, as if they were mirrors, and the days of rusticity, of that'll-be-fine woodwork, are gone. He catches himself shaking his head.

"Bobby, look. Look, here we go."

The sunlight turns through the entry and cuts up along the corner. They stand in bright silence, Bob with a thick-leaded pencil in his right hand. He sees one dimple and starts to mark it, watches it compound into another one, then another, as the sun shows every imperfection. The light is hypnotic and warm, and he catches himself watching it instead of the wall. He has seen it for decades, illuminating the spread of country he and his family have lived in.

BOB HAS MARKED ALL OF THE PLACES carefully, shading with the side of the lead. When the sun settles behind the peaks, he steps off the ladder and is left with Coke bottle–shaped drawings, waves made visible. Some look like topographic lines, concentric rings that show peaks and valleys, others abstract expressionism. He thinks of asking Ed for a beer.

"That's it?" he says, and turns to Ed, who has his hands stuffed down into his oversized shorts. Big Ed used to be a bum, ski type, and he and Bob pounded the slopes pretty hard years back. But Ed has found first money and then love, and lately seems to have confused the two, has become something of a clotheshorse and cash-monger. Bob would not be caught dead with him, and knows that it is mutual.

BOB'S TRUCK HITS A POTHOLE on the way home and the ashtray spills onto the floor. Later, he kneels in the driveway and gathers the contents. He finds keys to houses he is working on or has worked on and forgotten to return, a few coins, some stamps, several screw gun bits, some of which are broken. He flings those into the frost-stunted lilacs that border the drive. The ashtray is like an extra pocket, and Bob thinks, as he refills it and slips it back into the dash, that it might just be easier to smoke. An object on the floor catches his eye: a ring, small and silver, with a tiny clear stone, perhaps a sliver of a diamond. It holds him, and then things come with a rush—phone call, hospital, a small manila envelope of things that were Maggie's, her ring that he must have slipped into his pocket. That part is mostly a fog, a thing that happened in the deep heart of a perfect summer night.

Maggie. They had fought more than ever the year before her death. About clothes—lack of and type—money, about a high school and a car that were both too small and too slow, trips with and without chaperones to Disneyland and Santa Cruz, the car, about the fact that there was nothing to do in town, the shortage of video stores, the car again, the biker with the chains who lived in a tepee on the edge of town that summer, the tabs of acid Bob had found in her dresser, the fact that he was going through her dresser. The car again.

"SO YOU WANT A PITCH-AND-PUTT out at the trailer park?" He recalled asking her that on that last day of her life, just over a year ago. He had been cleaning his tools in a large bucket behind the house, near a ditch that held quiet irrigation water and middle-sized trout that all pointed one way. That day also held the longest light of the year, and he and Maggie were using the last of it to do what they did best. "Or maybe a water slide." She stood nearby, in stonewashed jeans and puffy, green L.A. Gears, her fists drawn at her sides, knuckle-white, and the little ring on her index finger. It was all he could see of her when he looked up from the bucket.

"I want to live in a place where something's happening, is that too much? You'd think I was asking for the stars." Her hands opened and closed in little bursts, feet loosened the dirt where she stood and left small circles. "Dad, not everyone wants to stare into space like you do, hike everywhere and ski all the time. Work like a dog for nothing." Bob looked over at Franklin. The beagle sat in his slumped way on the back step, as if he'd been poured there. He watched Maggie through watery clouds of eyes; he had done that since the day she had been born. "I don't see why I can't go live with Mom. Davis's got a great school, you said so yourself, there's plenty to do there and lots of kids. . . ."

"Lots of malls, you mean. Lots of traffic and crime, noise and bad manners." He rinsed his drywall knives with the hose water and set them into an empty five-gallon bucket. "Certainly an improvement over here."

She had tossed out her hand, pointed across the street and down the escarpment, to the bit of meadow a developer desperately wanted to call Mountain Echoes. It had become the center of local attention. "And that's why you're against that place?"

Bob had stood and turned the water off and she had followed him inside. He grabbed his beer and the fistful of crackers he had left on the kitchen counter, parked himself in a corner beside the refrigerator. He liked fighting from there. "It'll be no good, Mags. It'll change the way we live here, all we'll ever care about is having . . . no, spending, money. Yes, it'll have an equestrian center, a golf course, and a little mall, but it'll start turning this town into a place I don't want to live. Or you, if you really think about it." He waved the bottle and the crackers at her. "It's not why I came here. Besides, you've only got another year and then you're off to college. Free to go, off to paradise . . . the big city lights."

She had stood at the sink, looking out and away from him, and seemed more distant than the simple length of his arm. She built him a look, the over-the-shoulder one she had gotten from her mother, complete with dimpled scowl, folded arms, and slow words. "You're nuts, Dad. You just don't get it, do you? And I'm sick of you calling me Mags—I told you to quit it." There was a thick silence, the kitchen wall clock made its rounds. "I'm out of here."

"Just make sure you're back by twelve," he had said. Maggie stared at the sink, started to speak but pulled it back, pivoted on her heel and headed straight for the door. Franklin dodged its swing but almost tilted off the porch. The springs of Maggie's brown hair bounced with the two steps, snapped around her head as she spun and disappeared from his sight.

"Midnight," he yelled.

Bob is going through a new house that a friend is building, measuring it for drywall. It is small, a cabin-style house, with wainscoting and trim invented on the spot, and glass that gathers the sun.

"These lids get wood paneling, right?" Bob says, aiming his eyebrow and pencil at the ceiling. His friend nods, Bob hums and makes a note in a black plastic notebook.

"Except for the closets," Teddy says.

Bob flips the notebook under his armpit. "Okay, I'll call you tonight with the price."

"Why didn't you vote?"

"Vote?"

"Mountain Echoes. You didn't vote. You just sat there. Abstained. You were the swing vote. If a person were generous, they'd say you were asleep."

Bob looks down at the boot-worn plywood. He had hoped

Teddy would not be there at the planning commission meeting, had hoped few would be. But the room had been full and there had been heated, often circular arguments coming through the microphone from both sides of the floor. It had gone on for almost four hours before the vote, and no one had slept as they had at some meetings. No one had even yawned. Everyone was waiting for him, for the commissioners, to vote.

Teddy leans back against a doorjamb and crosses his arms, the hammer handle hanging from his belt tapping the wall. "This is the first large project around your town—it's a foot in the door." There is a hitch of silence that Bob is afraid to touch. "I've got to be honest, Bob, we go back some, and I . . . you were never like that. Why? I mean . . . you really believe all that, about how it'll bring needed jobs in, increase the tax revenues? You've been around long enough to know that's a lie. The shit never pays for itself."

Bob looks up at Teddy, whose eyes have flicked to quiet points. He knows they will not change back. Outside, the wind comes straight across the lake, leans against the house, and Bob spreads his legs to steady himself.

Bob sits on the top step of his front porch overlooking the disappearing lake. It is evening, and a quiet light mirrors the water, brightens its beach of white alkali and the sandy peaks to his distant right. Things stand clear. He thinks of the days he and Teddy and Big Ed lived together in the town where Ed now lives. They were unencumbered then, three men in their twenties, working for wages they would not even consider today. Back then, the other two drove county snowplows in the winter and Bob was a mechanic at the yard and they all worked construction in the summers. Three of them, and one young pup.

Of all the thoughts that tumble by, the one that stands out is the St. Valentine's Day Massacre, a February storm of proportion that dropped eight feet of snow in one night, one of several that just ran together.

He had gone home late one night from the yard, when Ed had called in from the road to tell him that Franklin had been gone when he had stopped by earlier. Ed's voice was broken with static and Bob could hear his plow running behind him, and beyond that, the roar of the wind.

Bob had closed his eyes and asked Ed to keep an eye out. He hung up and fell into the old black Naugahyde recliner they'd brought from the dump. Someone would be calling from the yard soon, someone calling him back to work. He closed his eyes and pressed his fingers into them and the burning eased. He didn't care that his Sorels were dripping on the carpet or that grease from his overalls would get on the furniture. All he wanted was to sit, to see no wrenches, no spun bearings, no shear pins, to hear no static, no wind, no air brakes. He thought about going out after Franklin, knew it would be a waste of time. All he could hear was the drip of the kitchen faucet and there was the smell of wood smoke—there'd been a house fire once and the Swiss owner was so cheap he'd never done anything about it. But it was warm and quiet at that moment and that counted for just about everything.

It had gone on for five days like that. When it was done, there was twenty-one feet of new snow, drifts three times that, and only one narrow lane out of town, closed but for emergencies. The old-timers threw I-told-you-so smiles at everyone, and snow shovels, any kind of shovel, were suddenly worth ten times what they had been a month before. Bob worked double shifts, sometimes around the clock, they all did, and he thought of Franklin in the slivers of quiet away from the shop. He saw the bowl in the corner of the kitchen, heard the silence instead of clicking toenails on the grass-green vinyl, and every time he went by the bathroom, thought of the slurp Franklin made when he drank from the toilet. Bob realized that what he had on his hands was a wanderer, more interested in going through trash cans, running deer, and looking for a new route to India than anything else.

Near the end of the heavy weather, before the last pulse had come pouring in from the Gulf of Alaska, he and Teddy had gone out looking in the big Kenworth that had a curved blade six feet high and threw snow six ways when the hydraulics were working.

The night was mostly clear, though they could feel the moisture in the air from the new front and see against the crystal point stars the leading edge of the clouds that would bring more of what they already had too much of. Teddy drove down toward the main highway where they had found Franklin a couple of months ago, cleaning up the reef along the highway as they went. The high cab lights were like flamethrowers against the whiteness, and the small clouds of powder that came up over the blade made Bob squint. Teddy chuckled, said it was as far as he'd been able to see in a week. Bob was amazed that he could drive the monster in good weather without hitting something, let alone the near whiteouts when they stumbled from snow pole to snow pole and often did so much guessing. If the county had ever done a thing right, he thought, it was in hiring locals who'd been here for some time, who knew the roads and curves and chain-up areas, places where tourists would most likely get stuck, who knew the road like Braille.

The blade growled to a stop on the white pavement, and Teddy shut down the diesel. They climbed down and walked along the plowed, blown snow corridor of the closed highway, listening and calling for Franklin but looking out over the pillow-soft basin. The sky to their left was already the lesser black of dawn and to their right, the dark range of peaks that they had skied and climbed stepped off into the distance like a chain of memory. The peaks seemed to stare back, like women, with looks that looped their hearts.

They had stood for a while, then turned with a dullness in their step, stole backward looks as they shuffled through the few inches of fresh powder. Ahead and sitting on the road under the right side door was a black dot in the growing light. He would be starving and thirsty, and more than a little chilled, but a survivor and a coming legend. Bob pushed him inside his jacket; the squirming paws tickled, the tongue was warm on the bristle of his neck, his nose a cube of ice.

"Careful, Scull," Teddy said as he climbed in, "he probably shit right there." They had laughed and hooted as the diesel roared under the fresh light of day.

"How's it going?" Ed says. Bob has his eyes on the wall, feels Big Ed's on his back. His knife scrapes on the stucco, feathering in the last patch.

"Good. This'll probably do it."

"Looks great."

"Your lady happy with the house?" There is a hanging moment and Bob wishes for the question back.

"Yeah, yeah. But you know women, never for long." Bob lets it go, cleans the tip of the blade on the mudpan in his left hand and wets it in the bucket at his feet. His hands are coated with white, like a baker's, though somewhat crustier. He remembers reading to his daughter when she was in her small white-framed bed, the one with the hearts cut into the headboard. Her favorite story had a baker in it, with soft-edged illustrations that Maggie would finger as he read, and he remembered the smudges they left. The pages were worn dark at the edges as well, and the book would open by itself to the large drawing in the middle, of the baker holding a pan of fresh bread, slipping on a banana peel or something like that, his hands white as snow. His daughter had asked more than once if she could come with him and help him make bread.

"Say, Bob, meant to thank you for the lack of your vote on that resort up by you. To be honest, I was afraid you'd knuckle under to those enviros and vote no. It'll be good business. At least a year's work, I'd think."

"Then what?" Bob asks.

"What do you mean?"

"Then what?" Bob stands facing the wall, spreads his arms, one hand with the pan full of mud, the other with the drywall knife lying in his open palm. "What do we do then, Ed, just keep going until everything's covered?"

"What the hell's the matter with you? All I said was thanks. . . ."

Bob can feel Ed behind him, rooted, hands coming up to his hips. The look will be vacant, his face more rounded than he remembers, though the beard is gone. He turns and sees exactly that.

"Do you remember, Ed, when you didn't have to lock the doors, and you could leave the keys in the truck, and you could just pile things up in your yard and not have to worry about them disappearing? When you didn't have smog alerts, or traffic lights, and we knew everyone in town? Everyone in town." Bob realizes he is pointing with his knife at Big Ed's chest.

"They're not smog alerts, it's wood smoke. . . . And you know, you make pretty good money off this, too. Christ almighty, you're starting to sound like Teddy. . . ."

Bob drops his eyes to a spot of mud on the terra-cotta tile and thinks maybe he does, a little. He waves at the house and feels his voice surge. "I mean, is this what you need? Really? Do any of us need this?" It isn't that at all—it's as Teddy had said—it had nothing to do with need and everything to do with want.

"I'll get my checkbook," Ed says.

HIS DAUGHTER IS BURIED NEXT TO FRANKLIN, on a point that overlooks the lake that is disappearing. He thinks she would have liked that. Franklin's life had been about the same length as hers, the two woven like fabric.

He stands on soft white ground, alkali earth, with his arms wrapped around his chest. The air is warm and swirls and makes strange noises as it travels around the white and brown tufa towers, like words whispered at a distance, too faint to know. Across the lake before him, rippled blue, the thumb of ground where they will build the resort. It is only a matter of time. He thinks of that snowy night among friends, looks at this calm day. Beyond the lake and the flats and the willows, the Sierra rise like a wall thrown up against heaven. He sees slope and ridge and a hemisphere of surpassing blue. It stops him, as it did that night, this excellent house in which he lives.

Bob cants his head and squeezes his eyes. He bites his lip and fingers the slippery ring in his pocket. She had stood in the kitchen, then shaken her head and gone her way, out the slamming screen door and into the twilight of moths.

There are flowers at her grave, a clutch of yellow rabbitbrush tied with a stem. Her boyfriend still comes once a week as he said he would. As Bob does. Franklin's grave is beside hers, a long arm's length away, about where he slept in her room, every night, even after she was gone and near his end, when Bob had to carry him up the stairs. It was where he had found him, still on that recent morning. There are no flowers on his grave. It is marked with a wire dog biscuit on a steel stake. It leans at an angle from the wind and Bob straightens it.

It brings him to his knees. His hands reach out to each grave, his arms span a certain distance of time. The warmth of the earth slips through his palms, eases knuckles that are stiff from the work of the knife. Bob closes his eyes and smells the ocean, sees the low sun bright on her face and feels her smile back, hears Franklin bark twice, shoot out after deer.

MIKE HENDERSON

(1946–   )

Veteran Reno journalist Mike Henderson has written on many aspects of Nevada life, from politics to personal interest stories, and at his finest, they are spare, straight-ahead, no-nonsense pieces. A Pensacola native, he has worked as a reporter, editor, and columnist for news organizations in Florida, Louisiana, California, and Washington, D.C. He received top journalism awards in three states and was nominated for the Pulitzer Prize. Over the years he has turned to fiction for its lyrical outlet, and hence the genesis of "Harmonica Man," the old story of a mob coming down on what is not readily understood, in this case a Vietnam vet trying to live out his days in the Sierra foothills. Like many Nevada journalists, he owes a great deal to Robert Laxalt, whose quiet hands coaxed the writer out of him and into public view. Today he works the city desk at the *Reno Gazette-Journal.*

Harmonica Man

The south fork of the Yuba River cuts deep into the Sierra Nevada's volcanic rock. The banks are etched in the rough by the travels of ancient glaciers and smoothed by the crushing weight of water from snowmelt that begins high in the Sierra and gathers force in its rush toward the sea.

As spring ends, the violent waters recede, slowing in many parts of the river to a swift current. The movement is nearly imperceptible where the river broadens into calm pools before rock walls funnel down to make it run violent once more.

This is gold country, abundant with places where the forty-niners staked their claims. Towns along the way bear names belying their boom-and-bust origins.

Near just such a town, where the river widens, summer encampments spring up in the shade of towering pines dotting the riverbanks.

Yellow pontoon boats bob like butterflies in the gentle current, playthings of the affluent vacationers who spill from their motor homes in search of gold.

They sift the sandy river bottom in quest of the shiny flecks that remain, hoping to recover enough to pay for their vacations, or at minimum, enough to show to the people back home. If their luck is extraordinary, they'll find a nugget. But the riches to be gained come mostly from getting away from the city and suburbia, parking the motor home in a shady grove on the riverbanks, and letting kids be kids on warm summer days while the adults indulge their own childish fantasies.

For this, Julie and her family came each year to the campground on the Yuba.

She and her brothers were too young to go along with their parents to play the part of prospectors. The children would grow bored with panning and sieving and beg to go home. So they were left in the safety of the camp to play with other children. Adults were always around to keep an eye on them, to invent games to keep them occupied.

But even at age ten, Julie was a bright and brooding child, too intelligent to be long interested in silly games, too dour to enjoy the laughter of mindless activity.

She was given to wandering off from the group, often retreating to the motor home to read, whiling away the long hours in the company of *Huckleberry Finn, Tom Sawyer,* and *Little Women.*

Or she would walk along the riverbank, gathering pretty rocks distinctive only to her because of their shapes or colors—gray streaked with purple, or worn smooth or flat, or resembling something in shape, a cloud perhaps. Or she would see in them a suggestion of a dog's head or the profile of a teacher she would not see again until summer's end.

These rocks, none larger than could be carried in her hand, she would wash in the river, turning them this way and that to admire them.

Then she would take them to her secret place in a grove of pines along the banks, near a point where a cottonwood stretched its smooth limbs out over the water.

She did not know it was also a secret place for the man called Hoppy.

A peculiar little man weighing no more than 130 pounds, he was not the sort one would take at first glance to be an outdoorsman.

Wiry, clean-shaven, well groomed, he had a shock of deep red hair and matching dark freckles. The combination played on his sun-creased skin, making him at once aged and ageless.

He would limp along the riverbanks from the upstream transient camp where he stayed, keeping his distance from others except at nighttime, when creatures of all kinds feel the urge to nest in numbers, a primal packing for mutual security.

By day, he would be out on his own. A relatively learned man in comparison with the others in his camp, he would spend the morning hours reading one of the dog-eared paperbacks he kept in his worn brown knapsack. Inside it, he also kept an extra pair of pants, a razor and other toiletries, and a good shirt he could wear into town when he went to get his disability check, sent general delivery to the little post office.

With him he carried only a pocketknife, a worn brown wallet with his Social Security card and his Veterans Administration hospital identification. And in his shirt pocket he carried his Marine Band harmonica.

Hoppy, the others called him, not knowing why he dragged the game leg behind him, not knowing of the havoc wreaked by a sniper's bullet as he waded knee-deep through a rice paddy half a world away.

Their meeting took both man and child by surprise.

Julie was in the quiet grove not far from the riverbank, gone to admire the treasures she had lain there so carefully yesterday before covering them with leaves.

She started at the harmonica's wail. But she was drawn by the mournful, reedy sounds emanating from just beyond her grove.

She crept close on what a child took to be soundless steps.

Then she saw him, knees drawn up to his chest, on the cottonwood tree's smooth limb reaching outward toward the river in search of the sun. She saw the freckled hands cupped against his chin as if he were blowing on them to keep them warm.

She took another tentative step and a pebble dislodged, tumbling down the bank and landing with a small "plunk" in the still, deep pool by the shore.

The reedy sound stopped, and she froze in place.

Hoppy took it all in with a glance, and he grinned.

"Well, little daffodil," he said, noting her bright yellow sunsuit. "You like my music?"

"I'm sorry," Julie said. "I was only listening. I didn't mean to disturb you."

"That's awright, Sugar. You almost scared me offa my branch. But it's OK. You like my music?"

"Yes, sir, but it's such a sad song. Why don't you play a happy song?"

Hoppy thought a minute, then said to her, "You know 'Row, Row, Row Your Boat'?"

"Sure," she said. "We learned it in Brownies."

"Well, I think I know it, too."

He played a few notes.

"Now, you sing it and I'll play along."

Together, they played and sang by the river on the bank next to the deep, quiet pool.

Again and again, through chorus after chorus, they played and sang.

Hoppy stopped for a moment and let her get a few words ahead, then he started playing from the beginning. The effect was in the style of a round, sung by men and young children for so many decades on hundreds of riverbanks and by thousands of campfires.

There is something about a song sung out of doors, in the

quietude, either a cappella or to the accompaniment of crickets or a simple instrument, that forges in men a kinship with each other and with nature. A song transcends speech, salving the psyche, nurturing the spirit.

Julie came the next day to the quiet grove and again they played and sang, whiling away a part of a long day.

And so the afternoon ritual was born.

One day, as she approached, Hoppy was again playing the sad song, the mournful, dirgelike wail that bespoke an inner sadness of long ago.

At her approach, he brightened, the sadness gone, and his spirits soared.

Julie longed for the afternoon visits as well, despite her parents' admonition that she not speak to strangers. By now, after all, Hoppy was no stranger.

And one afternoon, Julie summoned her courage and finally asked, "Can I blow on it?"

Hoppy smiled, remembering once, in a setting not unlike this one, when the cool metal of the mouth harp first touched his own sunburned lips.

"Jump right up here," he said, and he extended a hand to help hoist the child onto the limb.

As he straddled the smooth, cottonwood limb, he settled Julie into the saddle it formed, as if the two of them were riding double on a horse.

Julie giggled as she nestled in, ready for the adventure of blowing on the harmonica, a new way of making music.

Hoppy cradled the child against his chest and put his arms around her to hold her hands inside his own on either end of the mouth harp.

"Blow gently," he told her.

The result was three notes sounded together, a fuzzy, airy sound produced by the delicate, untrained lips.

"Again," he said, "but harder."

She filled her lungs and blew again. This time she blew too hard, and the instrument squealed in protest.

Julie giggled; Hoppy chuckled.

"Maybe not quite so hard this time," he said.

The third effort elicited a passable musical sound from the shiny silver harp that glinted in the sun filtering through the high limbs.

As the shadows grew long and the air grew cool, Julie was playing a rough approximation of "Row, Row, Row Your Boat" by herself, under the tutelage of her friend Hoppy.

Hoppy applauded her, praising her lavishly, promising that before the summer was out he'd turn her into a first-class harp player.

And so the dark and brooding child was transformed into a young girl confident and proud in her accomplishment. She skipped back to camp, her soul lighter, the world brighter.

As the weeks passed, her mastery of "Row, Row, Row Your Boat" was complete. She had graduated to "Red River Valley" and was learning "Camptown Races."

As summer vacation drew to an end, Julie was even learning how to make the "chuffa, chuffa, chuffa" sound of a steam locomotive as she forced her breath through the harmonica reeds. And Hoppy was showing her how to imitate the mournful sound of a train whistle by puffing out the cheeks, slightly overblowing the instrument, and deliberately moving the hand to and from the sound holes, bending the notes.

One afternoon she went down to the secret spot, and Hoppy was not there. He had been late before, so she waited patiently at first.

She remembered her treasure trove of rocks, which she had revealed to a much-impressed Hoppy, but soon she grew bored with the colored stones with the odd shapes.

At river's edge, she selected smooth, flat stones, just as Hoppy had shown her, and sent them skipping across the quiet pool to the current's edge. Once, she managed a triple skip, but Hoppy had not arrived to witness this grand feat.

Julie fretted and worried and imagined him sick, needing her, and still he did not come.

She straddled the saddle limb over the deep pool and peered into its darkness, looking for fish she knew she could not see.

Then she imagined herself an Olympian, walking the balance beam as she had seen the small Russian girls do on television. This was simplicity, she told herself as she placed one small foot in front of the other on the broad, smooth limb. Back and forth she walked, six steps out, then a turn, six steps back. Her confidence rose with each sure step, each agile turn.

Satisfied with the newfound prowess that would bring her fame and the adulation of her parents and classmates, she made the game more difficult, closing one eye. And after a time, this, too, became simplicity.

For a long moment she studied the limb, memorizing its polished white patina and gentle crook to the right.

Julie squinted both eyes shut tightly, took a deep breath and took one step, then another.

And another.

The fourth step out was a misstep.

She fell hard astride the limb's saddle.

The pain barely had time to register in her mind, for while at first she was teetering, stunned, now she was toppling to the right, as if in slow motion, unable to regain her balance, into the deep pool.

Its darkness enveloped her frail body, and as she kicked and flailed at the water with her arms, seeking a handhold, hoping to propel herself to the riverbank, she succeeded only in driving herself away from the shore and closer to where the water ran swift.

The current at first gripped her arm and then her leg, pulling her into it, surrounding her, holding her to its bosom.

Then it relaxed its grasp, for there was no longer a need to hold her tightly. It owned her whole being. She would go wherever it carried her, and it was carrying her to the rapids ahead.

Julie's head bobbed above and below the river's surface as if she were a fishing cork toyed with by a trout below. Each time her head came up she gasped, gulping as much water as air.

As the frothy roar of the rapids arrived, she was tugged first one way, then another.

A limb wedged between two boulders snagged at the light fabric of her sundress, then tore at the tender flesh high up her ivory legs.

Her right forehead glanced off a rounded boulder, stunning her, and soon her body, cold and numb, bobbed into a quiet, shallow place along the shore.

Julie grabbed at first one thicket, then another, but her hands could not make the connection. Finally, with two hands, she grabbed a willow bough and hung on, for fear her life would end if she ever let go.

The act was a triumph of the spirit; in that moment, she knew she would live.

Julie followed the trail beside the riverbank back to the motor home camp. She was hurt, cold, crying, and suddenly, inexplicably, hungry.

Her mother shrieked when she saw her daughter's torn, wet sundress and took her inside to warm her and change her clothes. She saw the scrape on Julie's forehead, the scratches on her arms from the brambles. And as she removed her daughter's dress, she saw the bruises on the thighs where Julie had fallen onto the saddle limb. She saw the cuts where the stick wedged between the rocks had poked at the tender flesh.

Still stunned from the blow on the head, hurting in every joint, teeth chattering from the cold, Julie was in no condition to answer the questions her mother asked. Her chest heaved with silent sobs, and she longed for the solace of sleep.

But her mother's conclusion was inescapable. Her daughter had been molested, probably by one of those bums in the transient camp upriver.

Julie's father was outraged, his anger beyond measure.

Children in the camp quickly confirmed that they had seen Julie with the red-haired man who walked with the limp, and word of Hoppy and Julie rapidly spread through the motor home camp.

Before long, men and women had gathered outside Julie's motor home to discuss what to do and how to do it as the child shivered under the covers and sought sleep to soothe the dull pain wracking her body.

The nearest sheriff's outpost was three hours away, and the angry group feared the man who did this thing would flee.

The attack was swift, deliberate.

The motor home men, armed with hunting knives and the pointed hand picks used to tap ore-bearing rocks apart, rained blow after blow on the small freckled body. They pierced his chest, his legs, his back, and where his hands rose in a defensive gesture in front of his face, his palms were penetrated.

It was death by torture. Hoppy felt every blow, saw the anger in the men's eyes, heard their curses. But as his life spilled out of him, etching the sandy riverbanks in filigreed rivulets of dark red, he never knew why it had happened.

In all, sheriff's investigators would learn, there were sixty penetrating wounds.

They would learn he had been to town that day to visit the post office and cash his disability check.

They found most of the money and a check stub in his pocket. They found the brown wallet with the Veterans Administration hospital identification and the Social Security card. They found the little pocketknife.

In his shirt pocket they found a slightly battered mouth harp.

And in his backpack they found a few personal items—some dog-eared books, a new bar of soap, a new pack of razor blades, and a small, gift-wrapped box.

They puzzled over the box, then opened it.

Inside was a shiny new harmonica, the Marine Band model.

ADRIAN C. LOUIS
(1946–)

Few writers have come out of Nevada to match the absolute candor and unrelenting, defiant prose and poetry of Adrian C. Louis. Like the unwelcome magpie, he constantly returns to haunt, and his days as a regional writer may finally be coming to an end. His long prose poems have recently been published in *Ploughshares* and the *Kenyon Review,* and his last three books were featured in the *Bloomsbury Review.* Among Native American writers (he is an enrolled member of the Lovelock Paiute tribe), he is working—particularly in poetry—by himself. There is no editor looking over his shoulder; he is not writing for "prevailing tastes." Against all odds he has sent his words into the world and, equally remarkable, they are being printed. The kingmakers are unsure of them, but they are printing them. Today he lives and writes on the Pine Ridge Indian Reservation in South Dakota, thanks to an award from the Lila Wallace/Readers Digest Foundation.

Bone and Juice (poems). Evanston: Northwestern University/TriQuarterly Books, 2001.
Ancient Acid Flashes Back (poems). Reno: University of Nevada Press, 2000.

Ceremonies of the Damned (poems). Reno: University of Nevada Press, 1997.

Wild Indians and Other Creatures. Reno: University of Nevada Press, 1996.

Skins. New York: Crown Publishing, 1995.

Vortex of Indian Fevers (poems). Evanston: Northwestern University Press / TriQuarterly Books, 1995.

Blood Thirsty Savages (poems). St. Louis, Mo.: Time Being Books, 1994.

Among the Dog Eaters (poems). Albuquerque: West End Press, 1992.

Fire Water World (poems). Albuquerque: West End Press, 1989.

Sweets for the Dancing Bears (poems / chapbook). Marvin, S.D.: Blue Cloud Quarterly Press, 1979.

Muted War Drums (poems / chapbook). Marvin, S.D.: Blue Cloud Quarterly Press, 1977.

The Indian Cheap Wine Seance (poems). Providence, R.I.: Gray Flannel Press, 1974.

Abducted by Aliens Inside Her Brain

RAPID CITY, SOUTH DAKOTA. A week before Christmas. Bitter, bleak, freezing, the white-trash citizenry hauled inside by the bitter cold. Late in the afternoon, Mariana watched the fat snowflakes slowly drift through the gray sky. Inside the downtown bus depot, poor people and students were scurrying to make connections home. Mariana was not homeward bound at all, but was only warming up, her feet swollen spongy and painful from bum-hiking the icy streets.

She had a shimmering hangover and her clothes smelled funky with grease, booze, and puke. Her eyes were red and the people in the bus station avoided making eye contact with her. When she lifted a half-smoked cigarette from a sand-filled ashtray and lit it, she was relieved that it didn't taste halfway bad. Even if it had tasted bad, she would have smoked it anyways. She had almost reached the bottom in her delirious descent into self-destruction. The blissful sewers of hell or some alien dimension beckoned. Sometimes, she told herself, she felt as if she had been cursed by being born an Indian.

Mariana was thinking about Charlie Boy Red Blanket and how she was glad she had left him. He beat her too much. He'd even hit her for calling him "Charlie Boy," although that was what all his friends and family called him. He demanded that he be addressed as "Charles," especially when he was drunk. And he was drunk all the time and bitter, crazy-mean during their last days together. His brain was poached in firewater.

"Only my buds call me Charlie Boy," he had shouted and then slapped her on three separate occasions.

Yet almost every time he got drunk, he would sit for hours and call her "Mariana banana, Mariana banana." Drunker yet, he would mumble, "Mariana ramma lamma ding-dong." If she gave the slightest hint of being offended, he would smack her. Mariana had come to view men as one of the great evils of the world—men, snakes, and breast cancer.

"I thought you loved me," Mariana would cry when he abused her. "I thought you loved me. This ain't love."

On one of his drunken binges, Charlie Boy had his friends shave his head like Charles Barkley and he'd kept it shaved for that whole year. He dressed in baggy clothes like an urban black gangster and that puzzled Mariana, but she was too scared of him to ever ask him about his taste in clothes or culture. Even when he walked around with his cap turned backwards, she said nothing. Charlie Boy was tall, dark, extremely muscular, and had scary eyes. She didn't dare cross him. You can never tell what a liquor-addicted fullblood man might do next, Mariana had told her Indian girlfriends.

"You got that right," every one of them had said at one time or another. "Don't *even* have to be a fullblood to be crazy," they added.

That last month with him, Mariana completely lost track of the beatings. They came often and were severe. A distant corner of her consciousness whispered that it was only a matter of time before he did the job right and killed her.

He came home drunk from an indoor rodeo at the Rapid City Civic Center one afternoon and screamed at her to "kill them black ants any time you see 'em." Mariana thought that was a goofy thing to say. She figured she was expected to laugh, so she giggled. Charlie Boy backhanded her and then kicked her in the shin with his stinky Air Jordans. She was still writhing on the floor when he staggered out the door.

"What'd I do?" she whimpered long after he was gone. "Dear God damn it all, what the hell did I do?"

THE NEXT MORNING HE STUMBLED IN and asked her to cook him some fried eggs and potatoes. He was contrite and hungover and he apologized. He had a black eye and his shirt was torn. "Them black ants ain't ants," he explained. "They're carpenter ants and they're eating the fuckin' foundation of this house. Don't you know nothing?"

Mariana was unsure whether to shake her head yes or no, so she simply nodded and began to cook his breakfast, afraid of saying anything lest they be the wrong words. She wondered why he cared about the house. It was a dump anyway. It wasn't even theirs, and Hank Goldberg, the landlord, never fixed anything that needed fixing. Goldberg, the grossly fat, blackhead-nosed landlord, had said she could do him some favors the next time she was late with the rent. She knew better than to tell Charlie Boy about *that*. No sense in getting beat up because of a horny landlord.

"Friggin' termites *and* ants can eat your foundation and stuff," Charlie Boy said, burped, and then went into the living room and passed out on the couch. Mariana spent the entire day cleaning house and watching out for termites or ants. She never saw a single one.

That afternoon, he awoke and asked for an early dinner. They ate sloppy joes and fried potatoes and then sat together watching television for an hour. Then he got dressed and left the house without saying where he was going. Late that night Charlie Boy returned lopsided, with his cruel eyes halfway rolled back in his head.

He came home like a devil in the middle of a tremendous thunderstorm. Lightning lashed out across the Great Plains trying to electrocute the Dakotas. The storm had knocked out the electricity, and Charlie Boy had fallen in the darkness of the front yard and lost his glasses. He banged on the door and made Mariana join him on her hands and knees on the wet, unmowed grass, helping him search for his glasses.

"Find the damn things before lightning zaps us," he yelled.

"I wish it would," she mumbled as low as she could.

"Keep lookin', bitch."

Mariana would never forget that night as long as she lived. The torrential rains had brought hundreds upon hundreds of foot-long nightcrawlers to the surface and her knees were soon covered with mashed worm flesh. She prayed for the lightning to strike them both dead. She gagged at the thought of those thrashing, slimy worms dying under her brown flesh, but she never complained. Wormy knees were better than Charlie Boy's fists. Almost anything was better than getting beat up.

"I don't find them damn glasses then I'm really gonna be pissed," Charlie Boy had shouted at her.

"I'm looking," she said in a voice that was barely more than a whisper. "I'm looking."

"You damn well better be looking," he said. "I don't find them I'm gonna knock the piss outta you."

Mariana had nodded and scooted quickly over the grass, smashing scores of worms before she located what they were searching for. She handed the glasses to Charlie Boy, and he walked inside without even acknowledging her.

"Thanks for nothing," she had mumbled when she was sure he was out of hearing range. Then she too went inside and made plans to leave him. It was either that or kill him, and that drunken shit-shorts wasn't worth going to jail for. Two weeks later, she packed two plastic shopping bags and left him in the middle of the night without a good-bye.

For a few days she stayed with her old boyfriend, Verdell Ten Bears, until his AWOL woman came home. Nine days after she moved out, she got the news that Charlie Boy had gotten his skull bashed by an aluminum baseball bat wielded by an unknown assailant outside an Indian bar. He was permanently paralyzed, but Mariana had no intention of ever visiting him at Sioux San Hospital. Mariana suspected Verdell Ten Bears had done her that favor.

LATE IN THE AFTERNOON, when the crowd of travelers thinned and only a few derelicts and students remained in the bus station, Mariana got up and checked the coin cups on a row of pay phones and found nothing. She shrugged, coughed, and hocked a loogie onto the green terrazzo floor and walked to the ladies' room. It reeked of Lysol and urine.

In front of a sparkling-clean mirror, she surveyed the ravages the passage of time had left on her young face. It had been five years since Sherman had died and four years since she'd had her tubes tied at the PHS hospital. She was now twenty-one and could drink legally, although she had done so anyway since she was thirteen. She needed a drink badly. She was beginning to hurt from the unpleasant creature of sobriety that was slowly quickening inside her body.

Mariana crawled under the doorway of a pay toilet and took off her jeans and removed her panties. She put her jeans back on and walked out the door, putting a small wad of toilet paper in the latch so it wouldn't close and she could get back in. She filled a sink with hot soapy water and washed out her underwear. Mariana held the panties under a hot-air hand dryer until they were no longer damp. Then she wet a red bandanna and went back into the stall to take a sponge bath.

She took a brush from her purse and pulled out the snarls in her short black hair. She even found an old tube of cherry lip balm and applied it to her cracked lips, although her aim was off and her mouth looked lopsided. Mariana Two Knives put on the black leather jacket a biker she'd slept with gave her and wiped some dried crud off the sleeves. She took a deep breath and walked back to the lobby and sat back down on a bench.

She rubbed her face and felt a pimple near her nose. She squeezed it between two fingers until it popped. She ground the white pulp until it disappeared and then walked up to an old man who looked like the last cowboy on earth.

The last cowboy seemed vaguely familiar, but then all *wasicus* looked the same to her. He looked exactly like Ross Perot's twin, and he was doing a crossword puzzle in a small booklet. Mariana interrupted his attempt at literacy and bummed a cigarette. The old wrangler had a *pachuco* tattoo on the webbing between his thumb and forefinger. Mariana had one there too, although hers was homemade with a pocketknife and a ballpoint pen. She had done it during her first jail time for public drunkenness.

The last cowboy said he lived in Rapid City and was headed up to Deadwood to do some gambling in the dorky casinos there. His bus wasn't due to leave for another hour, and he offered to buy Mariana a drink or two. She thanked him and declined and went back to her own bench. Sometimes life struck her so strangely that she was convinced that she'd been abducted and made crazy by space aliens. Aliens might even be living in her own brain. She looked down at her own *pachuco* tattoo. The cross with three sun rays above it gave her a slight twinge of hope.

Something in the blood of her people worshiped the sun. It

was something that the modern age could not destroy. The Lakota were children of *Wi*, the sun. A ray of sunshine illuminated the bus depot. The winter sun had broken through clouds. Mariana knew this was a sign. She knew then that she had to go down to the detox center and turn herself in for the cure one more time. It was always hard, but she would do it. She had to. She stared at the last cowboy across the way and focused her eyes on the tattoo on his weathered white hand. The spoked rays above the cross pulled her to her feet and she walked over to him.

"Can I bum another cigarette?" she asked.

"You're too young to smoke," he teased.

"No, I'm legal. Let me have one more smoke, please? I'm having a damn nicotine fit like you wouldn't believe."

"Sure, sure, you can have one more," he said and reached into his coat pocket and pulled out a pack of Marlboros. Strapped to the pack of cigarettes with a green rubber band was a wad of twenty-dollar bills. A thick wad. A wad thicker than Mariana had ever seen outside of television or in the possession of a crack dealer.

"You still offering to buy me that drink?" Mariana asked. Her mouth actually began to water from the mere sight of the cowboy's money.

"Listen, sweetheart, does a bear go poop in the woods?" The last cowboy laughed.

"I guess some do, the ones that don't live in outhouses," Mariana laughed and reached for his hand. They stood up together and walked outside. It had stopped snowing and the winter sun had completely broken through the fat gray clouds, but it was still cold, bitter cold. For a brief instant, Mariana thought one of the clouds looked just like her son Sherman's misshapen head. But the cowboy's arm around her waist made her forget everything except the deep dryness of her throat and the deep dryness of her soul.

"We're gonna have us a good time," she said.

The old white man giggled and squeezed her tighter.

"You betcha," he said.

"You got that right," she answered and asked for another cigarette. She wanted to look at that wad of bills one more time. Something about it gave her a delirious shiver of hope.

MARILEE SWIRCZEK
(1947–)

Pennsylvania native Marilee Swirczek has been a lighthouse for all things literary since coming to Western Nevada Community College in 1989. Her desire to bring words alive—in the students, among her peers, and in the community—led to the founding of the Lone Mountain Writers, which awards an annual fiction prize and continues to meet to this day. When she is not teaching English, or raising her family, she is working on drafts of her own fiction (which recently appeared in the anthology *The World's Shortest Stories,* and *The Sun*), perfecting the voice of a woman who is looking for the full range of experience yet who remains tied to the everyday. Her fiction simmers with restraint yet, as a reader, I know just how far it travels to reach me.

A Time to Gather Stones

I CAN'T KEEP HOLD OF TIME THESE DAYS. . . . I'm chopping onions for a chicken potpie and the next thing I know, I'm in sixth grade, and Mr. David is calling me up to the front of the room.

I'm standing in front of him, conscious of my flat chest and buck teeth, certain that I've been chosen for something special. He says, "When I'm talking, shut up. Now go back to your seat." I walk back to my seat—the last seat, naturally, a long walk—and wonder if I'm going to die right here in front of John Canonico and everybody, or if I'm going to live a long life and die in little bits every time I remember this. I sit down, trying to be casual, and then I'm back in my kitchen thirty-four years later.

I haven't missed a chop, and I've even started peeling a potato. I may be losing my mind, but I can be depended on to prepare dinner on time.

Or I'll be driving one of the kids to soccer practice and drive right on by the soccer field because I'm really thirteen years old, and I'm dancing a broom dance with John Canonico.

The broom dance is a brilliant idea of Miss Nugent's, our eighth-grade teacher. When the music stops, we have to change partners. If you're really dumb and don't watch out and plan your switch, you could end up dancing with a broom. Really dumb, but Miss Nugent's fiancé had been killed during the war (that's his ring on her finger, all these years later), and she never got married and has no kids, so how is she to know? John and Richard Marone plan it so we always switch with each other. That way John and I dance together mostly the whole time. He sure feels good, and I'm thinking I'll marry him in about ten years, and then one of the kids yells, "Mom, where are you going?" and I have to make a U-turn and go back to the soccer field.

I tell the kids I was just daydreaming, which is a dangerous thing to do while driving, but it's better than telling them I was thirteen years old and dancing with a broom.

Sometimes it's a smell that does it. Like last weekend when I decided that my kids should experience fresh lemonade for once in their lives instead of the frozen kind that's convenient. I actually went to the grocery store and bought a bunch of lemons that cost me an arm and a leg and was squeezing the juice myself, wondering if a little knuckle skin would ever be noticed, what with all the pulp—when I'm in Pennsylvania, standing in my front yard on Indiana Avenue.

The maple trees are little sticks, and I'm selling lemonade in Dixie cups for a nickel a cup. My dad's the only person who's buying lemonade from me until John and Richard show up. John is wearing dark pants and a white T-shirt that's rolled up on his shoulders. His arms are tan, his teeth are white, and he looks at me. I feel a little switch go on in my chest, and then my mother comes out and takes a picture. My dad, who must be broke by now from buying lemonade all day, calls John his son-in-law, and John smiles. I'm feeling shy all of a sudden, but really good—special—and then I feel a sharp pain in my thumb, and I'm forty-six years old, squeezing lemons.

I'm smiling, though, because it was nice seeing my father, who died thirty years ago.

I keep trying to understand why this is happening to me. I'm happily married, busy, have good kids. I think I've pinpointed when it all started, though—when Sherry Levine sent me a photograph of my twentieth class reunion. It was easy to recognize the faces; the girls were overweight, but their eyes were dead giveaways. The boys were all men, substantial-looking in conservative suits, except for Mike Rossi, who was wearing a tie and a T-shirt. And there in front, kneeling on one knee, was John Canonico. His hair was thinning, he had a beard, and his shoulders looked tired, but it was him all right. Next to him was an empty chair. On the back of the photograph Sherry had written: "The empty chair is in your honor."

Sometimes I even call my daughter by my sister's name. Like last Friday night, I was curling Jenny's hair for her first date, and then I'm calling her Sandi.

I'm curling Sandi's hair and waiting for John to call. He hasn't called all week, which is strange, because he's called me almost every day since kindergarten, and we're sophomores now. My best friend, Marjorie, hasn't called either, and I'm getting suspicious, just a little sick feeling that threatens to make me throw up if I dwell on it. I could pick up the phone and call, I guess, but for some reason I just don't. And then the phone rings. I don't run to answer it because I know I'm going to hear bad news.

Jenny yelps as the curling iron gets too close to her ear, and I say, "Sorry, Sandi" before I can swallow the words. Jenny rolls her eyes and accuses me of being senile, but she's smiling. She asks me what I was thinking about, and I tell her I was remembering the first boy I ever loved. His name was John Canonico, and we loved each other since kindergarten. He had beautiful dark eyes and white teeth, and one day when we were fifteen years old, he stopped talking to me forever. I never did find out why, I tell my daughter. All I know is my best friend, Marjorie, was jealous and told him something, and he never spoke a word to me again or looked at me straight in the eyes. "Some friend," Jenny says. "Why didn't you just ask him?" she wonders.

Why don't I just ask you? There you are, at your locker, alone, the perfect chance. All I have to do is walk up to you and ask "Why?"

You carried my books, caught fireflies with me, pulled my ponytail, defended my ten-year-old honor, held my hand, smiled at me, grew up by my side. I feel paralyzed.

"I just didn't," I answer Jenny. "Then my father died, and we moved away. Later I got married, and here we are. Anyway, all that happened more than thirty years ago."

That night I'm waiting for Jenny, ironing in the family room. The weatherman has predicted rain, and I'm hot and sticky. Next thing I know, I'm in Pennsylvania, walking along Judy Lynn Lane in my hometown.

It's August, and I'm wondering if my makeup will slide right off my face like a beige, rubbery mask, it's so humid. The kids and my mother are visiting with Aunt Marie. I haven't been home in twenty-five years, and I'm just taking a little walk, feeling like a girl again. I hear that John Canonico's new house is just up the road a bit, in that stand of maples and dogwood. Maybe I'll just walk on by, or maybe he'll be there, mowing the lawn or something. He won't recognize me; it's been so long since we graduated from high school. If it feels right, I'll walk right up to him and say, Hi, John, it's me, remember? And he won't recognize me at first, but then I'll smile and he'll say my name.

We'll walk a little together, close to each other, the quiet countryside serene and still. I'll ask him what happened, why he just stopped talking to me, and finally I'll know. It'll be something silly as we look back on it, something a jealous friend said, something that wasn't true but had hurt anyway. And he'll say he was hurt so profoundly that he was never able to look at me or say my name again, but he never forgot me.

I'll tell him I named one of my kids after him. He'll take my hand, press it to his heart, and thank me for that. He'll tell me about his little girl and his wife, and then we'll walk back to his house. We'll embrace, and he'll feel good in my arms, and then I'll walk back up the road to Aunt Marie's.

But I don't walk by his house. In fact, I stop at the turn, and I look up the dirt road as far as I can see. The road curves and is lost in the trees. I hear a dog barking, far away. A milkweed pod drops, and my heart is pounding. He's so close, so close after twenty-five years of wondering. I may never come home again. This may be my last chance to see him. A cloud scuttles across the sun, and the trees darken.

I can't do it. The heat is suffocating me. I turn around and quickly walk back to Aunt Marie's. The kids are eating ice cream, and Uncle Jimmy is playing "Turn, Turn, Turn" on the piano. Something is in my eye, and I go to the bathroom, shut the door, and sit on the edge of the bathtub for a while. I know that we'll be flying away, maybe forever, tomorrow. I know I just lost my last chance to look into John's eyes, which wouldn't have changed, and to see him smile.

The iron sizzles as a tear drops, and I'm back in the family room. I've ironed three T-shirts and a tablecloth, not bad for being three thousand miles away in a Pennsylvania woods almost three years ago. I turn off the iron and reach into my jeans pocket. I read the note that Sherry sent me: "Thought you'd like to know."

Then I read the obituary again, but the words run together. The photograph is a good one. He's looking right through the camera straight at me, and he's smiling.

EILEEN CLEARY
(1949–   )

A former journalist, construction worker, and miner, Eileen Cleary hails from Allegheny County—the coal-mining hills of Pennsylvania and the source of much of her fiction. After a long journey west, Cleary settled in Nevada and pursued a degree in English, worked as a tutor, a freelance writer, and an editorial assistant. For ten years, she owned and worked on the E & N Ranch in Diamond Valley. This experience gave her more than a cursory exposure to Nevada; when she writes about this place it is with an authentic voice, tender and gristly with no apology. In this opening section of her novel, set in northern Appalachia, Julian and Meave begin the slow spiral down the company mine. Their hands are literally tied, by bloodlines and poverty, to the coal dust beneath their shack. And we can only watch as the story plays out. Her fiction moves first to the imagination, the quiet country where these things must finally settle. She has recently completed a second novel, *Desperado: A Bedtime Story,* set in Nevada. In 1995 and 1997, she won the James MacMillan Award for the best piece of writing about Nevada.

Nearly three decades after leaving home, she has returned to her native Pennsylvania.

Ringgold's Run

(EXCERPT)

1984

JULIAN BOOSTS MEAVE ONTO HIS BACK and she rides him piggyback down the slant of the hill, her feet stuck through the bends at his elbows, his arms around her legs. She bunches her hands and hugs his neck. Her hair, escaped from its knot and wild, swings loose at her waist.

The glass embedded in the flesh of her feet causes blood to gather and run off her heels. The glass hurts Julian worse than it hurts Meave.

"I going to fix yer," he promises. He says it twice.

He carries her up onto the high front porch and uses the toe of his boot like a wedge to pry open the screen door. In the kitchen he settles his passenger gently into the exploded rip of a cotton-stuffed chair. His fat fingers pluck tweezers from a rusted Band-Aid box beneath the sink. He pumps a slosh of water over them and wipes them dry on the tail of his shirt.

Facing her on the seat of a busted plastic chair, he squints at the dirty soles of the feet in his lap. Meave howls appropriately as he grasps each shard and pulls it out. She bawls a little, covers the wet purple eyes with her palms. "He means to kill me," she says. "He'll do it next time."

"No ma'am, he won't." Julian peers at a stubborn point of jelly glass buried in the ball beneath her big toe. "I thumped him good and left him out there in the trees. He'll think next time." He catches the piece and lifts it and Meave yowls. She is giddy with fear and pain, but she trusts him. He is not inherited kin, like a husband-through-marriage, but real-blood kin, first-cousin kin. Their daddies were brothers.

Her shapeless dress dips between her bare thighs and she pushes it down to cover her knees. Julian stubbornly keeps his eyes on her feet until she moves the dress, then he looks. But only for a second.

Julian is big-faced and big-handed, his violet eyes are at the same time arresting and unsettling, between them the scar from a wagon handle thrown by his brother, a closed-up gash that nearly joins his dark eyebrows. And below it that other scar, the poorly stitched harelip that pulls the top of his mouth askew and makes him handsome in some flawed way. With hair black as blue ink and their odd-colored irises, he and Meave seem enough alike to be brother and sister. Except for a look that passes between them—an occasional hot caress in their eyes—that would have no business between siblings.

Meave wiggles her toes. The water is tinted vaguely pink. The enamel cook pot is serving double duty as a foot soak. Julian fusses clumsily, like a man, uses coarse bar soap to wash the soles. Meave sits still and keeps her dress bound tightly to her knees. The soap burns a little, but the cold water soothes.

The house is a mess. Julian's mama passed on, and he has been alone five years. Ashes spill out the bottom drawer of the cookstove. An electric hot plate rests on top of a stove lid, plugged into a dangerous-looking wall socket. A greasy chain saw is the centerpiece of the clutter spilling off the kitchen table.

Julian has sense enough to be embarrassed. "I got to fix that chain saw," he says. "Want a Coke?"

"You got Coke?" Her violet eyes are like pansies. Her husband never buys soda pop.

Julian is proud to be able to do something nice for her. He grins and gets a can out of the refrigerator, the big fingers fumbling with the ring top. The fizz splashes his wrist, and he licks it off and gives her the can. She takes big gulps. He watches her and the refrigerator hums softly in its corner.

"Boy." She wipes her mouth. "This tastes like heaven." She gulps again, and then her mouth slips into a frown. "I'm afraid. To go back up there."

Julian has been waiting for this. He knows what he wants to say. He has rehearsed the words two dozen times. But fear twists his tongue, makes his heart pound in his ears, renders him mute. He licks at the scar on his lip and Meave waits.

"You don't need to," he manages, but it comes out like gibberish.

Meave balances the Coke in the soup dish of dress between her legs. She looks up at him and waits.

"Here," he says stupidly, catches the scarred lip between his teeth and punishes himself by biting. He tries again. "You can stay here. Take care of stuff. Clean up a little. I'll bring you my paychecks from the mine."

She moves her eyes across the kitchen and then back to his face.

"They cheat me 'cause I can't do numbers," he says. "The store sometimes. The goddamn electric company, too. Because'n I can't read. If you was with me they wouldn't do it."

Meave is stiff with silence, even her fingers around the soda can are white.

Julian's voice jerks along over the words. "If you was here no one would hurt you. I'd bring you my paycheck. We could have Cokes all the time." He takes a breath. "That sonofabitch husband of yours, I'd knock him off'n the porch, he ever sets one foot—"

"All right," she says, and Julian stops talking. There is silence in the kitchen except for the humming in the corner. They stare at one another and he smiles first.

"You make me so nervous sometimes I forget how to talk."

"I know," she says.

Her agreement spurs him. He is excited and the nervousness leaves him. "You sit right here, soak those feet," he says. "I'll go back up there and get your stuff."

"My cat," she cries.

"Yeh, him, too, the old bitin' sonofabitch." He grins and goes out the screen door. It slides closed and she is alone in Julian's messy kitchen.

He takes the truck this time, she hears him start it, the red flatbed Ford without a muffler. He had come on foot before, quiet as an Indian, to catch Ardell abusing her, blacking her eyes and breaking the glass that would find its way into the bottoms of her feet. He is bold now, he takes that noisy truck and goes up the hollow to get her clothes and her shoes and Martin the biting cat.

She lifts her feet out of the pink and gray water and stands. She walks carefully, balancing on her heels, over to the table. She lifts the heavy chain saw, all her fingers around its handle, and struggles it out to the porch.

There is no fire in the stove and so she starts one. It is October. When the Pennsylvania sun sits down on the West Virginia border, it will get cold. She wads torn bits of grocery sack, finds kindling, sets a chunk of pine on top. Moments later the orange flames pop and lick at the pine. She closes the firebox and moves the hot plate off the stove top.

1994

A VEHICLE THUMPS ACROSS the wood bridge at the mouth of the hollow, and the sound is heard far up the mountain. It's a stranger's vehicle, Julian can tell by the way it hits the bridge, by the grinding noise the four-wheel drive makes, and the road isn't even muddy.

He perches on the railing and watches it glide by, an ugly Dodge Ram with a picture of trees and letters on the doors. The two men inside glance at him and don't acknowledge him. The tires scatter dry leaves and pea-size gravel and that grinding—Julian decides it isn't the four-wheel drive after all. Something else is about to go wrong with the Dodge. He grins and watches it disappear and hopes the wheels fall off.

Above, the road forks. The right fork trails off into a narrow path and ends where Meave used to live with Ardell. The left one meanders for another mile, twisting and turning back on itself, lined with maple and oak and thick with mountain laurel. There are four more houses up there, but they're all peopled with Ringgolds. It's Ringgold's Run from where the spring trickles out the side of the mountain clear down to where the creek crosses under the road, under the wood bridge.

It's not long, less than an hour—Julian is still sharpening the chain on his saw—when the ugly Dodge coasts back down from above, the engine working but one front wheel askew, the tire pushing gravel, the men inside craning to look at him balanced on the railing of the tall front porch. Julian can see it now, the back end crammed with surveying equipment, and he smirks.

Meave comes to the screen, stays just out of sight, only her eyes peeping around the door frame.

The two men step down, one blond and one dark. Both of them smart-asses. Gum chewers. Julian concentrates on the file working the chain teeth.

"You-all got a phone?"

Julian guffaws. "You see any phone line up here?"

The dark man seems local, the blond one very out of place.

"Lookit, now." The dark one advances a step or two up the bank. He jerks the bill of his cap at the Dodge. "She can't run on that wheel. Gonna need a tow. Gonna be dark in another hour."

Julian licks the scar, wets it, rakes it with his teeth. "Don't you come up here," he warns.

"I ain't aiming to." The man retreats the two steps off the bank, plants his feet on the road. The blond leans against the hood of the Dodge and shakes his head. The talker lets his eyes roam over the vehicles stacked alongside the house, the flatbed Ford, a Galaxy propped on cement blocks, another pickup with the windshield shot out.

"I'm thirsty as hell," he says. "Could I trouble you for water?"

Behind him Julian hears Meave brush the screen. Henny is beside her, his face in the stomach of her dress. Julian makes a generous motion with the hand holding the file. "Take all you want. The pump's aside the house." The stranger goes to the Dodge for a cup, tosses away whatever is in it, walks with deliberate care up the bank, trying to stay in one of the tracks leading to the flatbed.

The pump handle squawks; he pumps hard and fast, rinsing the cup and finally filling it, drinking twice. He lifts his eyes and spots Meave over the rim. She is looking out the window at him from the side of the house. She melts away into the darkness beyond the glass.

Julian sees where the stranger's eyes are looking. He moves off the railing and stands so both men get a good look at the size of him.

"We're surveying. Mapping," the man hurries to tell him. "USGS."

"Whatever the hell that is." Julian sets the saw at his feet.

"Geological." The man spits and wipes the rust out of his mouth. "If it's all right with you, we'll push that Ram off to the side, get it out of the middle of the road. We'll hike on out of here and get a tow."

"What's the matter with it?"

He shrugs. "Busted tie rod maybe. Wheel's ready to fall off. Gonna have to be hauled on a truck."

Julian grins, satisfied. "I'll ride you down. It's damn near six mile." He knows the talker will offer him five dollars. Maybe ten. The blond wouldn't think of it. Wouldn't know any better. But the talker is local. He knows the customs. His dialect is pure.

Julian is big. He takes up nearly half the seat so that the talker gets in front and the blond who hasn't said a word climbs into the club cab behind them. The interior of the pickup is crowded. Empty shell casings litter the floor. Empty Coke cans. The blond rolls a green Skoal container under the instep of his boot. A filthy miner's hard hat with a lamp in front sits upside down on the seat next to him. Two rifles clatter against racks on the rear window.

Uneasy silence while they jounce down off the mountain.

"Which Ringgold are you?" the dark one finally asks, and behind him his partner pokes his shoulder to shut him up.

Julian turns to peer with menace at the talker. He is kind enough to give them a ride. He doesn't have to answer their stupid questions, and is about to say so when the man smiles.

"I grew up ten mile acrost the mountain. Turkey Foot Hollow. I'm a Bettencourt."

It eases the tension in the cab. Julian grins. "I knowed you was local. My daddy was Clive. I'm Julian."

"Well, shoot." The man slaps his cap against his leg, an aw-shucks, good-ol'-boy kind of thing. "I probably kicked your ass in high school football."

"Not mine, you didn't. I didn't go to no school." Julian guffaws again and it stretches his lip tight over his teeth. The man sees the harelip, the ugly crooked scar running from lip to nose. He stares without meaning to.

Julian turns the violet eyes on him, looks him full in the face, dares him to keep staring. The man averts his eyes.

"What the hell you doing working for the goddamn government?" Julian asks him.

The man allows a full minute of uneasy silence to pass. "It's a living," he finally says.

Julian is menacing again. "Nobody worth a pound of salt works for the goddamn government. I bet you don't live in Turkey Foot Hollow no more, neither."

The man glances out the window, finds a spot on the road and fixes his gaze.

Julian drops them near the pay phone outside the cafe, and Bettencourt holds out a ten-dollar bill. It disappears into Julian's big fist and then he rumbles the flatbed into a tight U-turn, heading back the way he came.

Bettencourt watches him go, whistles, finally. Grins at his partner. "Did you see that woman? Back there—at the house?"

"His woman?"

"Somebody's woman. Wow." He rolls his eyes.

"Pretty?"

"Oh, yeah."

"I hate hillbillies. They give me the creeps."

"I give you the creeps?"

"No. You got away. You're normal. It's them. Did you see the arms on that sonofabitch?" He gazes after the flatbed, but it is gone. He fishes in his shirt pocket for a credit card, a phone card. "He'll strip that truck. By the time we get back it'll be in twelve pieces."

"Relax, okay?" Bettencourt takes the card. "He won't touch the truck."

JULIAN HURRIES BACK TOWARD THE HOLLOW. The flatbed slams the bridge and Meave hears it and knows he is coming. She uses a towel to jerk the hot skillets off to the side of the stove.

Henny hangs on her, his face in her dress again and she makes him stop it, pushes him away from the heat of the cookstove and into a chair. His eyes are as darkly violet as those of the parents who bred him, but they don't focus. He is cross-eyed, worse some days than others. He loves music, can say five words, is the size of a child half his age. He is ten years old.

"Poppy," he says when he hears the roar of the red Ford up the hollow road. There are other children in the house, three of them, but Meave did not birth them. They belong to her older sister. The sister has abandoned them, gone off to Chicago and never come back. The sister's husband dumped the kids on Meave and deserted the hollow soon after. Meave sews their clothes and cooks their meals and Julian supports them all without complaint. He mines coal and saws wood and protects his ready-made family.

There are two small bedrooms in the house; Meave sleeps with the girls, Julian with the boys. They can't risk it, the two of them sleeping together, making another baby that might turn out like Henny.

Julian steps into the warm kitchen, smells the supper she has made, sees that the floor has been cleaned. He wishes he could kiss her.

His son flings himself at him, Julian catches him, tilts the boy's head back so he can see into the unfocused eyes.

"Poppy," the boy says, pleased.

Julian rubs his dark hair, smiles down at him. Then his gaze moves to the boy's mother.

"He's nutty today," she says, "spinning around this kitchen like a top. A storm must be coming."

"Maybe," Julian says. "The wind's up. Papers flying through the street in front of the cafe." He goes to the sink, pumps a slosh of water to wet his hands. He uses the soap, works the pump handle, dries on the towel.

The table is set. None of the dishes or silverware match. There are two benches and four chairs at the table, room for twelve, and sometimes they need it. Julian looks to see if there is any pie left. Meave made pies from leftover apples, after she got done canning applesauce. There are half a dozen poke holes in the crust from Henny sticking his fingers in.

He sails by the table, hand at his crotch, and Meave grabs his arm and steers him out the back door to the outhouse. Sometimes he goes all by himself, other times he wets. Meave has to watch him. He is like an animal in some ways, nutsy and irritated before storms, hearing sounds that other humans don't hear. Henny's antennae are tuned to a different wavelength than the rest of the world. He has good days when he smiles and can see, his eyes don't loll so, he begs Julian to play his banjo, his mother her lap board.

But there are bad days, and bad nights, when he throws tantrums, winds himself into a ball and writhes on the floor, the violet irises far apart or pointed toward his nose. Sometimes the only way his mother can quiet him is with music. Julian has been roused many a night by Meave's fingers moving softly across the lap board, her voice, quiet, soothing, singing to Henny.

It kills Julian, sometimes. His only son.

MEAVE TUCKS HIM IN, zips him up, kisses her son's cheek. She boosts him out the door ahead of her and they walk together across the bare yard.

The other children come from somewhere, two of them at least, Kay-Anne and Mallow-Jean, six and eight years old. The six year old is a regular little lady, dolls and nail polish. Mallow-Jean has never been called anything but Marshmallow by her older brother; she wears chubby-teen-size clothes, has fat fingers and a slack mouth, curly red hair.

Mallow runs at Henny, pretends to stomach-punch him. He giggles, reaches for the red hair.

The clouds are low, pieces of them have opened and are leaking cold sleet.

"Let's eat," Meave says, and they follow her in the back door to the kitchen. Julian is already at the head of the table; beside him sits Meave's sister's oldest child, a freckled and towheaded boy.

Meave sets the skillets on the table with potholders underneath fried potatoes, venison, string beans from the garden. It is late fall, the bean husks are tough, the beans inside fat and gray. The boy turns up his nose and Meave sees.

"Eat 'em," she says.

"Ain't you got no butter?"

"Butter on payday." She sets a jar of preserves in front of him. "Use that on your bread."

The bread is crusty, homemade, sliced an inch thick. The boy eats it dry just to be obstinate.

Henny eats with his fingers, beans first, one at a time. Fried potatoes next, grease running off his chin. Meave leans toward him every so often and wipes his chin with her palm. He slides along the bench, steals a potato from Kay-Anne's plate, slides back. She doesn't mind. When he explores his father's plate, Julian uses his knife and fork carefully around the boy's fingers, allowing him to have what he wants.

Meave guides Henny back to his place, points to his plate. "Eat your own," she says.

THE GIRLS CHATTER, Henny hums and talks gibberish. Julian and Meave occasionally glance across the table at one another, there is hot emotion in the eye words. He cleans his plate, helps himself to more. Meave watches the fork go from plate to mouth in the big fingers. She tries to remember the touch. Those fingers.

The sleet turns to rain. It pounds the tin roof over their heads, and a minute later, a leak hole is saturated, water bubbles along the ceiling and finally begins to drip near the dish cupboard.

"Goddamn that roof." Julian gets up, finds a plastic lard bucket, sets it under the drip.

The rainstorm, driven by wind, thunders down the hollow. In minutes the creek will rise and tumble its banks, water will race down the road like a spillway, turning it to red gumbo. The wood bridge at the mouth of the hollow will drown in foaming brown water.

Henny plucks at his mother's sleeve and she pets him. "No lightning," she says. "Too cold. Maybe snow."

He says something unintelligible, his grunts and noises have no vowels to guide the words.

The wind rattles the glass at the windows; it moves the front porch swing to and fro. A cat comes to the ledge of the window, and Kay-Anne scrambles to let it in. When she opens the door a pregnant gust of cold and moisture sweeps across the kitchen. The cat is wet, offended. It goes behind the stove to lick itself dry.

The girls go into the bedroom and go to sleep without

Meave. But Julian has to lie down with the boys to make Henny sleep. Meave stays in the kitchen and wakes him at ten o'clock to get ready for work.

She makes him a lunch of the leftover venison folded in bread, the cold fried potatoes, a big wedge of pie, packs all of it into the tin lunch pail with a space for drinking water in the bottom. She wakes him by shaking his foot and he comes out blinking into the lighted kitchen. Rain still pours off the roof.

He needs to go to the bathroom and that means putting on boots, a hat, unless he wants to be drenched clear to his underwear.

"Shit," he says when he comes back in from outside. He slings the moisture off his hat.

Meave has made coffee for him. She pours a cup and adds sugar, hands him the cup with the spoon still in it.

"Gimme something," he says. "I'm hungry again."

The pie is gone, the leftover supper packed in his pail. She saws at the bread, cuts him a thick slice and spreads it with preserves.

Julian folds it in half and stuffs the whole thing into his mouth. He stands at the window chewing the bread and watching the dark drops slide down the glass.

"I'll be glad to go back on days. I hate this shift." He turns and looks at her. "I think Henny wet the bed again."

Her eyebrows frown. "I ain't going to wake him. I'll tend to it in the morning."

"You keep this door locked. Those two guys never came back for their truck." He smiles meanly. "Tow driver probably told 'em both to go to hell." He peers through the glass again. "Looks like that old Dodge done slid ten more feet down the road. The mud's washing her away."

"They'll come for it tomorrow," Meave says.

There's a shotgun beside the door, the shells for it lay up high along the top shelf of the dish cupboard. Meave has never had to use it. Julian is big and mean-tempered, fast with his fists. No one messes with her.

The urge to kiss her has been with him all day. He fights it, sits down on a chair to lace up his work shoes instead. His eyelashes are low but he looks through them, watches her. She is barefoot, wears wrinkled pants and a shirt that's too big for her. Her hair is untidy, wound up in a loose knot at the back of her head. She appeals to him, has not stopped appealing to him since she was ten years old.

He knows if he kisses her the other will happen. A few fevered sexual things have happened in this kitchen, always when he is on nights at the mine, always when they are alone and the kids are asleep. Meave is so afraid of pregnancy that she weeps for days afterwards, won't eat. Won't look at him.

Sometimes when he has the money, he buys condoms, thinking to sharpen her ardor. But Meave is still afraid. She got pregnant with Henny the first time they did it. She says his sperm are too strong, her eggs too willing. She wants to avoid sex.

The cost of the Pill is prohibitive. And Meave won't go get them anyway because she and Julian are cousins. People say things about that and it upsets her. Her own mother says they deserved what they got with Henny. That God punished them good and proper, kin screwing kin.

Julian ties the shoe and straightens up. He has been a long time without her, over a year. His body is tight with it, the longing. He tries once, explaining to her about other things they can do, slaps her legs apart one morning and quickly fingers her up under her dress. She likes it all right but never wants it again because it embarrasses her. Meave is not too savvy about sex. Ardell was cruel to her, made fun of her, beat her for not getting pregnant when the whole time it was his fault.

MEAVE LOOKS AT HIM. Sees the longing. She picks up the lunch bucket. "You better go," she says. "You're liable to slide off the road if you get in too much of a hurry."

He stands, pulls on his jacket. There is coal dirt in the seams of his work clothes that no soap will take away. He will come home black as the clothes, nothing showing but the whites of his eyes, the pink inside his mouth. He carries coal dust home in his hair and eyelashes and it slides off onto his pillowcase even after he's washed them.

He looks at her, at her eyes, and it's as good as if he kisses her good-bye. She knows.

She locks the door, watches out the window as he takes the flatbed down the bank and into the road. Her breath makes a film on the window glass.

STEVEN NIGHTINGALE
(1951–   )

The proud owner of Charlotte, a 1972 Blazer, Steven Nightingale has spent most of his free time roaming the Great Basin in his orange-and-white Chevy, looking, I suspect, for the predawn flight of the Last Buckaroo. Whether in Gerlach or Rawhide, it's to the vast open that he returns to nurture the fine prose that only recently came to life in *The Lost Coast.* For more than fifteen years he wrote in virtual isolation, sonnets literally stacked on the floor, stories, and novels, but published only occasional poetry. Then his debut novel came out in 1996 to wide critical acclaim. In this particular section, the band of wild ones are marooned at Beulah's Smoke Creek Ranch, where she regales them with the story of her firstborn—a lightning bolt. After hearing Beulah's story of a child come from the desert sky, the wild ones continue on in search of the lost coast. A long-ago student at Stanford, Nightingale returned to his native Reno, where he lives and works, plotting the next move of his fictional misfits, who roam the West in search of (who knows how much one tribe can attain) jokes, truth, work, and amusement.

The Thirteenth Daughter of the Moon. New York: St. Martin's, 1997.
The Lost Coast. New York: St. Martin's, 1996.

The Lost Coast

(EXCERPT)

The Story of the Infant Fallen from the Sky

"Sometimes when I was out on the desert I used to find little birds that had fallen from a nest, or had been attacked by some varmint, and I would take them back to the house and nurse the damn pecky little things back to health, even though I'd have to listen to all that peeping and chirruping. I liked it, though; I liked the little falcons the most. They had them bright eyes that made you think that they knowed everything that was goin' on outside the room and inside your head. I'm tellin' ya: falcons even when they're little can dive right into the middle of what you're thinkin' on and carry it away in their beaks. And a good thing too, since thinkin' is not so much damned use.

"One time, though, I was out in the east Smoke Creek and I saw this small gleamin', a little slip of sparkles, like a snake on fire. And I went over and there was this crooked little piece of light, I mean no longer than my forearm, but blazin'! I mean like dynamite goin' slow! Bright as a noontime packed in a stick—I mean if you took a rope and sowed gunpowder all through it so's it was more powder than rope, and lit the thing up, and it never stopped burnin', that's what it would be like 'cause this thing jes' kept firin' steady, crackin' and sizzlin' and singin' in its own heat."

Beulah paused and looked fiercely at Renato.

"Now what was I s'posed to do with the damn thing?"

"My guess is," said Renato, "that you're a good woman to have around when something weird happens."

"You're goddam right I am!" shouted Beulah, who looked like she was going to cuff Renato a hard one out of sheer happiness of recollection.

"And so this shining thing . . ." said Renato quickly, to get her back into the east Smoke Creek.

"And so," Beulah went on, "I was thinkin': now this ain't no rotten old bone, no old longhorn all polished up, no sir, and it's the kind of thing that mebbe I could use to rout out some of my old pipes, and so what are you goin' to do, Beulah?"

The ranchwoman glared at Renato.

"And so what did you do, Beulah?"

"'Bout time you asked, pussyface!" she retorted. And she stepped up and leaned her muscle and gristle against a saddle and looked out the doorway as she talked.

"I roped the little sucker and dragged it back to the truck and hoisted it in the bed onto some blankets; I left it on the rope and tied it down and then headed out. And as I was drivin' back to the ranch, with this thing fizzin' and sparkin' all over the place, all of a sudden I started to hear."

"Hear?" inquired Renato with extreme courtesy.

"That's right, hear! Are you calling me a liar?"

Renato envisioned Beulah writing her name in his flesh with the horsewhip. But we recall that the painter loved women; and so he had the good sense to shout back: "Beulah, you're a rock of a woman; but I know it's rock candy. So knock off all this bullshit!"

Beulah, who had stood forth in fury, now leaned back again.

"Don't you tell nobody!" she said grudgingly.

"What do you mean, hear?"

"I couldn't help listenin' to all the fizzin', and it were pretty soon that I could start to make out it was sayin' somethin'; in the fits and bolts and burstin' out, I could start to hear what the little thing meant. And that's not all. Because the ornery little thing had slipped off the blankets in the back."

"How could you tell?"

"I could tell because the whole truck was glowin'! I looked like a comet comin' down the road! And then I knew! I knew what was what! It was a baby lightning bolt! The cute little thing had fallen out of a nest of clouds and jes' couldn't strike back up into the sky. And *now* what was it going to do? Come home with me, that's what. . . . So's I had a big grin smack on my mug, I ain't never brung no lightning home off the range before. And then I thought, Beulah, you got a problem: how the hell am I going to get out of the truck without being fried?"

"It would take a lightning bolt to fry you, Beulah."

"I'll take that as a compliment."

Renato bowed.

"The trick is not to get grounded. And so when I pulled into the ranch I jes' threw open the door and hurled myself clean out of the cab, slammin' right down far out in the dust and rollin' away."

"Now *that* I would like to have seen," exclaimed Renato.

"And laying in the dirt I thought to myself: what does a woman do with a baby lightning bolt? 'Course, I knew right away what to do! 'Cause for the first time I was bustin' out with that mother-feelin'! Me, Beulah, I had got myself the baby meant for me. Mine! And there I was, all proud with lookin' at the way it made my truck shake, ripple, and glitter! My child!"

Slowly Renato got it.

"You mean that's what you've been doing out here all these years? Raising a lightning bolt?"

"You betcha!" said Beulah with satisfaction.

Renato paused to mull this one over.

"And so how many years ago was that?" he wondered.

"'Bout fourteen years now."

"So you have on your hands a teenage lightning bolt."

"Lanky. Wild. Strong," said Beulah with gusto.

"They say parents learn a lot from their children," he ventured.

"You betcha; he taught me how to strike out at things, if you know what I mean." And Beulah gave him a smile so hearty and strong that Renato felt like a little pipsqueak.

"And so . . ."

"It's a good life. I was supposed to be a mom. I done what I set out to do."

"And so where is he?" burst out Renato.

"Come with me," said Beulah, twirling Renato around and shoving him out the door of the tack room.

They walked, the painter and the ranchwoman, out in back of the ranch and straight through the sagebrush, moving toward some low hills.

"At first I didn't know what to do—hell, I hadn't had no kid around before. 'Sides, this was a boy that was goin' to take some figurin'. First thing: what the hell is his name? Well, what about Bolt? It says what it says. It is what he is. A good name for an impulsive boy, anyway! Next question: what does he eat? Then all at once it hit me. He eats everything standin'! If it stands, he'll eat it. Easy enough. So the next afternoon I took him out to where there was some little saplings in a draw of a canyon, and right there I jes' flipped him out of the blanket up in the air. It was kind of a windy day, the trees whippin' around, but that little bolt just hovered a minute and blammo! He made *ashes* of the tallest, skinniest one! And I thought, don't turn this little sucker loose in town! You don't want to be the tallest cowboy in the room around my kid, nosirree!"

Renato measured his height against Beulah.

"And so I took him home and laid him out in some insulation in the back room, he was a-sparklin' and a-cracklin', the dear little thing, a sizzlin' and beamin', the sweet thing, that was my boy! Now I always did want a child with some energy, some zip. And there he was. And so's he and I jes' settled into our life together out here on the Smoke Creek. It's been good. This was the perfect spot—when you're raising up a lightning bolt, you need some room! It's jes' not something you could do in some piddlin' little house in town. What a little beauty he was. Wait till you see how he's grown! It's been wild. It's been a blowout. I don't know how it coulda been stranger."

Renato thought: every orphaned piece of lightning should have such an upbringing.

"There was one time early on when I took him out to the Sierra in the truck—already he was gettin' so big that he would barely fit in the bed of the pickup, and I had always to cover him up with blankets, otherwise his light would damn near blind me as I drove. I remember one time when a police car pulled me over for speedin' on one of those faraway straight roadways all over the state, and this cop he came a-stridin' up to the car and Bolt knew that he meant no good. And he always was kinda protective. And so he started thrashin' around in the back of the truck, fizzin' and sparklin' heavy, clangin' on the sides of the bed, and the whole truck was shakin' with electricity, glowin' there in the road, the brightest thing in the Basin, in the middle of the day a star sittin' there in the high desert—the truck shinin' and buckin' and throwin' off sparks. There was a thumpin' in the air and the cop was standin' there wide-eyed, and all of a sudden the thunder cracked right in the road, I mean *blasted* this guy, it was like thunder growed out of the ground and the cop turned and he hightailed it to his car and drove the hell out of there like somebody who had seen God! But it was jes' my boy Bolt! Sweet thing! How we laughed about that one for years! And what a day that was, like so many other days. We went out in some open valleys where no one would see us, and Bolt would dart around, jes' snap and zip around, rambunctious thing, what a beauty.

"Sometimes I would stay all day with him waitin', waitin': fer there ain't nothing prettier than to see him play in the dark. I would jes' sit back, jes' sit back: and when twilight was gone he went sparklin' all through the valley and did his flashin' and jabbin' into the little canyons and shootin' down in caves, firin' back out, the black sky over us an' the whole valley singin' with light, my boy, he could *rock* those valleys, he could. He'd wear hisself out playin', he'd be plumb worn out and I would take him real soft and slow and I'd lay him in the back of the truck and cover him real careful and do a long slow drive back to the ranch. I don't know how I coulda been happier."

They were approaching the hills. Renato could see little whirlwinds of dust over soil and rock where it rose from the desert floor, and there was movement—the whole hillside was rolling, and steam piped from fissures in the stone.

Beulah smiled.

"Just how big is he now?" asked Renato as he heard the rumbling.

Renato and Beulah stood at the base of the smoking hills. Before them, the entrance to a cave. Renato could see flares.

"Bolt!" called Beulah.

—Stampeding of air, shuddering of hillside, parting of sky: even with a story to ready his vision Renato could not keep his feet before the roaring of the light.

THOMAS R. TURMAN
(1951–)

A woodworker by trade and a sculptor by choice, Tom Turman combines wood, metal, and Plexiglas to produce a visual architecture that lives long after first sight. When his hands are not in wood, he writes to reconcile his Texas childhood and, later, the years of timber cruising in the Oregon rain. He finally settled in northern Nevada to build a house on a ridge in the Virginia Range, where he works in his studio and raises his boys, watching the wind bury the anemometer. In his fiction, as in his person, reticence prevails. What is left unsaid remains the focal point of the story. A former volunteer fireman and student of science and math, he appreciates that while working with his hands keeps him grounded, he is now drawn to other forms of expression.

A Sunset

I NEVER REALIZED I HAD SO MANY TEETH until I saw a bunch of them scattered on the floor mat in front of my face. They were spread like some kind of dessert, like little marshmallows in a salty strawberry syrup, and I could feel numbly with my tongue that there were still more in my mouth. The motor was still running, but it was running loud and jagged, and I could smell fumes of hot oil down by the pedals. It was a cammed-up rig anyway, so it never did idle smooth, but now it was surging and clanging and making all kinds of strange noises. I figured the banging sound must be the fan whacking away at the radiator, since I could smell antifreeze in the oil smoke. That engine was going to be history pretty soon. I knew that if Bill was still in the truck he'd have shut it down by now 'cause he could've never stood to listen to it run that way. But from the way the light was angling through the smoke and dust down near the floorboard, I suspected his door was open or maybe even gone. Maybe he was on the outside already.

The desert can turn cold even on a summer afternoon, and the wind blew a chill draft down the back of the young man's T-shirt. There was nothing he could do about it. One arm was trapped against the seat edge and his stomach so that his hand hung down by his face. The other arm was bent up behind his back in a peculiar manner and was pinned hard by the the steering wheel. He tried to flick an empty beer can that had rolled down by his hand, but his arm was asleep; the fingers wouldn't move. So he just had to wait there and let the wind blow down his back, look at the teeth, and listen to the engine slowly seizing up.

The young man now hoped the state trooper they'd tried to outrun would catch up pretty soon. "You know," he thought to himself, "I've never been treated badly by one of those guys." But Bill knew he couldn't take another hit on his driving record. When the brake lights on the black-and-white cruiser told them they'd shot past the trooper too fast, they turned off the highway and made their run down a dirt road that cut through the desert. "Bill's a damn good driver, even when he's drunk." But this time they weren't drunk. "Jesus, we were barely buzzed." Still, another speeding ticket would be a fast three points on Bill's record and that'd be all she wrote: good-bye, license. So the boys ran for it. The young man spoke quietly from the mangled truck, "Three points, my ass. Now there's really hell to pay." Just the same, he was ready for the trooper to show up. "Piss on Bill's license. Somebody just get me out of here."

It was getting dark when he came around again. It wasn't evening yet, but it was dark enough that he watched flashes of red and blue and white illuminate the hand that still didn't move. The teeth now looked like little colored cotton balls, and his tongue was too swollen to move. He knew it hadn't gotten any warmer, but his back wasn't cold anymore. The motor was quiet. He could hear voices, young voices, but urgent, direct. Someone got their head down by his ear and told him they were going to pull the steering wheel out of the way to give him some breathing room. He heard a chain wrapped around the steering column. “Go ahead!” someone yelled, and a machine that sounded like a chain saw fired to life. He felt the heavy pressure easing against his back. A shallow uneven breath brought the bright but painful smell of sage. Then someone was back at his ear again telling him they were going to cut the steering wheel off. Rubbery hands covered his ears. This time when the machine fired up the noise was deafening and its exhaust blew hot across his back. He gagged on the oily two-cycle fumes that flooded the cab, and the ragged coughs shot razor pains through his chest and back. There were three muffled pops, then he heard the wheel bang into the bed of the truck. Hands still held his head and a voice called to someone else, “C-collar!” Another pair of hands in milky rubber gloves formed a stiff plastic thing around his neck. The voice from the man who still held his head, now said to others, “I’ve got traction. On three to the board. One . . . two . . . three!” Other hands slipped under his legs and arms, then lifted and carried him from the floor of the truck out into the cold desert air and down onto a very hard, flat board.

Hands were touching me and straightening my arms and legs. Hands felt up and down my body. Sometimes they pushed or squeezed or probed. Someone held my wrist, and I felt a blood pressure cuff tightening around my arm. When I looked up from the backboard I could see fuzzy sunset colors, but then somehow I realized I could look back and see myself lying there on the board. And I could look down and watch the firefighters carrying straps and pads and plastic toolboxes from their trucks. I thought I heard a young fireman ask me a question, but when I turned to him he looked quickly away. Then he focused his eyes on my forehead and asked again, “What’s your name?” I couldn’t speak. “Do you live near here?” I think I nodded no. “How many fingers am I holding up?” From the backboard I couldn’t focus too good, but from above I could see it was two. I held out two fingers on my hand that wasn’t asleep, but he didn’t see them.

Then they strapped me down to the board and stretched duct tape across my forehead. The lights from the trucks flashed bright colors that shone on my face and reflected from the helmets of the firefighters. The fireman shined a flashlight into one of my eyes, blinding me and pulling me back down to the board, but when he pointed it at my other eye it wasn't nearly so bright. It was just a dim little spot in a shiny chrome circle.

Bill and me was thinkin' the same thing when we came up on that rise. You know the way you spend enough time around someone and after a while you get to know what they're thinkin'? Well, we was thinkin' the same thing. We were bookin'; maybe sixty, sixty-five on that little gravel road, but Bill had it down just fine. And when we were shooting up that rise we could see the road go straight out ahead and then curve away easy to the left. Wrong! Man, really wrong! At the top of the rise that road cut hard left to a culvert, then cut hard right back, then it went straight, and then it curved easy to the left. We were screwed. Bill didn't even try to turn the goddamn steering wheel. I respect him for that. When the rear wheels cleared the road that son of a bitch roared like a dragster. Then I was thinking about last spring when we dropped the half-race cam into that truck. Bill's dad gave him a ton of shit for putting racing gear like that into an old pickup. But every afternoon as soon as he'd get home from work he'd get right out there under the hood and give us a hand. We'd never have got it running again if he hadn't helped. I'll tell you right now, Bill was thinking about his old man when that engine lit up. But he didn't get too much time to think about it.

You know how on TV you see those cars go sailing through the air with their noses up, almost flying . . . ? Well, don't believe it. The front of that truck was pointing almost straight down when we hit the bottom of the gully. And it didn't land straight, either. The right corner nosed down first. And then we hit. Goddamn it, we really hit. There was glass and lots of noise and dirt and shit flyin' around and then this goddamn branch was whipping me in the face, and then it wasn't. And then my feet were up in the air and my head was down bangin' the floorboard where Bill's feet should've been and then pretty soon I'm down there looking at my teeth.

The firefighter put his flashlight back into his pocket, but he kept after me with those questions. They'd put an oxygen mask over my mouth, so I couldn't have answered him if I'd wanted to. I was getting tired of that action anyway, and I'll bet he was tired of looking at me. Besides, I wanted to see where the truck hit. From where we left the road it must have sailed about fifty feet clear down into the wash, and then after it hit it ploughed up thirty feet of sagebrush before it started to flip. Now you could smell the broken sage and juniper hanging in the evening air. I could see pieces of the shattered windshield reflecting the emergency lights and I spotted Bill's door up in a juniper tree. Down the draw I could make out a wheel. And back over by the truck the fire engines and the ambulance and the cruiser all had their lights going around and around, throwing colors on the people and the desert. From above in the final reds of the darkening sky it was all just beautiful. Then a helicopter came up and circled everything and flooded the whole scene with its landing lights when it lowered past me. It touched down. The firefighters hustled two loaded backboards to the chopper. Then it rose up in a roaring cloud of dirt and sage litter, turned, and ripped away into the night. The red and green navigating lights flashed dimmer and dimmer in the distance.... But I didn't go with the chopper....

I stayed for a while and watched the men load their gear back into the trucks. Then I began drifting slowly westward where the last colors of the day had faded grudgingly into the darkness and a flat cold blue planet showed itself now that the sun was gone. There was one last fire truck stationed back down the road about three hundred yards. The fireman had shut down the lights and now he leaned quietly against the fender. He was looking up at the cold desert sky. He was thinking about his kids.

DOUGLAS UNGER
(1952–)

Doug Unger grew up in the West, living and working on family ranches. While a student at the University of Chicago, he began to report on the student protests during the seventies. This initial experience with journalism led him to pursue a degree at the Iowa Writers' Workshop. His debut novel, *Leaving the Land,* was a finalist for the Pulitzer Prize in 1985 (this excerpt is from the beginning of that novel). At times, the Hogans, the Midwestern turkey farmers at the book's core, seem every bit as desperate as the Joads when they set out to find California, but they are saved by Marge, the daughter who won't let the town of Nowell cage her wild self. His other passion, South America, has kept him busy chronicling the military dictatorship and the disappeared in Argentina. Together with his colleagues at the University of Nevada, Las Vegas, he has started a graduate program in creative writing, specifically with a focus on international students and literature. In 1996, he received the Silver Pen Award from the Nevada Writers Hall of Fame. Like Richard Wiley's work, Unger's fiction is informed by a world beyond our borders, and we are the richer for it.

Voices from Silence: A Novel of Repression and Terror in Argentina. New York: St. Martin's Press, 1995.
The Turkey War. New York: Harper and Row, 1988; reprint, New York: Ballantine, 1991.
El Yanqui. New York: Harper and Row, 1986; reprint, Ballantine, 1988.
Leaving the Land. New York: Harper and Row, 1984; reprint, New York: Ballantine, 1985; reprint, Lincoln: University of Nebraska Press, 1995.

Leaving the Land

(EXCERPT)

THE YEARS IMMEDIATELY FOLLOWING the war were fertile for weeds. There was a kind of plague of them. The white fluff seeds of the Canadian thistle and of the milkweed and dogbane filled the air like an invasion of tiny white parachutes. Hot winds swirled them through the streets so thickly that Marge gave up trying to pick them off her dress. She walked down the main street of Nowell, collecting seeds.

She hated this town. She hated the way the sun blinded her, glaring off the white adobe storefronts. She passed the high square wooden false front of the Baker Hotel and gazed up at five dark windows, one with an old white head leaning on the sill next to a box of withering geraniums. Clumps of cheatgrass made a shambles of the sidewalk as they broke through the concrete and spilled in wild tufts toward the curb. Weeds scratched at her ankles as she walked. Sharp seeds prickled under the collar of her dress. She would have to comb them out of her hair like wedding rice.

White, she thought, *white . . .*

Marge had trouble with her high heels as she stepped off the curbs, crossing unpaved side streets more like ruts with manes of weeds. Houses along those streets were mostly white, save the few that were left an unpainted gray, with rusted tin where they ought to have shingles. If she watched for them, she might see a yellow house with black shutters, a small brown house with white shutters. She hated the thought of houses. She passed the double doors of the municipal bar with its black-on-white sign that read NOWELL hung over the wide frames of screen. She glanced in at the men shooting pool. Somebody hooted. She had no way to tell if that sound was meant for her, but whenever there was hooting she liked to believe it was meant for her. She moved her body in a certain way when she heard it, not even sure there was someone watching her in the street.

Marge didn't believe in love. She hadn't believed in love since Thursday. That was the day she decided to accept Burt Cooney's proposal for marriage. Now it was Monday. She was on her way to his mother's house to fit her wedding dress. She walked, alone in thought that love was over before it had ever been. She used to think love was a feeling of romance. Both romance and what she had been taught to believe of love—that all love was somehow the same as a spirit in her hands as she worked, as she curried the sides of a show heifer and shaved the face just right, even when she was sure she couldn't do anything right; or in her hands as they toughened with other chores, getting the bum lambs through the last suckling weeks, working in the dust and swelter of the fields, cooking her family's breakfast when her mother was ailing. Years ago, she believed all love was the same as the love in the rhythm of her mother's sewing machine long into the nights, as in the early morning sound of her father's boot steps amid the high, sirenlike whining of the cream separator. Years later, alone in the darkness, she discovered other meanings.

Burt Cooney was a just a boy. All she had ever known were boys. He was like the boy she had gone to the movies with and didn't go with anymore because once he brought a jar of pig's knuckles along and offered one to her as if it were popcorn. He was like a boy at a party once who sat on the log next to her. He slugged down whiskey out of a pint bottle. He stared down for a long time as if at the stitching of his cowboy boots. Then mumbling into the firelight, he tried taking her hand, afraid to look her in the eye. And when she so much as squeezed his hand back, he asked her to marry him. He was like the boy she used to cruise with from the blacktop junction and back to the Dairy Freeze at least once a day, parking somewhere so he could cup her breasts, suck her neck, ply her clumsily with his fingers. She might have gone all the way with him if he hadn't told the whole damn town it had already happened. He talked the way boys did of how many beers he'd had that day or he offered to drive on out to the butte for a sloe gin screw under the northern lights. Or he told her for the umpteenth time how he'd shot the front tire of his truck out from under him huntin' jacks or how next month's winner-take-all jackpot rodeo was gonna be another story, and on and on he went until she thought she was fit to die of boredom. There was nothing better to do than give in to him, but only up to a certain point. She draped her arms over his shoulders and kissed him. Her nostrils filled with the acrid odors of sweat and shaving lotion. Her lips recoiled at the bitter tastes of beer, smoking, cheap whiskey. She carefully raised an elbow to protect her breasts. She rested her head against his neck, wiping her lips on his shirt in the process. She felt a film of hair oil on her face and hands.

"Shit," Burt Cooney complained. "We been at this three months now, three damn months now, honey! What in hell's wrong with you?"

She gave in and kissed him again. They fought each other on the musty car seats. As much as she wished it were different, her mind was always somewhere else.

She usually had him drive her home as early as possible. Then she lay awake in her bedroom, trying to imagine her lover as almost anyone else. She imagined him with her in that small, orderly bedroom. Then he led her out to some weedless pasture all high brome and crested wheat grass, and like in the movies, he spread his coat in that deep rug of grass. She heard the high-pitched drone of the insects in waves of sound. There was a sudden, high chattering as a covey of mourning doves exploded up out of the pasture. They lay down on his coat. He played a kind of game in which he knelt over her and spread the long grass around her face, weaving it over her cheeks and over her eyes. She tasted it. She ate a little grass. He gripped her hands with a strength almost painful. He kissed her and it was different, as if the sun shone with a summer's wholeness in sunflower gold. She raised one bare knee, imagined he set his chin there on it and eyed her deeply. Then the image dissolved, a palmful of chaff scattered in the winds.

Sometimes he was comforting. Nights when the yapping chorus of the coyotes kept on because there was no answering call. She had heard that sound all her life. But she found herself turning on the lamp to search her room, turning it off again to settle into her bedsheets, then a howl might burst out closer, just beyond the yard fence, the family dogs in a sudden uproar, and she'd reach for the lamp again. Sitting up, she'd try to imagine her lover there so she could hide her face in the muscles of his chest. She wanted anyone's voice in that room, in that old clapboard house where her father and mother slept, scratching themselves, tossing in their sleep. Sometimes, it was enough to close her eyes and think he was with her, warm and holding her close into sleep, his voice a comfort to her until he had gone. Other times, nothing helped. She lost all vision of what it was she really wanted. She lay awake and dreamless, filled with the unhappy sense that she would always be alone.

Mornings after a night out were always the same. She faced her parents.

"You been out some," said her father. He was at the breakfast table, scooping eggs into his mouth with a spoon. "You got home awful early." He glowered up at her. "You won't get nobody, you come home so early."

"There's nobody to get," she said. She picked the biscuit plate up off the table.

"You go on and say that now. You just go on and keep telling me that!"

"There's no more than that to tell," she said.

"I don't like you 'round here like you are."

"Then I'll move on into town."

"Now that ain't what I mean," he said.

"You won't have nobody to cook your breakfast!" she snapped. She watched her father nod his head back toward his plate, using a knife to chase a fried potato through the grease. She shrugged. She went into the living room to fetch her mother's plate. Her mother held the plate stiffly in her hands. Her head was laid on the chair back, eyes wide to the ceiling as if it might fall with the pressure of the next rain.

"You can't get a thing done here without me," Marge told him. "Who's going to help you herd them turkeys out of the rain?"

"I expect that won't make no difference soon," he said.

"Well, it sure as hell better," she said. "When I'm done sticking you in the grave, I want to have something."

"Shiiiiit . . ." Ben Hogan said, and laughed.

"I mean it," she said.

"But that's what I been telling you all along for, dammit!" he shouted.

"Well, then why don't *you* try riding around with him?" she shouted back. "Go on now! You just try an evening with Burt Cooney! Go on! That boy doesn't know scours from hoofrot! He'll tell you about the way he rides, sure he will. He couldn't stay on a corral fence! He doesn't know a solenoid from a voltage regulator! There just isn't nobody . . ."

Ben Hogan coughed and laughed at the same time. "That's what your own ma kept telling her folks about me," he said. "And all the while, we was spending nights in her daddy's harness shop. He's all right, that Burt Cooney. He just needs feeding up some. He'll show right. Now you might have to teach him how, but he'll take to it. Besides, I think I'm getting me a bit of the emphysema . . ."

"You hush up," she said. "We'll do just fine on our own."

"*Marge.*" Her mother's cracked voice came from the living room. "Marge, you got the Gel-u-siiil? . . ."

Ben Hogan sighed and rose from the table. He hooked the straps of his overalls up and over his shoulders, then stretched and yawned. He caught his daughter by the arm on her way with the medicine.

"You be out in a minute and help with them turkeys," he said in his gentlest voice, playfully slapping her behind.

When the boys started coming home, Marge tried her best to get married. She put on her new clothes. She drove her father's pickup to the municipal bar. She perched on a stool, her legs held in perfect S-curves sheathed in seductive nylon, her elbow gracefully leaning next to her drink. She did her hair like the movie star Veronica Lake so that it covered one eye, swept over the point of her cheek and spilled smoothly over her bared shoulders. Silver and turquoise dangled from her ears. She drew her lips in deep red and powdered her face. She flared her nostrils. She exuded clouds of L'Origan and Lilac Mist and dragon trails of smoke. She left the top of her dress unhooked to suggest encounter. She fluttered her eyes. One night, she even pretended there was hayseed in one of her eyes so Ron Ballock could lean in close, probing with a corner of his oil-stained handkerchief and listing drunkenly on his heels.

"There now," he said. "That's got it, I betcha." He patted her on the head like a dog. Then he hobbled back to his game of pool, feeling his war wounds.

Marge tried learning to shoot pool, rolling the soft melons of her behind with each ridiculous shot, peering down the length of her cue at the impossible angles.

"You go on and leave the table to the boys," Ron Ballock grumbled. "Either that, or put up your five bucks just like everybody else."

Marge lost twenty dollars that way.

Burt Cooney started coming in nights, covered with diesel, the grasshoppers crawling in his pockets. He sat up at the barstool next to Marge. He bought her beers and sloe gin cocktails. He swaggered around the pool table, spitting tobacco and teaching her how. Marge won back her twenty dollars. Burt Cooney invited her to the dance in Whitewood.

She went with him. It was a forty-mile drive, south into the tree-covered hills. They passed a pint bottle. He belched at the wheel. He pounded his hand on the dash in rhythm to the crackling of the radio. He threw his chest out proudly under the pink flowers of his western shirt. Before they left the car to join the folks packed into the main street of that town, wildly kicking their heels to the music of fiddles and Hawaiian guitars, Burt Cooney arranged each grease-coated strand of hair in the rearview mirror, pushing his thick glasses higher on his nose.

They danced. He waved his hat like they were riding in the rodeo. He did tiny quick steps to either side, gripped her hands, then he swung her dizzily on the axis of his cowboy heels. He pressed in closely for the slower numbers, oblivious of the elbow raised to protect her breasts. That street was too crowded with hooting range boys tossing women in bright clothes and the music was usually too fast to keep up with unless Marge let Burt Cooney drag her in circles or lift her perilously in his tottering arms. He grinned each time he lifted her, as if surprised at himself, then he bore in to try again until he tossed her up just a bit too far and with a high-pitched scream of amazement he fell on top of her, as stiff and heavy as a pine log.

"Marry me," he said, parked under the fireworks of the northern lights on the way home. Marge still held an icepack to her head. "I love you, gal . . ." he moaned.

"I'm not any goddamned *gal,*" she muttered, then lit a cigarette.

She tried another man. He was a huge bear of a man named Clemmie Bosserd. He worked for the Homestake Gold Mine in the town of Deadwood, fifty miles south, but he had grown up on Marge Hogan's mail route out of Nowell. He stopped for Marge one day to help her change a tire. He invited her up to the historic mining town in the picturesque holy hills of the Sioux for drinks and dinner, for an evening spent reaching a compromise while holding hands and exchanging personal histories. His eyes were the color of blue steel. They looked her over through the dim amber candlelight of the restaurant as if she were a piece of fruit.

He told her his war story. She laughed at how he had been standing in the noncom club when it was bombed. He dove under a table. The sergeant cowering with him had a Scotch in his hand and there was a full bottle of it on the table above their heads. He was ordered to rescue the bottle. He reached up to grab for it just as a bomb sent a shower of fragments through the canvas walls. He wondered how he would ever explain to his kids that he had received the Purple Heart while reaching for a Scotch.

She pressed him at the mention of children. He said he wanted at least ten, though he couldn't afford them. She sympathized with his hard life in the mines, his days spent using a steel bar to pry loose rock down from the shaft ceilings. She told him about her father's farm, his predicament, the deaths of her brothers. Clemmie listened quietly for a long time.

"There just doesn't seem to be a man worth the bother," she said.

"You come home with me now," Clemmie said, "and I'll show you who to bother with."

She rose immediately to go to the "gals'" room. She was in there long enough to smoke four cigarettes, and by the time she was back at the table, her fingers working nervously at the clasp of her purse, she had made her decision.

"Let's go now," she whispered hoarsely.

There was a long walk half up a mountain through that old western town with its brightly painted buildings, each with an old hitching post anchored to the sidewalk in front of a brass plaque to explain which gunfighter had bit the dust in that very location. Clemmie Bosserd pulled her along as she tried to stop and read each memorial. He drew a finger like a gun and playfully pushed the barrel against her back.

His small cabin smelled of the sour union suits hanging on the door. It was lit by a glass lantern filled with green oil, swinging slowly from a beam near the old blackened coal stove where bacon rinds and potato skins sat molding in a skillet. Marge stumbled over the rough, unpainted floorboards, looking for a place to hang her hat and purse. Clemmie began to shed his clothes quickly, with his back to her, tossing them in a pile on the floor, then he turned, raising his eyebrows like some comedian in the movies, as if surprised she hadn't undressed the same way. Her fingers went cold on her neck as they worked at the hook of her dress.

"That's it now," he said. "You ain't scared. You're the gamest woman in these hills, that's a fact. And one of the prettiest I ever seen. Don't think old Clemmie here don't know. You're the kind of woman that jumps on a man like a dog jumps on a bone." He laughed. He sat down on his narrow cot like some four-limbed fish, dangling his hands between his knees. She turned her back to him. She spent an interminable minute picking at the elastic of her garters with hesitant thumbs.

"Come on over here now," he said. He stretched his arms out. She froze. Then she thought what the hell. She looked over her shoulder at him perversely. She peeled off her underwear and spread her smooth legs up over his knees and folded herself into his arms. He wrestled her to her back, throwing her giddily over his mountainous body. She was breathless under his weight. She felt him try for her immediately, probing and missing at least twice before he grumbled, "What in the hell can't you gimme some *help* now, baby?"

She felt a warm trickling in the creases of her thighs.

"I never been with a man," she said, and felt him stiffen. With sudden revulsion, she tried to push him away. "What in hell do you think I am?"

"Shiiiiiit," he groaned, a sound she felt as much as heard by a violent movement in his guts. He vise-gripped her arms. "Shiiii-iiit," he said again. He turned her body like a shock of straw. He pressed his weight so hard against her she couldn't move.

"Let me go!" she screamed. She squirmed, used her nails, kicked her feet at him wildly. One of her feet landed home. He responded with a blow into her side. She saw the next blow coming at her head and her body went suddenly limp in a dense, ringing whiteness. . . .

Arms about her breasts, Marge weaved like a spinster's shadow through her room. She began to give up hope for any love but the love in dreams. Her parents rocking in the living room wouldn't say it, as though they thought it was a kindness not to, as though their silence wouldn't do the same. She slept each night curving her spine a little more, curling her body into its own warmth. Sometimes, she wept. Other times, she beat her pillow, crying *Damn, damn,* and still she didn't say it even to herself, that, loveless, nothing could make her beautiful again.

"Marry me!" shouted Burt Cooney in front of the municipal bar. He followed her down the sidewalk on his knees. Sick from drinking, she was searching for some bushes, anyplace, to relieve herself discreetly.

"Noooooo," she croaked, staggering down the walk.

She decided to give herself at least a year before she married him. Exactly one year from that hopeless night. She circled the date on her calendar. It was a Thursday in the hot month of August.

MARGE DIDN'T BELIEVE IN LOVE. She hadn't believed in love since Thursday. She continued down the main street of Nowell, collecting seeds. It was useless to pick them off her dress, her blue flowered dress sewn from five-and-dime material. Hot winds swirled the tiny white parachutes by the thousands through the streets. She would have to comb them out like wedding rice.

She walked past The Cove Café with its door fan blowing hotly at her legs. She walked past Foos's garage, past the voices of men with wrenches and the clanging of machinery. Buster Hill stood huge in the parking lot. He tipped his straw hat. She tried walking past him like he wasn't there. She tried walking through the whole town as if it wasn't there. Burt Cooney's mother waited in her white house at the end of town. As she drew closer to the house, she knew more and more inside that she could never marry him. And there was nobody else.

She slowed her pace. She stopped and spent a long time adjusting the straps of her shoes. Breathing was hard. Thick air pushed her diaphragm slowly and forcefully inward. She felt faint as she stared off into the hot white grain of the shimmering sidewalk. Grasshoppers hummed. She was stopped there, sweating, unable to move.

Suddenly, she heard the distant throbbing sound of machinery. Her hand moved to straighten her dress, then fluttered nervously at her hair. She started toward the Cooney house again. The Cooney house was just down from the Dairy Freeze. She saw the drive-in had half a dozen cars parked around it. She felt she was being watched from them.

The Cooney house was just across the street in the shadows of its elm. Marge stepped off the curb and felt one of her heels slip in the gravel. She bent over to fix her shoe again, then stopped. She looked around in the middle of the street. There was a loud noise coming from somewhere. Horns were honking from over the rise of the highway that skirted town just past the Cooney house, big diesel truck horns. Everyone at the Dairy Freeze heard it. The high school kids were leaving their cars to stand out closer to the highway, sipping their milk shakes and jabbing at each other, asking, *What's that? What is that sound?* Her eyes found the roll of prairie over which the blacktop disappeared and from which the sound of horns and clattering steel rose to a deafening pitch. The lead bulldozer, pulled along on its trailer, a gleaming yellow in the afternoon sun, rolled up over the hill. Then one by one, a convoy slowly appeared—three bulldozers, several trucks larger than she had ever seen and loaded with bulk under gray canvas, a long road grader, three tank trucks marked with flammable-liquid warnings, two trailer houses as wide as both lanes of the road, then several smaller trucks loaded with tools and materials of construction followed by a tractor trailer pulling the two halves of a high steel tower decked with red flags. And in the middle of it all, looking as if he couldn't possibly belong there, thick brown scarves of dust rising up around and nearly covering him, a man in a black convertible wove in and out of that line of machinery in search of some way to pass on down the hill, but the trucks weren't leaving him any room.

Marge watched that man from a distance. His image wavered in the heat. She could see him shout something to one of the truck drivers ahead of him. He leaned on his horn. He wove out again wildly, trying to pass, and the truck moved over to block his way. He gave up and pulled back into line. Dust shrouded him. A pair of sunglasses covered his eyes with glaring reflections. She could just make out a sports jacket thrown over the seatback next to him, and the way he used its sleeve to wipe the sweat and dust from his face. He turned his head stiffly. He stretched his neck as if it pained. He drew close enough so that she could see his hands beating a tattoo on the wheel in impatience, his mouth set grimly, one hand raking through his gray hair, his features badly sunburned and looking worn by an early middle age.

The lead bulldozer was pulled off the highway onto the main street of town, followed by the convoy. She was surprised to see that small black convertible make the turn with it onto Main. The car slowly approached the Dairy Freeze. She watched the man in it turn his head and consider the small crowd gathered there. She was close enough to notice the gray shadow of his beard, the rings on his hands, his crumpled necktie draped over the rearview mirror. She felt his eyes pass first over her and for an instant, through his sunglasses, she caught his eyes with her own. She looked back at him weakly as he grinned, then he faced the crowd of high schoolers in the parking lot behind her, raising one hand to wave at them energetically and with a politician's smile.

The horns trumpeted and the engines boomed. Huge tires

dug furrows in the gravel streets. It looked like a circus parade of caged machines. As the convoy moved down Main, the drivers shouted, waving their arms out the truck windows. The sidewalks filled with people. Knots of children ran out of the houses and down the street. A group of farmers shuffled out of The Cove, even Mrs. Nilsen out there with them, wiping her hands on a flowered apron. Then closer up the street, Larry Foos and his mechanics stood, apelike, and watched, tools in their hands. Sheriff Meeker, farther down, staggered through the double doors of the municipal bar. Jim Fuller stood wiping shaving cream off onto his jeans. An old man with a pool cue climbed up on a bench and shaded his eyes.

Marge stood on her toes to catch sight of that man again. His car pulled up in front of the Baker Hotel. He climbed out of it and stretched his legs a minute, walking stiffly in a small, casual circle, then he moved around to the trunk for his luggage. The convoy passed on its way to the turkey yards at the end of Main, everyone out there gaping at all the new Nowell-Safebuy plant machinery. Nobody was there to greet him. Nobody waved or shouted at him. It seemed as if no one knew this man.

She looked around her then, amazed. She found that she had followed the trucks down Main Street almost one full block. She stood there, sweating. Her head ached. The damp straps of her brassiere dug into her skin. She started for the Cooney house. She stopped. It was early yet. There was bound to be some uncommon action at the municipal bar. She told herself that she had the time at least for one drink, just one drink before Mrs. Cooney's fitting. Around her eyes, internal tremors suddenly inflamed her eyelids. She felt the tears about to burst over her cheeks.

Somebody hooted. She turned on down the street and saw an arm waving at her from a truck window. She swore at it under her breath. She caught her heel in the gravel again and stumbled. She threw off her shoes. In bare feet, she elbowed through the mechanics in front of Foos's garage. She pushed her way through them and came up against the crowd in front of the municipal saloon.

Mose Johnson, just retired from the Nowell-Safebuy, stood at the center of the crowd. He tottered drunkenly. He opened and closed his fists like he was ready for a bar fight. He waved a fist at that caravan of machines, pointing them out for the turkey farmers gathered around him, grumbling something that she couldn't hear. Across the street, the man in the car was setting his bags in front of the Baker Hotel for Hiram Baker to carry up the stairs. Hiram said something, and the man looked toward the crowd in front of the saloon.

The commotion gathered force. Marge pressed in to listen. Whatever Mose Johnson was telling them, something about a speedup at the plant and the loss of jobs, the others reacted with laughter, cussing, an uproar of disbelief. Then Will Hartley, as if convinced enough to humor him, reached an arm out to steady Mose and guide him back through the door. "Why I'll be damned, Mose," he said. "Why I'll be damned."

MONIQUE LAXALT
(1953–   )

Reno native Monique Laxalt studied English at Stanford and later took a law degree in Iowa before returning to northern Nevada to raise her family, write, and practice law. When *The Deep Blue Memory* was published, it took many people by surprise: it was quietly eloquent, poetic, and like the memories from which it was woven, rich in texture and intent. To her credit, it was more than a first book, written in the shadow of her father, Robert Laxalt. It was her voice, set clean against the page, not the imitative voice of a young novelist but that of a seasoned writer. This is the opening chapter of the book, in which the narrator vividly recalls growing up in a Basque family. Today Laxalt lives in Reno and is working on several new fiction projects.

The Deep Blue Memory. Reno: University of Nevada Press, 1993.

The Deep Blue Memory
(EXCERPT)

The Family Table

I

UNDER GRANDMA'S DINING ROOM TABLE it was dark and warm like the earth. The legs of the table were deep brown and thick. They were woven among one another, like the limbs of a jungle, leading everywhere and nowhere, within a circle. We played in them silently, timelessly.

The top of the table Grandma would have covered with a round tablecloth of white lace. She would set white, gold-rimmed cups and saucers around the circle, the cream and sugar in the center.

They would be seated around the table, drinking coffee and smoking cigarettes. The men wore khaki pants and wing tips, the women slim-fitting dresses and stockings and sleek shoes. They spoke intensely, in voices that rang with certainty and success. They were young, younger than we are now, and adult, more adult that we are now.

In the corner by the window, Grandma would sit and watch the afternoon Nevada snow fall quietly outside.

In the other corner, next to the blazing window of the stove,

Grandpa would sit upright, straddling the oak straight-backed chair turned backward.

Grandma would bring fresh coffee from the kitchen, and Grandpa would stand and add wood to the stove. The windows would steam up, and the room would fill with the smell of the coffee and the thick white cream, the smoke of the cigarettes, the warmth of the blazing stove.

In the dark of the underneath, the thick, interwoven legs of the table connected them. We could hear the pure, clear, crystalline ring of their voices. It sheltered, encircled the darkness, like a sphere.

2

IN THOSE DAYS, Grandma was strong and sturdy, imposing. On Saturday, when they had left us for the weekend, she would be up early. We would awake to the smell of steaming chocolate, and bear claws warmed on the woodstove in the kitchen, lit hours before.

While we ate, Grandma would disappear into her bedroom. She would reappear in her elbow-sleeved dress made of black wool, looming above us, her hair braided neatly across the top of her head, wearing stockings and thick-heeled black shoes.

After we dressed, we would leave through the dark entryway at the front of the U-shaped house. We would listen in vain for sounds of the small Indian family who rented the other side of the U living silently in what was called the "apartment."

We would emerge from the screened front porch of the old white frame house and would walk the chilled back-street sidewalks of Carson City. Grandma would wear her black purse over the forearm of her left coat sleeve, her chin high and her face turned forward, and we would proceed at a march to Main Street, then left one block to Gilbert's Drug.

Once arrived, Grandma would browse in the birthday card section and visit formally with the proprietor or his wife while we scanned the toy section, made our selection, and brought it to her. We would choose such morbid things as a rubber tarantula on a string, and once home we would choose the moment to dangle it in front of her. She would start with fright, then scowl furiously. Then she would smile in her twinkling, mischievous way as we paraded the spider, on its string, through the house in search of Grandpa.

In the afternoon she would sit by the corner window, working her crochet needles quickly and mechanically, producing more and more of the round lace doilies that ornamented the house. We would play in the back porch area outside the kitchen, the small area between the two wings of the house that trapped the afternoon sun. We crept slowly, silently in the direction of the woodpile, in ever futile attempts to seize one of the wild kittens that lived there. Grandma would bring warm milk in bowls, and we would crouch inside the kitchen door, waiting, as the kittens ever so tenuously appeared, and approached, and began to drink. Then we would emerge in a burst of glee, and in a split second the kittens would vanish. We knew they were in the woodpile, and were watching.

In the evening, after dinner, Grandma would dress for bed at the same time as we. She would emerge from her bedroom in her long robe, her braids taken down, draped behind her shoulders, down to her waist. We would stand by her chair in the window corner where the shade was pulled down now, and we would brush out her hair from the braids. It spread in silver, crimped waves down the front of her robe, more beautiful than anything we knew.

In the later evening, we would crawl into the double bed in the large far-back bedroom, and would shiver under the covers. Grandpa would come with wood, and he would light a fire in the small alabaster fireplace not far from the foot of our bed. Lying there, in the glow of the fire, we could hear the distant, quiet, enchanted sound of the old language that we did not understand and that was a part of this house. Later, over the quiet sound of the fire, we could hear Grandpa rattling in his attic bedroom above us, and the floorboards in Grandma's room next to us creak as she got into bed. At some moment, in the still, pure air of the bedroom and amidst the glow of the fire, we would cross over into sleep.

We would awake to Sunday morning sunlight, the alabaster fireplace cold, the smell of hot rum permeating the house. Grandma would seat us at the dining room table, at the white lace tablecloth. She would bring rolled pancakes soaked in a blend of maple syrup and rum. They had a taste that, like the distant sound of the old language, went only with this house. We ate them voraciously, gluttonously, searching for the sweet taste of the syrup.

Grandma would help us wash and dress in the bathroom, and send us to the dining room to wait. She would appear in her black wool dress, a black wool scarf tied around her head. She would hand a rosary to each of us.

We would walk the back streets to Saint Theresa's Catholic Church. We would ascend the steps, and once inside we would reach up, into the marble basin that held the holy water, and cross ourselves. We would proceed in Grandma's wake, taking a pew toward the front of the church, and kneeling, and crossing ourselves and taking the rosary beads from our pockets. In the quiet before mass began, we would bow our heads like Grandma, fingering the rosary beads and mimicking the silent movement of her lips. At some point we would break into muffled, uncontrollable laughter, and she would throw a black scowl that went through us.

She would proceed, whispering, with the infinite succession

of rosaries that stretched right on through the mass. Grandpa would arrive late, and would stand at the back, even when the church was half empty. He would vanish just after communion, and afterward we would find him waiting outside, on the sidewalk, outside the little wrought-iron fence that bordered the churchyard.

We would walk the back streets home, some up front with Grandpa, some at Grandma's side. It was like this time and time again.

3

ON CHRISTMAS DAY, the house would be transformed. The families would begin arriving in midafternoon, carrying packages. We would come through the gate in the front hedge, rattling the little wooden address sign that hung on its front. We would come through the screen door and cross the old front porch. We would turn the brass knob on the heavy wooden door at the entrance and flood into the dark, musty entryway. We would take an automatic sharp turn to the left, away from the wing where the Indians lived. We would proceed through an open door, and then make a sharp right into the long stretch of living room used only on this day. We would deposit the packages under the little Christmas tree that sat on a table in a bay window and proceed on past the couches and the oak rockers, past the old black baby grand whose top was a mass of family photographs. We would head through the white double doors that were opened up wide, into the noise of the dining room where family was everywhere. Grandma and Grandpa somewhere in the heat of the kitchen, aunts and uncles bustling from kitchen to dining room with martinis in hand, nineteen cousins crawling, toddling, darting every which way underfoot.

Later they would pull out a long folding table, setting its end against the old round dining room table, stretching it through the open double doors and down the length of the living room. Grandma would cover the entire length of the table with white tablecloths and would set the endless number of places. People would take seats all along the table, and Grandma would appear with steaming oval platters bearing the Christmas dinner. They poured red wine for all of us.

From where we sat along the stretch of table, we looked across to the photographs that covered the top of the baby grand. We ignored our own photographs, which were in color and were too recent, too familiar to have significance. We studied a brown-and-white print of a family of seven: the figure of the young, slender, delicately featured woman whose dark hair was braided neatly across the top of her head, the sculpted, dark-haired figure of the man seated next to her, the young children in obsolete clothes, all with the same round, deep brown eyes as the infant.

While we ate, Grandma would appear with ever more of the steaming platters. Grandpa would remain invisible, somewhere in the far corner of the kitchen, washing pots and pans.

Later, when the fresh coffee had been served up and the cigarettes lit, we would sneak safety pins from the middle drawer of a Mission-style dresser in the dining room. We would creep quietly into the large dark, far-back bedroom, and fully clothed, we would climb into the double bed. In the dark, we would pin our clothes to the sheets and then to each other's clothes. We would giggle quietly, ecstatically, with the thought that they would be unable to extricate us from the bed, that they would be forced to leave us there, together, until morning.

We would sleep amidst the distant ring of the voices, the distant clatter of more coffee being served up, unable to hear whether Grandpa had yet gone to his attic room above us.

4

THE FAMILY IN THE BROWN-AND-WHITE PRINT, the mother and the father and the five children with the round brown eyes, they were the immigrant story.

The father, of chiseled face and dark hair as thick as a horse's mane, and the mother, of delicate face and delicate body, of the dark braids wrapped about the head, they came from the green hills of the Basque Country of southern France, long before our own existences. They had come separately, fifteen years apart, crossing the Atlantic by ship and then the United States by train, he as a young sheepherder headed for the desert hills of the American West, she as a young woman hired to cook for a sheep ranch in western Nevada.

By the time they met, he had built his way up in a manner that could be done only in America, from lone herder to owner of a small band of sheep, to co-owner of a network of ranches that spanned eastern California and western Nevada. They married at Saint Thomas Aquinas Catholic Church in Reno, and a year later their first child, a boy, was born in a mansion on Reno's Court Street, high above the Truckee River. The mother would dress the infant in lace, and tuck him into a carriage fit for a king, and stroll on quiet afternoons through the parks that rimmed the river.

But then in the midst of the boy's first year the sheep market had plunged, and they lost everything to the banks. A second child arrived a year after the first, a boy also, born in a sheep camp outside of Alturas, California, in the desert hills where the father had found work as a herder. They lived in shacks and tents throughout eastern California and western Nevada, in country that was as harsh, as barren, as any you would want to know.

But when the boys were one and two, the mother herself seized on what it meant to be in America. She wrote home to the old farmhouse in the green hills, asking for the one hundred dollars that had been kept there for her, and two months later the money arrived. She took it and moved herself and the two baby boys into Carson City. She took a lease on a boardinghouse on Main Street, just across from the capitol grounds. She hired a girl to tend to the boys, and for eighteen hours a day she cooked and served and cleared and washed. The father would appear at intervals, tending bar until he became sick with cabin fever, then disappearing back into the hills.

Over the next eight years she bore three more children, all boys, standing over steaming kettles and dishpans until the moment the labor pains came, delivering the babies in the family quarters of the boardinghouse.

It was when the older boys were five and six that she made the decision to speak only English to them, and within a year they had lost all comprehension of the old Basque that their mother and father still spoke quietly to one another. She purchased the *Encyclopaedia Britannica* soon after the eldest started school, and then the works of Victor Hugo, translated. She sent the boys to roam in the room where Nevada's senators and judges drank and talked business over hot meals. In the end, all that the children had lost of the old Basque was made up for twice over in their command of the English language, because they knew the English of the books, and the English of the senators and judges, and the broken, accented English of their mother that had expressions no English-speaking person had ever uttered.

She raised them Catholic, in the church that was the link between this country and the green hills from which she came. Rain or snow or sun, at a quarter to seven on Sundays and on each of the forty days of Lent, she could be seen parading the brood of five out the back door of the boardinghouse, along the back streets of Carson City, headed for mass. One after the other, the boys served their stints as altar boys and never lost their ability to recite the Latin liturgy.

When the older boys were twelve and thirteen, she took all that she had in savings and bought the U-shaped house, which came with a full inventory of Mission furniture, and bedding, and china and silver. She moved the five children into the first real home she had had since the mansion on Reno's Court Street, even if it meant that she would rise earlier, walking the back streets to the boardinghouse in pitch dark.

The father would come in work shirt and Levi's and laced walking boots, bearing the scent of the Nevada hills. He would sleep in the attic room at the top of the steep, narrow stretch of stairs that led up from the back porch. He would stay for two days, three at the most, then load his Ford pickup and disappear back into the hills.

As the mother's body lost its delicateness, as the father's face grew more and more weathered by sun and snow, the children shone with all that the father and the mother had hoped to find in this country, all that was strong and young and unrestrained by a hundred generations of sameness. They flourished in school, in sports, in popularity, increasingly with each progression from grade school toward high school. And then onward, the boys one by one heading for a Jesuit university in California, the income from the boardinghouse making its way unfailingly to the school's office for tuition and fees. The children learned things, saw things, knew things that went light-years beyond what their parents had any hope of knowing.

This, from the green hills to the university degrees, we grew up knowing like a catechism, never formally instructed, but acquired in bits and pieces that we seized on and held in our minds with solemnity. We knew too that at the heart of the story was the dining room table, the table that was round and made of dark wood and lace-covered, the table where early on the children of immigrants had formed a circle that protected them, that strengthened them, that over time had become a place of privilege, where only family was allowed.

5

In our own house in Reno, in our family of five, it was a world apart from the U-shaped house in Carson, yet somehow connected with it.

For the three of us children, our earliest memory was of the sound of the typewriter, because it was there always, in the early-morning hours as we woke, in the late night as we slept, in the background as we played. It had its own rhythm: a steady, continuous rap . . . then a slower rap . . . then a stalling, uneven rap . . . then silence . . . then an endless silence . . . then explosion into a flurry of sound . . . then quiet again.

It came from the charcoal black Royal typewriter that sat on our father's desk in a far corner of the house, and it was the same typewriter, and the same distant sound, during all of our growing-up years.

We were six and four and two the day when in midafternoon our mother sat us on the front step of our little subdivision house in Reno, and our father rushed home early from his work at the university, and we drank champagne, there on the front step, the five of us. The words *book contract* and *Harper* and *New York agent* became fused with the warmth of the afternoon and the way time seemed to have come to a halt. We sat there on the cement step, the five of us, in our own impenetrable circle of celebration.

Then one evening our father's brothers came to our house and sat on the couches in our living room and listened as one of them read aloud the chapters that had been written thus far. They listened closely, with expressions of intelligence on their faces. At the end there was a silence, our father even more somber and tense than he had been throughout the reading. Then came the words of approval, and the exhaling, our father's face taking on a glow, a radiance, the room filling with the air of celebration.

When we were a year older, our father handed to each of us that which you could actually hold, a little book that had form and weight, that was deep blue in color, to each our own copy inscribed separately.

Even before we were old enough to read, we knew what the book was about. We knew that it was about our grandfather, about a trip our father had made with him back to the green hills of the old country, after a lifetime in the desolation of the Nevada desert. We knew that it had to do with the beauty of the green hills, but somehow, too, with the strange, rugged beauty of the desert hills and of the man who had grown old in them. We knew that it had to do with our father, too, that it had to do with his own voyage of discovery, of his father, of the gentle beauty of the distant land from which all of us had sprung.

The deep blue book was that which each of us, if ever a fire had struck our house, would have taken first.

6

OUR FATHER, WHO WAS THE SECOND-BORN, was most devoted to his elder brother. We knew this from things that were never said, like the innumerable times that the telephone rang and our father said, "If it's for me I've gone to Tahiti," and then on being informed that the caller was his elder brother, said unhesitatingly, "I'll pick it up in the bedroom." We knew it from the way we would pack up and drive to Carson unfailingly when invited to his elder brother's house, even if it meant that other commitments had to be canceled. We knew it from the way our father would change demeanor when in the company of his brother, his face taking on a look of strength and peace and promise.

People would say that the two of them were so alike yet so different, and this was true. Of all of the five, they had the round, deep brown eyes that were the most indistinguishable one from the other. They had hands that were indistinguishable too, strong hands with defined bones and pronounced knuckles. They had frames that were the same too, just under six feet, square-shouldered and of medium weight, and they sat the same way, one foot to the ground and the other crossed over, square-like. They each had the familial good skin that tanned the color of rawhide in summer.

Yet in ways equally fundamental they were as different as night and day. Our father, named Anthony, was quiet and craved privacy, and it was for this reason that he, of all the brothers, had chosen to live at arm's distance from Carson. In the face of his family's skepticism he had followed a career as a writer. He had married our mother, a fair-haired beauty who had a love for the arts. He had forged himself a position as director of a fledgling press at the University of Nevada in Reno and bought a modest house in a new subdivision on the edge of town. On weekends he took his wife and children shooting in the foothills west of town, and he loved his dog, a male collie with fur the color of autumn. His closest friends were a cowboy artist-professor from Oklahoma who had ridden the bulls in Madison Square Garden, and a fiction writer, nationally known, twenty years his senior. He sang "Clementine," "Home on the Range," and "My Old Kentucky Home" to his children at night. And his family ate dinner by candlelight.

His elder brother, named Luke, was the first to have taken the path to law school. He had married the daughter of a Carson City attorney, and after law school had returned to his hometown. He was a good young lawyer and prospered. To the west of Carson he built a hundred-thousand-dollar home where there were people coming and going at all times of the day: strangers emerging from the guest bedroom at nine in the morning, vaguely familiar faces helping themselves in the kitchen, Indian girls folding laundry and serving up sandwiches, people standing with drinks in hand at the pool table, more people lounging by the swimming pool as the six children arrived home from school. There were parties where the entire grounds were lit up and the children and their cousins ran wild until one in the morning, where our uncle moved through the crowd with a warmth, with a confidence, that seemed to infect people.

Our father said it so many times that we had no memory of the first time, how such and such a person had remarked that our uncle was prime material for "political office." We knew the term long before we had any idea of what it meant, except that we knew it had to do with the difference between our father and his brother.

But for us, it was the sameness that prevailed over the difference, because we felt the same in each of their laps. It was a sense of something that went far back, long before our own existences, somehow connected with the old country, with green hills and dark earth.

7

IF OUR FATHER AND HIS ELDER BROTHER were a paradox of sameness and difference, so too was the third brother, named Mitchell, an enigma of likeness and unlikeness to our grandfather. He had the height of our grandfather, and an identical face, chiseled and strong-jawed. He had the hair of the young father in the brown-and-white print, black, and thick as a horse's mane.

Of the five of them, he was the second to have taken the path to law school, following the steps of the eldest brother but then veering off on an altogether separate path. He lived the life of a bachelor, a life apart from us and of which we knew little, relocating time and time again to new jobs and to apartments no one ever saw. In this too there was something of our grandfather in him, appearing and then disappearing from the U-shaped house.

But in a sense far more fundamental, he was the opposite of our grandfather. And it was this that shone in his face as he appeared at the U-shaped house, the expression that like the others' seemed to change as he crossed through the double doors into the dining room. It was as though he came there for sustenance, to refuel and rekindle. And in this he was as different from our grandfather as night from day.

8

JUST AS OUR FATHER AND HIS OLDER BROTHER bore the scent of the old country, the two youngest of them were infused with the light of the new world.

In the fourth-born, named Mark, it was a lightness of heart that found its place in his smile, the smile that shone from the face of the two year old in the brown-and-white print. The smile that was pure sun. At the Jesuit university he had married a girl of Italian descent, and on returning he had followed a career as a history teacher at Carson City's high school. They had five children, one after the next, who had the sunlit smile and the sweetness of heart from which it came. The bunch of them would come bounding out of their station wagon onto the sidewalk in front of the U-shaped house, carrying ribbon-tied packages from the bakeries of Carson. As they burst into the house it was as if the shades were being opened up room by room, setting the house aglow.

And then Francis, the baby of the five, of the same round brown eyes but of more delicate build, whose mind bore the light of the new world. Since childhood they had said he was the one who would outshine them all, the one who had gone on to graduate *maxima cum laude* from the Jesuit university in California, the one whose books filled the old Mission bookcase that lined the back wall of the entryway to Grandma's house. He had married a young woman who was as delicate in face and body as a porcelain doll, and his five children were the youngest, and the best dressed, and the most Catholic of us all.

In our earliest years he was completing that which our father called the *doctoral degree in English literature,* teaching high school in Carson while writing that which our father called a *brilliant dissertation.* He would come through the double doors of the dining room, and behind his black-rimmed glasses there was a look of intelligence in his eyes, pure and analytical, safeguarded from emotion.

Then suddenly he had changed paths, he had taken his family and headed for law school in the wake of our eldest and middle uncles. He had returned for the summers to work for Uncle Luke, and at the end of three years had returned permanently. Our father said it over and over again, how he had the golden mind, how he of all of them could have chosen any path and shone.

9

THE NINETEEN OF US, we had the good skin that tanned dark in summer. We had the eyes. We had the same rosaries from Grandma. We knew the music of the old language that we did not understand, we had eaten the same pancakes soaked in syrup and rum. We had the same connection to the mother and the father and the five children in the brown-and-white print. We had the same connection to the deep blue book that told our grandfather's story, we had the same link to the old earth and green hills from which our grandparents had come. We had the same blood.

10

In the quiet of Grandma's bedroom, against the ring of the dining room, and the small group of us there around the bed. And the old dark rosaries that hung from the bedpost, and the warm scent of Grandma that filled the quiet of the room. And the sun-darkened limbs of Uncle Francis's fifth-born. The dark limbs reaching, touching the rosaries and rattling them. And the face of him who was the most beautiful of us, round-eyed, brown-eyed, good-skinned, angelic. Freshly diapered, at play, and the dance of the rosaries in the quiet of Grandma's room. The sun-darkened limbs beside the white of his mother's dress, against the pure white cotton dress. And the young mother resting, there on the bed beside the child against the crystalline ring of the dining room.

Angelic, this one was. And the group of us hovering there. He was our favorite. He was all that was good in us.

11

In spring, we would make the hour's drive south twenty miles past Carson, then southeast through the little town of Wellington, pulling off the highway at midmorning and heading down the straight strip of dirt road that led to one of the sheep ranches. We would find our grandfather there in the corrals, amidst the dust and the ewes and the new lambs.

He would take one of us up in one arm and a new lamb in the other, and standing there in his dust-covered Levi's and brown denim work shirt and round-toed work boots, his sun-darkened face and snow-white hair framed against the clear blue of the Nevada sky, he would break into a smile that was as radiant, as pure as the spring sun.

In the warmth of the late morning, he would bottle-feed milk to the bummer lambs, those whose mothers had died or rejected them, and they would take it in one swoosh, filling the bottle with foam. We could smell the dust and the warmth of the Nevada desert, and the sun-cracked wood of the corral posts and the denim of our grandfather's work shirt, mixed in with the bleating of the newborns, with the sight of the snow-white wool and the spatterings of blood and the clear, clear blue of the Nevada sky.

12

AT OTHER TIMES WE WOULD walk with Grandpa into a canyon that lay in the foothills of the Sierra just west of Carson, that smelled of sun-warmed sage and pine in fall, fresh snow and cold pine in winter. It had a wide, sagebrush-covered promontory that our father and mother dubbed the "peninsula" and a steep forest of straight pines that rose up just where the dirt road crossed the back of the peninsula. A wide band of aspen ran along the side of the peninsula and on up into the heart of the forest, following the path of a freshwater creek that wound down from the mountains beginning with the first snows. By late October the creekbed would be dry, its fine sand twinkling with specks of fool's gold. And the bank of aspen would have turned, stretching like a blaze of light up the depth of the canyon. It was family land.

Grandpa was like a young deer there. He knew the land, every inch of it; he knew the road in and the best place to leave the pickup and the best path across the peninsula, the place to be on the alert for rattlesnakes, the exact degree of coldness at which you no longer needed to watch for rattlers. He knew the best path up into the heart of the forest, and the best spot to stop and break out the picnic lunch, and the best spot for Christmas trees this year. He was like a solitary young deer that welcomed the company of our visit, that beamed with pride as he stooped and seized a piece of petrified wood and handed it to us. But at the same time like the young deer he would bound up the mountain free of us, disappearing from us, and with our father and mother we would follow with our slow, laboring steps.

It was what our father had written in the deep blue book. Our grandfather was at home here, his soul did not reside in any house, it could not be kept in any house, it was part of the land, it was one with the snow and the pines and the sage and the autumn blaze.

13

On a morning in July would be the gathering at the gate, just past the junction at Spooner Summit on the road from Carson City to Lake Tahoe. The cars would pull off the highway into the dirt area just outside the gate. Our father would call out that our grandfather had buried the key just to the side of the right gatepost, and then the horde of us would emerge from the cars and begin the search. One time we dug up the entirety of the right hillside, and then the left for the possibility that our father was mistaken, without finding the key to the padlock. We ate lunch sitting cross-legged all over the road inside the gate, the parents and aunts and uncles mumbling under their breath that one of these days we had better get some duplicates of the goddamn key made.

But at other times the key was found just where it was supposed to be, and the gate was swung open, the cars heading through in a cloud of dust, those in the last car stopping and locking the gate behind us. Then time would stand still, the caravan heading in, winding its way from the hum of the highway, silence descending inside the cars. We passed a quiet meadow lake, taking the left fork at its far end, and then a gentle slope upward. We headed through pines that were tall and straight and so thick that the sun broke through only in threads of light, and then we broke onto a clearing, a grass meadow crisscrossed by streams, rich with wildflowers. We passed an old abandoned cabin that sat on the edge of the meadow, and then we began the steeper climb, through more of the straight pines and then into the aspen, past the gray-white trunks that bore the initials of sheepherders long dead, through the dance of the sun on the quaking leaves. And then upward, out of the aspen grove, the road riding a high ridge until it broke onto a high valley floor covered with streams, specked by wildflowers pale in color now, rimmed on the far side by mountains more massive, more bare, than we had ever known. Then the first snowflowers, one or two at the most, bright red against the patches of snow here and there beside the road. Then upward from the far side of the valley floor into a forest of gnarled, twisted pines, the road ragged from fallen trees. We listened to the hum of the car and breathed the air that was pure and cold now.

At the moment we broke the ridge and looked down on the hidden lake, deep blue, glimmering, it was a spell broken. Inside the cars was the sound of deep breaths being let out, and then the yipping began. The caravan plowed downward, descending to the rim of the lake and veering to the right, the sunlit blue of the lake visible through the aspen, the road following the rim of the lake and then heading upward, away from the lake.

At the crest on the far side of the lake was a flat, sandy area called the *lookout,* where the cars would pull off the road and the doors would open up and we would come piling out. In the chill of the high mountain air we would button our coats up to our chins, and we would stand with them, looking down on the deep blue lake and outward, beyond it, a thousand feet below it, to the gentle, pale blue expanse of Tahoe, maternal, rimmed by mountains so distant they were purple in color, the whole earth stretching out below the clear, sun-filled blue of the Nevada sky.

We would pile back into the cars and head onward, taking a left fork and curving around a last, sandy hill. And from there we looked down on that place tucked deep in these mountains that was our grandfather's summer camp, that place that like the canyon in the foothills was *family land.* We could see from afar the shape of the canvas tent. We could see the shape of the huge stock truck that had made it in fifteen years before and was not expected to ever make it back out again, and we could see our grandfather's pickup, faded green. We could see the little stacks of wood that would supply each of the families for winter, and in the distance we could see the small band of sheep that he would have taken to the high mountains for summer. We could see the shape of our grandfather, his right arm waving, his snow-white hair blowing in the mountain air.

In the night, the campfire aglow, they would pile us into the canvas-topped bed of the huge old stock truck, innumerable cousins placed every which way under blankets. We would lie in the dark and look out the open back end of the truck to a sky so laden with stars that at places they seemed to be blended together. Against the distant ring of the voices that surrounded the campfire, we could smell the dust and the gnarled pines, and we could feel the cold mountain air on our faces and the warmth of each other's small bodies that filled the bed of the truck. We knew that this place, hidden deep in the high mountains, like the other things, was in our blood.

In the morning, our mothers would cook bacon and eggs over the pit that Grandpa would have rimmed with fresh white rocks just for this visit, and make hot chocolate from canned Carnation milk, and we would romp in the sand and on the rocks that surrounded the camp.

In midafternoon, dust-covered and sunbaked, we would pile into the cars, and the caravan would head out again, leaving Grandpa alone with the wood and the small band of sheep and the chill breeze that blew quietly through the camp. We would roll out slowly, passing the lookout and heading down through the aspen that rimmed the lake, veering up away from the lake and over the ridge, descending through the forest of gnarled pines, crossing the high valley floor, moving down the high ridge and through the aspen grove, down through the straight pines and out past the old cabin and the meadow, past the meadow lake, to the place where the dirt road led back to the gate. The driver of the last car would emerge and head up to the gate and swing it open, the caravan moving back onto the highway.

Then the drive down the highway that led back to Carson, and the regathering at the U-shaped house, Grandma in the swing on the screened front porch, aproned, standing to greet the boisterous crowd that smelled of dust and pine.

Then the quiet half hour at the dining room table, and the smell of the fresh coffee and the thick white cream and the smoke of the cigarettes, and the sound of the voices that surrounded the underneath.

14

We had no word for it, yet it was always there, at the heart of everything they said and in the very tones in which they spoke. It was what made their faces change when they came together, it was that which made the circle hold.

It had to do with something infinitely old, that went back to the dark earth that bore our grandparents, and their grandparents for ten thousand years back, something that bound the circle back to the old earth. Yet, too, it had something new and enlightened to it, like the gold rimming on Grandma's coffee cups.

It was there always, at the soul of the creature called family, unconditional, unquestioned. It was that which, from the dark underneath of Grandma's white-laced table, made their voices ring purely. It was that which lingered at the center of the table, atop the white lace, at the very place where the cream and sugar sat.

TERESA JORDAN
(1955–)

A woman whose reverence for the almost silent West has filled a score of occupations, Teresa Jordan divides her time between a small northeastern Nevada ranch and a mountain cabin above Salt Lake City. The Wyoming native has edited two volumes of writing by women and has written a widely praised family memoir. A 1994 National Endowment for the Arts Literature Fellowship enabled her to explore fiction, and this is one of several stories that came out of that year. In 1996 she received the Silver Pen Award from the Nevada Writers Hall of Fame. She is an active volunteer in ecosystem restoration collaborations among ranchers, environmentalists, and natural resources personnel. Like so many who make their living with words, she has turned to painting as a kind of artistic foreground from which to gain perspective. This interest in painting, particularly the watercolors of Chiura Obata, has led her to work on the *Field Notes* series about western landscape. Together with her husband, Hal Cannon, founding director of the Western Folklife Center, she created the radio documentary series *The Open Road: Exploring America's Favorite Places.*

Field Notes from the Grand Canyon: Raging River, Quiet Mind. Boulder: Johnson Books, 2000.

The Stories That Shape Us: Contemporary Women Write About the West. New York: Norton, 1995.
Graining the Mare: The Poetry of Ranch Women. Ogden, Utah: Gibbs Smith Publishers, 1994.
Riding the White Horse Home. New York: Pantheon Books, 1992; reprint, New York: Vintage, 1993.
Cowgirls: Women of the American West. New York: Anchor Press/Doubleday, 1982; second edition, University of Nebraska Press, 1992.

St. Francis of Tobacco

Horace McWallis and I were the only gringos at the funeral. I knew Horace would come since Francisco had worked for his family for more than sixty years. Horace's wife, Louise, would have been there, too, but her phlebitis was bad and she had to keep her feet up on a hassock.

There were maybe thirty of us in the little white church. Francisco's daughter Eléna, her husband, Jésus, and their four small daughters sat in the front row, the girls all dressed in white dresses, their dark hair hanging in thick shiny braids. I recognized an older couple who, like Francisco and his wife, had come up to Sky Valley from Mexico as young marrieds looking for work, and raised their children here. They never learned English so well, but their kids graduated from high school and some went on to college. Their oldest daughter practiced medicine in Reno. And then there were folks I recognized from restaurants and casinos in town, dark faces without names. I wished more of my neighbors had come to note the passing of someone who had lived among them for so long, but I guess to many of them Francisco was no different, just another dark face without a name.

Father Hernández drove over from Winnemucca and gave the mass in Spanish. His words were as foreign to me as Latin had been in high school the time I'd gone to Catholic church with Hazel O'Callahan. But I'm old enough to know something of love, and I got the meaning just fine.

We emerged from the service and, as Father Hernández crushed a flower over the grave, and then let fall a handful of dust, I felt old. I looked out over the valley shining in the clear autumn air, the gold meadows just melting from the morning's frost, the rusty lines of coyote willow, the pale stretches of desert dotted with sagebrush beyond the reach of the mountains' generous watershed. I knew that behind us, the Rubies were wearing their first shawls of snow, that white would blanket the meadows before long. After Father Hernández said the final prayer, I found myself drifting down to the fence of the small cemetery, resting my hand on the cold wrought iron.

I turned back to the chirping of young voices and saw Francisco's four granddaughters leaning over his grave, tossing in petals from their white floral crowns. Perched on the edge with their white dresses billowing out behind them, they reminded me of birds, ibis or swans. Angel birds, Francisco would have called them.

A different, more familiar sound drew my attention skyward, and I looked up to see two sandhill cranes. They looked ancient, almost prehistoric, with their long, thin bodies silhouetted black against the sun and their slender wings hesitating slightly at the top of each stroke. I'd never found words to describe their strange wooden cooing before, but that day they sounded like sad geese, gone hoarse from grief.

FRANCISCO USED TO TELL ME THINGS I thought might be true. "You know how hummingbirds go south?" he asked not so many weeks ago. It was the end of the summer, still hot, but the meadows had faded from green to gold and the aspen in the mountains were just starting to turn. We sat on the porch of his little shack, drinking lukewarm iced tea and watching the bright specks of birds hover to suck from the feeder he had made out of a plastic Mrs. Butterworth's bottle and some bright red ribbon. "Such tiny wings," he said, "so many miles. You ever wonder how they make it?"

I shook my head. There were a lot of things I'd never thought about.

"I don't know for sure," he said, "but I think they burrow in the feathers of snow geese and catch a ride. I had a friend once, he tell me he see this. So if I ever see a snow goose, I look, and maybe I see it too." He laughed, softly, and light caught in his dark, watery eyes. Then he started to cough, a wracking, phlegmy cough too strong for his thin body. He reached out blindly, adjusted the knob on the oxygen bottle next to his chair. It was on wheels and followed him everywhere, like a puppy on a leash. The coughing seemed to last forever, and I looked away, toward the mountains.

"No good, no good," he said when the spell was over. He gasped for breath, and I could see him consciously trying to remember to breathe through the little tubes strapped to his nostrils. He leaned his head back, closed his eyes. Tears streamed down his face.

When he had recovered, he reached in his pocket, pulled out a pouch of Bugle tobacco, started to roll a cigarette. "Francisco"—I couldn't help myself—"don't do that."

"Oh, it's bad for me, I know, but I learn too late. And now—what difference does it make?" He finished rolling the cigarette, reached over and turned off the oxygen, struck a wooden match with his thumbnail, and inhaled. He didn't cough, which surprised me. He blew out a thin stream of smoke. "I feel better," he said. "Don' worry."

A barn swallow flew onto the porch, landed on the arm of Francisco's chair. "*Hóla, pájarito,*" he said as the bird cocked its head and looked at him through one eye. Then it plucked a flake of tobacco from his sweater and flew through an open window into the house.

"They will go south soon," he said, with a note of sadness in his voice. "I wish I could go too. Winter don' seem so good to me this year." I murmured in agreement and felt a wave of loss. I didn't think Francisco would see another spring.

FRANCISCO HAD STARTED LIVING WITH the birds a couple of years earlier. He'd grown too weak to work, but Horace told him he could stay on. I like that about Horace and Louise, they have the sort of loyalty you don't see much anymore. Francisco was grateful. The Valley had been his home all his adult life. Years ago he'd told me he'd like to return to Mexico, but now that he was ill, the desire seemed to leave. "This is my home," he said to me. "I don' really remember the other anymore."

Horace and Louise worried about Francisco's ability to take care of himself. They talked Eléna's husband, Jésus, into coming to work on the ranch, and the young family moved in with Francisco. "I don' want to get in your way," he said after a few days, and he moved out to what had once been a grain shed. Eléna and Jésus were distraught. They wanted their daughters to know the old man and besides, people would think they had kicked him out. They enlisted Horace and Louise, but Francisco held fast. "No, no, no, you need room," he insisted, and finally we all came to realize that he was the one who wanted privacy.

He cleaned the shed up slowly, as his breath would allow, sweeping out the droppings of pack rats and spiders, sprinkling baking soda to soak up their musky smells. But up in the rafters hung a line of mud cups, the nests of barn swallows, and he left these alone. "This is their home," he said. "They don' need to worry 'bout me." He left his windows open from the time the birds first arrived in the spring until they migrated south in the fall, and they flew in and out at their will. "*Mi otra familia*," he said with his soft laugh. To tell the truth, I think he moved out of the house to be close to them.

"You know what this is?" he'd asked when I had visited him early in the summer. He showed me a handful of tiny feathers, the same buff color as my buckskin mare. "These are *escrituras* —how you say?—deeds. Or maybe name tags." I looked at him as if he were crazy. "No, really," he said. "Last fall, I watch as each bird, before she fly away, pluck one feather from her breast, leave it in her nest. And just now, the birds, they come back, each one take up her nest, drop the feather on the floor."

"Francisco . . ."

"Really," he said, his dark eyes twinkling. "Where else you think I got these? This fall, you come see. And then you believe."

I'D KNOWN FRANCISCO SINCE I WAS SIXTEEN and he was only a year or two older. It had been the middle of the Depression and strangers roamed the country, dropping off the freights, hitchhiking, looking for work or for food. My parents told me to be careful and so I was afraid, especially of the men, and most especially of the Mexicans. I don't know how I got this last message so clear, but it came through.

I met Francisco during the first snowfall of the season, a nasty day, cold and windy. I was driving the truck to town to lay in our winter groceries when I saw a young Mexican couple on the road. The girl was pregnant and they looked so cold and miserable, I stopped. They both started talking very fast, though I couldn't understand anything they said. The girl burst into tears. She held her belly and the boy kept pointing at it and talking louder. I made out the word "*médico*."

"I'm going to town," I said. "I can take you." They looked at me blankly, but I waved them into the truck and they understood. They climbed in and I realized they were shivering. The girl wore a thin cotton dress with no stockings, and a man's wool coat, several sizes too big. I guessed it belonged to the boy. It was filthy, stained with mud and grease and I didn't know what else. I found myself inching away from it. The boy wore no coat at all, just a dirty cotton shirt with a right-angle tear on the shoulder, like he'd caught it when he ducked under a barbed wire fence. The girl's teeth chattered and he held her hands to warm them. The truck had no heater, but I pulled a wool robe out from behind the seat, though I admit I hesitated for a minute before I handed it over. *Gracias, gracias,* they both said as they unfolded it.

Snow slicked the road. I had to keep stopping to clear ice from the windshield. Once the boy understood what I was doing, he'd hop out before I even had the truck stopped, and clear it with his bare hands. There was no arguing with him, even when his hands turned blue. I gave him my gloves and they fit fine.

Though I didn't speak their language and they didn't speak mine, I came to know a few things about them during that long ride to town. Their names were Francisco and María Sanchez. It was too early for the baby, but something was wrong. I thought I understood that María was bleeding. Francisco worked for Señor McWallis—that would have been Horace's father—and he feared McWallis would fire him for leaving.

"It's okay," I said. "I'll talk to him. My father will talk to him." I didn't think they understood.

Mostly, we drove in silence. I kept stealing glances at María. She looked so scared. She was no older than I was, maybe even younger. I tried to imagine what it would be like to be married, to be having a baby. But I couldn't.

By the time we reached town, María was pale and trembling all over. I took her to Dr. Phelps, who took care of our family. "Do you know these people?" his nurse asked me.

"No," I said. "They work for Mr. McWallis."

"Can they pay to see the doctor?"

"I don't know. I don't think so. Mr. McWallis will pay for it. Or my father will."

"Does your father know about this?"

"Oh, yes," I lied. "He sent me in."

"Well, all right, then. . . ." She looked dubious, but she gestured for María to come into an examination room. Francisco followed along. The nurse tried to get him to stay in the waiting room, but he insisted and she gave up.

She came back in a few minutes. "She'll have to go into the hospital," she told me. "You might as well go home."

"And Francisco?"

"I don't think he'll leave her." I must have looked worried, because she added, "It'll be okay. We'll call the priest. There are other Mexican families in town. They won't be so alone."

I went back to the truck and climbed in. A small pool of blood marked the place where María had sat. It must have soaked clear through the coat. It was as red as my own.

"WHAT WERE YOU DOING, picking up people like that?" my mother demanded when I started to tell my folks about the day. "They might have killed you." But she calmed down as I told the whole story, and when I finished, my father said I'd done the right thing. He talked to McWallis, and he must have smoothed things over, because when Francisco finally came back from town, he still had a job.

I didn't learn for a long time that María had died. She hemorrhaged, I guess, and bled to death. She was my age, we'd been shoulder to shoulder, and now she was dead. They'd been able to save the baby, a little girl born five weeks premature. Francisco named her Eléna and a family in town took her in. I didn't speak to Francisco; even if I had had the language, I wouldn't have known what to say. Sometimes I'd see him from a distance, forking hay off the sled to the cattle or, when spring came, walking the irrigation ditches with a shovel in his hand. Always, he wore that dirty wool coat. It struck me it was all he had left.

THE YEARS WHIRL PAST, DON'T THEY? I graduated from high school, went to college for a couple of years, came back and married the boy next door, Isaac Place. We worked for his folks for a few years, and then, when my father died and Mom moved to town, we took over the home place. Isaac's folks died and we inherited half their ranch, bought the other half from Isaac's brother. Bought some more land, built up quite a spread.

Isaac loved land, loved buying and selling it. He loved buying and selling anything, really: cows, horses, ranches, buildings, stocks and bonds. Union Pacific, he loved Union Pacific, bought another share of it every time he had an extra dollar in his pocket. People said we were in the ranching business and it was true: Isaac was in business and I was on the ranch. He wasn't around much, always off chasing after one deal or another, and to tell the truth, that suited me fine. I was always glad to see him. He was loads of fun. The minute he'd get home, the house would fill with people, with stories and laughter and whiskey. And ideas. He always brought home a lot of ideas, of new machinery we could buy, improvements in irrigation, new breeds of cattle. For a while he wanted to build a new house, a real showplace. I liked living in the home place, in the house I grew up in. I let him talk me into a new kitchen—that didn't take much talking—and I loved my up-to-date appliances, but that was enough. Lucky for me, he had a short attention span and I was always glad to see him go, to let him put that energy into something else.

Isaac liked being known as a rancher, he just didn't like ranching, didn't like the cold or getting manure on his lizard-skin boots. There are a lot of people like that, men and women both, and I don't blame any of them. But I felt just the opposite. I liked manure. Well, not really, but I liked the critters that made manure, and I liked what manure did for the grass. As far as I was concerned, as long as I had my horses and cows, Isaac was welcome to all the fancy boots in the world.

That was the only real fight we ever had. Isaac liked to live on the edge, to wheel and deal, to *leverage,* to use one of his favorite words. I didn't know he'd "leveraged" this place, didn't know he could, until one day the banker showed up with a handful of papers and told me we no longer owned the ranch. I didn't even know where Isaac was—he was in Tucson, as it turned out—but I tracked him down and read him the riot act. I don't know what he sold or what he traded; things were nip and tuck for a year or two. But in the end we kept the ranch and, at my insistence, he put it in my name. I didn't care about anything else, any buildings or ranches or herds of cattle in distant places. I just wanted to know that *my* home and *my* herd were safe. I could sleep again. Isaac was a decent man. I think he would have done anything he could to make me happy. Except stay home or stop trading, and I never asked him to do either of those things.

Francisco was invisible in those years. I'd see him sometimes if I went to help McWallis's brand, and sometimes when he was irrigating, I'd pass him on the road. We'd nod or wave at each other; well, everybody out here did that. But I was busy all the time, putting the ranch together, making things work. And then Isaac and I were trying to start a family.

I could get pregnant easy enough, but come the second or third month, I'd miscarry. The third time, Dr. Phelps said, "No more." If it happened again, he said, I might not survive. He took everything out. When I woke up from surgery, Isaac sat by my bed, holding my hand. He was sweet and kind, and he nursed me through the next few days. When I got back on my feet, he left again, though he called every other day or so and sent funny little gifts.

But I was feeling blue. Empty, you know, and sort of worthless. To make matters worse, my two-year-old sorrel filly, the one I was so proud of, ran through the barbed wire and impaled herself on a fence stay, ran it almost clear through her shoulder. The vet sewed her up and managed, for the most part, to prevent infection. But as the wound healed, it made proud flesh, sort of like it didn't know when to stop healing until she had this raw outgrowth on her shoulder the size of a grapefruit. The vet told me there was nothing much I could do about it. He could try to surgically remove it, but it would probably grow back.

I had just stepped into the corral to nurse the filly when Francisco rode in, trailing a couple of my heifers who'd walked the fence and turned up in McWallis's meadow. "Señora," he said—he always called me Señora now—"you got trouble?" He swung off his horse and looked at the filly. *"No problema,"* he said. "I come back in a little while." An hour or so later, he turned up with a poultice made out of cayenne and tobacco and I don't know what else. He put it on the wound and just held it there for a while as if warming it with his hands. Then he laid gauze over the swelling and taped it. Every day after that, he'd show up with more herbs, and I could see the proud flesh recede. The vet said it was impossible, and then he said it was a miracle. The red swelling disappeared almost entirely, just a faint ridge of scarring remained, and the filly's coat came back to cover it, only the hair came in white, shaped like a human hand. I joked about her war paint, but it made me think she healed more from Francisco's touch than from his herbs.

"Oh, yeah, Francisco's something," Horace said when I mentioned it to him. "He can fix anything. We hardly ever call the vet anymore." He told me that the Spanish have a word for someone who heals, *curandero.* It usually refers to someone who works with people, but Francisco was a *curandero de animales.* After that, I started calling on him every time I had a lame horse or a wire cut or a calf coming backwards. He always knew what to do. If he had to sew something up, his stitches were as fine and precise as a blue-ribbon quilter's. And no matter how frightened or how badly injured, the animal calmed down the minute Francisco came around. After he treated one of my critters, I always tried to pay him, but he never accepted it. I started baking him pies and rolls and cookies, giving him little gifts of coffee and tobacco, handing them to him when he was here, or sometimes taking them over.

I remember, that morning of the accident, I was mad at Isaac. He'd just called from Denver to tell me he'd made a deal on our steer calves—on *my* steer calves—and I was furious because he hadn't consulted me first. "You were going to sell them anyway," he said, "and I didn't think you could get a better deal." But they were *my* calves, *my* deals to make. We had plenty of hay that year, and I'd wanted to winter them over as yearlings. I was unleashing my temper on the chopping block, splitting a load of piñon into kindling. I looked up for a minute and saw Francisco coming down our drive with a big bird on his shoulder. It had to be the red-tailed hawk with the broken wing he'd been doctoring. Francisco had told me the bird was almost healed, and I figured he was bringing him down to show me before he let him go.

I kept swinging during the split second I looked up. I'll never know exactly what happened, but I missed the piece of wood and the axe hit the edge of the chopping block. The head broke off and I remember the blade soaring back through the air as if in slow motion, dark and heavy, clumsy, like a wounded pigeon. It landed deep in my thigh, just above the knee. Everything blurred from that point on. Francisco started to run. The hawk took off, and I remember feeling this great sense of exhilaration to see it fly. At the same moment, I saw the blood gushing out of my jeans, and I knew I had done something bad.

"Aye, Señora," Francisco said, and he whipped off the bandanna he wore wrapped around his neck. He ripped open my jeans and as he tied a tourniquet, I could see red red blood spurting out of an artery and, beside it, the white of my bone.

Dr. Phelps told me later that if Francisco hadn't been so quick to reattach the artery, I would have died, or at least risked losing my leg from the tourniquet by the time he could have gotten me to town. The doctor said he had never seen such an expert job of sewing. But what I remember is Francisco's great gentleness, the quiet murmur of his Spanish, the calm that washed over me, the sense that everything would be okay. And I remember, too, those next few days and nights in the hospital, a strange heat overtaking me, and a wild dreaming, images of exposed white bone, of hawks in blue sky, of Francisco and me together, riding, working with animals, touching. In waking I felt dizzy, almost drunk with a yearning for something I'd never required of Isaac.

Francisco came to see me. He held his hat in his hand, deferential as always. He motioned with his chin at my leg. "It is going to be okay, no?" he said. "You heal soon, yes?" He was formal and shy and I ached to have him close to me again, murmuring, caring for me.

"Francisco, you saved me," I said, and I found myself stammering on the words, flushing and giggling like a young girl. I reached out. I wanted to draw him close. But he looked at my hand, gripped the rim of his hat more tightly.

"Francisco, please, I want . . ."

I didn't know what I wanted. I did know what I wanted. Francisco knew, he had to know.

He said, "Señora . . ." and his voice trailed off.

"Anna," I said. "Don't call me Señora. I'm Anna."

He touched the bandage on my leg, softly, tenuously. "Señora," he said again. "You are my friend. My very good friend."

I could feel the heat of his hand through my bandage, or I thought that I could.

"Your leg heals fast, and we work together. I look forward to that time. But now, I must go." He took my hand then, for just a moment, and then he turned and walked out of my room. When the nurse checked in a while later, she found me sobbing hysterically. The same nurse had attended my hysterectomy, and she took hold of me with a hearty authority. "It's shock," she said, dabbing my face with a cool wet cloth. "You've been through a lot in the last few months."

RULES, EVEN THE UNWRITTEN ONES—perhaps especially the unwritten ones—keep the walls of our ordered worlds from caving in. They are a scaffolding of sorts I guess, and we should probably be grateful for them. But sometimes they feel a lot like prison bars. I came home from the hospital. I used crutches for a while, but I healed up good. I didn't see Francisco for some weeks and then he showed up one day carrying a young cat with a bandaged leg. "Someone hit him on the road," he said. "I fix him up, but he needs a home." I took the cat and he leaned against my chest, started to purr. He was a fine black fellow with a pure white belly. I felt a sense of great relief. Things were as they always had been. We'd be okay.

So we went along, Francisco and I. He helped me with my animals, I helped him with his birds. He brought me tomatoes out of his garden, I gave him zucchinis out of mine. Isaac died, Francisco and I grew old, we could joke with each other more. "It's that handsome vaquero," I'd say when he arrived; he called me *Señora Pájarita Bonita,* Mrs. Pretty Little Bird. He smoked and wheezed, I complained about my arthritis, we both started having trouble remembering people's names.

AND NOW FRANCISCO IS GONE. Today is cold and overcast and spitting snow; I can't help thinking how much this air would have hurt his lungs. I visited his shack the other day, to see if the barn swallows had left, to sweep up the feathers and close his windows if they had. Maybe I was looking for the *escrituras,* the breast feathers that marked their departure. As I approached I saw that the meadow was filled with big white birds. Swans, I thought at first, but then I saw the black tips on their wings. Snow geese. I'd never seen them in the valley before. Most of them were hunched over with their beaks to the ground, pecking for grain or for grass, and they reminded me of something, though I couldn't put my finger on it. Then it came to me: Francisco's granddaughters at the graveside, angel birds. I watched for a while until, of a moment, the geese took flight, circling higher and higher, finally forming a vee, heading south.

JOHN ZIEBELL
(1955–)

A writer for an electronic news service, John Ziebell grew up in Green Bay, Wisconsin. An accomplished landscape photographer, former shoe salesman, and marine, he lived in northern Arizona before moving to Las Vegas in 1993. While living in Flagstaff, he began to write short fiction. He recently earned his M.F.A. in the University of Nevada, Las Vegas, creative writing program. A student of the Southwest and its people, he has had his fiction published in the *Red Rock Review* and the *Tucson Weekly.* There is a subtle, almost unspoken quality to his stories that gives them an imaginary horizon on which to lie. When we last spoke he was midway through a novel, anchored in his two recurring themes, place and relationships.

Yellowjackets

OLIVER IS ON A GUNSHIP NEAR VENUS when the screaming starts. He's in command of that gunship, but he's not really paying attention because the woman downstairs is playing her flute. She's been practicing for about an hour and he's listening to her with his eyes closed; right now she's playing Beethoven, a piece composed originally for violins and cello that he loves the sound of. The notes drift into the hot Saturday air that stands outside the house, eddying in the shade. When she rests he can hear the birds in the tree outside his window. She stops playing when the kid begins to scream.

He opens his eyes to look at the enemy spacecraft that traverse the screen of his computer monitor. His weapons are locked on. The cursor is blinking, asking for his decision. He doesn't remember what his plan was. He's gotten good at these games, over the past few weeks, but he can't think with all that noise outside.

Oliver knows the kid, knows him by his voice. His name is Arnold Robert and he belongs to the people next door. Arnold is nine, maybe ten, but he's already got a history. Once he found a snake in the garden, a diamondback about three feet long, and poked it with a stick until it began to strike. The snake missed

Arnold but got the dog that was watching him do the poking, knocked it flat right then and there. Another time he got the brake of his mother's car loose and rolled it down the hill, across one street, and into a telephone pole. He's got a round face, Arnold, and eyes that are too close together. He hardly speaks. Oliver figures he'll be a bully if he lives long enough, but Kathleen, his wife, feels sorry for the kid. When she sees him alone in his yard she buys him ice cream from the vending truck that cruises their street. Since she started her summer contract the kid has said nothing to Oliver at all; he just stares, like he's been betrayed.

Arnold is still making noise so Oliver gets up from the computer and wanders out of his apartment and down the stairs to the hallway. He never knows if anyone is home at the house on the corner where the kid lives; the man works nights, and his wife says she's a designer of some kind. He usually sees them only when they walk to one of their cars. At the bottom of the stairs he passes the door of the woman who plays the flute. She's a graduate student at the university, renting a downstairs apartment for the summer. Her name is Renate. She has soft dark hair and a tan that's baked deeply into her skin. She's friendly when she sees him. They talk and sometimes have a beer together on the front steps, waiting for rain on these long afternoons.

He'd seen her, the other night. He'd come in late and climbed the stairs quietly and was standing there with his key in the lock when she opened her door to let a man out. Oliver heard the sound of boots on the old hardwood floor. By the time he turned to look down the man was a shadow passing out of the building. Polite, though; he closed the screen door gently behind him. Oliver could see Renate's dark hair and the lighter curve of one naked shoulder as she stood in her door watching the doorway. Something about the way she was standing let him believe she was unhappy. He waited, sure that she would look up and catch him there, staring. He was holding his breath. Then the hair disappeared, and the bare brown shoulder, and the door closed behind her.

OLIVER STANDS ON THE SHADED FRONT PORCH, looking over at the lot next door. The house where Arnold lives is set well back from the street, small and faded. The yard in front of it is hard-packed earth, covered with unruly patches of wild grass. Sunlight filters through the branches of trees down the rest of the block, but there, at the house on the corner, it falls flat and without shadow across that grass. It's one in the afternoon. The air is so still that Oliver can hear softball games from the American Legion park six blocks away.

Arnold's father is coming out of the house with a yellow can in one hand. He wears black shoes and loose pants and a white shirt with short sleeves. The whole family dresses like that, in inexpensive clothing without style. Arnold's father has short hair and black eyeglasses, the kind the military gives to people in boot camp. Arnold is gone, silent, and Oliver figures that he must be inside. The birds have started up again, in the trees in front of the old house where Oliver lives. He doesn't know what birds they are but Kathleen, his wife, does; she knows them by their calls, knows which of them return to the feeder she has set out. She has favorites among them.

Arnold's father is shaking something from the can onto the ground. Oliver steps off the porch and walks around the fence. Arnold's father is named Paul, Paul Robert. Robert without the s, he always says. He looks up, the can bright in his hand. His glasses are dirty. The dead grass, where he stands, comes halfway to his knees.

"Hornets," he says. "Those fuckers bit Arnie."

Oliver is close enough to see them coming out of the ground now, out of a bare patch of hard dirt where they have bored holes. They are black, with dull yellow stripes, and they fly away slowly. He thinks that they are not hornets, but yellowjackets; he thinks that there is a difference, but isn't sure if it matters. More of them, whatever they are, land and crawl into the holes. They seem indifferent to everything around them. Oliver wonders what it is that the kid did to piss them off.

"Is he all right?"

"Yeah," Paul Robert says, "but they bit him four, five times."

"What is that stuff?"

Paul Robert looks at the can in his hand.

"Roach killer," he says, "but I figure it should work on regular bugs too."

The bees are coming and going, slowly, one or two at a time. They appear to be ignoring the white powder that Paul Robert has sprinkled around the holes.

"Maybe not," Oliver says.

It's hot there in the sun and he can smell the dry grass in the Roberts' yard. The air is thick and he looks across the hot blue sky, searching for clouds. This is the end of summer, the rainy season, but so many of the days begin like this.

"One way or the other," Paul Robert says, "they're leaving."

He tosses the can to one side and stands there, an uncertain soul. Oliver turns and walks away. There are bees around his place too, around the flowers that stand in pots on the porch behind their upstairs apartment. The bees there are larger, brighter and harmless. They walk across the wide brim of Kathleen's hat when she is reading in her chair. When they settle on her book or hover near her face she brushes them away, gently, with the back of one hand. Kathleen is like that. She's not one to let things bother her.

Oliver and Kathleen live on the top floor of the old rock-and-timber house, split now into three apartments but still sturdy and dense enough to be cool in the heat of the day. The tiles of the walk are hot beneath his bare feet and as he climbs the steps he can see Renate standing in the hallway, her figure indistinct behind the screen door.

"What's going on out there?"

"The kid got stung by bees," Oliver says.

He opens the door and moves past her. She's wearing a loose skirt and a silk tank top that is a brilliant green. She doesn't look, he decides, like a person who is unhappy.

"It sounded worse," she says. "I mean the way he was screaming."

"I know. I guess he's all right, though."

They stand there for a moment. He's leaning against the mailboxes set into the wall of the hallway just inside the screen door. She's next to her door in the green silk top, standing there with a flute in one hand. Shadows that lie on the hardwood floor, cast by sunlight falling through the leaves of the tree in the front yard, shift gently. A subtle breeze passes through the screen.

"I like to listen to you play," Oliver tells her.

She smiles, all those teeth so white against her tan. There's something about her, the way she stands, the way she smiles; he doesn't know what it is. An aura she has, something that moves across her body like the fabric of her shirt. He thinks she's charming. He takes a step toward the stairs.

"Come on in and have a beer," she says. "I'll play something for you."

He hesitates, but only for a moment.

"All right. I'd like that."

He follows her inside. Her apartment is dark and cool, furnished with old and heavy things. There are photographs on the walls, old programs, calendars. The back of her couch is arched like the upended shell of an oyster; she sets the flute on its cushions, bright against worn burgundy fabric. There is another flute beside it, shining softly in a box lined with blue velvet.

"Sit down. I'll get your beer."

He sits in a low chair with wide armrests that end in carved wooden balls. Renate brings beer from the kitchen, two green bottles. She hands him one, drinks deeply from the other, and sits on the couch. She sets the bottle on the floor, picks up the older flute, leans forward. Her feet are pressed neatly together.

"See if you know this," she says.

When she plays her head moves, just slightly, and her fingers race across the instrument. Oliver watches her play, the bottle cold in his hand. He drinks and listens. The notes from the flute roll out around the small room. When she finishes she sets the flute across her knees and picks up her beer. She leans against the back of the couch and drinks from the bottle.

"Well? Do you know it?"

"I don't know it," he says.

Renate laughs.

"That's a safe answer," she says.

She smiles and plays something else. She tells him about the flutes. They sit there, talking about nothing, until their bottles are empty. She moves the flute from her knees to the couch and stands fluidly with the empty bottle in her hand.

"I'll get us one more."

He watches her walk past him, into the kitchen. He hears the door of the refrigerator open, hears her pop the caps off the bottles.

"I haven't seen your wife around lately," she says from the kitchen.

"She's still in Los Angeles. She was supposed to be back, but her grant was extended; they found more money for the museum acquisitions."

"Is she having a good time?"

This is the question that Oliver doesn't ponder. The whole thing has begun to make him uneasy. Kathleen has become hard to reach. She returns his calls days later, if at all. At night, sometimes, he listens to that phone in L.A., listens to it ring, through what must be the emptiness of the place where she stays.

"I'm not sure," he says.

"You must miss her. I don't think I could do it."

Renate comes from the kitchen with two more bottles of beer. She hands one to Oliver and stands there with her weight on one leg, her hip resting against the back of his chair. He can smell, faintly, the fragrance she wears.

"I think it would make me crazy," Renate says, "a relationship like that."

The American Express bills come to the house with eighty-dollar dinners on them. Receipts from shoe stores, airfare to Catalina. Her friends don't call him anymore to ask how she is doing. And she doesn't honestly know, she tells him, how soon she can get away. There are times when Oliver actually wakes up at his desk; he doesn't remember getting to work but he's there, looking through his office window at the mountains to the west, his necktie and a mug of coffee waiting on the desk in front of him.

"She usually makes it home every couple weeks," he says, "for a day or two. And with this project I'm working on, I spend most of my spare time at the computer. It's not as bad, that way."

He's used to the computer games now and he's risen quickly through the ranks in the current one; he's a Strike Force Leader, taking his ship deep into enemy territory. He's gotten rich on the spoils of war and has made a name for himself in the galaxy.

Her body straightens and moves and he feels silk, that bright green silk, flow against the back of his hand. She walks to the window. He watches her profile as she raises the bottle to drink from it.

"If I were you," she says, "I'd be having an affair with someone."

Her voice is quiet, but carries conviction. He sees her head begin to turn. She rests her beer on the windowsill and looks toward the house on the corner.

"He's doing something else, now. That man."

Oliver gets up and moves across the room to stand beside her at the window. At this range he can smell the components that make up her scent; the aroma of spice coming from her body, the tang of citrus from her hair. He can see Paul Robert, next door, walking from his house with a five-gallon gasoline can in his right hand. His body is sloped to the left—not a man who is used to carrying heavy things.

"It looks like he's going to pour gas on them," Oliver says. "The bees."

"He gives me the creeps."

Paul Robert sets the can down and wipes his right hand on the leg of his baggy pants. The sky outside is as unblemished as a sheet of glass, but in the distance, out over the mountains, Oliver can see the ragged edges of big clouds building fast.

"I wish it would rain," Renate says.

She sees them too, those clouds; on days like this they are something you look for, a salvation of sorts.

"They said it would," he tells her, "on the radio."

The breeze has stopped coming through the window. It's warm in the apartment. Renate turns slowly, her body facing his. The silk of her blouse has formed itself to her body. He looks down. He knows already how those breasts will feel, the weight of them, and how her nipples will look. She takes half a step. Her eyes are dark, but they have paler golden flecks around the pupils. They're looking right at him. A dark wing of hair falls to lie along the line of her cheekbone. His fingers slide down her arm. She breathes, deeply. He can feel the warmth of her body, settling around him like the heat of the day.

The thudding sound of mass ignition rolls across the neighborhood. Black smoke coils across the driveway, bending to follow the wall of the house. Oliver leans past her toward the window and sees orange flame racing across the lot next door where Paul Robert lives.

"That asshole," Oliver says.

Renate walks quickly into the bedroom, and he follows her. From the bigger window there they can see the whole lot burning. Paul Robert is moving around the perimeter of the fire, shaking his hands. Oliver speaks quietly, already turning to leave.

"I better go out there."

He can feel her standing beside him. When he turns from the window he looks, for a moment, around her bedroom. The bed has a headboard that is six feet tall and a hundred years old, carved from cherry wood. Blue blue sheets have been thrown back carelessly. He thinks he can smell her on those sheets, thinks he can see the imprint of her form on the mattress. The top of the dresser that matches the bed is cluttered with small bottles and jars. There are books stacked on the floor between the bed and the dresser. Hanging from the knob of the open closet door there is a bra the color of gunmetal, skeletal and elegant.

Come back, he thinks he hears her say.

By the time Oliver gets outside he can hear the sirens. Paul Robert's wife is standing across the street with her arms around Arnold, like she's holding him in place. Robert is still waving his hands, and when Oliver gets closer he looks down at them; they look like they've been sunburned, red from the heat. His eyebrows are melted down to stubble and his eyeglasses are sooty.

"I didn't think it would catch fire," he says to Oliver. "Not all of it, like that."

They stand there, watching the paint melt off the five-gallon gasoline can. Oliver can see the fire reflected in the lenses of Paul Robert's glasses. He's watching Robert and is surprised to see him smile.

"I guess I got those bastards," Paul Robert says. "This time."

And then Robert walks down the driveway to talk to the firemen who are just pulling up in big yellow trucks with the sirens wailing.

Oliver watches the firemen work for a while, watches them uncoil heavy hose and send water out across the lot in thick streams. The smoke changes color. The firemen keep spraying water long after the flames are gone. Some of them are talking to Paul Robert. His wife is still across the street, still holding on to that kid. Oliver figures that he's had enough for one day. He walks back to his house and moves quietly inside. He can feel his face flush as he passes Renate's door. He hesitates, there in the hallway, for just a moment. He can't imagine going back upstairs, back to the computer game, but he does.

On the wall above the stereo components there is a photograph of Kathleen, one a friend made years ago. The photograph is black and white, but when Oliver looks at it his mind gives color to those features; chestnut to the hair, hazel to the eyes, tan to the freckles that run across the bridge of her nose. Those same freckles are spilled across the tops of her breasts, and across her shoulders in the back. Her skin is fair, her body so lean that it seems to fall in planes.

He's looking at the photograph as he sits in a chair holding the telephone. The blinds on the windows click and hum as wind, still warm and heavy with ozone, pushes through them into the room. He dials the number of the place in Redondo where she stays. Kathleen rents a room from two other women who seem, also, never to be home. He holds the phone to his ear. It rings and rings. He's listening to it ring when someone knocks softly at his door. He hangs up the telephone and carries it with him, cord trailing, to answer the knock.

It's Renate. She's standing there in old soft jeans and a loose top and, over that, a bright foul-weather jacket like the kind sailors wear.

"Come in," he says.

"I can't," she says. "I've got to go out for a while. But I'll be back in a couple of hours. If you want to stop down. Have a drink, maybe."

"I'll see how things go," he says. "I'm in the middle of something right now."

They're standing close to each other, but the doorway is between them, an abstract plane. He reaches through it. He straightens the white string that is meant to pull the hood of her jacket closed. She hooks one finger into the placket of his shirt and stands slowly on her toes to kiss him, once. Her lips are soft. Her eyes are like amber, just that still, with highlights trapped inside them. He can't read a thing in those eyes. A car horn sounds. The bright jacket swirls, her hair flaring against its color. She moves down the stairs, through the hallway, then outside with the screen banging closed behind her.

Oliver doesn't know what to think. He carries the telephone

over to the desk and sets it on the floor. He sits in his chair. He turns on the computer, makes his selections, brings up the status of his gunship. He checks weapons, fuel, supplies. The command display flashes on the screen. He plots a course and heads toward the enemy stronghold.

When he hears the thunder, later, he's doing poorly. He's outnumbered, and his craft has taken damage. He hears the thunder and gets up from the computer to stand at the window. Lightning flickers softly along the bottoms of the clouds. He turns off the lights to watch the storm. The computer glows behind him, pale light that lines the edges of the furniture. He can smell the rain. He watches it fall on the incinerated lot that had been Paul Robert's front yard, glad that it is here. He is still watching the storm when a car stops at the foot of the driveway. The car sits there for a while. He can see the blue of its exhaust, the rain falling through the beams of its headlights. The passenger door opens, and Renate gets out to run toward the house with her jacket held up over her head. The car pulls away, headlights cutting a path through rain.

He moves to stand near the door of his apartment. He listens to the screen door close behind her. He listens to the sound of her shoes on the hallway floor. He hears her open the door, then, what seems like a long time later, hears her shut it.

He dials the number in Redondo again. A voice answers, one of the roommates. She doesn't know where Kathleen is. She doesn't know when Kathleen will be back.

"This is her husband," Oliver says. "Could you have her call?"

"Sure," the woman tells him.

"Thank you," Oliver says.

He hangs up the phone. He sits in the chair and listens to the rain. It would be good, he thinks, for that rain to just keep coming down.

The telephone beside the bed starts ringing and brings Oliver out of a crushing and dreamless sleep. He picks it up, his body thick and unresponsive. He speaks into the handset, uncertain of his control over the words he's trying to use. Kathleen is on the other end. It seems that she's just now getting in. He tries to focus his eyes on the blue numbers of the clock.

"Jesus, it's almost daylight here."

"You wanted me to call," she says. "That was the message I got."

Oliver sits up, taking the base of the telephone from the table to set it beside him on the bed. He tells himself that he's not really sure how late it is on the coast, one time zone away. The vision is there in his mind; Kathleen sitting in a chair, still wearing her party clothes, unfastening her earrings as she speaks. Trapping the telephone handset between her head and shoulder to pull off, with relief, the shoes that she wears. Her feet must be throbbing by now.

"I just wanted to talk to you. I wanted to know how you are."

"I'm fine," Kathleen says. "I'm tired. My feet hurt. I had to go to a reception, and people stay up all night out here."

There is silence. Oliver is beginning to think of that silence as a curse that haunts the telephone lines between Los Angeles and where he is.

"I miss you," he says.

"I miss you, too. Listen, I'll call you tomorrow."

He's awake, now. His wife is in L.A. and her feet hurt, the way they do. He thinks about how good she looks when she's dressed up like that. How she would get home and take off her shoes and light a cigarette, needing it badly because she didn't smoke in public. Sometimes she would step out of her shoes and let her dress fall to the floor leaving it there like a black puddle. She would sit with her feet up, her head back, her body sprawled. She would close her eyes and smoke would trail away from her, winding out into the room.

"I love you," he tells her.

He can't imagine her doing those things with other men.

"Good night," Kathleen says.

He hangs up the telephone and sets it back on the table. He watches the blue numbers change, flashing across the face of the clock. It is quiet outside, and the rain has stopped. It takes him a long time to get back to sleep.

ON SUNDAY MORNING OLIVER WAKES UP after eight and walks slowly through the house to put coffee on. When he looks out the window he sees a day that is not yet committed; the sky is blue but the clouds that move across it are heavy and gray, dark at the edges. He gets his bathrobe and puts it on. He walks out of his apartment and down the stairs to where the fat newspapers lie stacked just inside the screen door, under the mailboxes.

He picks up his paper. He pushes the door open and steps out onto the porch. He looks over at Paul Robert's yard, at the blackened rectangle still wet from the rain. Paul Robert is at the curb talking to a man in a uniform. They're standing next to a red car with lights on the roof and a fire department decal on the door. The fireman is talking to Paul Robert, pointing his finger at him. The fireman writes something on a clipboard and rips the top page off. He hands the page to Robert, who takes it. Robert's shoulders are slumped. He's got the look of a changed man. Oliver watches the fireman get into his car and drive away. Paul Robert walks back to his small house with slow steps, staring down at his black shoes.

Oliver goes back inside. On his way upstairs he stops at Renate's door. He listens for a moment; he can hear a radio inside, quiet noise, and nothing else. He climbs the stairs slowly and is at the top when he hears the sound of her door opening. He stops, turns. His hands, holding the newspaper between them, rest on the railing.

She moves to stand in the bar of sunlight that falls through the screen door. She stretches, hands fisted behind her head, elbows out. Her bare legs look strong beneath the short cotton robe she wears. She stands in the sunlight and then crosses the hallway. The robe opens to bare a long brown line of her body. She tucks it closed again, holding it that way with one hand as she bends to pick up her newspaper with the other. She's humming, softly, one of the duets she plays on the flute.

Oliver stands there with his hands on the railing, waiting for her to turn. If she turns and looks up she will see him there, at the top of the stairs, watching her. That's all she has to do, he thinks. Just turn, and look up.

SAM MICHEL
(1960–)

Sam Michel moved to Reno as a boy and stayed for fifteen years before leaving for the University of California at Berkeley, where he earned his B.A. in philosophy. He later studied in Montana, and it was at this time that he began to pursue his writing seriously, publishing stories in *The Quarterly*, *Cutbank*, and *Neon*. He has received grants from the Sierra Arts Foundation and the Nevada Arts Council, and his first collection of stories, *Under the Light*, was highly praised. The following story is from that collection. Michel is now at work on a novel set in Winnemucca. Nevada, in his words, "inhabits my fiction." He and his wife live in western Massachusetts, where he is a visiting writer at the University of Massachusetts.

Under the Light: Stories. New York: Alfred A. Knopf, 1996.

Willows

It was easy, really, the business with the willows. It was the colonel who wanted the willows clipped. They'd all seen him. Each fall season they had all seen the old man burn and spray and hack at the stand of willows, which would always grow back thick along the ditch bank over the course of the following summer when the water ran fast in a flowing gush the color of mud. From the downside edge of the grassy slope that the colonel kept mowed close to the ground behind his big-windowed house, you could see each season the sunlit glint of steel that marked the slashing motion of the old man's spit-shined machete. Thrashings, you could see, animals in the underbrush. But never the colonel himself clear and complete. Songs, and whistlings, you could hear, signs, and you could see the boys spying from the span of bridge passing over the dried-up ditch, Harry and Tom among them, stretching their necks to get a glimpse, listening close to pick up the best of the colonel's pirate curses, the boys keeping their noses covered against the black clouds of green willow smoke and the windswept spray of poison.

There were rumors. People said the old man used a rifle—that he shot squirrels and rockchucks and rabbits. And cats, they said he shot, though mostly spraying males nobody much blamed him for. But the fathers winced at mongrels, then claimed the old man was crossing the line at purebreds, and some of the mothers wondered about the child who cried of nearly being missed by one of the colonel's whining bullets. No bird sang or shat upon the colonel's property. He fed rice to the birds to watch their stomachs explode. When Harry himself was younger, he used to believe the old man existed only as an apparition, a nighttime traveler hanging in the billowed forms of curtains, waiting at the window to claim the first sleeping child to open his eyes and get caught looking where he ought not to have ever looked.

The truth was—what you could count on and know for certain—that only once for some weeks in the willow-cutting season of the year did the old man appear from out of his big-windowed house, and yearly were Tom and Harry there to witness his workings. So it was easy, really, if you could come in those years to see the old man as any other man made out of the aging flesh and blood he really was, stripped of story, minus the mask of magic slipping slowly away from his unseen face as the years passed and the boys came to see themselves as growing wiser with the seasons—was easy, really, if you saw Harry as one of those boys, the way the job of clipping the colonel's willows was handed on down to him.

What was harder was the boy. You could call him Lester, or Maurice, or Sydney. Any name to practice a lisping tongue thrust too long and held too soft on the front of the teeth a person rarely saw on him in either speech or laughter. *Lethter, Maurithe. Thydney,* you could call him. You could know him by his lisp and by his hands placed resting lightly on his hips, thumbs pointed forward after the girlish fashion that he had. *Oh, Lethter!* you might have heard. *Thay, Thydney!* Harry remembered. But what Harry thought of even more than a name, when he remembered the boy, was paper doilies, say, lacy, delicate things,

things like silken sheets and shade, white skin and cool breezes, lips, kisses, slim-waisted ladies showing slips from dresses, and shaved legs, and arms, too, Harry would think of, the boy's arm, twisted, pushed up and turned behind his back in the grade-school way, his face pressed into the playground sand and a crowd surrounding around Jackie Price, who early on had made it his job to pound the boy into saying the names they gave him.

But the boy never said the names. Not for Jackie Price, not for any of the other boys who stood shouting there behind him—Harry and Tom included. Because it was true that Harry and Tom were no different from any other person who ever saw the chance to bully the things he was most afraid of. Harry and Tom had helped to paint the boy's face with lipstick and rouge, helped to hold the boy still while waiting for the glue-lined wig to dry on his head. It was Harry who taught the other boys what in the world a hermaphrodite was, and it was Tom who supplied the circus freak pictures. But it was Jackie Price who pushed the game further by trying to make the boy drop his pants and show them whether or not it was true. In every game and in every way it was Jackie Price that Harry remembered as being the one to take things with the boy to the point where Harry found himself, even before the willows, wishing to hear the shrilling of the teacher's whistle calling them off the playground.

But for all that Jackie Price had studied to come up with to do to the boy, the boy still never said the names, nor ever showed them the private parts of himself either. The boy kept instead more and more to himself through the years, and his eyes took on a fishflat blackness that always held its look no matter what they all thought he must have felt as they witnessed Jackie Price's weekly beatings.

Nobody told. Nobody told because, as Harry had said, there were none of them at the time afraid of the boy so much as they were of Jackie Price. It made sense to be afraid of Jackie Price. It made sense to be afraid until the season Harry took the job to cut the colonel's willows.

THEY WERE COMING FLOATING DOWN THE DITCH, Harry and Tom, in the summer when the colonel asked them. Against the sun in their eyes they could see the shape of the colonel hot-footing it down the grassy slope of his close-mowed lawn. It was Harry's idea from the beginning, Harry suggesting that he and Tom grab hold of the willows to wait and see what had brought the old man out before the ditch was drained and it was time for the blade. The old man wore a Panama hat, Harry had seen and remembered, and he carried not a rifle but a cane, and he dressed in a shade of black that hid his face in shadow. Harry turned and saw Tom staying back in the cover of the willows as the colonel's clawed hands clasped the bridge railing from where he addressed them, making the offer, to either one or the both of them together, of a hundred dollars cash to cut the willows down.

Harry could feel the tug of the summer's muddy water on his calves. He looked at Tom, and he looked at the shape of the colonel standing there above them, and then he tested the supple toughness of the willow in his hand and figured it was worth it, never seeing the sweat it would take to earn the hundred-dollar bill the old man had dangled off the bridge in front of Harry's nose. So Harry said he'd do the job and he turned the willow loose, and together he and Tom passed underneath the darkness of the bridge, hearing the colonel whistling in the summer sun from up above, singing, *We'll see you in the fall, Drake, we'll see you in the fall.*

IN THE FALL IT WAS WHEN Harry first heard the boy's voice from up on the trail. It was while sitting underneath the bridge where they had floated through not so long ago that Harry first heard the boy and knew by the leafy lilt and birdsong of his words exactly who it was. It was while scraping the aphids out from his ears and shaking the tiny spiders from his hair, mixing willow grease with the sweat on his face, bitching and moaning and figuring from what work he had done and what was left ahead that in Harry the colonel had bought himself a one-bill slave. But it was not only the boy's voice, not the big-lipped lisping of the boy that Harry listened to on the high side of the willows, but the man's. Not in Harry's house, or in any of the houses of all his friends, had Harry ever heard a voice like the voice of that one man's. Cancer, Harry heard in the man's voice, quick-killing disease and back-alley danger, knives and fists and a tone pitched to straddle the border of what is recognizable as human. Harry could hear the voice speaking to the boy in a language that made the colonel's seasoned curses seem the callow work of a halfhearted actor. Harry listened, and listening he could know right off how it was that Jackie Price and his schoolyard beatings had never got the boy to come out from where he had hid himself, could know that neither the number nor the kind of years that Jackie Price had lived could match the hauntful rasp that Harry heard cursing the boy up there on the trail.

Harry began to follow the boy and the man for much the same reason and much the same way as he had followed the colonel in the years preceding, keeping himself nearly side by side with the two up on the trail above him. He picked and hopped his way along, and was careful to miss the lingering pools of water and the sticks and twigs that would give him away. He stepped around the stones where the sun never shone and the water clung concealed in the slippery sponges of lichens and moss that had set him flat on his backside more than once in the past. He spotted out the loudest yellow-baked leaves fallen from off the cottonwoods. Harry bent his knees and held his breath whenever he came up near to where they walked, peering to get a clean glimpse of the man and the boy through the wall of willow green that grew thick up there between them, straining his ears to hear what in the circles of his own life he had not.

But quiet as Harry was, the colonel had been quieter, the colonel who had come from behind on the silent treadway of his close-cut lawn to show Harry the old man still had some words left in him to bump up the flesh on a young boy's arms, the colonel catching Harry two knuckles deep, digging willow grease and aphids from out of his nostrils as he leaned to listen to the boy and the man. Snot Fuck! the old man called Harry. Lily Shit! he called him. What did Harry mean by being such a Limp Dicked Ass Jacker? the colonel wanted to know. What kind of a Snoopy Bitch Gossip Queen had he hired here? the old man asked.

Harry spun to see the colonel then not as a shadowy shape against the light of the sun, and not as a cane-wielding, Panama-hatted elder statesman, either. What Harry saw was to his knowledge the first clear sighting of the colonel by any among the pack of boys that Harry ran with. He was there, the colonel, framed for Harry by the one-eyed window of the old man's house that loomed watchful in the upslope background. He was standing in a pair of sneakers and a jockstrap and a regulation set of aviator sunglasses that Harry could see himself reflected in. Harry saw himself in the aviator sunglasses hustling back to the bridge, where he had left the machete and the tree shears, explaining to the old man that, no, sir, he, Harry, didn't personally himself think he was any of what the colonel had suggested he might be—Snot, Lily, Limp, or Other—but that he was only thinking he maybe knew that boy to talk to. Harry worked himself from a hustle to fairly running back to the bridge as if he believed the old man might have the rifle somehow stuck inside his jockstrap, Harry keeping an eye out to watch as the colonel came on slipping down the ditch bank in his slick-bottomed sneakers. He hadn't paid Harry to talk, the old man was saying—and he said he wasn't any impressed with the way Harry had been working when he wasn't wanting to talk, either.

The colonel took the machete and it wasn't technique that Harry watched as the colonel fell to working—it was the colonel's hair. Harry had never seen the kind of body hair he saw the colonel sporting. It was silver and white and it was everywhere where there was skin to grow it. Arms, chest, shoulders, back, ass and legs and stomach, hands, and maybe even palms and nails, thick and curling and really no sort of hair at all, Harry thought, but fur. It was animal fur, and they were animal sounds the colonel made as he worked his way deeper into the willows, cleaving the willows easy at the trunk, never retreating from the retaliatory sting and slap of branches Harry himself had ducked from on the little he had done. Grunts and growlings and stuck-pig squealings shook the brush and caused Harry to recount to himself the stories he had once believed before the years had led him to his newfound wisdom.

The old man emerged from the willows panting and hacking up some yellow stuff from in his chest, and Harry saw the colonel seemed to notice neither the willow grease that matted his fur, nor the teeming life of unnamable insects that his body had since become host to. Harry watched as the colonel made himself a willow switch, saw the colonel flick the switch through the air, whipping up a cutting sound that seemed to please him, and then the old man held the machete out to Harry and told him it was his turn.

Harry took the machete and felt the colonel's sweat on the leather handle and heard the cutting of the colonel's willow switch. Harry picked the smallest willow and swung a chop that hardly nicked the trunk. Harry raised the blade for another swing, but felt the colonel's clawlike hand grabbing at his wrist to hold him back. The old man's other hand held on to Harry's waist, and Harry could smell the stale-meat smell of the spit on the colonel's breath as he whispered now in Harry's ear to stay away and leave the man and the boy alone. Just leave them be, the colonel whispered, let them do what they will do. Nearly every day, the colonel whispered, the man and boy passed down this ditch trail, since long before Harry had seen them today and before Jackie Price had made it his job to work the boy over—never mind how the colonel knew about that—since clear back to the time when the boy was small enough to ride astride the man's shoulders, the colonel had seen them coming. He could see it all, the colonel said, from the big-windowed view up in his house, and he was watching, and he was watching Harry until he finished with the willows—and maybe even after.

So Harry passed it on to Tom, the job of finding out about the boy and the man, and Tom followed the two for a time before seeing the place where they disappeared from the ditch trail and down into the tallest bitterbrush at the bottom of the gully. Tom would squat, reporting what he had seen back to Harry, talking down to Harry from the ditch trail through the daily growing, stump-dotted space where once were the willows Harry had clipped and hacked. Tom told Harry that never once had there been any contact between the boy and the man, no pushing or shoving or hitting, but that what Tom had seen was the boy moving forward in prodless shocks of motion. The voice was the prod, Harry had said, along with all that the man's voice promised, and what was promised, Harry knew, must be what went on between the two at the bottom of the gully.

Tom kept following and Harry kept waiting underneath the bridge to listen, and it got to where he thought he might be looking forward to hearing the man's voice, got to where, when the boy's lilting lisp came on ahead of the man, Harry could hear the run of bubbles popping in his stomach at the idea that he might one day ignore the sticks and twigs and slippery mosses and come up on the ditch bank to give himself away on purpose.

And it wasn't, as Harry remembered it, the fear of giving himself away that kept him under the bridge, so much as it was the fear of the colonel's watching.

AFTERNOONS, HARRY SPENT WITH ONE EYE checking always upslope for signs of moving life behind the giant glass of the old man's watching window, listening in the lapses of his working through the birdless quiet for the colonel's footfall coming daily on the yellowing pad of grass. Nights, Harry saw the colonel in his dreams, Harry carrying with him into sleep the thoughts and scenes the old man had put into Harry's head during the dusking hours when he worked. Harry would hear the colonel speaking from the spot where Harry had looked to see no living soul not three swings previous. Harry would see the old man standing even in the cold and rain of the later weeks wearing nothing save his fur to warm him. The old man would hiss and spit, and Harry would wish for just one time for there to be a witness other than himself to the manner of the old man's appearance and the strangeness of his words. The colonel, Harry learned, had always known about the rumors flown around him. The cats, the old man knew about, the dogs, the children, and the birds it was said he shot at. The colonel neither confirmed nor denied the rumors but gave instead to Harry new things to think and dream, what the colonel called his military secrets, which he posed to Harry as questions. The colonel would crouch, prowling, eyebrows raised above the rim of his aviator sunglasses, asking Harry did he notice the concrete mowing strips, or the tin-sheet siding on his house? The colonel would slow his prowling, lower his voice so Harry had to come up close to listen, the old man asking did Harry care to guess the number of dry goods in the old man's cellar? had Harry thought yet why in the colonel's yard you would never see a tree? And then the old man asked the question no one had ever thought to ask, wondering had Harry considered this—considered why in God's world the colonel would ever want the willows cut down in the first place?

Harry never guessed and he never got an answer, and each day he would watch the colonel to make sure it was two feet and steps the old man had to take to get back to the top of the slope and the big-windowed house from where he sat and watched. Harry waited, watching, listening—the colonel on the one side of the ditch, the boy and the man on the other—and the leaves turned from green to red then gold and dying amber and the insects fell away in a single night's freeze and each day passed the same as the last with Harry working his slave wages way through the willows that bent and swayed in the late-autumn wind even as he cut them, hacking and clipping and chopping the living willows at the ground, the stacked and severed branches stiffening in mounds, and what was once the thick and thriving wall between Harry and the man and boy now became a void, a row of tough and bloodless stumps.

IT HAPPENED NEAR THE END, near the time when Harry had nearly cleared the willows completely, that Tom reported back to Harry that Jackie Price was following now, that Jackie Price had gone where Tom could never get himself to go, trailing the man and boy to the bottom of the gully. It happened near the end, too, that Jackie Price began finally to get the boy to say the names they gave him. Without a single arm twisting, no head banging or punching or any other kind of schoolyard drubbing—you could see the boy's eyes light up from the fishflat blackness they had all become accustomed to, and he would set his hands to resting slimly on his hips to do a mincing little two-step, saying, *Thydney, boys, I'm Thydney, look at me, Maurithe!* And the boy showed himself to those who stood behind Jackie Price, and even still with knowing what they knew, Harry and Tom did not step out of line but looked on with all the rest. It was a looking without seeing, as Harry recalled it, Harry recalling not wanting anymore to be a part of whatever it was that Jackie Price had learned to use to make the boy come out, Harry not wanting to see any of the things that had been made to be shown.

Whatever it was that Jackie Price had learned to use it was not to last, as they had all seen in less than one week's time the boy go back to what he was, then on to something worse that even Jackie Price could see and had no more nerve to touch. And it was not only Jackie Price who had changed his bullying ways but the man as well, whom Tom reported now as seeming to follow the boy rather than prod him down the trail. It was the boy Harry had heard from beneath the bridge, the boy ceasing with his lisping—and the man, whose voice had helped keep Harry all this time in the darkness where he was, leaving off in turn. It was the colonel, though, who seemed somehow to Harry to make the whole thing final, coming around now to burn and brush over the countless willow stumps, dipping to paint and rigging the pump and wand to spray from his bucketful of poison, whistling and singing to Harry now that *It's coming to a head, Drake, it's coming to a head.*

So that Harry was not much surprised when he heard the shots that came up from the gully. Six shots Harry counted but never told of hearing. Neither, when the time came, did Harry admit to seeing Tom, who had met Harry running down the ditch trail from where the shots had sounded. Tom had grabbed at Harry's arm, pushed at his back, trying to get Harry to run with him for home. But Harry would see what he had heard and know what he had guessed at, and so he had gone and he had seen them, seen all three—Jackie Price, the boy, and the man stretched dead in the clearing near the bitterbrush at the bottom of the gully. Harry had seen the boy standing naked with the gun and with the man that he had shot laid out there at his feet. Harry had seen Jackie Price, his face paste-white with fear, stumbling and lunging up the gully, the only one among them to testify against the boy in court, Jackie Price claiming those six shots were not in self-defense, that the boy had made the man to kneel before him and beg his pardon before he ever pulled the trigger.

THERE WAS NOT MUCH SURPRISE IN ANY OF IT, really, Harry figuring that these things have been happening since past when any single person could remember or even guess. They were the things that you could think on till you could see that you would never see the end and it was too late to go back to the start. Ten, fifteen, twenty years further in your life, you could know in it all no more or less than when you stood with both feet squarely in the middle. You could know that the man was dead and buried, that the boy had been sent and was gone to someplace far away. You could know that Tom and Harry had, in the winter of that year, lost their fear of Jackie Price and pushed him face-first onto the frozen ditch water to trip and knock his teeth out. You could know that the colonel had finally died and the willows had grown back along the ditch bank with nobody yet to try again to cut them.

And if you were Harry, you would often remember and think of the colonel in the way that he was when last you had seen him, Harry sometimes thinking that maybe the colonel had known it all from his big-windowed house, where he had sat the years and watched, the colonel pointing his finger at Harry and

Tom and the bloodied gums of Jackie Price, the old man laughing, bending at his silver-furred waist, lowering his voice then and speaking through his spitting to them all, the colonel seeming to Harry to be like nothing else but the hissing in the willows next to where you walk, whispering to you in your listening ear the things best left kept secret.

VERITA BLACK PROTHRO
(1964–   )

Freelance writer and Reno native Verita Black Prothro grew up in northern Nevada and attended the University of Nevada, Reno, where she received a degree in journalism, and Lesley College, where she earned a master's degree in education. The editor of the National Judicial College alumni magazine, she also teaches a class on excellence in journal writing. When she is not writing freelance articles, she works on her fiction and poetry, trying to find the balance between mainstream America and the voice within, a woman coming of age in a sometimes unforgiving world. She is passionate about politics and reading, and her fiction is concerned with an old truth—people are people—no matter what their color. As a black writer who grew up in a small family among Italian friends and neighbors, she felt as if there were only "blacks and Italians, collard greens or lasagna." What little time she has left when she is not working is spent with her new husband and two stepdaughters, and her nephew, whom she adores.

Porched Suitcases

"I HAD ANOTHER DREAM LAST NIGHT. I dreamed that ol' hussy was throwing grenades at me. She was pullin 'em right out of that ol' raggedy suitcase. Them grenades would come right up on me and I was tryin' to get out of the way but they just kept on comin' but they didn't hurt me. Ain't God good? I sure hope that heifa ain't tryin' to work no root on me," said Mama Jenkins as she sat in her ripped pine-green vinyl recliner and talked on the phone to her sister friend, Mrs. Carrington. Part of the reason they didn't like Loodybelle was, although she attended Mission Society, she never came to church and she gambled in the casinos.

"Girl, that dream was as clear as day. I never did like that ol' nappy-headed heifa. I better get my sista to send me a geeree bag from Louisiana to put around my neck at night, just in case she's tryin' to work a root on me." (Geeree bags were supposed to keep away bad spirits, but they were most successful in keeping away people because of their high garlic and dead weed content.)

Mama Jenkins seemed to have always been old. Everyone called her Mama even though she never had any children. She was feisty. She moved to Reno from a small country town in Louisiana in the early forties in an attempt to make her life better. She was never a pretty woman, but she had always been striking because of her odd combination of features. Her skin was smooth as silk and black as night, and her baby blue eyes could peer right through you, especially when she was angry. The years had changed her bone-straight hair to a salt-and-pepper color, but she wore it as she had done for a thousand years—French-braided back into a roll that looked like a cinnamon bun.

She and Mrs. Carrington had been friends since they first came to Reno. They couldn't remember how or when they met, only that they couldn't stand each other at first, but now they loved one another more than sisters could.

Mrs. Carrington was fiery (her first name was Ollie but she refused to let anyone call her anything other than Mrs. Carrington). She had one daughter who lived in New York. They didn't talk because they didn't get along; they were too similar. Mrs. Carrington was nearly as old as Mama Jenkins, but she had had many advantages that most black women of her day weren't afforded: education, travel, and fine clothes. She was still fairly attractive. Her creamy yellow skin had few wrinkles, and her silver hair and perfect English made her look and sound as distinguished and as uppity as most people thought her to be. Despite being opposites in looks and backgrounds, they were both black women, their experiences were common and their struggles were what bonded them.

"Girl, my rheumatism is bothering me today but Mission Society is tonight, so I'll press my way. You better bring your ol' self. You know that hussy Loodybelle will be there, tryin' to be cute and workin' on my nerves."

Mrs. Carrington replied, "You know I never miss."

The Mission Society, a Bible study for the church ladies, met every Tuesday evening at six o'clock at one of the ladies' homes. Mama Jenkins and Mrs. Carrington played host more than most because they didn't drive and it was just more convenient that way. Mission Society was mostly just an excuse for these ladies to talk about the old days.

Mama Jenkins loved to cook and play hostess because it gave her a reason to bake one of her famous butter-laden, melt-in-your-mouth pound cakes. She loved to add an extra stick of butter and an extra half cup of powdered sugar to make it even richer and sweeter.

It was a clear, hot summer evening in the Truckee Meadows. The ladies began to file in at exactly 5:55 P.M. About fifteen minutes were spent on the Bible lesson. The ladies were so predictable. One never wore her false teeth because "they hurt somethin' awful." Another one pretended she left her glasses every week; everyone had figured out long ago she couldn't read, but they played along—they would never damage her pride. Mama Jenkins trudged into the kitchen to bring out the pound cake and iced tea she'd made for the meeting.

They were spending the remaining hour reminiscing about life down South and about loves they'd once had, when Loodybelle made her entrance. The room grew quiet as she sauntered in with that old suitcase. The truth be told, no one liked her because she was so pretty and so strange. She didn't have one wrinkle in her cocoa-brown skin. All of the ladies thought she must be working a root to make herself look so young. She obviously dyed her heavy hang-down hair—it didn't have a hint of gray, but it looked so natural, it glistened. Even though she was in her early seventies, many men would snub a young woman to be with her. She was one of the first and few black women to work in a casino, and not as a maid. She worked as the powder room girl, and rumor had it she used to mess around with the white men. She always angrily denied this accusation. She claimed she was a beauty queen down South, and no one doubted it. But with all of her beauty, she had sullen eyes.

"Glad you could make it! And your black ass knows not to bring that suitcase mess in *my* house," snapped Mama Jenkins.

"Chile, I'm sorry to be late but I see I'm in time for some of your good ol' down-home pound cake. Girl, that cake will make you hurt yourself," she replied as she walked back outside to set the suitcase on the porch.

"What was the Bible lesson about?" she inquired, pleasantly, considering she was a woman under attack.

"It was about letting your light shine. Bearing fruit of the spirit. You know, like not gambling and drinking and carrying on, so that people will know you *got* the Lord," Mrs. Carrington replied, knowing this would irritate Loodybelle.

"Sounds like it was a right nice lesson, Ollie!" Loodybelle snapped.

"*No-You-Did-Not-Call-Me-Ollie!*" She stood up and put her hands on her hips. "My name is Mrs. Carrington and you best not forget that. You might be old as black pepper and your memory might not be that long"—she quickly snapped her fingers—"but nobody calls me Ollie." By this time Mrs. Carrington was apple red. "Don't make me get my pistol out." She looked around for her pocketbook.

"You know, Mrs. Carrington, they didn't stop making .38s when they made yours!"

Mama Jenkins interrupted, "Now listen here, I won't have this dog mess in my house. This here is a Christian home and we respect folks up in here. I tell you I've never seen the likes—Christian women carrying on." All the other ladies looked relieved.

Loodybelle had steam coming out of her ears, but she took one bite of the cake and pretended to cool off. She could understand why Mrs. Carrington insisted on the white folks calling her Mrs. Carrington, but she couldn't understand why they all had to.

One of the women tried to ease the tension. She started talking about her grandchildren. "You know my little grandbaby, Malcolm? He's going to play Frederick Douglass in the community center play. He's smart as a whip and only five years old. You know he's the one who was born the day Dr. King was killed."

"Ain't he the one with the white mama?" someone asked.

"Yeh, girl. She's white but she sure is nice. And as long as my son is happy, I'm tickled."

Like calling Mrs. Carrington "Ollie," white people were a subject that sent Loodybelle through the roof.

"If that don't beat the bugs fightin'! That's what's wrong with church folks now. They is too complacent—'if he's happy, I'm tickled.' What you gonna do when she turns on him? Will you be tickled then . . ."

And as always, when she would go into a tirade, someone would break into the monologue and ask the same question. This time it was Mama Jenkins. "Loodybelle, ain't none of us in here crazy about white folks, but girl, you got a problem. Why you hate white folks so much?"

"I told ya'll a hundred times—I don't hate nobody."

They all had seconds of the pound cake and continued to reminisce. Some talked about how rough it was leaving the South to come to an unknown place. Many talked about how they liked living in Herlong better because it was small and more like the South. Mama Jenkins always lamented, "But when that 'dog' Eisenhower got in office and cut all the jobs, everybody had to move to Reno to make a living. Just don't make no sense."

An hour or so later, everyone left, except Mrs. Carrington. She always stayed late so they could gossip about Loodybelle. Everywhere she went Loodybelle toted this old small suitcase, and these ladies desperately wanted to know what was in it. Mama Jenkins blurted out, "I bet she has all kinds of mess in there. I once knew a woman from down home who used to carry a bag like that. Everybody knew she was working roots. People would go to her and buy potions—potions to make people love you, to make people get sick if you hated them, and potions to make people fall dead if you owed them money. I never went around her. I was scared to death of that old woman."

Mrs. Carrington added her part. "A woman I knew of in New York used to write people's names in red pepper and fry them up in a skillet, when she got mad at them. Sure enough, those people would fall dead when they heard she'd done that. Everybody was scared to walk by her house."

"Do you think that old she-devil has a man's privates in there?" Mama Jenkins wondered.

"Girl, she might. She might have an old dead man in that thing," Mrs. Carrington retorted.

"No, it would stink to high heaven if it was a body and 'sides, it ain't big enough for a whole damn body," snapped Mama Jenkins.

Mrs. Carrington looked puzzled, "I wonder if she really keeps a mojo in there?"

"I don't know, but that's why I won't let her bring that mess in my house. I make her ol' self keep it right out there." Mama Jenkins pointed wildly to the porch.

Mrs. Carrington scratched her head and looked even more awestruck. "Child, she might have some money in that thing."

"Well, if that old heifa has some money she oughta pay somebody else to carry it around for her sorry self. She looks as crazy as I don't know what, carrying that thing around *all* the time. It's so raggedy. It has more tape on it than leather."

Mrs. Carrington replied, "Think it don't! She's just pitiful," and they roared in unison.

They agreed as usual that one day they were going find out what was in the old suitcase.

The week was a typical one of much prayer and gossip.

Sunday morning rolled around, and Mama Jenkins and Mrs. Carrington headed for morning worship service. They lived next door to each other on Quincy Street, and for years one of the younger women in the church had been picking them up every Sunday.

Mrs. Carrington always looked like she had just stepped out of a fashion magazine on Sunday morning. She would always go over to Miss Ema Jean's to get her hair done up on Saturday night so the curls and finger waves would look fresh for church. She always wore a small flowered head ornament and gloves, and she had shoes to match every outfit. She said that's the way they did it in New York. She was the only one who wasn't from down South. And she was proud of that. She was also proud that everyone knew she could never have been a sharecropper's wife or child.

Mama Jenkins tried to wear nice clothes, but she never looked nice because every Sunday before she would go into church she would dip snuff. As the deacons would start singing the hymn "What a Friend We Have in Jesus" to signal that devotion was beginning, she would spit it into her snuffbox, an old Del Monte green bean can with a partially ripped label. She'd stuff a wad of tissue in the can and tuck it in her purse. She looked much like a man because of her thick moustache and the snuffbox, but the gaudy hat, big purse, and tacky fur stole let everyone know she wasn't.

She and Mrs. Carrington always sat on the Mothers' Bench. It was a place of honor in the church. For most of these women, it was the only honor they would ever receive. They sat proudly, as erect as Father Time would allow, flaunting their hats and sporting their pretty togs.

As the church clerk got up to read the weekly announcements, Mrs. Carrington's jaw tightened, as it did every Sunday at this time. "It doesn't make any sense for them to have her up there," she fumed quietly. The clerk continued to stumble horribly through her reading. "They just shouldn't have her country, 'Bama self up there *trying* to read those announcements. You just wouldn't see this country mess in New York. . . ."

She was about to continue when Mama Jenkins hunched her in the side and told her to hush up. She conceded, albeit unwillingly.

The choir sang their newest song, "Oh Happy Day," and then the offering plate was passed. Mama Jenkins and Mrs. Carrington were always stretching their necks and their eyes trying to see what people around them were giving. Later they would gossip about how cheap Sister So-and-So was; it was a Sunday afternoon ritual.

After the offering the choir sang "We Have Come This Far by Faith." That is when the Holy Ghost entered the building. Sisters started shouting and speaking in tongues, especially Sister Smith. Every Sunday, she would knock the pews over in her excitement over God's goodness. Many people thought most of her spirit came out of a bottle. While the choir was singing, the mood of the entire church changed. Suddenly sisters who'd spent a lot of money on their wigs didn't care if they flew off—in fact, they would snatch them off. Women who spent countless hours selecting shoes would run right out of them. People would yell, "Ain't God good?" "Thank ya, Jesus!" and "Won't he make a way, ya'll?"

After the choir sang, Pastor Gibbons got up to give his sermon; but he felt too good to talk, so he just sang, "Amazing Grace, how sweet the sound, that saved a wretch like me. . . ." Whenever Pastor sang that song, Mama Jenkins would stand up, wave her white lace handkerchief, and cry. Those who knew Him understood; those who didn't sat in bewilderment.

She would declare, "I thank ya, Jesus, I just thank ya, Jesus, because last night my covers didn't become my winding sheet. I just thank ya."

Pastor would always wait for her to get her issue of the Holy Spirit before he would move on.

"Today, I'd like you to turn with me to the Gospel According to Saint Matthew seventh chapter, seventh verse. 'Ask and it shall be given to you. Seek and ye shall find. Knock and it will be opened unto you.' My subject for today is 'Why Don'tcha Just Ask Him?' Before I start my sermon, I would like my lovely wife to bless our souls with a solo."

The pastor's wife hopped up to the front microphone and began to sing, "It's a highway to heaven, none can walk up there, but the pure in heart . . ."

"Now she's gonna chase the Holy Ghost out of here, with her no-singin' self. Bless her heart, she sure can't sing," Mama Jenkins said as she began to come off of her spiritual high.

After the song, the preacher whooped and hollered and put on quite a show for the congregation at the Greater First Baptist Church. After the sermon he offered the Invitation to Christian Discipleship; no one accepted. There was one more offering and church was dismissed.

People fellowshipped outside for a while, catching up on the week's news. By twos and threes they all left.

During the ride home, Mama Jenkins was still complaining about the pastor's wife chasing the Holy Spirit away.

"She's simple as the day is long. She oughta know she can't sing no better than me. Poor soul. She's right pitiful, gettin' up with that solo mess," she complained.

Mrs. Carrington wouldn't let a good complaint session go without adding her two bits: "I don't know what's wrong with him, putting her up there all the time. Poor thing, he must be pussy-whipped. Ooooo, God forgive me, I should not talk about

Pastor like that, he's a good man and he sure did preach today. Blessed my soul."

When the car stopped at Mrs. Carrington's house, they both got out. They'd already decided to have dinner there. Mrs. Carrington's house was ragged and old from the outside, and the inside too. It was dimly lit because she never opened the drapes; the walls looked like poorly done papier-mâché, and the floors creaked when you walked. But she had fine antique cherry-wood furniture, sterling silver utensils, the finest china, and European crystal stemware.

Mrs. Carrington walked with the assistance of a four-pronged cane. She always wore long dresses to cover her knees, which time and arthritis had grossly misshapen. Mama Jenkins, on the other hand, was at least a hundred pounds overweight and moved very slowly. No one could be as patient with them as they were with each other. They *always* helped each other along.

Mrs. Carrington didn't like to cook, and she didn't cook nearly as well as Mama Jenkins. So today, thanks to Mama Jenkins, they feasted on Southern fried chicken, homemade macaroni and cheese, freshly snapped green beans with a little salt pork added for flavor, cornbread, and lemonade.

It was another excruciatingly hot day. After dinner the weather turned moody and electric as a thunderstorm moved across the heavens. The ladies knew the danger of storms and as soon as the first flicker of lightning raced across the sky, everything electrical was turned off and they sat in silence. As children, both had seen schoolmates struck by lightning and killed. Each time the thunder would roar, the ladies would quietly call "Sweet Jesus" in unison. Mama Jenkins slept in the guest room that night.

Tuesday rolled around again and the Sisters were meeting at Pastor's house. He was out of town, the church sent him to the national baptist convention. The pastor's wife picked the old women up.

"How are you ladies doing tonight?" she asked.

"Baby, I ain't a bit of good today," Mama Jenkins answered.

"Oh, I'm fine today, but I'm not as young as I used to be," Mrs. Carrington mused.

Mama Jenkins said, "Girl, you sure did sing that solo Sunday."

Mrs. Carrington could barely hold back her laughter.

When they arrived at the house, the other ladies were arriving also. Loodybelle appeared later. She brought the old suitcase in, and Mama Jenkins started rubbing her hands together and rocking back and forth like a parent waiting on a delinquent teenager. She knew she couldn't tell her to take the case outside because it wasn't her house or Mrs. Carrington's, but she didn't want that thing near her. Finally she could no longer take it.

"Girl, why don't you take that mess outside?"

"If Pastor's wife wants me to, I will."

The pastor's wife pretended not to hear the exchange.

This week the Bible lesson was forty-five minutes long since it was at Pastor's house. His wife served store-bought cake and the ladies took a piece to be courteous. But later they would gossip about her being too lazy and trifling to bake a homemade cake.

"Sister Gibbons, I'm not the meddling type, but you need to stop spoiling Pastor so much," one of the ladies said.

Mama Jenkins was glad to jump in on a man-bashing conversation, "Yeh, girl, you are young and one thang you needs to know is that the two easiest things in the world to spoil is a dog and a man."

They all laughed hysterically.

Sister Gibbons was curious. "But didn't you ladies spoil your men when you were young? You know it's so hard being a black man in a white man's world. I just want him to feel extra special when he's at home. That might be the only time he feels special."

Mrs. Carrington jumped in and answered before anyone else. She loved to talk about her late husband. "Yeh, girl, my husband was a good man. The best one God ever put on the earth. And I spoiled him somethin' terrible. Folks said he worked himself to death." Her eyes filled with tears. "All I know is, when he died—well, I've never been the same. And I tell you *one* thing, another man better not come up in my face trying to be too friendly. That's all I know."

Mama Jenkins loved to talk about her love-affair battle wounds. "Well, my man was a skunk. Hear me what I say? He drank *and* chased women. I thought if I spoiled him he would leave those other women alone and only love me. He wasn't worth two dead flies. He hurt me real bad. And it sure hurt me real bad when I had to chase his black ass away with the rifle that day, but, girl, I'd had enough. I tell you, I'd had enough. I say, you just can't spoil 'em, you just have to be slouchy and nasty. That's all. Men love slouchy, nasty women, I don't know what it is about 'em, but men love themselves a no-good woman."

"What about you, Miss Loodybelle, did you spoil your man?" Sister Gibbons was the only person who called her Miss Loodybelle.

"She probably killed him off with that mojo mess she carries around," Mrs. Carrington jabbered out.

Just as she said that, a flash of lightning streaked across the sky and thunder roared wrathfully.

"My man was a good man." The storm apparently didn't frighten her. She kept on talking and the other women listened. "He was the best man God ever made. *He* was fine, dark and tall, and his eyes—oooo, they were the kindest, prettiest eyes in the whole world. I mean, all the women wanted him. He was also strong and kind. And he only loved me."

"Well, I don't think they make men like that. Sounds like that Superfly fella, if you ask me. If he's so good, where is he?" Mama Jenkins asked, obviously forgetting the storm.

Loodybelle looked out toward the thunder and just talked.

"One day he didn't come home. That wasn't right. We hadn't married yet and his mama, she was so worried. He was reliable. Late that night the sheriff came and told his mama her boy was hangin' from a tree down Thompson Road. He told *her* to go cut *him* down. Lord, that woman hollered, screamed, and called on Jesus. Everybody came runnin' when they heard all the commotion.

"The pastor, he said my man must have done something—talked crazy to the white folks, looked at a white woman—something. I knew he hadn't done nothing. They cut him down. Since we weren't married, I couldn't even sit close at the funeral, so I went back and got that long rope they hung him with."

"Is that what you carry in the suitcase, Miss Loodybelle?"

Miss Loodybelle just looked off in the distance, not crying, just gazing.

They shared each other's pain, but she was too strange for them to share hers. Loodybelle's pain was too deep and too close to home for them to acknowledge it. So, seemingly ignoring her, they went on talking about church business and the weather.

After the meeting, Pastor's wife took the ladies home. They sat in Mama Jenkins's house and talked about the night's conversation.

"You know why that ol' crazy-behind heifa wouldn't answer, don'tcha? 'Cause she got root workin's in that suitcase and she didn't wanna admit it in the Man of God's house. That's what it is," Mama Jenkins insisted.

Mrs. Carrington had sorrow in her eyes. "That ol' woman needs to learn to pray. We've all been hurt, but we don't carry it around with us all the time. Won't do any good. Next thing you know, she'll be at the nuthouse over in Sparks."

ERICA HECTOR VITAL
(1967–)

Virginia native Erica Hector Vital came to Las Vegas in 1993 after receiving her master's degree in creative writing from Virginia Commonwealth University. The recipient of literature fellowships from the Virginia Commission on the Arts and the Nevada Arts Council, she is hard at work on her novel, *Natural Causes,* from which this opening chapter is taken. She describes her novel as "almost mystery," featuring a young black female protagonist, Asa Bridges, "who for most of her life has been afraid of what it means to be a woman and black." The genesis of the story, which is rooted in a decaying East Coast city, came from the news and the unconscionable acts of violence that can destroy the life of a community. But Vital chose to tell the story from the black woman's point of view—a perspective that rarely finds its way into newsprint. Her fiction has appeared in *Catalyst* and *Obsidian.* She teaches English at the Community College of Southern Nevada and the University of Nevada, Las Vegas.

Natural Causes

(EXCERPT)

ASA'S BOOTS SANK INTO DAMPNESS, her heels striking against patches of ruin in the grass where the November crunch of the leaves had been bleached out by the rains—vitality long gone—emptied out like the partially clothed body lying on top of a nearby leaf mound. Its arms were stretched wide, its face to the east, crushingly ornamental like a bad Renaissance painting or, thought Asa, like some of the latest in art nouveau: hard dashes of color on canvas hung in awkward positions in some of the more fashionable galleries in town.

A detective stood across from the mound in a wrinkled hunting jacket; he coughed without putting his hands to his mouth, his breath a puff of white on the breeze. He was gray-haired, tall but slightly bulky—an upstate idea of the Marlboro Man. Face creased by the wind, jaw set tight. He put his hands in his pockets, pulled his gaze away from the body on the mound long enough to stare at Asa instead. She thought she saw him wink, papery pink lids opening and closing above a smile that would almost have been fetching if it weren't for the circumstances.

He'd introduced himself as Mankewitz, Mank to his friends. To Asa the nickname brought to mind small rodents, close-smelling dens.

She'd seen the way Mankewitz had let his off-colored eyes

trail over the body on the mound, coming to rest on particularly vulnerable places—the hardening breasts under a torn party dress, the ripped coffee-colored hose and the slim legs beneath. What bothered her most was that he didn't appear to get much pleasure from these glances. He was bored, unimpressed by the brutality, as if he had expected just this type of woman to be found half clothed, lifeless, and without any known identity in Tannen Heights Park. And when he looked in Asa's direction his gaze remained unchanged. It was the same act for him as looking at the lifeless woman on the leaves. The same slightly bored expectation, the same level of no-surprise.

The skin around the detective's lips was shiny and pink, an unhealthy stretch of chafing that he bit into over and over. He held a notepad in one hand and cradled a ballpoint pen behind one wind-reddened ear. He'd set his pen in motion just once since Asa had arrived, intent on getting down exactly who she was, where she lived, and what she was there for. He'd bitten into the fresh layer of peelings along the side of his mouth, jaws and teeth working as he scribbled, like a child who can read only if he's allowed to mouth the words, the connection between thought and action so tenuous, so unsure.

Now Asa's full name stood alone at the top of a lined page. No list of clues, or hastily scribbled thoughts of inspiration. He was just looking, biding his time, and perhaps if the victim was lucky, he was taking mental notation, an orderly list of suspects behind the chaos of thin lips and wrinkled hunting jacket.

"Think she'd mind if I took a look?" He smiled over his shoulder, his eyes seeking out Asa, finding her and holding on while he leaned over the body on the mound as eagerly as he would lean into a lover. He lifted the hem of the woman's dress. The fabric, caught on a sudden breeze, whispered seductively as Asa caught sight of one tea-and-spice-colored thigh and the scalloped edge of black lace underthings.

Mankewitz knelt into the leaves, the caps of his knees close enough to bump the dead woman's hips. The hem of the black dress rose further. Asa stood by, sickened by the sight, but saying nothing. Finally, she looked away and into the distance, where she could see the detective's crew several feet away, leaning on squad cars, combing the sand and grass idly for evidence. Their blue uniforms dotted the park in patches of stately order. Blue arms, blue caps, deep blue winter jackets on deep blue chests almost serene, while in the foot of space that separated Asa from Mankewitz, and Mankewitz from the deceased, there was confusion, the flurry of the black velvet party dress rising, the erratic notion of Mankewitz's probing, before he stopped.

"Nothing there." He dropped the hem, but the wind coming in off the Hudson refused to let the fabric rest. The velvet hissed hotly, the hem rippling like water. Mankewitz winced as a sudden breeze snatched a string of salt tears from his eyes. He blew onto his palms for warmth, rubbed them together, a sound like paper tearing. Asa raised her camera, wanting to take his picture, needing to take it. Her finger was light on the shutter, his penny profile filled the frame.

At the last moment she changed direction, catching sky instead.

If her camera had been a weapon she wouldn't have been able to fire.

"It's gonna be a rough winter," Mankewitz growled into the cold. "People coming out of their skins." He flicked at the hem of the dress, chuckling softly to himself as if death were a joke and only he knew the punch line.

It was Asa's guess that Mankewitz had taken one look at this woman and had already decided exactly what she'd been. The flash of the dress, the teetering high heels, the thick lips drawn in thicker and redder still against dark skin. Mankewitz bit at his own reddened lips, the roar in his throat combative, like garbage being thrown on a truck. Asa held the stout body of her Nikon close and aimed again at the back of his head. But again there was nothing—no final pressure on the trigger. From the beginning she'd had trouble photographing living things.

She huddled inside her jacket, the denim above and the knotty cardigan underneath doing nothing to muffle the blow of the wind. She'd loaded up with colored film this morning, yet she was sure the shots she'd develop later would come out in black and white. The morning was that quiet, that still. Devoid of any warmth. The night had been even colder, so cold that a fine web of ice lay over everything, the leaves, the individual blades of grass. Even the Hudson was sluggish, the tide weighed down with a light coating of crystal. Ironically, the deceased was without hat, coat, or scarf, but her skin was still warm. At least that's what Mankewitz had declared, only half interested. The warmth something to be remarked upon like the weather, like the itch behind his ears. Just a comment, nothing that would make any difference to anyone else, not to the family of this woman when and if they could be found, not to the thousands of subscribers who would pick up the afternoon edition and see the body on the front page. Just a comment. "The vic' is still warm . . . what's for lunch?" Mankewitz was impervious and Asa was afraid of him.

As she watched him dig around the body, sifting through the leaves, she felt the throb of a headache setting in, a burn that started at the base of her neck and worked its way forward. She squinted against the pain, wanting badly to scream or to cry. The best she could do was to lightly touch her forehead with the tips of her fingers, letting the cold sink in.

One of Mankewitz's guys looked her way, almost sympathetic. He was young and black, one of the department's affirmative action babies, of which there were two types—churlish and brisk or cautiously diligent. This one was of the latter group and handsome; his face a dark rock being buffeted by the wind. He had the decency to hold his cap in his hands in the presence of death, while bursts of cold from the river plucked at the creases of his dark pants. Asa looked away, not wanting Mankewitz to think she and his colleague knew one another, for the detective was sure to be the type to think that all blacks were acquainted, slapped hands, waved to each other, gave secret soul shakes to signal the start of a revolution that had yet to come.

As it was, Mankewitz probably believed that she and the victim were related, long-lost half sisters, common-law twins. At best he would think that Asa could identify the woman, pull a name fragrant and piping warm from her inside pocket... Lequia, Tracy, Anita, Djani... when half the time Asa could barely recognize herself.

No, Asa couldn't name her, had not seen her before. But there was something familiar about the woman, something that made Asa want to look too long or not look at all.

Mankewitz eased his way up and away from the woman's side, his joints creaking as he dusted wet leaves from his jacket, arched his back. He nodded toward Asa, then back toward the body. "Throwaway," he said, the skin of his lips parting.

Asa flinched at the sound of his voice, her headache moved up a notch. "Beg your pardon?"

"Right there," he looked down. "Throwaway."

Asa followed his gaze. The throb in her temples trickled down the back of her neck, curled into the nook above her spine.

This was her fifth body. Enough death to fit each of the fingers on one hand. Enough death to keep her thinking about the ends of things instead of the beginnings.

It should have been simple by now. But this was just as hard as the first time, maybe harder, though you'd think she would begin to understand what death looked like. That it came in so many different faces, colors, ages. The first one she'd seen had been a suicide, the body of a young painter stretched out on the pavement. He'd leaped from the window of his four-story loft, leaving behind a stack of unsold canvasses and a suicide note that said simply, "No more." His work consisted of studies of dark egg shapes painted over and over, sometimes black, sometimes gold. "Death taking a look at itself," was one of the many phrases they'd come to use for Asa's style after she'd taken the shots. What she'd captured, they said, was his weightlessness. The bands in the neck and in the knees dangling, broken, like the filaments of a light blown out.

It had been an accident on both their parts: Asa wasn't really working until she'd taken those photos and the painter wasn't really an artist until he'd fallen.

That's how Asa's career was going. Someone else did the hard part, the dying, the grieving, and she came in afterward, put their tragedy into neat phrases, sealed the eyes shut with the click of her camera—life and death both coming to her secondhand.

Asa's father had been a Southern Baptist who believed that the soul was housed within the body and was therefore naked when the body was naked. He would not have approved of the condition in which this woman had been found. He would not have approved of Asa's role as a witness, as a recorder of what had taken place.

But he would have welcomed the detective's coarseness, the offhandedness of his remark, simple, basic, and said in no particular way—"throwaway," as if he'd stumbled upon an object that had already been named.

It was close to six now and morning crept above the water. The Hudson was a dirty theatrical cape on the park border, woolly and gray. In the distance Asa could see a stream of commuters making their way out of Tannen. They'd turn onto the connector at Lasalle Avenue for a beat through the Palisades, then pay their toll at the George Washington, leaving the much talked about serenity of Tannen Heights for the bustle of Manhattan.

Not knowing what had been found here this morning, the locals who took the route over the bridge would get into their cars and pull out of landscaped drives without checking to see whether someone lurked in their backseats. They would forget to lock their driver's side doors. Most of them thought that the danger lay elsewhere, over there, in cities cut from stone. They walked through their days believing they were immune to this kind of thing as long as they had the shine of Corinthian leather, the novelty of crystal imported from Sweden, and the warmth of double-sided fireplaces.

This evening, they would pick up the *Tannen Courier* and the first thing they'd see would be Asa's shots. They'd browse through the story and "tsk" themselves through dinner. Rationalizing even as they bit into their vegan platters that such a terrible thing could happen only to a suspect someone, someone who had no business being in the park, a woman alone at night, someone who possibly didn't belong in Tannen Heights at all. They'd dip the proper fingers into the proper bowls and they'd forget. Just like the reporters from the local television station, just like the cops in their fresh-pressed uniforms, and hopefully, just like Asa.

She wanted to forget it too.

She began to pack up, disconnecting her lens and the antiquated flash on top. Mankewitz saw her slipping away and stopped her. He was a blur that blocked her path, his fingers covering the bend of her arm, roughlike, holding her still. The tilt of his head and the prim set of his mouth were almost matronly, a schoolmarm about to impart a pivotal lesson. Learn or you stay after, learn or you get left back. The papery lids blinked in the wind, the lips parted. "Do you know what I mean?"

Asa shook her head, clutched her camera bag close, sad protection as she stared into the unforgiving recesses of the detective's face. She'd seen a llama once, long-lashed and delicate on cloven feet, spit into the face of its keeper at the Bronx Zoo. One minute there was the ungainly grace of the llama's features blinking sweetly, oblivious, as a man with a baton steered the animal where he wanted it to go. Asa had looked on expecting to see more of the llama's chewing, more of its passive response, but then there was the sound of the keeper screaming, his hands flagging in front of his face. He thought he'd been blinded. The llama's venom had been that strong. Asa was ten, and she'd been envious of what the llama could expel without holding back. What would it have been like to scream when she felt like screaming, to shout when she wanted to shout, to spit in the face of self-appointed keepers?

She pulled her arm back, slowly, imperceptibly as if she had need of both hands. Mankewitz dropped his hold and smiled. He smelled of lime and tobacco, of something freshly burning. "Know what I mean?" He smiled a secret smile. "Throwaway?"

"No," her response was tentative, barely above a whisper. "I don't know what that means."

Mankewitz came in close, close enough for Asa to see the individual strands of old flannel in the weave of his jacket. The smell of cut limes grew stronger. "Means there are too many like her to go around. Means that if one of her boyfriends didn't do it, her dealer did. This one was through before she got started... a throwaway. Nothing to waste the paperwork on." He winked again and nodded toward the body. Asa followed his gaze downward, imagining a baton steering. "Know what I mean?" His hair ruffled in the breeze, the sky was ice, his eyes and the veins beneath the surface of his wind-chaffed skin were ice.

Her eyes held. What she saw was a fairly young woman, possibly her own age, no more than thirty. Dark skin, skin with an almost purple texture. The hands were manicured, glossy tips dipped in oxblood polish; she saw the lean legs in coffee hose.

This was someone she could've passed on the street or at the supermarket. Someone she might have seen in the halls many years ago at the high school tipping her head back against a locker, showing the dark bend of her throat to the boy standing over her. What she saw was a woman who looked too much like herself, who had probably sounded too much like her, too, and who had lived, at one time, too much like her as well. But all the same, wasn't it obvious from where she was and from what was left of her that this woman was exactly what Mank had said? A throwaway. Nothing to waste the paperwork on.

Asa opened her mouth to say something to him, but a voice inside her squelched it. Her own personal keeper. Instead she found herself backing away from Mankewitz and the body. She was moving toward the police tape that circled the mound, stepping over to get out to the other side, to cross the official divider between the living and the dead, between Mankewitz and herself, when the heel of one boot seemed to slide. The damp leaves and ice shifted. She slipped, her body twisting so that she landed back where she started from, within reach of the mound, so close to the woman lying there that she could see for herself the negative circle where flesh had been. What Mankewitz said was a bullet from a .38 had gone in cleanly at the soft spot between hairline and jaw—the temple. Sounded so restful—a sweet spot; a spot to be kissed, to worship, to pet.

Asa closed her eyes, trying to keep out the sight. She was shaking. She could feel her bones turn into something pliable and quiver with the cold. The mush of leaves and ice bit into the soft tissue of her palms. She could feel the ice seeping in. But when she opened her eyes she was standing, feeling blooms of blood where she'd scraped her hands.

Mankewitz steadied her, holding her a bit too hard around the arms before he let her go. His teeth worked deliberately on that bottom lip. The laugh was there and something hard around the eyes. "You okay?" he asked without real concern.

Asa's teeth chattered out an answer that was not an answer. She drew a deep breath, paused to wipe bleeding fingers across the leg of her jeans. She was thinking of something to say, something biting and confident. The words were on her lips fighting their way forward, but before she could get herself together, Mankewitz was walking off, his slightly hunched shoulders receding, the red plaid in his hunter's jacket growing brighter the farther away he moved. He didn't look back. He had nothing else to say, no new notes to jot down, no new evidence to list. He'd already done his duty, the case could close. She'd seen exactly what he'd wanted her to see.

313